RHESUS

POSITIVE

GAVIN FEATHERSTONE

Rhesus Positive

Published by Faaronheigt Publishing

ISBN 978-0-9935266-2-6

© 2020 Gavin Featherstone

Printed and distributed in the UK by Witley Press Ltd., 24-26 Greevegate, Hunstanton PE36 6AD www.witleypress.co.uk

Rhesus Positive is available from Amazon Books at amazon.co.uk

ACKNOWLEDGEMENTS

Editors: Paul Sorensen and Belinda Dickinson.

I would like to express my thanks to Paul and Belinda. They really did have to smooth over my all too many rough edges, but may I say they did it with much aplomb, detail and humour.

It would seem to many that writing a novel is a far reach away from heading up the coaching of top hockey teams. I was not surprised as I had armed myself with two of the finest assistant coaches. In addition my technical coordinator was Kelvyn Skee of KS Digital who brought even more colour to the book with his organisation of the illustrations.

Finally many thanks to Avril at AP Solutions and Services for her devoted secretarial work in deepest Somerset.

Much appreciation to the Peek Freans Museum for supplying two photographs from their HQ in Bermondsey, and to Author Peter Damian (Wikipedia) for the Thames Walkway in Bishops Park SW6, attribution – Sharealike 3.0 Unported (CC BY-SA 3.0).

CONTENTS

Gavin Featherstone hails from Wandsworth in south-west London. Educated at Kingston GS, Durham & Oxford Universities, he progressed to becoming an England hockey international and to lead the coaching of the USA & South Africa at two Olympiads.

After penning three books on hockey and sport, he has diversified to write this first novel, *Rhesus Positive.*

The Walkway by the Thames in Putney

PROLOGUE

His bearing was unmistakably military, sharply defined and so well preserved after all those years. The new century had eased his stride into more of a stroll as he negotiated the Middlesex bank of the Thames. He managed a cursory glance at the starting point of the Oxford-Cambridge varsity boat race. On this grey day in early winter the waters, devoid of craft, assumed a choppy swell bouncing off the walls beneath him.

The river could always be relied upon to remind him of the world he had faced for over half a century. It had been fast, it had been slow, with high tides and low tides, but in its murkiness it had always been live and dangerous.

He was punctual by nature and well prepared for an afternoon appointment at the Duke's Head public house on the Surrey side. Mr Jones was to meet a man from the writing trade, a scribe on whom he could trust with the heavy load he had been carrying for so long. There had been countless times when he had landed up in London to perform his duties but in his bones he felt that this visit would yield a haunting finality.

Fixing his gaze on the All Saints church clockface he climbed the concrete steps from Bishops Park up on to the bridge at Putney. Over old father Thames he was met by a stiff icy breeze before veering right towards the Young's hostelry and his impending nemesis.

The octogenarian entered the river bar at once recognising the journalist. He greeted him warmly, "At last we meet, your pen is at the ready?"

"Yes sir but just one question before we start. Why have you got me involved?" replied the scribe.

"When it comes to family I make it our business."

CHAPTER 1

SOUTHAMPTON COMMON: 1940

"Heads or tails, Ray?" The dishevelled young upstart asked of his big brother.

Heads was his response, but he had it wrong. Young Phil had goaded his fuming sibling as he announced to his gang that he, Phil Bristowe, would captain the England football team, whilst Ray had been relegated to being in charge of the Germans.

For two young kids of six and eight years, this was to be their war fought out on the battlefield which was Southampton Common. That Thursday afternoon when school had finished, Phil had begged Mr Latchford, the PE teacher, to lend him one of his laced-up leather balls so he could practise his developing skills. The 7 a side game was to start exactly at 4.15pm and it was to be refereed by Ray as there was no way he was going to play for Nazi Germany.

The other kids didn't care much for it either but Ray, even at this age, had an air of seniority about him and with his Dad's railwayman's whistle, they knew he'd be fair. This was a quality that his younger brother did not share: Phil was ruthless and rules were an irrelevance to him. The boys had put down two bikes as goalposts at one end and Ray and Phil had put their jumpers down at the other, on this warm, humid September afternoon.

The big match was going well for Phil's England when Ray's attentive ears heard the familiar sounds of a deep, thudding, repetitive drone. He took his eyes off the game, peering into the skies above him and into the distance towards Southampton docks, three miles away.

His Uncle Cyril had, earlier in 1940 for his eighth birthday present, given him a comic book which had detailed pictures of all the World War 2 fighter and bomber aircraft with all their norms and characteristics.

Above him were the trails of the dogfights at that point high in the sky as Hurricanes were chasing in pursuit of the Luftwaffe's Dornier or was it Heinkel Bombers?

The blue sky was criss-crossed at all angles with white foam and Ray just sensed he had smelt the preliminary whiffs of aircraft fuel. He now believed his senses; his nose, ears and eyes could not be mistaken. This was a big 'un, a German air raid.

Another feeling had gripped him, the sensation of fear.

Meanwhile, Phil had burst into the penalty box and was chopped down mercilessly by one of the local county Wessex boys, masquerading as one of Adolf's "Stormtroopers".

4

"Penalty, Ray, you must have seen it with your eyes closed?" Phil complained vehemently to his blood brother. Little did he know that Ray was miles away, up in the sky, fearful not only for his own life but for the two teams innocently unconcerned as yet with the battle that was to unfold hundreds of feet up. No penalty awarded, especially to his brother!

His mother had warned the two boys about playing out in the open, unsupervised. German planes had already wreaked havoc earlier in the month down by the docks and she knew that their new home in Chandler's Ford was too far from the Common for her to take a hold of her two sons eager to bike to a big open space.

By now all the boys on the field were glancing up as they were hearing the screeching of accelerating engines getting nearer and nearer. Then suddenly, just above the Common's treeline, at such a low level, they witnessed a Heinkel climbing furiously clearly having dropped its load just three minutes from the target, the Woolston factory by the water of the Solent. Ray blew a long big whistle, acknowledging that all the boys should make a run for it to a prefabricated changing block or to take cover in the nearby wood. His younger brother would have none of it, exclaiming that his England team were winning one goal to nil and itching to score more. The referee was to have the last word, running over to his brother and giving him a clip round the back of his head.

"Everyone off, scarper, including you Phil," he ordered.

The boys now were running but not at any speed because their eyes were trained on the skies. They could pick out the silver black cross on the sides of the German bombers and even glimpsed at the goggle protected eyes of the pilots in the cockpits. The noise was intense, the smell overpowering, as Hurricanes with lightning speed were gaining on the fleeing bombers. Up they scaled into higher elevations with the higher pitched noise of the Hurricanes rattling out machine gun fire.

By now the boys, some of them stopping in their tracks, simply watched the theatre of war, cheering on the faster, more fluid Allied planes. Even if England's football team were halted from winning on the Common, these lads were cheerleaders for the RAF above. They all still thought it was a game, a big adventure up there with winners getting medals as they shot down the hapless opponent.

All except one. That was Ray, who even at his tender age, had read up on air duels and the fallout literally from the uncompromising savagery of the conflict. He knew that the Luftwaffe trying to escape from Southampton Water, would have already delivered their bomb load and he was also cognisant of the local fighter aerodromes at Eastleigh, Tangmere and Middle Wallop, that were the bases for the hunters. His Dad had already been heard to say at family tea-time that the Germans had knocked out the early warning radar system at Ventnor on the Isle of Wight. This meant their bombers for a short period could fly low under any signal uninterrupted to the south coast cities of Portsmouth and Southampton to attack naval and commercial dockyards.

So, Southampton was gonna get it. Ray was experiencing it all first-hand when suddenly something rained down on the football pitch, their Wembley, from the smoke-filled sky. The boys had just escaped in time. The dreaded shrapnel, which could cut a boy in half, fell like confetti from the tail of the bomber. It was hit, as the Dornier with plumes of black smoke rearing from its wings, was descending with a terrifying screeching higher pitched sound which intermittently spluttered. Now out of control, the plane all on its own was heading at 45 degrees, then more, just beyond 'Wembley' but still hurtling towards open ground.

Ray's natural reaction was to keep the group sprinting away from the inevitable explosion of the aircraft hitting the ground, but the kids were now away from the red-hot shrapnel zone and nearly 300 yards from the resting place of the plane. It hit the grassland in a ball of fire which engulfed the plane to such an extent that Ray could not recognise the type of bomber that had just perished. The crew couldn't have stood a chance.

Curiosity had got the better of him. He started running away from the players towards the stricken aircraft. As he timidly approached the scene of desolation with fragments of destruction and petrol fumes dominating the scene, he was struck by one thought. The thought that enveloped him, like a bolt from the blue was "Where is my little brother?"

Did he really care a fig about the younger Bristowe? More likely was the certainty that he would have to face the music from his Mum when he got home. After all, she had always laid down the law that if anything should happen to

Phil, he, Ray, would have to take the rap. He winced at the thought that he was going to take a hiding.

Janet Bristowe was Bermondsey through and through, a docker's daughter, the eldest in a family of seven. She had never been out of the Borough of Southwark, a London borough only a mile from the heart of Westminster and all its riches and influence. South of the river, it was a world away, a blue-collar enclave that was the hub of all commercial goods in and out of the pre-war British Empire.

Janet was schooled as the eldest to bring up her younger sisters and brothers. If they stepped out of line, it was her duty to clamp down on any errant behaviour, and in 1920s and '30s Bermondsey there was much a plenty of that. So, it was the same for her own family as she led the codes for discipline in her household. She had married a crane handler on the Surrey Docks. Freddie was his name, a man who would provide for the four of them, come what may.

Ray, now panicking, retraced his steps across the 'Wembley' surface heading for the mini hut which acted as the changing room, and then onto the wood, but nothing on Phil. He asked all the departing players there, but none of them noticed a thing, their attention being drawn to the theatre of the skies throughout the entire air raid. He ran back noticing that a crowd of adults had gathered like bees round a honeypot by the smouldering bomber. He approached one of the older folk and told him he had lost his brother called Phil. The adult reassured him that he would inform a Constable or Home Guard Official as soon as they would arrive. Ray was happy with that and, clambering on his Raleigh bike, headed off the six miles home to Chandler's Ford.

Phil Bristowe kept running and running and, as he came close to his target, accelerated to a sprint. This, on his own, was his big chance. His classmates at school had better believe this, and here was a real opportunity to put one over his elder brother.

His eagle eye had spotted in the opposite direction to where the Dornier had been driven to the ground, something that came out of the sky, a dot, a mere dot had caught his attention as he headed rapidly towards its path. Then suddenly, the dot enlarged and decelerated into a beige coloured parachute. The Luftwaffe pilot had escaped the burning inferno and was drifting onto the waste ground the other side of the wood.

Phil knew what he was going to do. The pilot hit the ground beyond the trees, rolled and then just sat in an upright position with his unruly parachute cascaded behind him spread over open ground. The young Englander, shy and reserved, faced him just five paces away. It was a stand-off between the cream of the Nazi bomber formation and a little wee blond boy with baby faced blue eyes.

The pilot had removed his headgear to reveal bruised and burnt, strong features, but nothing could mistake his blond, razor cut hair and piercing blue eyes. He looked, almost fixing his gaze on his mini-sized enemy and thought, contrary to his training, that this was all madness as the boy could easily be mistaken for his own son in Berlin.

Phil, unscathed and without an ounce of fear, met the German's eyes, never even blinking an eyelid. The pilot's blood and burnt condition never even bothered him. Then, the change of face in the German suddenly occurred as he watched young Phil pull a tiny packet out of his pocket, offering the pilot a gesture of peace. It was a small packet of Woodbines, cheap but popular cigarettes that he had nicked from the sweetshop earlier that morning.

The German indicated positive by placing his index and middle finger on either side of his lips. "Haben sie feuer?" he naively asked the six-year-old, for a much-needed light.

Phil whipped out a tiny box of matches, but in doing so, stared at the pilot's uniform and pointed to his crumpled beige over-jacket. He wanted his 'German wings' insignia from his chest and the Nazi Swastika emblem from his lapel.

'Hans', smiling, guardedly complied, ripping off the two invaluable artefacts and duly handed them to the young extortionist! What happened next deeply, but amusingly jolted the pilot. His Englander 'son' lit up two cigarettes, handing the other one to the desperate German.

Phil stared hard without a glimmer of gratitude into the eyes of Germany's feared Luftwaffe and just turned on his heels and headed north across the fields, the short-cut to Chandler's Ford and home.

* * *

'Home' for the Bristowes since April of that year was to be a converted flat above the baker's shop on Bournemouth Road in the hamlet village of Chandler's Ford. Since 1936 when the small settlement had been incorporated into the borough of Eastleigh, it had acted as a rural enclave only one mile from the railway hub of Eastleigh and a further six miles from Southampton Central. Janet and Freddie Bristowe had been offered a billet right across from the railway yards in a terraced house in York Road in Eastleigh, but the mother just did not fancy the built up lines of adjacent plots. As far as she was concerned, if she took up that option, the family might have just as well stayed in the cramped tightly knit streets of Bermondsey.

She did not want to leave home in London. There was the comfort of her own home, which was now 'invaded' by two sisters and a brother, and in addition there was the extended family of her parents. They were a sound buffer zone between Freddie, 'always at work', and the grandchildren, Ray and Phil. Whatever the MOD and the wardens warned, not a concerted bomb had fallen on London in the winter and spring of 1940.

So why did Freddie accept a posting to the south coast, interrupting family life and the kids' schooling? The answer was clear: Freddie Bristowe was going up in the world. If ever there was an example of shop floor, in his case a crane operative, to junior executive, his was a classic example of a rising star. For the head of the family and the sole breadwinner, he had been a stevedore, a crane handler, then onto an operative on the port directing import and export inventories, to finally just before the war, becoming a Chief Administrative Officer within the day to day running of Surrey Docks. In short, anywhere where rail terminals offloaded and received their load or cargo at the port of entry or exit, he was an essential cog in the management and successful transit of goods, both agricultural and industrial in nature.

As Janet's Dad would often reassure her with his Cockney tones, "The boy done well, Jan, stick with him and you'll be all right girl". She respected her father, but inwardly wanted the two boys out of the Bermondsey bubble of scraping a living from the docks.

The Armed Services had requisitioned all men under forty, but Freddie had the luck to be born in the last year of the nineteenth century. He had to undergo interviews for how the over-aged were to serve the war effort. Bristowe's interview lasted no more than fifteen minutes. Dock managers were a high priority as the Ministry of Defence and Port Installations knew that, sooner or later, Herman Goering would be lambasting the life blood of the British people, the external ports. It was just a matter of months before London, Liverpool, Hull, Edinburgh and notably the South Coast, were all in for a pounding.

Thus, back in April, it was not a surprise to Freddie that he and his family were issued with papers to resettle to the principal target and the closest to German occupied France, the city of Southampton. From the very outset, as far as Freddie was concerned, the 'Blitz' he was to experience, was the constant carping and nagging of a beloved wife chained to her family back in Bermondsey. He was as happy as Larry, as his day to day bike ride into the Eastleigh depot was only quarter of an hour away. On the days he was needed in Southampton Docks, there was a bus available up and along 'the Avenue' and down into the centre of town, a trip of just five miles from home.

That September afternoon, Ray had lost all his usual calm. After all, he had just witnessed the jaws of war bite into his life, had lost his kid brother and then panicked to escape home as quickly as he could to tell his Mum. He got hold of his bike and jumper, and just pedalled as quickly as he could muster, away from the 'Wembley' pitch and the destroyed Dornier.

He flew past the lake and entered the weird world of the Old Cemetery. The densely packed hallowed ground spooked him out as he would always remember Phil's constant taunting of his fear of the dead and this particular burial ground. It was unkempt, murky with no particular shape. He journeyed along a narrow, bumpy pathway to the Chapel in the south-west corner of Southampton Common. He was fearful of all the Victorian ghosts that might swoop down on him, a fear that hastened his leg speed over the two hundred yards of purgatory he was to face. He had to get out of the Common, and at last he glimpsed the Chapel. Surely this would put an end to his first misery, the Cemetery.

Then his second misfortune bore down on him; he was at the wrong end of the Common. His Dad had once told him that if he wanted to know where he was, and which direction he needed, he was to look at the sun. It was another clear sunny September evening. So through the array of airplane discharge in the sky he, at near on nine years of age, worked out his location. He was going south-west, he needed to go north-west. Easy, he thought, just turn right out of the rectangular open Common, and he should be heading north and sooner or later, hit 'The Avenue' and home to 'The Ford'.

It worked! However, then there was his brother's disappearance to contend with. He hoped the police or the wardens had found him by now, delivering him home. That was his best chance to escape the belt. Phil would get it instead, or maybe miserably, as well!

Ray parked his bike by the side of the baker's shop, it was just before 6pm. He poked his head inside Mr Griffith's shop for goodies leftover from the day's business. Maybe a pie here or a jam doughnut there. They were his favourites, but all sold out, it just was not to be his day.

Now to face his mum! She was over the stove, putting the final touches to a mutton stew when he climbed the stairs to enter through the side door. Janet turned her attention off the culinary delight to be shared amongst the four of them later when Fred got home.

"Where's Phil then?" Ray did not reply.

"Raymond," He hated it when she said that name as it was the sign of the tempest to be let loose on him, "What have you done with him, where is he?"

Ray then almost on the point of tears, could only say that he disappeared when the plane had crashed on the 'Wembley' pitch and burned everything alive.

His mother lost control completely.

"Disappeared, what plane and where the hell is Wembley? And who was burned alive?".

"I don't think Phil was near the German bomber but the pilot, he had to be burned. Ask the wardens, they were there, and I told them to look for Phil, they'll find 'im".

Janet, lost for words, could only come out with the safety valve system for all mothers, "You wait 'til your father comes home".

Ray knew this was serious, but he was clever enough to have noticed that his dad had never laid a hand on him nor his misbehaving brother. He had an hour of respite until Freddie would appear, so he whizzed up to the tiny box room which he and Phil shared as their bed and play room. Besides, he was earlier angry with himself for not fully recognising the downed plane, so he raced up to the bookshelf to seek out Uncle Cyril's birthday present.

Freddie arrived spot on time, given that he had been at the railyard all day. He parked his bike slightly mystified that one small one was missing. Hardly in the door, Janet came close gushing with tears, "Phil's missing! He disappeared during that air raid on the docks and shipyard. Ray's ok, he's in his cave, go and speak with him".

From manager man to father Freddie in just twenty minutes, he had endured a hell of a day as the Luftwaffe had mounted its biggest daily raid yet in September with dozens of bombers with fighter escorts. Gradually, throughout September, he had noticed that the bombing had become more systematic and targeted on the plant at Woolston and its neighbouring shipyard of Thornycrofts, producing Royal Navy destroyers. What he didn't want to tell Janet was that the potential targets of Eastleigh

Railyards and the assembly plant of the Spitfires adjacent to Eastleigh Airport were next in line!

"Well lad, just where is your brother?"

"Dunno", the Bermondsey Boy glibly retorted, "But I did tell the men, the wardens that I hadn't found him, can't you ask them?"

Freddie was able through the baker's downstairs, in an emergency, to use the phone. He did just that, but all his enquiries to police and wardens had met with no reply, and he knew why! He had been told earlier at 5pm after the raid, and by the evidence of the multitude of planes high above Eastleigh in combat, that this was a serious raid with untold damage to factories, property, utilities and people. Phone lines were down.

"How can we eat when all this is going on?" sobbed Janet. Her precious little boy, only six years old! "God knows what's happened to him?"

The family were helpless, only Ray was unfazed, telling his mum that Phil knew how to get home and his bike was still there at the pitch when he left for the cemetery gates.

Six o'clock became 7pm and then onto 7.30pm. It was slowly getting dark even though it was a clear blue sky evening. They sat motionless, waiting, hoping, praying. Ray interrupted the silence, offering a suggestion that Phil might be at Jimmy Fowler's house as it was just outside Chandler's Ford on the way to the Common.

"Let's go, you show me the way," said Janet.

Just before dark, they commenced their ten minute bike ride, desperate to see if Phil had decided to stay with Jimmy. Again, no luck, but at least Jimmy's uncle was a policeman and staying at the house, so he decided to rapidly raise a posse of fathers as a search party. They could cover a lot of ground in the twilight zone of the evening.

Two doors away, in The Parade, was positioned the highly-rationed butcher's shop. This was a social tragedy not only for the local community of Chandler's Ford, but also for Mr Yates' black Labrador called Bilko. He had come to enjoy pre-war all the trimmings and leftovers that the generous butcher would throw his way, including such delicacies as tripe and sumptuous bones. Bilko had won over everyone in the neighbourhood, but only one, just one person was his mate for life, and that was the little blond boy two doors down. They did everything together, walks, swims in the local ford, even the dog played in the local kickabouts. Bilko and Phil were inseparable.

The dog could sense when Phil was nearby. Mr Yates always knew when the boys came home from Chandler's Ford Primary, even though they had only been there for three months. Sat in the butcher's shop, Bilko would bark and bark, without even seeing outside and then do his circular twirl, a kind of welcome war dance as his master let him out down the street to meet and greet the two boys. Yet it was always to Phil that he made a beeline.

It was ten to eight exactly as Mr Yates was listening to the wireless before the eight o' clock news when Bilko, kipping quiet all evening, reared up excitedly barking, squealing, then barking twice again. Mr Yates recognised the sequence as he sped down the stairs almost being rugby tackled by Bilko! He unlocked the side door. The dog

17

launched out at the bedraggled boy in front of him, jumping up and licking his hands and giving the youngster that funny kind of dog talk. He was ecstatic to see Philip Bristowe.

"Look Mr Yates, what I got," Phil rumbling through his pockets.

"Bet you've never seen nuffink like these."

Mr Yates set his eyes on Phil's souvenirs, astounded at what he was witnessing, a fully-fledged German Luftwaffe pilot's wings and a dreaded Swastika. He and the dog, ushered Phil outside onto the pavement and marched the tired and hungry mite to his baker's home. The butcher knew Freddie well, and not even bothering to knock on the door, barged into the flat. Freddie spun round, elated, to behold his youngest staring right through him and stressing,

"They're for you, Dad – I got them from a German pilot."

How could Freddie resist such an offer, and how could he have explained that Phil had been so naughty to go missing and upset his mother so? Dad knew then that like any parent, he could never have a favourite, but whereas Ray had inherited his mummy's striking dark looks, it was the boy Phil that took after his dad.

Within minutes, two deranged figures reappeared at the door. Janet couldn't believe how crowded their little lounge had become with father, son, Bilko and Mr Yates all tucking into the warmed-up mutton stew. She was beside herself with joy, hugging and kissing her young devil. Ray wondered how long the theatrics would last before he would get a lashing for letting the little one out of his sight.

Mummy pulled out another dish from the cupboard for herself and commenced her tasting of the stew she had so pristinely prepared all afternoon,

"As for you, Ray, no supper for you. If I've told you once, I've told you a thousand times, if you go out with young Phil, you are responsible for him. You were too careless today, so it's early to bed, now go!"

She added, "Phil, off to bed once you've finished that stew, and keep Bilko away from it as well".

No one was spared, no doubt without hinting at an exit, "Thank you so much, Mr Yates. I've got a lot to speak to my husband about. He's got a great deal to answer for!"

Freddie awoke at just before six am that Friday morning with the bells still ringing in his ears from the previous evening. He did not have to recover from the all out attack of the Luftwaffe with all its deafening intensity. No, it was the two hours nagathon from Janet, far worse! Freddie took off to the docks at pace.

Not long after him, Janet acted as the kids' alarm clock. She made a point of bathing them in the regulated depth of water, notably after the events of the Common. Friday was the half day at the primary school, starting early at eight, but finishing at one o'clock. She walked the boys the short distance to their recently acquired 'Ford' school. That done, Janet made her way back to John Yates' butchers' shop where she gave him a hand as a part time assistant.

Her duties were mainly of a presentational nature. For a start, she had always taken pride in her appearance and polite demeanour. To John, it was a bonus that in her previous job she was a fashion window dresser in the Elephant and Castle. She had presented a lay out of his poultry products in the shop that was really striking to the customers. The trouble was they were all on rations and by Friday in any week there was precious little left!

"John, can we spend lunch hour together today?" she mused, "I want to quiz you on a few matters before I pick the kids up".

"Up for a cuppa and some lemon curd tarts in your flat, yes please," he retorted with customary optimism.

From time to time, she enjoyed and valued his company so much. Somehow, he filled the deep void in her life that had been missing since departing Bermondsey and all that entailed. She missed her father's reassurance, and maybe John, a widower who had lived life to the full following a twenty year career at Thornycrofts, acted as a positive father figure replacement.

She was still very much in love with Freddie, and as the mother of their two children, was devoted to her family making it on their own in the real world. That was until Adolf Hitler stepped in and wrecked the stable flow of their marriage. Freddie couldn't have done more for her and the boys. He was a great role model and turned the heads of many a woman in the street and was a very young forty, priding himself on his appearance and well-cut tailored suits.

John Yates had retired from his senior role at Thornycrofts as a result of the tragic premature death of his wife in a boating accident. The pair of them had always planned to own a small commercial holding in the village of Chandler's Ford. Her untimely death did involve some self-assessment for John, but he decided it was what she would have wanted for him. As time moved on, he acquired a cute little Labrador puppy to keep him company that evolved into the scatty adult that had become Bilko.

Janet popped next door before midday to put the kettle on and prepare some sandwiches. Minutes later John appeared with his companion, the sandwich hungry 'Bilks'. She opened the conversation very directly.

"John, after yesterday, I don't think I can take anymore. The bombs are falling more regularly, the planes are right above us and I just cannot keep a twenty four hour watch on the boys all by myself. Freddie's work requires total dedication to the docks and railways".

"I know, have you read The Echo this morning? Nearly a hundred dead with scores injured. As for the boys, I cannot blame you. Do you know young Phil walked nearly six miles all on his own to get back last night?"

"Yes," she whispered in faltering tones, "and he even trudged back forgetting all about his bike and jumper".

She knew that John would have a handle on what they could expect from the Germans in the coming months there in Southampton, but could he, and would he tell her?

"John, please tell me what you do think will happen here in Chandler's Ford and Eastleigh?"

"Janet, it's bad news. They're going after the docks, especially to destroy the Supermarine works where component parts of the Spitfire plane are made. They must know that the final assembly is up here next door to

Eastleigh airport and that all the parts are moved in via the rail tracks of Southern Rail at Eastleigh. My money is the bombing will continue at the waterfront but then move up here with our lads in the RAF trying to protect the skies and us below".

She hesitated to ask much more, whilst John had clearly noted the anguish his reply had created on her downward gaze. He had realised that she was caught in a trap, a dilemma that by supporting her husband's patriot work in the war she was endangering her life and the life of the two boys by remaining with him. It was just a fact of Freddie's life that wherever they sent him to, whichever British or foreign dockyard, he was to face bombs, mines and destruction.

War was about to make deep inroads into her family's life. For the sake of Ray and Phil and her family's very survival, something had to be done and done fast. It just had to be her decision. Bilko forlornly was peering into Janet's eyes totally unaware of his master,

"Ok, Bilks, let's go and get the boys home before anything else happens".

Janet took the lead, and Bilko led the way.

CHAPTER 2

THE FIRST CUT IS THE DEEPEST

"My Darling Freddie,

By the time you read this, I will be well away on the train to Waterloo. I do realise that we spent half the night discussing the matter, but I just have to get the kids back where they belong, with Grandma and Grandpops. We mustn't have a repeat of yesterday. They need to be around all the family.

I also know that London is under fire as well, but down here your work is taking us to live right by a Spitfire factory, a rail centre and an aerodrome, all round the corner near Eastleigh. Blanket bombing will soon be on us here in Chandler's Ford.

Whenever you get days clear, come up and see the family in Bermondsey. We all understand your work situation: you're forever in our hearts,

Love Jan and the boys."

Freddie peered down at the fireplace, then staring out of the window in the gathering gloom of evening, read the note again before throwing it in the fire. He was angry but not shocked by Jan's precipitous haste. That was her through and through. It was always going to be her children and any mention of the word family would mean her mother and father, sisters and brothers. More than anything he wanted to see Ray and Phil as growing boys with a backbone and an independence of mind. All Freddie could foresee was that they would be cossetted, namby-pamby style, under the stifling care of Jan, her mum and her sisters.

Danger and its impending force on London's dockland never really worried him, simply because he had no idea of the scale of the Luftwaffe's bombing that was to be unleashed on the capital that 1940 autumn. He had seen the sporadic raids on Southampton at first hand and appreciated that some of the south's principal airfields like nearby Tangmere were taking a pasting as well. He, like many others at the time, thought that major bombing of civilian residential parts of cities would be minimal.

In a funny sort of way, Freddie was a traditional type of fellow believing that war was directed at power centres like shipyards, aerodromes, industrial plants, ports, oil supplies and ocean shipping. What sort of a people would hit defenceless women and children in mass attacks? He was in for a big surprise. The dockmaster just did not seem to connect factories with people, and that they were mutually located side by side. His work was at the dockside, with his outlook directed down the river and out to sea. How he omitted to note that processing of all the ports' goods was completed and finished in places like Stepney, Bermondsey and Hackney, but he did, and that was a fact of his life.

Whenever he could, he would get back up to the streets he grew up in but it was to prove a rare occurrence. With no active telephone in service at her end in Kimberly Street or at her parents', it would be a matter of Janet updating what was going on through letters to the bakery in Chandler's Ford. For Freddie, no news would always be good news.

"Janet Bristowe, please can you come forward and see the officer?" exclaimed the local evacuation officer for Southwark Council. For some weeks right through October at the height of the Blitz, she had moved heaven and high water to get an interview with a representative of the Evacuation Committee. It was said at the time that Londoners could take it, the incessant night and sometimes day blitz on the city. Nearby Silvertown over the Thames beyond Rotherhithe had really copped it, whilst the margarine and sugar processing plants in Bermondsey were hit directly with the ongoing pong around the place for weeks. Rows of nearby terraces had been demolished and the community hall was part damaged. Rubble was everywhere and the roads were often made impossible through unexploded bombs, gas main leaks and water supply difficulties.

Janet's extended family, only two hundred yards apart would get together in her mum's back garden as they had invested in two Anderson shelters small enough to avoid

25

any direct hits, big enough to take up to seven at a time huddled in silence listening to the mayhem unfolding from above. In the mornings the Bristowes would appear at the local primary school, but it was a haphazard affair with no real consistent supply of electricity, heating, food or even teachers. Most of them were either at war or had returned home to look after their own nearest and dearest.

Nearly 800,000 kids had already been evacuated from England's cities, many of them at the start of the war in 1939.They had made a mistake of returning to the crowded cities in the summer as no bombs had materialised. They had sleepwalked into a perfect storm when the Battle of Britain was to begin from mid-August over London. Huge casualties in London's southern and eastern boroughs had hastened all the forced evacuation committees into full action again.

That was Janet Bristowe's objective. If only Southwark could see their way clear to get her and her kids out of the firing line. She had heard, that in other boroughs, entire schools with their teachers alongside them, had been dispatched from the city. Southwark was slow in that respect, after all it was a bureaucratic process. Yet again at her meeting, she was held in a queue and the long wait continued. However, one glimpse of light appeared when she was recommended to visit the parish church of St. James where the vicar had access to rural rectors who were taking small families on a private basis.

She wasted no time in banging on the Reverend Oliver Banting's door at his own private hostelry aside the church. Again, it was a short meeting with an outcome snapped up by the desperate Janet. The high churchman could get her and her two kids up to a northern enclave called Bingley, but it had to be the next week commencing November the 13th. Although the train journey would be long and circuitous, it would be complimentary but as was the custom there would be a statutory charge of 10 shillings and 6 pence for the weekly board and lodging at Park Road, Bingley.

Thank God the Reverend Banting had shared digs with his ecclesiastical 'roomie' at college, who had subsequently dispensed his duties to the flock of the mill town of Bingley, thought Janet. She was overjoyed; maybe it was true that God worked in mysterious ways.

Although her first thoughts were with the children, after all they were still only six and eight years old, she still mulled over what would happen with Grandma and Pops. She was reconciled to the fact that, like her two brothers and sisters, they would rather live in Berlin than leave Bermondsey. Oh yes, then she would have to consider Freddie. She had only seen him once since Chandler's Ford and that was just for one Sunday, so he would just have to go with the flow.

More important things were at hand. She needed to know how much clobber she could take up there. Clothes were easy as there was not a surplus on that front, but what about kitchen utensils, and Ray would want to know about his precious Raleigh bike? Surely the Reverend would know. What really concerned her were the effects of moving between three schools all in one year on the poor mites. Ray could handle it, but she was not so sure about

Phil. She would check in that coming week the details of the accommodation and the local Bingley schooling. She knew Bingley would be the big move, there would be no short-terming, no turning back. The vicar would be left in no doubt about that, even if her kids turned out to be Yorkies with "ee buy gum" accents!

The Reverend Banting had to contact Janet, and contact her quickly, so he himself walked the mile through the dilapidated streets of Bermondsey to find her at home. It was a Sunday evening with that fact alone reflecting the danger he would encounter if the air raid sirens were to disturb the air. She was delighted to see him of course, thinking it was some good will mission with some final pointers to her escape from living the hell of the Blitz.

"What I am to tell you will no doubt be disappointing. At this late juncture, the authorities at Euston Station have informed me that there will be no trains leaving 'til Wednesday morning: The Works parties are still working on the two platforms, the roof and the station's hotel after the bombing on Thursday night."

Jan, now bordered by Ray and Phil, was grief-stricken. Everything was ready to go with all the tearful goodbyes administered over a Sunday lunch of bread and dripping and a potato soup over at her mum's place.

She turned to the boys, "Just two more days, don't worry, we'll be on that beautiful steam engine train: it'll be worth waiting for."

The vicar reasserted that all was set for Wednesday on the evacuee express from Euston to Stoke on Trent, then onto Manchester London Road where they would change for the cross Pennine route to Huddersfield, Bradford, then Bingley.

"How long will it take, mister?" enquired Phil, not having been on a train for more than an hour and a half,

"You'll be at Lyndhurst by tea-time."

"I thought we were going to Badley," replied the uncertain child,

"No, no, no, my dear boy, 'Lyndhurst' is the name of the house, the special house you'll love, and don't forget, Philip, it is Bingley not Badley," laughed the Reverend.

Phil knew that boats and trains had names, but still asked the question, "I never knew 'owses had names, why doesn't our 'owse have a name Ray?"

"Cos it's surrounded by 'owses that all look the same. We're going to a big 'owse all on its own," Ray offered with some clarity.

* * *

It was bedlam that morning at Euston, but the Bristowes finally made it. What with the hooting of train horns, the loudspeaker announcements, and all those steam filled platforms hissing and spitting a mild fog over hundreds and hundreds of excited kids. It was a sight for sore eyes. Against the backdrop of such activity, evacuation officers, with the help of elderly guards and a multitude of mums, grandmas and grandpas, organised their children all neatly dressed in their best into ones and twos. Ray and Phil were inseparable, and even though they never ever really held hands together, Ray guided his little brother into line.

At first, this simple manoeuvre had proved difficult as all the younger Bristowe wanted to do was run down the platform to the front of the train to stand next to the steaming engine which even at rest devoured the attention of young Phil. He had never seen a steam engine at close quarters. The sheer size, power and smell of the Pullman powerhouse he was witnessing made Phil a train fanatic for life.

Janet put the boys into the carriage with dozens of boys and girls, some with their mums and others, mainly the older ones of twelve or thirteen, with no accompanying adults. She made a point of wanting to help them on the journey as much as she could, thinking all the time who in their right mind would abandon their children to their own devices, like that? Maybe they had grandparents or guardians at the other end; she hoped so anyway. As she boarded her carriage, she faced the stark reminder of her overall situation noticing the label on the train's exterior stating

'Third Class only'. She wondered, was that for life?

Her kids clambered into the fourth compartment along the corridor, chucked their bags up high on what looked like soft netting, and then sat down alongside a family of four which included an elderly grandad. Suddenly the train jolted with Phil soon annoyingly imitating the rhythm of the chuff-chuff train. Never had the children experienced such speed and mechanical noise, even drowning out the playful yelling and screaming of up to fifty young kids in their carriage alone.

The adventure had only just begun. The train accelerated, whistle blowing a deafening shriek of a sound in the damp November air. Inside there were Beanos and Eagle comics strewn across the seats, whilst the kids would sprint up and down the narrow corridors opening and closing the hatch doors to every compartment with gay abandon.

Luckily the mothers were used to it all. Janet started up some loose talk with the family sharing their booth. The grandad explained that he had come down the week before to pick the two girls up with their mum as their elder brothers were of service age and had enlisted as trainee pilots in the much depleted Royal Air Force. Their father had been a survivor at Dunkirk serving with the Staffordshire regiment. Janet soon realised it was not just the Bristowes that would be split up as a family because of the war. It was even worse for some with brothers and sisters displaced over a long term period. How the mothers could allow their kids to be separated she never knew; it was bad enough not having the father around.

The green English countryside was serenely passing by as the train hurtled towards Stoke on Trent, the first drop-off and pick up of more evacuees. Janet drifted half in a dream world, and half in an incessant assault on her thoughts working overtime. It was true what they said, she surmised, that the female of the species always felt guilty about something. She chided herself all through the journey that she was on the chicken run. Real cockneys would never abandon London town. Then she descended into a dream with floating faces of her mum, her two brothers,

Anderson shelters, the vicar and the Elephant and Castle shop where she had previously worked. The faces would fade into each other.

Half asleep, half awake, she blurted out, "No, Freddie, no, we have to go, where's Phil, Phil, where are you?"

Suddenly she was yanked by the elbow with that ever-loving stare expressing reassurance,

"What's wrong mum? I'm here, look, wake up, I'm here with Ray," the little boy interrupted.

It was raining outside. Well it was November, and Ray had already warned his younger brother that all it did in Manchester was rain. Indeed, this time it was Stoke that loomed on the lunch-time landscape. Ray's idea of going north previous to this journey was crossing the River Thames. Waterloo was his package port to another country which started at Charing Cross.

"Blimey, what a dump, Phil, look at those 'owses with little lanes between them, and d'ya see all that smoke coming out the chimneys. They goes on for miles and miles."

It was midday, Ray thought, but it was dark, dreary dark with the rain now horizontal. The coal-fired soot had ascended to mix with the low cloud of a rainstorm which had resulted in a near permanent fog, a dirty grey blanket as far as the eye could see.

Janet had only told the good things about the North. She had made no reference to the cobbled narrow streets with the factories belching out the poisonous fumes of Josiah Wedgewood's Stoke on Trent, the Victorian gateway to the industrial dirty promised land of the North. She knew

32

Bermondsey was built up enough but the South London landscape had hope: it had the river, the effervescent flow of the docks and theatres with colourful people, the cockneys and the pearly queens. This place on the Trent was just a drab workhouse!

"I'm glad we're not getting off here," muttered Ray as he searched for his satchel. He was to grab a few pencils to go with the notebook, blank with no lines that his grandad had given him as a going away gift. He could now stretch out and think about what he could reproduce on paper in the hour and a bit before Manchester's London Road Station.

The accompanying family had just disembarked at Stoke scurrying along the platform to take cover, this time from the pelting precipitation. Their war was to be staged in the foothills of the Lower Peak District, mainly oblivious to the crash, bang, wallop of their North London home.

"Why do they call it, The Peak District, Mum?" asked Phil, always inquisitive on things he'd never heard of, or about.

"Well a peak is like a hill you know, like Crystal Palace on the way to Auntie Edna's. So it's hilly where all those girls are going, but not as high as where we will be staying in Bingley, well away from those nasty Nazis."

When the Bristowes arrived at the terminal stop at Manchester they had to change trains and platform for an hour before the onward journey to Bingley. Mum broke open some sarnies for Phil but Ray wasn't hungry. The elder boy just wanted to sketch the locomotive that had brought them there to Manchester. The engine was at its resting place and luckily for Ray, there was no onward journey for that loco for a few hours. Janet kept Phil busy with a game of 'I Spy with my little eye', whilst Ray contentedly perused the giant black engine which looked like, but was not, the famous 'Flying Scotsman'.

Forty minutes went by as Janet collected the baggage to pile onto the new mini-train to Huddersfield and Bingley. She screamed at Ray to put down his enlarged notebook and hurry up. He was, however, detained by the station master peering over the eight year old boy's shoulder.

"Listen young man, you wouldn't let me have your sketch, would you? I'll give you half a crown," he pleaded.

Ray couldn't believe his luck, pocketing the large round coin, re-joining the family and informing his mum that the station master wanted a word with her. Janet approached the kind, elderly gent who sheepishly addressed the mum,

"Eh, lass, that boy of yours has a special talent. Have you seen the detail, even in pencil, he has put into this loco engine portrait? Never seen 'owt like it in me life, especially for a lad of his age. What's your address? I'll frame it for you."

"Lyndhurst, Park Road, Bingley," she retorted.

She and he would come to never forget that line.

"By the way, his name is Ray Bristowe."

It was dark by the time the trans-Pennine subsidiary train pulled into Bingley station. Pitch black was how Janet described the weather conditions, but at least she was afforded a warm Yorkshire welcome from the local vicar who had known the Reverend Banting so well all those years ago.

"Welcome to Bingley, no bombs, no sirens, no black outs and no damage, let me take you up to Lyndhurst."

He offered luxury in his five seater Morris car.

Surprisingly the two brothers were excited at the prospect of their new home at the top of a very steep incline. Many boys and girls of their ilk had fought tooth and nail in leaving their toys, friends, play areas and even their little primary school behind.

The house, as explained by Mr Crawshaw, was inherited by his family as vicar to the parish from an old mill owner who had made his fortune from wool and worsted cloth at and before the turn of the century. The front gate opened onto a trim front garden with plenty of open space to the sides of the property which on one side gave way to a steep dip to a running stream fifty feet below. By six o'clock on their first host evening, Ray and Phil were unable to note any of these features, but inside there was light and noise from the downstairs kitchen communal area.

The Bristowes were the fourth and final family to be housed in what Ray described at first viewing as a big mansion. The London family put down their heavy loads at the invitation of Mr Crawshaw and were duly led into the kitchen/scullery, and briefly introduced to the assembled throng of three separate families, a total of nine adults and children.

Janet, in turn, politely asked Ray and Phil to let the other kids know their names. Two of the three resident families had a mix of boys and girls who spoke with strong northern accents, later to be discovered as Liverpool and Hull dialects, but the final family, two boys of the same age as Phil with their mum, had familiar notes as they sprang up from deepest Kent near Dover. Right from that moment on, there seemed to be a chemistry between the two sets of brothers.

"Don't they look the same," Phil suggesting to his mum.

"Yes, they're twins, identical twins," offered Janet with a sideways glance over to their mother, Mrs Berlinger.

"Double trouble!" added their mum, almost with a glowing sense of pride.

"Lovely to meet you all and I hope you don't mind, but we've had a long journey and we had better settle in this evening. See you all in the morning," said Janet.

The Bristowes occupied the upper quarter of the house which was reached by a wide central staircase. They would turn right at the top, the Berlingers were to the left. After all the preliminaries, Janet packed Ray and Phil off to bed, a double bed in their own bedroom. While the boys slept soundly, it was just the ticket for Janet to show her true appreciation for all that Reverend Crawshaw had done to place them. She was delighted and told him so.

The rooms were spacious, a little cold upstairs but with plenty of space for the boys to play in and a back garden with apple trees and sycamores to explore in the daylight.

Strangely, in the morning, they came down to a childless home as all the kids had already gone to the Mornington Road Primary at the foot of Park Road. It was an easy walk or bike ride in the morning, but murder getting up that hill on the way back at 3.30 every day.

Janet would not place her boys in the school until the next term in early January, so that they could adjust to the town, its people and their fellow families at Lyndhurst. So for that day in mid-November, she suggested they take a long morning walk around the town. Firstly, after Bermondsey they found little evidence that the town was actually at war. There was no rubble, no road closures, no holes in the road nor damaged houses. They also noticed something they had not enjoyed in months, fresh air. The Borough of Southwark reeked of either gas, the glue factory or the food processing plant, all of which had been bombed at one time or another during the Blitz.

Once the mum and two boys had got to the bottom of Park Road, they now could see what there was to behold of Bingley town. For Ray and Phil, even Janet as well, it was a revelation. None of them had seen mills, canals, locks or tin bridges before. There were sawmills and tanneries as well, and all of them though ancient, were in working order.

Beyond the dozen or more mills with their chimneys active, the centre of town was criss-crossed by two further hills at the top of which were the Assembly Rooms and the Hippodrome Theatre, and at the base of the hill was the Cosy Corner Picture House. Stretching down on the lower road were twenty-seven acres of parkland with tennis courts, a bandstand, a bowling green and the Princess Hall swimming pool.

The two boys were dumbfounded, but ecstatic. In turn, Janet was relieved that this little textile backwater was such a self-contained town, an oasis from the daily troubles of the city and with so much to offer two active growing boys. She ushered the boys into a teashop, and as with the adjoining shops, there was so little choice. Rations were biting hard, it being obvious by the look in the eyes of her two small children, that it still was to be an adventure, but a hungry one at that! She ordered a pot of tea and two buns from the waitress. Did Janet detect a certain look of mild animosity from the server? She certainly was very abrupt, or was that just the down to earth ways of Yorkshire folk out there in the sticks?

That was the one area of concern for Mrs. Bristowe. Would the local folk, and particularly the occupants of Lyndhurst, take to a London mother and her two very cockney kids? Once January came, Ray and Phil could be in for a difficult time with the northern schoolkids. She knew that children could be so cruel at times, especially with two city boys who might have been deemed to invade the space of such a small town. It was so important that they made friends.

Over the coming months, in many respects, Jan need not have worried. Inside Lyndhurst, the twins quickly befriended the Bermondsey boys, in fact the four of them were inseparable. For the foreseeable and unforeseeable future, the Berlingers provided a soft landing for the boys from South London. Yes, there were petty squabbles and rivalries at times but in those early times, Peter and David were showing the new boys the ropes, even though they had only been evacuated from Kent three months earlier.

Second World War children in those circumstances through mutual and collective play were allowed to develop through their dared and shared experiences. Whether it was conkers and tree climbing in the autumn, snowboarding in the winter, football in the spring or the Myrtle Park swimming baths in the summer, they really were an independent, self-reliant bunch of young kids. They would risk, invent and innovate new games, secure in the knowledge that if anything did go wrong, they could rely on their mates for help.

Both the twins, and Ray and Phil, seldom ran to their mummies to bale them out. They would never tell or snitch on one another, and if found guilty, take their punishments. Janet was a past mistress at reading the riot act to her two, but she had nothing on Mrs Berlinger, a very robust woman married to a sergeant major in the eighth army, who would have won an Olympic gold for belting the hell out of the twins!

There was no doubt that the twins and especially Phil loved the sporting and outdoor feel of Bingley. All of them excelled at school sports to a point of excellence, and their constant 'daring' of each other around the house and the garden simply drove them on to bigger and more dangerous acts and options that defied all levels of common sense. Yet, this was where Ray came in as the senior boy, always the one at eighteen months older who demanded respect from the 'Three Musketeers'.

At this stage, Ray provided that common sense and an understanding of fair play that brought the others into line. That was, while they were infant seven year olds. Ray, through his bellyaching at his mother, had saved enough from his pocket money to buy a second-hand bike from one of the leavers of Mornington Road primary by the end of the 1941 winter. One of the reasons for this was his continuous sketching in Bingley. He had recognised so many unfamiliar elements that he could draw within easy reach of 'Lyndhurst': he had waterfalls, the famous stepped locks of Bingley, Myrtle Park and the grouping of woollen mills as all of these landmarks fascinated him.

One or two other areas of encouragement really helped him. Firstly, his mum gave him permission to ride the bike anywhere as long as it was not in the dark and not in anyway loaned to Phil. Secondly, once in late spring, a package arrived with a Manchester delivery stamp on it, and opening it up, it was the framed picture of the 'Pullman' Engine that had transferred them up from London Euston. Signed at the bottom was the autograph of the Manchester, London Road station master, with the message,

"With best wishes for your future career in art!"

Once Janet showed the piece to Ray's art master, known as Arthur, 'Art' Brown, Ray was to spend many after school sessions fine tuning his skills onto canvas.

To Phil, this was water off a duck's back. He had started at Mornington Road and was pleased to be in the same class as Peter and David. They walked to the school together whilst Ray of two years above, cycled. At the ages of six, they at times, were mistaken for triplets. For wherever there was a football, a school outing or a physical challenge, the 'Musketeers' would take it on and win. They were a team within any team, and despite the efforts of the local classmates who really did not take to the three abrasive, confident southerners, they staved off any mickey-taking or bullying.

As far as they were concerned, if any local Yorkie touched any one of them, and that included Ray, they would react and spring into action as a team. Theirs was a thorough physical education, one which they wholeheartedly enjoyed as an adventure in life and a very happy one at that.

Inside Lyndhurst, Ray and Phil played to the rules in what was more like a commune. They would 'dig for victory' in planting vegetables, notably the potatoes which had become a staple diet. They would pick fruit, and even go down into the town to collect the milk from their householders' jugs.

Hand me down clothing was ever present as were the dreaded patches on trousers, jumpers and coats. At least the mums and the girls would mainly attend to those tasks. Rations were tight and their energy levels meant they were constantly hungry. For treats they would go with the Berlingers to the Regent or Cosy Corner picture houses (The Hippodrome was more upmarket for the adult theatre buffs and concert devotees), where their favourites were inevitably cowboys and indians and listening on the newsreels to the infamous Lord Haw-Haw making his latest pronouncements from Germany.

Indeed, the war was passing them by. Unlike the early evacuees that were received in the Bingley and Keighley District, a total of over 21,000, of which 10% went home within the first fortnight, the Bristowes were there to stay for the whole course if necessary. It was a far cry from the situation in London, where back in 1941, Janet had heard the tragic news that half her street at home had been pancaked from an isolated bombing raid. Her house was gone, but thank God, all her brothers and sisters had been holed up at her mum's Anderson shelter that weekend.

In short, she was homeless with the kids. What was hers and Freddie's was gone. They would have to wait till the end of the war before anything could be sorted out. Until then, they as a family would continue to experience the three way split: Janet and the boys in Bingley, her mum and family in Paradise Street, Bermondsey. As for Freddie, goodness knows, in Egypt, Sicily or Italy, but by his very irregular communications, at least he reckoned he was winning the war!

Time was moving on and her boys were growing, but to her mounting concern, by 1943, in very differing directions. It had come to her notice that young Phil was not sleeping or using the same bed as his older brother but sneaking out in the middle of the night to stay with his twinned chums. She would turn a blind eye to this, as did Mrs Berlinger, but alarm bells were sounding when she noticed they were ganging up on Ray, now they were all ten years old or so. They were merciless at poking fun at Ray, teasing him all the time about his more academic and artistic talents. Physical frustrations were boiling over and cuts and bruises on all parties were explained away by the boys as mere accidents.

The split between the three and Ray was confirmed when the latter won an academic scholarship to Bingley Grammar School. This prized achievement was held in high esteem by all at Lyndhurst and across Bingley as a whole. Ray had augmented his prowess by continued trips via cycle rides to the neighbouring Keighley's celebrated library. This listed antiquated building had all types of treasures for Ray, including the full set of the Encyclopaedia Britannica from which he boasted he had already read the first eight volumes. By the autumn of 1943 Ray was peddling across town to the highly renowned grammar school, whilst Phil with the Berlingers plodded their way to Mornington Road with no academic pretensions of their own.

Boys will be boys, it has often been said. Here, there was a widening gulf that the educational system was rather inadvertently expanding. Whilst Phil kicked around in the playground with his mates, Ray was reciting his Latin verbs and skilfully placing brush to canvas. Janet only hoped that time would return the two together, but for now, she was happy if they were happy.

There was no doubt that by early '44, even the civilian population of the mill town knew that the Allies had the upper hand. Troop movements, tanks and armoured equipment were all heading south through the Yorkshire market town ready for the expected invasion from the south coast, as it turned out in June of that year. The first to go at the end of the primary school term in early August were the Berlingers. Both Janet and clearly Phil, with watery eye, bade farewell to the family that had been part of the Bristowes' life for nearly four years. Ray stood impassively as their train pulled out of Bingley station. Janet, as the Head of the Bristowe family, had decided only to go back south when Freddie's overseas work had finished and that was scheduled for, hopefully November. Til then, the boys had to continue with their education and Phil now was to enter his last year at Mornington.

It was the quiet summer holiday that was about to unfold with victory in Europe as the backdrop. Without the Berlingers, Phil was collecting a new set of friends, local boys who already had been in real trouble at the school for thieving, bullying and fighting. In the height of August, boredom would often set in as the brothers had enjoyed all that Bingley had to offer. Ray was soon to be a teenager, whilst Phil was starting to find pleasure in unsavoury and dangerous pursuits.

One weekday afternoon, they had been swimming at the Myrtle Park Swimming Baths with Ted Gilbert, a local rough and tough acquaintance of Phil's. On a spare patch of grass, they rested up with Ted suggesting to Phil, "How about a game of splits, Phil?"

"Have you got a knife?" replied the younger Bristowe.

"Sure have, look at this, let's play," suggested Ted

They, then, standing opposite each other with legs together, faced down three yards apart. The aim of the game was to throw the elongated penknife into the ground adjacent to the opponent. At that point, he would place one of his legs on that spot. They would do this alternately until one player bowed out because his legs could not reach the penknife. Hence the name 'Splits'!

"OK, you win Phil, that's because you can throw this knife with either hand, you lucky bastard. Now play your brother at reverse splits."

Ray stood dumbfounded but for some reason, maybe to impress Ted, he agreed to face off against his brother. The two stood diametrically opposite, but with legs as far apart as they could go. The aim was to fling the knife inwards, again alternately as near to the other foot as possible. Ray went first and he halved Phil's stance. Then Phil, a very similar inward throw, then Ray, who shortened the distance again so that Phil's feet were only seven or eight inches apart.

Phil, this time left-handed, threw to four inches. Now even Ted was worried; Ray flung the sharp implement to the two inches between Phil's feet, but the knife had not entered the ground, therefore not counting as legal. The younger Bristowe now would aim with heightened intensity. Tongue hanging out, he spun the knife at speed straight into Ray's foot between the end of the shin bone and the start of the fine ankle ligaments.

Ray looked down in agony as the knife had penetrated by at least an inch. He screamed, losing complete control, and lowered his hand and yanked the knife from the gaping hole, blood oozing from the wound. He glimpsed up at Phil, who had never seen his brother like this and now was ready to hunt him down. Phil Bristowe retreated at pace with Ray in pursuit, almost frothing at the mouth. Ray erratically whizzed the knife through the air. The blade slammed deep into the side of Phil's neck as he collapsed to the ground, more Bristowe blood cascading down his cotton shirt. Ray was screaming, Phil was almost still. What could Ray do?

He dropped down, and for the second time in a minute pulled the knife, red with blood and brown from the dirt, out of Phil's neck. He then whipped off his vest and wrapped it around the wound and pressed hard. His mood had changed,

"Go to the pool, quick, get the lifeguard, he'll know what to do and be quick," Ray ordered the startled Ted.

With no emotion Phil whispered in Ray's ear:

"One day, I'll get you for this."

* * *

Later that night, Janet visited both boys at Bingley Hospice. She wore a headscarf more out of embarrassment than need. For the first time, she held a calm and collected air, for she was not going to quiz her boys on what had happened. No, she would never do that nor tell any of the family, let alone Freddie.

That was the Bermondsey way. Any shameful acts within the family would stay within the family. To admit that the boys had fired the first shots of war at each other would only mean to Freddie, her sisters and her neighbours that Jan was failing as a mother. That would never do.

In time she would hand out the punishment for their crime with the principal target being Ray, the elder brother. He always knew what was coming. How he hated that his avenging mother in her own spiteful way would never let it go, never let him forget his occasional flare up with his wayward brother. She would always shift the blame onto his shoulders with her favourite slight of,

"Raymond, you should be ashamed of yourself!"

Nevertheless, to Jan it was a sign, a signal to move on from Bingley even though the town had been more than kind to her and her boys. The war was coming to an end,

Freddie was coming home for good, they all could start afresh in a new home with a new start. Things like this can happen in wartime – yet deep down in her mind's eye, she knew the damage had been done.

Things between Ray and Phil would never be the same.

CHAPTER 3

THEY EAT RATS, DON'T THEY?

It was just another clear blue-sky morning in early May over London town. The sun had returned out of the gloom of a desperate winter. Yet this burst of springtime was unique, unique all over a jaded Britain. Victory in Europe Day was to be celebrated across the continent as fighting ceased from the nasty grip the Nazis had held over lands as far as Poland to Spain, and from the fjords of Norway to the islands of Greece.

As for Londoners and for the Bristowes of Bermondsey, they had endured a bellyful of war. As Janet used to stare up at her print of Mister Churchill on her kitchen wall of old, she would burst out with the rhetorical question,"Well, Winston, what has war done for us Bristowes?"

And then she continued to provide the answer,"Bombed out house, two boys brought up never seeing their father, a family pulled from pillar to post all over England, no money, no clothes and precious little food."

Nevertheless, Janet sensed a new feeling that May morning. It was the warming all around her, not just in the glow of the sun but also in the sanctity of relief. She knew and recognised the signs of closure as she took an early day walk from her sister, Edna's house in the small village of West Wickham, beyond the suburbs. She had settled in with the boys just off the High Street in Kent Road and apart from two families living together in Edna and Cyril's home, there was a real air of normality over the spring months of 1945.

Gone were the days and nights of air raid sirens and Bermondsey's continued bomb damage along with the dreaded doodlebug rockets that had rained down on the southern parts of the capital over the autumn. For her, also gone were the times when she and the boys were estranged to the desolate cold moors of Yorkshire, stuck out on a limb away from her parents and most of all from the love of her life, Freddie Bristowe.

Jan strolled down the High Street in the fresh air passing smiling faces bidding her 'Good morning' and 'Lovely day' as she surmised over something she was still getting accustomed to; there was, happily, no damage to West Wickham! In strict contrast, Dockside Bermondsey was always in recovery. If it wasn't bombed out houses, it was gas leaks, water losses, the smell of sewer exposure and the endless rubble along the pitted streets.

Thank God, she thought, she had left her dad's home back in November, and with Freddie back from Italy and

North Africa, she was ready to start afresh. For the moment though, it was time to celebrate. It would be a West Wickham street party like no other before, based around Cyril and Edna's house. Freddie had resumed his work up around the Millwall Docks which had taken a pounding over the duration of the war. The one good side effect of this was his appropriating, legally, some of the docks' contents directly onto the dinner table of Mrs. Bristowe!

Freddie was now honoured by the provision of a military car which he shared with two other officers. He would pick up early, and drop off in Croydon at six thirty evening time. Some of their snacks included bananas, sugar and oranges, straight off the boats. So with Cyril's friends in high places working in the food ration distribution centres, the two families at least had something to celebrate with!

The tables were set out with the Union Jack flags decorating the adjoining gate posts along Kent Road, and with all the mothers mucking in, VE Day was a late lunch punctuated with spam and a small number of cheese sarnies, followed by home-made cakes and scones and fresh fruit. What a novelty! For Ray and Phil had not seen such luxury since 1939, so like the other kids in the street, they ate like there was no tomorrow. What was missing from the frivolity were the servicemen still marooned in Europe somewhere. What men were there, were grandads and the likes of Cyril and Freddie, workers on the home front. For the latter, it was a sober affair no booze, just tea and lemon squash and now, plentiful liquid in the form of English rain!

They all rounded off the party with a sing-song as one of the mums had brought her piano alongside the tables. All of the favourites were played out with gusto as the lyrics of George Formby and Vera Lynn were second nature to this band of happy war survivors. Ray would wonder at how they would just continue on from one frivolous song to another, never missing a beat nor a line of words. The songs would go on uninterrupted for half an hour at a time. Phil could never understand what all the fuss was about and just wanted to get away from all those frolicking women with bright red lipstick. He hated it because of the lack of men. He would be forced to dance with some old bird he never even knew and at the end of such an embarrassment, receive a big whopper of a kiss on his cheek for his trouble.

The party moved on a pace throughout the afternoon, gradually dispersing as the evening approached with still a nip in the air. Most of the families returned to their abodes, but there was a rumour that Mr Turner at Number 36 was offering some of his locally renowned and infamous home brew beer. Freddie couldn't resist it even though it was like rocket fuel with the next day hangover absolutely guaranteed. He needed no convincing to get inside out of the rain.

He hoped that his inebriation would only affect his morning duties at the office set aside for him at the end of the wharf. Freddie had only been back a month after dispensing his expertise with Britain's 1st Army up the east coast of Italy throughout 1944 and 1945. Not wanting to alarm Janet in any way, he remained silent about not only his direction of travel, but also the perilous work he had undertaken. His unit was known as 'The Mop Up Squad', with their primary function of making good the ports and docks vacated by the retreating German armies.

Freddie had pushed north up through Bari and Brindisi with the familiar pattern of harbours that were mined and routinely attacked by Stuka dive bombers. He had lost count of the number of occasions he had to dive into harbour waters to escape the screaming Stuka loads. The German army would take just hours to leave and then deliver their pay loads whilst his Army mops needed a week just to make the harbours safe from mines. Additional weeks were required to make them functional to be able to import the goods and services of a mobile occupying Army. Freddie never talked about his near scrapes with death, but just told anyone interested,

"Thank God for the Yanks. Without their equipment, we would have got nowhere fast."

So, why was he so anxious about the length of his hangover from 'ole git Turner's hooch? He was to appear across the water that very afternoon at a Ministry of Defence briefing up near Charing Cross; not so much a briefing, more an order from the top brass. They, in their considered kindness had given him the afternoon off from dealing with the last set of cranes that had broken down!

He never told Janet. Anyhow she was too busy trying to get Ray and Phil sorted out for schooling for the following September. With both of them now at the secondary stage of education, they had been to just too many schools, and their return to Bermondsey the previous autumn was another destabilising feature of their behaviour after four years in Bingley. She had withdrawn them from their local school and was now seeking a better and more suitable place away from the educational nightmare and environment of schools surrounded by bombsites, displaced kids, truancy and wild west behaviour.

"Sit down, Mr Bristowe, although for the purposes of this afternoon, it will be Sergeant Bristowe of the 1st Army," said the duty officer.

Freddie stiffened as it already felt like a court marshall. The surroundings were drab, just a portrait of King George or 'Bertie' as he was affectionately known, set in a high ceilinged room at the back of the third floor building, just a couple of hundred paces from Scotland Yard.

The duty officer, a Major, clearly was on a mission, his demeanour positive and straight to the point. He said, "sergeant Bristowe, you have had a good war. In fact, outstanding service to the war effort wherever you have been, and I understand your work has taken you from the London Docks, to Southampton, Liverpool, Greenock, Tripoli, Sicily, Bari, even Anzio. Once a docker, always a docker, would you say?"

"Yes, sir," Freddie nervously replied.

"Enjoy the work eh?"

"It's hard graft, sir, but yes from driving a crane, loading and offloading to the desk work organising it all, I suppose I have come a long way."

"Exactly, Bristowe, and we're not finished with you yet. There is work to be done from this day forth, with a salary to boot, and most important of all a real opportunity for you to climb in the ranks of the British Army."

"How would that 'appen?" Freddie lapsed into dropping his aitches.

"We have been posting men into probably one of the most vital areas of work and in one of the most strategic cities of wartime and post-war Europe. Your overseas experience has to be exploited and we need men in these trouble spots who have plied their trade under pressure and achieved nothing but positive results. You have done that since 1940, Bristowe. We want you to be one of our top dogs in resurrecting the Hamburg Docks, the first phase of the full recovery in our British sector of Germany's powerhouse port on the Elbe."

Freddie was speechless.

"Don't just sit there man, what do you say?"

"Just how long will it take? I know the RAF decimated the place."

"Correct. You will be working from a blank canvas with and alongside a huge number of MOD departments to get that city up and running. It will not just be a port job, you will be part of a Brit effort to resurrect this city from the dead. Your career can now be launched for life. We need you for a minimum of two years. I understand you are a married man with two kiddies. The MOD will do everything to give them a stable upbringing whilst you're doing your duty in Hamburg. You know, provision of housing, placement of schooling, and of course scheduled visits on a regular basis to you in Germany.

"You mean, I can't take my family with me?"

"No place for a woman, especially with kids. You will be hands to the pump for six days a week, twelve months a year for a minimum of two years," informed the major.

"Crikey, you do tell it as it is, sir."

The major knew from his own experiences that an army career, however short, was a passport to 'Civvy Street', and the more specialised your talents, the more likely the rewards, the money, the pensions. For a family in any post-war austerity period, this was an offer Freddie couldn't refuse.

"If you take a step next door, the sergeant will give you the terms and details of the placement. Any queries, could you put them in writing to me here, to Major Jim Swinson, within seven days?"

"Goodbye Bristowe, and good luck with the Krauts."

Freddie ambled down the stairs totally unaware of his dour surroundings after his briefing with the sergeant. Not for the first time this dockmaster had been torn down the middle between his enduring family that were true survivors of six years of deprivation and the challenges, the real buzz that he got every single day from being a docker. The incessant noise and smells of the waterfront and the activity of a long-lasting camaraderie had filled him and his forefathers with a true loyalty, even love for being by the quayside all their lives.

There was more to it than this sense of belonging. He was also a slave to construction and recovery. For Freddie, being a docker meant you were building something every time you went to work. You were, in reality transferring goods to the workshops and dinner tables of a nation.

Without you, nothing or very little could get done. His work ethic was one of delivery. He and his like delivered for a living with their bare hands. Yes, with every year passing he was getting further away from the lifting of the crates of his stevedore days to the newly mechanised cranes that would take the loads. Add to that, the improved facilities at the wharfs with more suitable vehicles and access roads to the docks, his rise to the administrative sector was coinciding with faster and more efficient procedures.

Post-war would need standardisation to handle all the mass-produced materials arriving from America. Instead of war machines, it would become an era of perishable goods, food and household materials to meet the demands of the inevitable recovery. His nature and personality wanted, even needed a slice of all that. Freddie had to be central to it all and that is why he was very tempted by the sergeant's offer, all be it on 'enemy territory'.

The army orderly had motivated him further not only with a salary reward to be paid into his family's account in British sterling, but also, as the major had hinted, that they would attempt to place his children in suitable schools. Surely this would convince Janet first and foremost. He knew, as he would put it, that Jan would initially go bonkers at this proposal. Once she heard that they would be put at the top of the list for a new prefabricated house of her own, and still located in the borough of Southwark with her kids in decent schools, she would just come around. Anyhow, that was the plan!

Just two more years and they would be made for life. He had recognised that salaries in the army came with rank and given that he would be up for demobilisation soon, for him it would be in 1947. He figured that even England would have settled down a bit by then. In short, a transition period in Hamburg for Freddie Bristowe would be a passport to prosperity for his family.

Jan did hit the roof! Freddie experienced 'the usuals'. The screaming and the shouting was always followed by a long period of sulking and the no-talk zone, in this case weeks of a non-communication tactic. Only when she had exhausted this line would she then go missing with Ray and Phil for days on end to stay away from Edna's place in West Wickham back at her mum's. The two kids in this period, out of school, loved to briefly go back to their Gran's to revisit their true home with most of their old mates they had left behind when they were evacuated to Bingley.

Nearly a month had passed when Jan finally cooled and then even warmed to the idea. Freddie knew she would, and he proved it by accepting the posting after seven days! Still, he had written requesting the provision of the prefab and an answered notification of where exactly the boys would be placed. This was to prove a little awkward!

Ray was a bright boy academically; Phil was not. The scholarship that the former had received to Bingley Grammar School back in 1943 had pushed Ray and had the impact of stimulating his interests into wider studies that only a Grammar could provide. He was studying Latin and Chemistry for God's sake at Bingley. There were few schools within five miles of New Cross in South-East London that got near the appropriate educational provision for him.

However, reportedly, the trains were starting to work again with track repairs a priority for the new government. A twelve-mile journey to outer London to a place called Beckenham was a real possibility, especially as this suburb was also handily placed not far from Edna's house.

Ray sailed through an entrance exam that summer. He was accepted as early as June but would continue his grammar school education at the age of thirteen in September.

What of Phil?

"I don't wanna go to no grammar," he would say to his mum, not understanding that he didn't have a cat in hell's chance of achieving such a goal. So far at Mornington Road Primary in Bingley he had flunked all tests and moved onto the town's only secondary modern, then called elementary, for just one term in the autumn. To put it mildly, here was a very unsettled boy, taunted in Yorkshire for his cockney accent with no academic leanings and no sympathy from rigid 1940s schoolmasters. Did he moan about it? Never!

Yet, with Phil, there was one chink of light. He was physically gifted and had been widely admired for his prowess at sport. He had been miles ahead of his peers and even elder contemporaries at football and cricket. Any individual challenge put before him, he had relished. Never to be pushed around he was now at the end of the war back on his manor. Whereas Ray had loved the bike rides in the open country around West Yorkshire, Phil was looking for much more than books, libraries, theatres and school societies, and he knew he would find it in the dim light and rocky streets of post-war London. Back streets of Bermondsey, they were his!

Simply put, Phil journeyed to the local elementary school, one of many boys at the age of eleven, who would count the days and months until they were released from their prison at the age of fifteen or sixteen. Would he, like his dad and grandad before him, just walk down the docks and enrol, or perhaps even learn a trade? Only time would tell but Phil had never listened to the superior teasing of his elder brother. Ray had continued his banter over time of belittling his kid brother, with the divisive English school system just reinforcing that prejudiced stance from the age of eleven upwards. "Phil, you've had it mate, you've got nothing up 'ere," Ray used to taunt, pointing his index finger to his temple. The younger sibling always kept it inside. He remembered the pen knife incident: he had told Ray what to expect for the rest of his life. Phil Bristowe, even at eleven years old, was a man of his word. He would wait for the right moment in time.

Freddie secured everything that June and July. Janet would leave her sister's house down in Wickham and take up residence still only three miles from her parents not far from New Cross directly on the rail link to Beckenham and the suburbs, and the boys would be back on a stable school footing. He was to have a number of briefings in early July to familiarise himself with the situation in Hamburg and Germany as a whole. His family had landed on its feet in a

London that was truly stuffed, but he was out of there by the grace of divine intervention.

He boarded the plane, an RAF transporter on July 15th 1945, his first ever time on a plane as all his movements in the war were inevitably by rail and water. Whatever the briefings or assimilations, nothing would have prepared Freddie Bristowe for what he was to encounter in what was left of Hamburg in 1945.

At the outset of the war, the city acted as the water hub of the Third Reich with the greatest proportion of all ship building and external trade alongside the Elbe waterfront. Landward side the Elbe had linked the port to Berlin and what was then the industrial double heartlands of the Ruhr in the west and Leipzig and Cheminitz in the east of the country. This was effectively achieved by the huge dependence on a canal system linked to the river, and a network of autobahns that were in widespread construction as the Nazi government programme of Hitler came to power from 1933. The city housed a major university, a number of historic museums, and for centuries was one of the major focal points of the Hanseatic League, as the dominant northern Europe trading block founded in mediaeval times. Hamburg was Germany's window to the world, and with Rotterdam, Antwerp and London, it shared the bulk of European trade hitherto in the twentieth century.

The British military picked up Freddie with little fuss off the runway, an uninterrupted flight with fair weather, clear skies and no bombardment from below. Bristowe spent the time airborne thinking darkly of what it had been like for the British RAF bomber crews, and the thousands that had lost their lives in 'Bomber' Harris' aerial campaign. Horrendous explosions in the sky with decimation for the cities of Dresden, Cologne, Hannover, Berlin and Hamburg.

Now as the army's American jeep travelled south through the suburb of Barmbek to the centre of the city, he was to witness it all in full daylight. He was bounced around all over the place, not just by potholes, but holes in the road nearly two feet deep and by regular accumulations of rubble, piled high alongside the road everywhere. There was no straight route to their destination as they were checked at points of entry into each suburb. There was no doubt that his driver, a British staff sergeant knew the route and knew the checkpoint guards.

The smells en route were awful. The tenement buildings were either destroyed and pancaked flat, or were left like a skeleton in no real recognisable form. Mile upon mile of a newly familiar pungent air of entrenched burning was experienced, with what people were to tell him was the stench of death. Thousands had died in the bombings, burned alive, or even seeking solace in the nearby canals, still would perish in oil stained waters on fire. More than 50% of housing lay in ruins with 80% of the port area totally destroyed.

In the jeep there was no conversation. Silence had pervaded the atmosphere inside the vehicle. Freddie was just an onlooker. If there was a hell, this was it. The stillness he was experiencing was in strict contrast to the mobility he was overtaking on both sides of this so called road. Alongside the Alster, the dammed water lake, hordes of bedraggled people were limping in the opposite direction getting away from the city with makeshift barrows. Occasionally this long line of mobility was interspersed with a huge throng of humanity huddled together. All was directed to a man, always a man on a box, and always a man with his arms aloft, hands displaying either pieces of food or items to trade with an assembled rabble.

"What are those people doing?" he asked of the driver.

"Black market, mate, the only way to survive over here," the sergeant replied.

More and more masses moving north, why? He pondered. The staff sergeant recognised his inquisitiveness,

"They've gone into the city, most of them refugees to beg, trade, exchange, even steal to survive. They're all Germans, displaced from the East getting away from the Russians. They are all now heading for the open fields to sleep in. If they're lucky, they'll stay on a farm. Most of them walk seven miles in and out each day. It's a day to day existence."

"Why are so many of 'em, women and kids?" Freddie inquired.

"That's an easy one, they'll never see their husbands again, millions of soldiers dead on the eastern front, and as for those in the west or north here, many of them are Nazis on the run who do not want to be traced, wife or no wife. Nearly there!" exclaimed the voice of occupation.

Freddie muttered under his breath as the jeep pulled into the only building left standing alongside the east flank of the Alster. "What have I done to deserve this?" he thought.

The attractive, five storey building which was to be his home for the next two years was decorated with a huge sign by the street entrance, announcing, 'Welcome to the Atlantic'.

Freddie ventured gingerly through the lobby to be met by Lieutenant Colonel Tim Sinclair, a man with a neat little moustache and a firm services handshake.

"Mr Bristowe, I presume, but let me tell you that you must go by a military rank over here. That will arrive by formal letter, BFPO, very shortly."

Sinclair got down to immediate work by showing Freddie every one of the downstairs rooms and their respective functions – there were spaces for meetings, liaison, planning, dining and of course the Officers' Mess. All the master of docks had noted was that all the rooms were spotlessly clean and all decorated with long, large mirrors.

Walking back to the lobby with a large reception area made grander by the high ceilings, and to the right, a spiralling staircase with two elevators, Freddie was introduced to the military concierge to sign his life away and collect the keys to his second floor billet. He could hardly get to the stairs through the throng of civilian German men and women standing in a disciplined line.

"Interviews started yesterday!" exclaimed Sinclair.

"What for?" Freddie had no idea.

"Since VE Day, there have been strict night curfews in the city and a non-association with its population. You cannot believe how much the paper pushers have taken over us military chaps. Roughly half of the six hundred in the Atlantic here have been sent over to run the place. Trouble is they need the local Krauts to carry out the law, rules and regulations. All this lot, you see, are the upper crust Hamburgers, you know, the town planners, surveyors, civil servants, accountants and the like. They've also interviewed cooks, chamber maids, chauffeurs, cleaners and general hotel staff as well. Never mentioned the real problem, did I?" beamed Sinclair.

"Which is?"

"How many of these bastards, now the two-month non association has been lifted were, or even worse, are Nazis! Within the week Freddie, you and I will be interviewing former tug men, stevedores, crane personnel, drivers and dock masters ourselves! Ready for it ole chap?"

Sinclair, though right out of the English boarding school tradition, Marlborough evidently, had a down to earth demeanour for a prospective colonel, but first impressions for Freddie were that here was a boss he could work for.

"Dinner at seven in the dining room. Number Ones only please," Sinclair added.

Freddie peered out of the window as darkness fell on a city that epitomised a black hole. He had witnessed death and destruction across the desert and in Italy, and even in his home ports of London, Southampton and Liverpool, but they were different as he was always passing through. Here he was stuck, he was to be an honoury Hamburger until further notice with no family, kids or home comforts. Yes, the Atlantic hotel was a bastion of affluence compared to the dilapidation of daily life in Hamburg. He would never get used to these extremes.

Freddie soon became Lieutenant Bristowe, which really meant he could get stuck into his duties over in St Pauli, Altona and the dock areas on the western downstream stretches of the Elbe. Or could he?

Sinclair was right. The repatriation of original Hamburg citizens mixed with refugees, former Nazis and petty criminals exploiting the black market was a nightmare. In those early days, there was an even greater danger that all over the dockyard hundreds of unexploded RAF bombs had to be dealt with before any remedial or reconstruction work could take place. The Army engineers were just brilliant in combatting and detonating huge bombs, and sadly lives were lost on the way. Once the OK to proceed was given, clearance meant that the goods could be offloaded by a combination of mass human labour with the increasing amount of imported ramps and cranes with connective vehicles, all from the U.S.A. People claimed it would be a miracle to restore the port, indeed the national economy of Hamburg and Germany, but Lieutenant Bristowe knew the conditions were ripe. The gradually assembled work force laboured for food and shelter only. The Yanks were piling millions of dollars into the infrastructure, and the last component was where the Brits came in, that of civil organisation. They had run an Empire from Bombay to Barbados and from Cape Town to Hong Kong.

For the next two years, by hook or by crook, Freddie acted as middle management to get things done. Working parties and liaison committees were everywhere to connect the life of a destroyed dockyard with housing, agriculture, roads, rails, industrial plants, water and power, and all manner of tele-communications. Moreover, all this was managed without any official currency as the Reich-Mark had collapsed. The main form of remuneration for Germans was exchange, swapping goods, gifts and skills for food whilst the British authorities and squaddies were building makeshift, temporary Nissen huts as homes by the tens of thousands. Rumours were rife that a newly commissioned currency was to be implemented for national use, but this was never to be introduced in Freddie's time in Hamburg.

Lieutenant Bristowe had Saturday evenings, and most of Sundays clear for any amount of personal and leisure time. Right through the first year his weekly duties were never a slog as the time passed very quickly, so quickly that he had to keep reminding himself that there was an England and that he had a family back there. Jan wrote every month mainly to complain about the dreadful winter conditions in the damp prefab, but at least she would wax lyrical about the family day trips to the seaside and of course, to her mum's. Occasionally she would worry about the scrapes that Phil would be getting into, but she put that all down to his teenage years. As for Ray, he was just top of the class at Beckenham Grammar with flying colours, a dedicated academic 'A' streamer.

Freddie realised that he was now essentially a single man at the Atlantic and in Hamburg as a whole. He was desperately lacking in female company, but this was all compensated by the officers' mess on Saturday nights and by the weekly gatherings for Sunday lunch at the Atlantic which became their only luxury meal for the week. Still, he reprimanded himself during these mini feasts as he glanced out of the window to witness the beggars and the abject poverty of the streets.

Saturday evenings by the summer of '46 were becoming quite musical with dance bands and an open floor for the British servicemen to enjoy. The high ranking officers who, by then, had their wives cohabiting their hotel suites, glided gaily across the floor jealously perused by the inebriated single men of lower rank. This still included Freddie who occasionally would intercept and claim his two-minute foxtrot with many a major or captain's wife.

What was, however, noticeable was the gradual increase in numbers of young German women. They were all even after a year of occupation treated with surly suspicion by all the ranks. The main reason for this was their association with the general flow of the same local women who were selling themselves one night on the infamous Reeperbahn district and the next evening as partners in dance at the Atlantic.

Still, there were many who rightfully did not fit into this duplicitous double life. The German ladies who had done sterling work as typists, reception staff, chamber maids, translators and even as tutors to some of the older children of officers all testified to leading a normal life, if still ensconced in poverty. It was however noteworthy that the higher the rank of the British army officer, the more numerous the amount of professional attachments there were with the indigenous female population. Sinclair, for instance, had his own chauffeur and chamber maid which perhaps explained his immaculate physical appearance and absolute affinity to punctuality at all staff meetings!

Maybe Freddie could be indulged one day? The saving grace was the forthcoming visit from Jan and the boys for their august summer holiday. There was always a surplus of army family dependants at this time of year, but this extra was easily catered for by the only other hotel that was left standing at the city dam end of the Alster, the Hotel Streits. Built in 1838, it was a massive structure and had been hitherto a staging post for celebrities including Marlene Dietrich and her more infamous contemporary, the Fuhrer himself!

Janet refused to travel by air. "You'll never get me up in one of those things. I've seen too many burned out wrecks."

She made her grand appearance at Hamburg Docks overnight on a liner from London. Her erstwhile husband paced the jetty itching to welcome the boys and their mum, but inside he was beside himself on how this would all transpire. The port was half up and running, but the city was still a shambles with all the evidence of desperate people and vast areas of dereliction open to the naked eye. Hamburg was better than in '45, but not by much. It had survived the knockout blow but was still reeling on the ropes.

The very good news for Freddie and the family was that he had been awarded an upgraded apartment at the Atlantic and that included an administrative assistant, a local German accountant called Dieter Muller and a bright young housekeeper called Helga Semmler who had the run of the kitchenette on this top floor residence at the Atlantic.

68

For Jan, Helga was a godsend as it was her only intent to yet again re-establish a relationship not only between herself and Freddie, but also to reintroduce Ray and Phil to their father. To achieve that, she could leave the apartment and its well being to Helga. The young German would work a six-hour day cleaning the rooms, washing clothes, preparing beds and snacks. The place was pristine, but little did the Bristowes know that she was just another unfortunate who made the long six-mile trudge northwards six days a week every late afternoon. Her home was a barn, normally a storage space for hay on a dairy farm. As for food, it was milk in the early mornings with any scraps from the Atlantic kitchen she could reassign later in the day.

Like Dieter Muller, she had one major asset. Her English was passable, not to his technical standard, but her schoolgirl 'englische sprechen' was to improve rapidly within the confines of her job. More to the point, she was street wise enough to know that her English was her means to upward mobility.

Janet was already experiencing problems. She was used to getting around the country lanes of West Wickham or even biking along the river by Bermondsey. Having recovered from the shock of losing her home back in 1941, she was lucky to have the freedom of her own prefab. Here in Hamburg, the days were punctuated by trips with junior drivers, but trips for the boys in Hamburg meant only gloom and visual mayhem. Hardly anything was left standing. She just couldn't let the boys out of her sight even though they were used to adventure and the freedom

69

of play back in England. Here in Germany, there were just too many real dangers.

One day, Jan invited Helga to join the family whilst Freddie was at work. The corporal assigned to them had suggested a drive up to Uhlenhorst, a suburb that had not been too badly affected by bombing and then come back along the Alster to the Hotel Streits, where he had a pass for early evening supper. Another brilliant summer's afternoon allowed the two ladies time to get to know each other whilst Ray and Phil tried to convince the corporal to stop the vehicle and let them have a go at driving the jeep!

Just a mile before the Streits, the driver succumbed to their demands to get off at one of those black markets inundated with dozens of Germans offering exchanges. Beyond the lead man on the box, Phil noticed puffs of smoke and a definite smell of something burning which reminded him of Uncle Cyril's 'sossidge' barbecues. He tapped Ray on the back nodding his head in the direction of the heat. They followed their noses to find a fire built up over wood, paper and motley lumps of coal. Over the basics was a crude spit with an elongated string of flesh being turned to culinary perfection by a group of what Ray told Phil were gypsies. Phil was hungry and could not wait for tea at the Streits. Ray quizzed the lead gypsy, "Was ist das?" pointing at the burnt offering.

In fluent English, the German replied, "Rat, the best rat from the Hamburg waters."

Phil couldn't believe his eyes, "They don't eat rats do they?"

From behind him, a shrill voice firmly slammed the 'door' shut on him. "Come away from those people, Phil. You must come away now, they are bad Germans," said Helga, clearly upset and dragging the boys back to their driver.

The lead gypsy angrily pointed at Helga and gave her a chilling stare, screaming, "So you're one of them now Helga – Lead your little crawling life as you like, but never forget where you came from!"

Ray, in retreat, tugged at her elbow and wanted to know if she knew that dirty, bedraggled man, whilst Phil just kept rolling his eyes and head at the turn of the rat on the spit!

All she could do was to grab the boys and return them to Jan who was now intrigued in the throng of people by the activities of the black market. As soon as Phil clapped eyes on her he shouted repeatedly,

"Mum, Mum, come and see the rats, the Germans are eating rats!"

Janet had enjoyed her tea and scones with Helga and the boys at the Streits that afternoon but realised there and then that the month in Hamburg was to be one big struggle. Even her relationship with Freddie was to prove awkward in all parts of their days and nights, especially the nights. She in many ways could not recognise the man she used to know. His smell and touch, his warmth were no longer the same, and though she knew he would never look at anyone else, his look was a distant one totally tied up with what he was doing for King and country in distant Hamburg.

Every other day Dieter Muller would bring his thirteen year old son Pieter with his Hamburg mates to come to the

Atlantic for the day. It really was a highlight for them all. Dieter could work as the German liaison man within the hotel for all the constituent parts of the British administration, a body that trusted him and his family's history implicitly, notably as all his family had been reprimanded by the local National Socialist Party throughout the pre-war period.

There was one other huge plus. Phil, true to form, had persuaded his mum to smuggle an old leather football in his travel bag. Across the road from the Atlantic was a small snippet of grass, big enough for a four- a-side game. Between Phil, Pieter and surprisingly Ray, they attracted more and more strays from officers' boys from the Atlantic and friends of Pieter to complete the numbers. Phil struck up a real rapport with Pieter and it was noticeable they were always on the same team! Both were gems of embryo young footballers and Phil was sure that one day Pieter would play for Germany.

After a while more and more local waifs joined in with nothing on their feet and ill-fitting clothes over painfully thin bodies. Both Ray and Phil would fill their pockets full of anything from the kitchens to force feed their young German team mates. Those boys were starving and existing on half a meal a day. Ray wondered how they would ever survive the winter.

Janet had made up her mind. What with her kids stealing titbits out of the Atlantic kitchens and her boys exposed to daily black markets, beggars and widespread poverty and crime on the streets, it was time to go home. Her boys had a sixth sense for adventure but they both had severe up and down moods, clearly upset and never accepting the plight of the Germans. For them so young, she recognised the experience would stay with them for the rest of their lives. Phil began having nasty nightmares.

She was to take the next boat home. Freddie knew that a month would always be too long for her in Hamburg. She hugged him passionately at the quayside, kissed him like never before and looking him straight in the eyes said,

"I want you home for Christmas, for good, Freddie. Otherwise it's a divorce."

CHAPTER 4

PREFABS AND PANTOS

Janet always tended to overestimate the value and the condition of her Bermondsey home, notably when conversing with Freddie over in Hamburg. Strictly speaking, of course, she was now residing in neighbouring Rotherhithe, having secured one of the early prefabs hurriedly assembled twelve months earlier. A whole year had passed since the war's end, and there she was, in a modern reinforced concrete structure bolted together in panel form.

They were described as temporary dwellings, by the Ministry of Housing in the new Atlee government that was quick to act in building over 170,000 of them during the immediate post-war years. Jan's prefab in Rotherhithe was typical in supporting a family of four or five at a push, and she was particularly ecstatic that it supported electrics for a cooker amongst other kitchen utilities, and an inside WC and hand basin.

Whereas the Luftwaffe had hit the Bermondsey riverside docks and outward rail lines from London Bridge, Rotherhithe had experienced even worse extensive damage to residential areas by the Surrey Docks. In between these two dock sectors were where, unexploded bombs allowing, the authorities had to build up swarms of prefabs. Jan's main priority the previous winter had been to keep hers warm as there was no provision for coal fires within her structure. The Bristowes as a result of Freddie's investment intervention had to rely on three tiny electric bar fires for warmth, and light as well, as the family's supply was dispensed by a shilling coin meter.

So Janet was financially stretched and it was obvious to her that if the boys were not to have another shivering winter with long walks and bike rides to school, she was going to have to get a job and work the system to rise above ration book day to day living. After Ray and Phil's sojourn in Hamburg, they returned to face one egg a week, two ounces of cheese, no meat and two pints of milk per family. They were fed on stews, potatoes, cockles and whelks out of the Thames and live eels from the tanks outside Lipton's every Saturday.

Their mother took the bus on one such Saturday morning that late August in her Sunday best. She was to face an interview with a certain personnel manager at Peek Freans biscuit factory, close to the centre of Bermondsey in a district called The Blue. How the journey was to startle her every time. If only Freddie could see the intermittent

75

gaps of former houses and entire terraces no longer there, he would be heart broken. Four of Bermondsey's pubs, Manse's Pie and Mash shop, the Old Palace cinema, the tannery and all the food factories like Crosse and Blackwell, Shuttleworth's chocolate, and the furniture shop had all been bombed out, very badly damaged or obliterated altogether.

As the bus continued west along Jamaica Road, she daren't look right towards the river and the streets bordering the old wharves. One of these streets, running narrow and parallel to the Thames, was the place of their old family home, Paradise Street, just seventy yards from The Angel pub and the waterside. Bombed to oblivion, that little enclave would now be buried in her past. Jan kept her gaze left as she spotted the intersection ahead of Drummond with Jamaica.

It was a short trot in the direction of The Blue. The Peek Frean factory was directly in line with her well-trodden path to the Saturday market where she fully intended to go after the interview. While she hastened her pace down Drummond Street, she couldn't help noticing that where houses had been, there were now very attractive patches of gardens covered in flower beds. Rumour had it that the incendiary bombs hit the edge of Southwark Park in such a devastating fireball that the fires had enriched the soils. The former edges of houses and commercial sites had given way to gardens and playgrounds.

She was ushered into a third floor waiting room, and nicely she thought, offered a cup of tea which she gratefully accepted. Within minutes, she was ready to face

Mr Williams. He gave the impression of being a kind and genial man, about sixty years of age, and most definitely had worked at this most celebrated of biscuit manufacturers since the turn of the century around 1900. His office was inundated with commendations, posters, models and biscuit tins, most beautifully decorated in all shapes, colours and sizes. World famous custard creams, cheeselets and bourbons grew out of the posters, and Jan was actually beginning to feel quite peckish!

"Before we go into detail, Mrs Bristowe, you are aware that we run three eight hour shifts here, twenty-four hours a day, and you may not always be offered the day time popular ones. Also Peek Freans now have almost more female workers that men but I must inform you we only employ single women. Only in exceptional circumstances do we sway from that policy."

"Oh, yes, Mr Williams, but essentially I am just about single these days with my two boys growing up and my husband, major Bristowe, working abroad," impressing her host, Jan thought.

"Well that's as may be, but any married woman, especially in these difficult times, must prioritise with her family. We do find single ladies far more, how shall we say, pliable and affable," he posted.

"I can be all of those things, Mr Williams, and I do have the relevant experience in promotions and display work of products. Packaging and imaging are my specialities," Jan offered invitingly.

Frank Williams then suddenly stood upright, offering his arm to Jan for a tour of the factory. He was keen to show her some bomb damage at the rail side of the triangular shaped commercial area, with the view that they were hoping to rebuild that section into a factory display shop area, notably as rationing could hopefully be consigned to the history books in the near future.

"We now must make full use of our floor space so every inch here counts for a successful range of products that, as you can see, are separated into specific brands of biscuits and the processes involved," he enthused.

On return to the office, he laid down the terms of employment and also the benefits that such a large, but family based firm could offer. She could not believe her ears when they included a full sports and social club membership and total provision of insurance with a company group of doctors and dentists available to her and her family. She was overjoyed when offered a position as Peek Freans was a very paternal institution that seemed to value its workforce which was to climb to 3,000 daily workers on the factory floor.

What had started as a merger between two families importing Norfolk flour, West Indian sugar and West African cocoa, had brilliantly expanded to exporting all over the world its biscuit packets, tins, cakes and Christmas hampers. After all what was tea without a biscuit, and who didn't like a bourbon or custard cream?

Jan was to start straight after the august Bank Holiday. For the moment, she would continue on to join The Blue market. At its heart was the old Blue Anchor pub along Southwark Park Road. Even though car use was increasing by 1946, that didn't matter a jot as The Blue market just converted the roadway on both sides to a long line of uninterrupted stalls and barrows flogging scarce snippets of foodstuffs, second hand goods and locally manufactured clothing. Items of legal and illegal origin were all up for grabs together!

Jan used to drag the boys around most Saturday afternoons. Phil would joke that you never needed to know how to get to The Blue, you just followed your nose and ears. The pungent smells of flowers, fruits, leather and breads filled the air. As for the noise of constant banter, the calls and stories from the stallholders drew crowds from all over south and east London. It was one of the few points of interest and mutual enthusiasm that did attract mum and both boys. She was even able to convince one of the stalls selling paper and pens to take on some of Ray's sketches of Tower Bridge taken from Butler's Wharf downstream. His charcoal drawings were selling like hot cakes until Ray terminated the arrangement when the winter days drew in at the end of November.

By 4pm Jan and the boys would leave the 250 stalls behind laden with supplies for the week and return to the sanctuary of the prefab two miles to the east. The family of three had settled into a regular routine that autumn, but as was the case in many families in these post-war years, the composition of the family unit was anything but regular. Some like Jan had husbands working in Europe still part of the armed services, but many wives found life intolerable with men they had not seen for four years, and returning husbands from the war hardly recognised their kids.

Divorce was rampant in city areas like Bermondsey, five times the number in 1946 than in 1939. In addition, it must never be forgotten that 3% of Bermondsey residents had perished in the bombing and the aftermath of the Blitz and the V1 and V2 rockets. Couples married shortly before the outbreak of war had lost parents. Children losing the stability of grandparents had also split up families. Government agencies were trying to recommend to mothers like Jan to relocate downstream to the Essex marshes or down Medway way, but she, like many other Bermondsey parents, would never leave their home and roots behind. She had endured enough of that temporarily in the evacuation years.

Jan had found some kind of security at last with Ray catching the train out to Beckenham and Phil using the family bike to get to Tower Bridge Secondary for their schooling whilst she was able, because of the nature of her role at Peek Freans, to get the 8 til 4pm shift. At weekends Phil would play in his junior club football team with Ray spending Saturday mornings back at Beckenham with extra specialised art classes. She really did try to get the three of them together on a Sunday but in the back of her mind she had hoped that Freddie could be the answer on his return to bring the two boys closer together. He had been very regular in his communications and seemed to have yielded to her final ultimatum in Hamburg.

* * *

The early westward movement of the Siberian High had prompted a premature Christmas present for Hamburg.

This horrendous weather system had the force to plague northern Germany and the Baltic region for winter months if it took hold. In the second half of December the signs were ominous. Freddie, half packed to return to London, peered out of his penthouse window at the Atlantic hotel and what met him, was a sight for sore eyes. There was a six-inch blanket of snow following the Friday evening's first winter deluge. December the 16th had not started well.

Rapidly changing into his winter work dungarees, he nipped downstairs to what by then was a fully functioning restaurant to grab some piping hot porridge and black coffee. Across the hallway was the general office for the British administrative sector for the city and it acted seven days a week as the communication hub. The place was overrun with telephones, telegram access points and all manner of links to the BFPO (British Forces Post Office). Freddie wanted an up to date 7-day weather forecast and the state of play along the Elbe river and its feeder canals. Even more important was the condition of airstrips.

The port management office also accommodated the meteorological centre. Later that Saturday morning Freddie received the bombshell. The canals supporting the flow of barge traffic from Berlin and into the Elbe had frozen up in temperatures of -20 centigrade. In the Baltic shipping was encountering icebergs and the wind chill factor direct from the Russian wastelands was so cold that it was prohibiting any transit activity on the ground. In short nothing was getting in or out of Hamburg with the exception of one cleared airstrip north of the city.

Only eighteen months after cessation of war this Siberian high pressure was set to last for three months with vital food supplies, perishable by nature, trapped in ports. Refugees, still abundant in numbers, many homeless, would have to survive on 650 calories per day with no coal imports to supply any degree of heating.

In British service terms, all leave was cancelled. In German, it meant 100,000 souls would die in a never-ending hell that was to be known as The Hunger Winter. Freddie did not hesitate to act. For a start, despite Jan's ultimatum in the summer, he could never hand in his notice as he knew that would decimate a potential Services pension which he was due on completion of his two years in June. He had always banked on talking Jan round over what he convinced himself would be a Christmas break only.

It was a sad irony that the Hunger Winter of '47 would save, or at least postpone the possibility of losing his family. He wasn't very good at letters, so he would send an extended telegram. Jan would have to cope until he saw out his contract. It read;

Darling Jan,

Terrible news, all leave cancelled until further notice. Shipping crippled, port iced over, -20°c here, supplies at a premium, people starving. Watch out, because it is heading your way. Only good news is that I have been awarded a full pension on the completion of duties in June.

Please understand, Jan, I never wanted it this way, but we've got to hang in and see this through. Will send extra funds through to cope with this worst of winters.

Love to the boys, stay strong, Freddie xx

* * *

Jan was distraught. How was she going to give the boys a proper Christmas? What with the misery of dark, dank nights that were becoming increasingly frozen over these final days of 1946 and the terrible food shortages, there was only one course of action – back to mum's and sisters. If they could pool resources, maybe the boys at the age of fourteen and twelve might have a Christmas of sorts? That plus the fact that her parents would be sympathetic to her situation with Freddie. It really was beyond either of their control.

Her work at Peek Freans had been going very well, and already the new shop was taking shape as were the services that the company was offering. Although she never fell ill nor took a day off work, the Bristowes were still making use of the medical services of the doctors. Phil, as a result of his junior football team getting together with Mr Murray, the team manager, was playing on any available spaces, including the countless number of bomb sites where detonation squads were kept busy for several years to come.

Luckily, Phil never got blasted, but in kicking balls around very near to the fragile house walls of such sites, he inevitably courted danger. Twice the Peek Frean husband and wife team of doctors, Drs Tinter, of Austrian origin, were rushed in to remove rusty nails from his feet along with the painful inoculations. Not only this, but many of these dilapidated slums housed mattresses and pillows that were still alive with bed bugs and fleas. So, because Phil had contracted them on a regular basis and was sleeping nightly in the prefab with Ray, his innocent elder brother also had the indignity of being deloused on too many occasions as well!

What really saved Jan's family that Christmas was the candlelit dinner the weekend before Christmas Day at Peek Freans. It was an annual event, originally instigated by the company's owner's Quaker religious roots and was known as the Children's Dinner. All the kids of employees under the age of fifteen were invited to maybe the biggest feed up of the year. How the kitchen procured the range of food was a mystery to all but the items that were plentiful that evening included oodles of biscuits. No expense was spared for the waifs of children that filled the tables.

The Bristowes, both Gran's and Jan's families were up against it those winter months of January right through to the April of 1947. Jan doubled the number of electric fires in the prefab despite there being a run on them, because there was a coal strike. It was a disgrace as absenteeism resulted in productivity being two and a half times less than in 1939. The coal shortages resulted in February in stockpiles for less than four weeks. All houses were down to less than fifteen hours of electricity per day with irregular power cuts. Civil unrest, amidst frozen temperatures for forty-five days running, was a regular occurrence as power stations across the nation were shutting down. Even the Minister for Power, Manny Shinwell, needed bodyguards as he had received death threats.

Poor old Phil, there was to be no football for three months but at least he could delight in Tower Bridge Secondary closing down for nigh on two months. Ray, on the other hand, was singularly depressed and really was a misery to all around him. For him, life without school and his art was not worth living. The local libraries were shut and his mum just wouldn't allow him on the icy snow covered roads to ride his bike. Phil would delight in watching ice blocks float down the Thames and building his own sledge and snowmen with all the accompanying snowball fights. None of that nonsense appealed to Ray.

Like her parents, Jan toughed out the winter. She had reluctantly relented on threats to Freddie, who eventually returned in June, the conquering hero. Apart from a week's long frivolity party, it was Jan's wish to resume a family life, one of normality and routine as soon as was possible. Freddie was to comply as he always seemed to do. And it happened. The balance of husband and wife, new home, both parents working happily and two children settled in schools at last was achieved. Money did not seem a problem now that Freddie had resumed his dock work allied to his services pension and of course Jan's extra salary was another big bonus for the family.

Sounds good, eh, so far? As the two sons approached adolescence, unfortunately more problems emerged.

Arguments and squabbles turned into fist fights between the brothers which were a serious matter at fifteen and thirteen years old. Part of the problem was Phil's errant behaviour and like it or not it was the reporting of these crimes by Ray to mum and dad that exacerbated the big divide. Throughout the summer, Phil had taken to smoking and had got himself in with the wrong crowd at Tower Bridge. His smoking habit was being subsidised by joining a gang that was pilfering lead and slate off damaged roofs away from Bermondsey down in Eltham and Sidcup, which had suffered from the V1 and V2 rocket attacks near the end of the year.

Ray was on next to nothing in terms of pocket money. Freddie always believed in his kids earning it through their own invention and initiative, and he made it clear he was pleased that Phil was taking the lead in that direction, and that Ray should learn from his younger brother. In one tempestuous week in early September, Ray had had enough. He grassed on his brother and his activities to his mum. Jan never believed him. Well not until the 'ole bill' arrived at the prefab and along with his mother escorted the boy to Bermondsey 'nick'. The cops were on to Phil and his gang all through those summer school holidays.

Jan didn't tell anyone, but the police sergeant took her boy away, put him in a cell for the afternoon, then gave him a clip round the ear and the threat of borstal before releasing the miscreant. "That should do the trick, Missus, with your young tearaway. We have the ringleaders in custody," boasted the sergeant.

Phil never really learned. All he could think of was his elder brother had grassed on him. It was to be the same pattern over the following twelve months as the boys drifted further and further apart. Ray with the two years age advantage could look after himself with Phil still waiting for the right time to wreck his elder sibling.

Freddie started to appreciate the problem when he decided to take the family to a Christmas play later that year in 1947 up along Tooley Street where a new theatre company for children had opened at a small performing theatre. They were doing a version of 'Dick Whittington,' under the supervision of a tour group led by a real gem of a lady called Caryl Jenner. This early production was to be on the school stage of St. Olaf's grammar school before she was to settle her mobile theatre at the Unicorn down the road in Tooley Street.

Caryl had pioneered theatre for children, continually battling with the Arts Council for supportive grants. They would in these early days only sponsor her if she would combine her work with adult productions as well. The children of the Unicorn were 'her children'. She was expert in this field, because she had observed the children's reactions to which sequences would hold their attention. How did she register this? Unsurprisingly, by the noise levels! Jenner was to become an icon, eventually creating four touring companies, discovering lists of new plays and talented young actors and actresses.

All this was to be lost on the night with Phil. He saw plays as a bit of a joke and notably with the interactive pantomime format, he was able to sneak away during the interval to join his Tower schoolmates to raise merry hell in the second half of the performance. Freddie, Jan and Ray were rooted to their seats and just too embarrassed to be associated with the hellraising and disruptive noise of his brother's group at the back of the hall.

Ray was calm. He observed every element of the production. His parents knew he might take to live theatre. He responded to the banter, the irony and the humour as an adult would do every time they accompanied their children. Yet what really took Ray's senses was the production, the set, the costumes and the colour-inspired enjoyment of those involved. For the first time in his life, he had been transformed from a black and white nobody to a colour-centric participant, even though he was just a voyeur at this stage. Could or would he ever get over the war, its misery and his family? Maybe not, but it was the panto in December 1947 that would act as the trigger to joyfully introduce him to the possibilities of another world.

Later, then in 1948, Ray received the JS Stanley prize for Art at Speech Day one September Saturday morning at Beckenham, an event that Phil had refused to attend much to his parent's disdain. Phil didn't hold any academic envy of his brother, he just did not respect art and artists. He thought they were wasters and worse, in the main, weirdoes. By this stage, Freddie used to take the boys up west periodically on Sundays to see the post-war recovery sites of London. He would walk them from St. Paul's to Westminster Abbey, The Monument, Fleet Street, Theatreland, The museums, Soho and sometimes a boat trip, or a scrummy chocolate éclair at Maison Lyons in

Marble Arch. The boys seldom tired of it. Phil in particular was imbued with a patriotic pride which Ray could never match.

Nevertheless, Phil's football team would take preference in the autumn of '48. He had to play for a new team that was made up of a lot of the kids of Peek Frean employees. So it was mum who escorted Phil on Saturday mornings with Freddie sharing the delights of the art galleries with Ray. Jan, in particular, felt that this division of labour was winning the day in acquiescing the boys, that they would soon settle the old scores by at least accepting their differences.

The 'Ray' visits on weekends continued with his father. They would leave together usually early on, but for an unaccountable reason would never be back before dark at 5pm. Phil noticed immediately asking his mother why dad would give Ray a full day's attention. Jan did ask the question of her husband with the reply that art galleries were giving way to matinee shows at some of London's most famous theatres. She never found any programmes or ticket stubs in their pockets on wash day which compounded her doubts.

Then one day in early spring for the very first time, Jan fell ill with a dose of latent flu, missing her early eight o'clock shift at the factory. For over two and a half years, it had always been Freddie's job to pick up the morning mail delivery, normally about 9 o'clock, then he would head off to his office at the docks for a 9.30 start. That morning he took Jan's role of walking Phil early to school.

Jan was on the downside of a fever, so she was up and about when she heard a loud double rap on the front door. She was aware she was on her own and, slipping on her dressing gown, answered shouting out, "Who is it?"

"Royal Mail, special delivery, you have to sign for it, luv."

She pressed open the door, grabbed the official brown envelope with a formal typed address made to one, Raymond Bristowe. She had to think twice before signing the receipt note as she was sure the postman had got it wrong. She signed, on the top left side where there was a heavily smudged print which was part obscured by mail lines, but she did make out the words, "His Majesty's".

What would his Majesty want doing with her Ray? she mused opening the envelope with scant hesitation. There it was, from that day forward within a trim navy blue booklet, on the inside cover, the inscripted words:

"His Britannic Majesty's Secretary of State requests and requires in the name of His Majesty all those whom it may concern to allow the bearer to pass freely without let or hindrance, and to afford the bearer such assistance and protection as may be necessary."

The name inside the passport, Raymond Frederick Bristowe. Her eldest boy, unbeknown to her, was to leave the country!

Janet had not heard a single word on the matter. She would hide the passport until she was able to get Freddie and Ray to the dinner table. They were not going to get away with this and it was they, as she knew Ray could not have arranged this without the consent of a parent. No, this deeply underhand plot had Freddie's fingerprints dabbed all over it and like so many times before, he had some explaining to do.

This time she had the element of surprise and timing. With the lighter April evenings she would ensure that young Phil was out of the way. For her, it was imperative that the kid brother would not hear the impending war of words, otherwise even he might get strange ideas in his own head as well. The next morning Phil would go off to school which dovetailed into an early evening of football practice. Seldom did he tear himself away before seven o'clock. She gathered it was the climax of the season.

It was a perfect fit as Freddie was as regular as clockwork in clambering in for his supper at six on the dot. Her preparation of a simple meal that evening of egg and chips would lend itself to a brief period of digestion before the gathering verbal storm. As the men weighed into their mugs of tea, their contentment was shattered by the appearance of a pristine passport flung into the centre of the table.

"What the hell is this for? A boy of seventeen with his own passport, just what are you two up to? And where on earth do you think you are going Ray?"

"Australia, mum", he retorted with some juvenile pride.

"What, just what has got into your head? You're not going nowhere my boy. You're not running away from family just because the going is tougher these days. You want to quit on Bermondsey and the Bristowes? How on

91

earth do you think you are going to get there? You'll have no money, no job, no family, no roots, nothing, and so far away," she posted.

"Sorry, mum, but you're wrong. We have been accepted on the assisted settlement scheme which pays for the entire journey for just ten pounds. There is a job waiting for me on a farm in New South Wales with an Aussie family. They will pay me for the work and act as my sponsor for two years," Ray informed her,

"Two years in Australia, two years! I suppose you put him up to this, Freddie. Not satisfied with breaking up our family for your years of gallivanting in Germany with your army pals, now you want Ray to do the same, anything to desert his kith and kin," said a tearful Janet.

"You know that's not true, Jan. Look, darling, he's nearly a grown man now with his own ideas. Here's a real chance to see the world, do something really productive, earn some money. Think, Jan, Australia's a young country, unaffected by war. It's crying out for youngsters, and don't forget, they're all ex-Brits, our people out there," Freddie interjected.

"The way you're talking, you'd think he's intent on going for good. Two years is so long to be away from home, he'll get homesick," she suggested, now aware that the two of them were equally as keen.

"Jan, whether you like it or not, Ray would be leaving home to do his National Service, anyway. You'd see precious little of the lad. He'd be posted to Germany or Aden or some dark patch in Africa. Far better off in the open air, healthy on a farm in Australia. You've always said you didn't want your boys in the British Army, over your dead body, you used to say," he teased.

Freddie glanced across at his eldest and most assured boy,

"My boy's got talent, he's bright, he's got his exams and a true passion for art. He can develop all those assets in Australia. Here it's nearly five years since the war's end, and he still has to witness squalour, temporary housing, deprivation and rationing. Can't you see it's suffocating him?"

A short period of silence ensued, and in a faltering voice, Jan tentatively placed her palms on Ray's shoulder. "So, Ray, you really want to go and leave London?" she asked

"Yes, Ma. I've thought of nothing else these last six months and when dad took me up with him for the interview at Australia House, it was marvellous, a different world of sun, sky and open space. I kept, but hid all the brochures and posters, and dad and I thought it best we didn't tell you or Phil or grandma 'til they accepted me," said Ray.

"Ray, I only want what's best for you and the family. I wish you had told me. I can't let you go until I know all the facts and you must promise me it will only be for two years. Freddie, you can arrange another interview with the migration officer, with his mother present, can you?" She pressed hard the hand of her husband.

Freddie felt then that one of the chords had struck home with Jan. He didn't know which one, but he suspected it was his point about avoiding National Service as she just hated the army and all it stood for. At the back of his mind he had the knowledge that Ray did see his move to Australia as a two year introduction to a new and more active lifestyle, an introduction to a more permanent life down under. He could never make Jan aware of this at such an early stage as there was always the threat of the unknown. Nevertheless, Ray had always been a mature boy for his age, and it was clear that his intent was solid, based on his research into everything Australian, from the nation's history, geography and cultural background to its politics and economics.

From the practical angle, Ray had an uninterrupted passage, a gift of an option to become what was to be known as 'a ten pound Pohm'. Ray even quibbled with that expression, never accepting the abbreviated version, Pom. The educated Beckenham boy knew it stood originally for 'Prisoner of His Majesty' (POHM). He was never going to be that in Australia. Ironically, in late 1940s Bermondsey, he did feel like a prisoner. The winters of '47 and '48 had just about killed him off despite all attempts at a healthy cultural life at Beckenham. Once the nights drew in for seven months of the year, the lack of sun and heat on his body drained him, detached him and disintegrated his spirit.

For Ray, there was precious little difference between post-war London and the squalour of Hamburg, and we were supposed to have been the victors of a struggle that had dug deep into his psyche of what it meant to be an Englishman. He would walk down to The Blue and smirk at the irony of those attending the market. Humanity on those Saturdays and all through the week was colourless, monotonous, and poverty was everywhere. When his clothes from the war years would just be duplicated onto Phil as hand me downs, when power cuts always occurred at the height of the winter months, and when he had not eaten protein-enriched meat for weeks on end, this was not the England, the noble England that Churchill used to vividly portray to the world.

He also knew, through his mum and dad's work ethic, that he and Phil were the lucky ones. His parents had employment, full employment and there were at least two full meals on the table per day. Unlike Freddie, Ray was not overly physically self conscious, but one thing he had noticed and become alarmed about was that for the first time in the Bristowe's recent family history, the son had not grown to be as tall as the father. The eldest son would look in the mirror, and had only reached five feet and eight inches, a full three inches below fearsome Freddie. Ray, of course, blamed it on his sparse upbringing devoid of vital protein, and always being hungry in Bingley in his growth years.

Jan had achieved her insistence on an interview with Mr Bob Fowler, a very cheerful if somewhat abrupt Aussie migration and settlement officer. She had entered the outwardly positive building in Kingsway inundated with posters and magnificent photographs decking the walls of Bondi and Bronte Beaches, the sun, the surf and Sydney Harbour and its awe-inspiring bridge. All these pointers were there to take her away from sombre Britain to a land of opportunity for those willing to partake.

Indeed, the magic over that two hours had thawed out Jan Bristowe. She was very much reassured by the tight organisation and scheme that Ray was to participate in, a sponsored assisted passage for teenage single men. In short, at the interview's end, she turned to Ray and Mr Fowler, and simply said,"Well, Ray, it looks like you're going!"

The Aussie looked Jan in the eye with steely determination and said, "Listen here, Mrs Bristowe, it won't be no holiday camp for Ray, but I can tell you, with his talent and if the boy mucks in, Aussie will take care of him and he'll love it!"

Freddie and the Bristowes face down the Luftwaffe. Southampton's port was a principal target from July to September in 1940.

Since the 19th century the Peek Freans factory housed up to 3000 workers in Bermondsey on a 24 hour schedule.

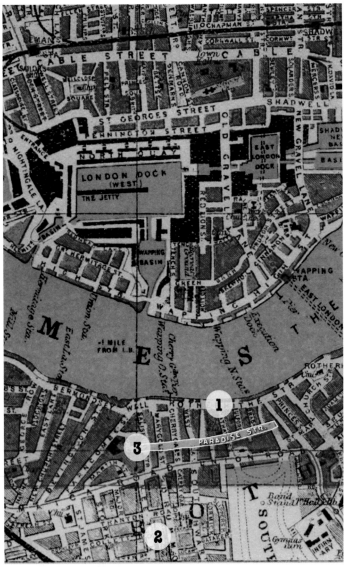

1 The Angel Pub, 2 Peek Freans Factory, 3 Paradise Street, home of the Bristowes of Bermondsey.

Peek Frean & Co Ltd

Peek Freans: "Anyone for custard creams or bourbons with your tea?"
Janet's saving grace for post war employment.

Helga's everyday journey to 'The Atlantic' through the desolation of Hamburg in 1946.

CHAPTER 5

THE TEN POUND POHM

Ray, now could prepare. With his mother on board and Freddie acting almost as a liaison officer for his travel arrangements, he could get down to the vital priorities that he could set himself before his departure in January. This elder son just seemed to look at life differently from the rest of the Bristowe family. For a start, he had sailed through his Higher Certificate exams in the summer fully qualified to enter a professional office job or even to gain university entry. They would act as distinct trump cards in his back pocket.

For the moment, however, he had recognised that within months he would be met by a rural New South Wales dairy farmer who would have invested and risked a substantial amount to take on an untried urban urchin from bomb-ravaged post-war London. All Ray had gleaned at this stage was that it was to be a two year physical employ in the

Hunter Valley with the Sykes family on the edge of a town called Scone. He was to be afforded full board and lodging with a small remittance for his labour and a minimum of one day recreation per week.

What would have been the alternative for a young teenager leaving school in 1949? There were two definite options, neither desirable at this stage, which were university study or far worse, national service. He had to evade the army's clutches where, after basic training, it would have been the possibility of a one way ticket to the world's trouble spots. In 1949, he might well have been cannon fodder in Korea, Malaya or Kenya. Ray had inwardly acknowledged no liking for foreign ways, religions or cultures. He had scant experience of them despite the overwhelming numbers deposited into England as an aftermath of war for military men from Britain's colonies.

Australia was untainted and anglicised. At that stage in her history, her ways had been passed down through a direct association with the British crown and government. Following the war the Aussie authorities had assertively pushed the boat out to receive British young aspirants, white and Christian. They knew as a country where they were going with a huge expansion in agricultural and commercial development based around their common English language and British cultural values. Ray was aware that he stood at the front of the line. In short, he was wanted and needed.

Still, he was intent on contributing and making an early good impression on his hosts. Ever the pragmatist, he would spend that autumn preceding his voyage early in the New Year in preparation. The first task at hand from the base of the tolerable prefab was quite predictable. He would aim to develop his art in a very singular manner. Away from the gaze of his mother's eyes, he had found a newsagent next to 'The Blue' that sold 8 by 5 inch blank white postcards. Ray purchased twenty of them in bulk. He had the idea to take his functioning bike and pencil and crayon to draw as many landmarks and scenes from London life as he could muster in the three months before setting sail. He had the notion that these could act as very useful gift cards to his expectant new Aussie friends, notably members of the Sykes family and their community in Scone. So off he would pedal two or three days a week to internationally famous venues along with visits to hill or river viewpoints that had artistic value to the eye of potential connoisseurs.

The second area of time consumption was quite surprising really. He had contacted Phil's junior football manager, Mr Murray at Peek Freans, to ask him if he would consider Ray as a football referee in September. Murray got to work, and with a referees course held at Sidcup every Wednesday evening while it was still light in September, he registered Ray as the youngest ref in the local clubs U16 league. Ray's main motive was to gain as much running fitness as possible prior to his migration. It was a fact that New South Wales was to afford young Bristowe an outdoor way of life on a farm which necessitated daily physical labour. He had to be ready for that.

Ray's seniority in age over the fourteen and fifteen year old players was not to be a barrier. His only foreboding was when it was announced he had to officiate his younger brother's team. If Phil was bad enough around the house in the family, on the football field he was an absolute nightmare! It was to be Phil that led his team, but his idea of leadership focused around acting as a physical enforcer in competition. Constantly carping at the officials, and instead of handing around the complimentary Peek Frean biscuits at half time, Phil would gather around his cronies for a group fag session!

It was these two activities that really made the time go fast that autumn. Ray took a free hand around the prefab as both Phil as a schoolboy, and Freddie and Jan were committed to parallel daily routines basically orthodox nine to five schedules. He flourished in this independent environment whereby he could decide early in the day his intended itinerary. He was enjoying the fact that he could visit the local library, clamber onto his bike for variable rides, mill around the market stalls of 'The Blue' or apply the final brushstrokes to his art projects.

Supported by Jan and Freddie's double salary, at last he was achieving a sense of freedom, a quality he was to experience as part of his forthcoming life in Australia. That was what he assumed it would be. No armed services, no tight academic commitments, no parental interference, Ray saw this autumn pass as the prelude to his Australian adventure. Christmas came and went and the big day was imminent. Inevitably, Jan was all a fuss in her valiant attempts to pack Ray's trunk. His idea of what was required was quite different from his mother's, knowing full well that his work clothes in Scone would be provided by farmer Sykes. Jan, for some unknown reason, had scurried around to supply her son with winter apparel despite the fact that the average temperatures for January through to May were to be 82°F!

That last evening the Rotherhithe freeze was continuing with frosts at night and grey heavy anticyclonic cloud dominating the days. Freddie had managed to add some special additions to Jan's meagre offerings for the last Bristowe supper. So there it would be, the family feast of stew, oranges and bananas, but at least they all would be there including grandma and granpops. It was to be their final farewell to the departing Ray which was definitely one way emotional. As a result of evacuation, he had never built up a close relationship with his grandparents in the vital years. So it was Freddie who decided that the journey to Tilbury would be too much for them.

"All set then, Ray, we won't be making a fuss tomorrow, just your Mum, Phil and me. You'll be glad to know we've all got the afternoon off including a chauffeur from our stock of cars at work," he said.

"And you be at the school gates, Phil, two o'clock sharp," warned Jan.

"We've got a lunchtime football practice. As soon as that finishes, I'll be there," added Phil.

Phil had taken his brother's break from the family with a pinch of salt. Secretly he thought that Ray was chickening out of national service. The younger boy was already exerting some degree of independence by making quick exits at meal times by scoffing his food in the knowledge that the bedroom would finally be his; no more art décor or certificates mounted everywhere for anything that Ray had achieved. He just saw his elder brother's absence as a selfish extended holiday. The Aussies would sort him out, he was confident of that. The only downside was Ray would come crawling home with his tail between his legs pleading for forgiveness. To Phil, it was just a matter of time.

Other than Phil's antagonism it really was an evening of mixed emotions, of tales from Freddie of his times during the war in the Med, which of course was to be navigated by Ray's liner via Port Said in Egypt, then Aden, Colombo and onto Fremantle and Sydney. The entire table recognised what an adventure young Ray was about to embark upon, but they still impressed upon him to be ultra-cautious around the dreaded foreigners. And what about the nigh on 2000 British travellers, some of whom would be desperate people scarred by the post-war era?

Ray's mind was already in a whirl, the balance of which was falling down on the side of adventure and of discovery. Across the table was his past, whatever the family ties. The future was crying out for him with the dark shadows of his past firmly blown away. He was never going to sleep a wink that night. The one thought that occupied his swirling brain that cold damp prefabbed night was that he had never been on an ocean liner a ship that would take five weeks to reach his destination!

"Where the hell has that boy got to, it's already ten past two?" a furious Jan complained.

"I'll nip into the school office and get Phil," said a forlorn Freddie.

For Ray, this was par for the course with his brother. He knew Phil was not too bothered about waving him goodbye, and the feeling was quite mutual. Another five minutes passed with Jan, wary in the knowledge that he had to be at the embarkation point by three o'clock, rising to fever pitch!

Suddenly Freddie jumped into the Humber automobile's driver seat, his face grimacing with nervous agitation. "Practice my arse, the little bugger is playing in a full school away match in Brixton! That is in the opposite direction. We can forget about him for the day," he cried.

Jan's expression said it all; she was fuming. How ironic it was that the only calm in that fine leather upholstered vehicle was from a seventeen year old about to board a ship to sail halfway around the world. Freddie put his foot down through the Rotherhithe Tunnel and turning right at a temporary roundabout, headed due east following the line of the Thames north bank all the way to Tilbury.

To be quite frank, even though encouraged by the family war time housing placement officers, Freddie and Jan had never been down the river as it widened and deepened towards the Essex marshes and estuary. Quietly he knew that places like Dagenham, Grays and Tilbury were the future for the docks with their open expanse of land and their handling ability of these new container ships.

Cargoes were exploding in size, much of their content coming from North America and the colonies. The whole set up needed deeper water, easy access and grander roads and rail transport in and out of these ports. Ocean liners dotted the harbourside as Freddie steered his car within a hundred yards of the embarkation reception area. He was amazed at the ease with which he was able to complete the journey, for out there he had noticed there were no pot holes, no rubble nor road blocks. It was out in the sticks.

Ray was relieved to walk into the departure lounge, even though it was bedlam in and around that area with over 1600 noisy and excited souls scrambling around and awaiting their turn to board their ocean liner, the Maloja. His agonies were prolonged as he would be amongst the last to board. It was families first, then foreign passport holders, then finally in small hundreds the single passengers with assisted work passage visas.

Jan's tears were ever flowing as she hugged and pampered her eldest to the departure gate. All she could think of was what were Freddie and she doing in despatching her son into the complete unknown amongst thousands of strangers. She kissed him farewell reminding him to keep all his papers for Mr and Mrs Sykes in his passport. "You will write, Raymond, from every port on the way and as soon as you get to Sydney with a return address?" she cried.

Freddie hugged his lad, proud of the fact that he had the guts to take on the unknown. He was sure as the boy walked up the distant gangplank, that one day he would return as a man. From the docker's point of view, he felt sure that he had done exactly the right thing in encouraging his son to go and search for his dreams. The couple joined the multitude of hundreds of families and friends and well wishers with streamers cascading from the liner as it blurted out its foghorn in a cacophony of long blasts. As the Bristowes waved from the quayside, all the mixed emotions of loved ones were left behind with the excitement of those onboard leaving for a new life. They created an exhilarating scene of joy, tears, screams and genuine expectation for what the future would hold.

The blurts from the ship's horns became shorter and shorter as the Maloja pulled slowly and sedately out of port. She was a huge vessel, but very much a ship of 1950. Ray made mental notes amongst the 'football' crowds on five accommodation decks. By the time the liner had worked its way clear of the Thames estuary he knew where the food halls, the entertainment lounges, the cinema and the on-deck swimming pools were located. Was it to be a holiday camp on water after all?

Reality checked in with him on finding his six berth cabin with three double bunk beds inside on a narrow corridor on the port side of Level 4. The berth was situated just above the water line and had little room for manoeuvre for the six of them who would be ship mates for five weeks. Four of the five he was to meet straightaway and luckily they were not too old but in their twenties. The two lads from Birkenhead were gardeners having just missed active service in the war, but had completed their two years national service already. They had got thoroughly fed up with crossing on the Mersey ferry every day to work in and around Aigburth Park for Liverpool City Council's grounds department. Both young and free, they sought a better life away from ravaged Merseyside to the sun to develop their outdoor skills. They had landed jobs working to the same type of job description in Melbourne.

The other two were related but a bit older and had worked as riveters on the shipyards of the Clyde in Glasgow. The two cousins had built up quite some expertise during the war in working in a specialised preferential job as shipwrights, a job which kept them away from the eager clutches of the military. Ray at first struggled with both sets of accents as these lads were down to earth and had put their backs into their living. Hence the humour and all the regional colloquialisms. It was never going to be a dull voyage!

The missing person, Chris Carlson had already parked his trunk. The four lads had explained to Ray that he was from Spennymoor in County Durham and had come aboard earlier with his wife and young son. "I don't understand, I can't see where she's going to sleep," said Ray.

"Oh, don't you know, son, this is a segregated ship. We'll only see him first thing in the morning and lights out time at night," joked Colin Buchanon, the burly shipbuilder from Bellahouston.

"Yep, take note, the female quarters are all on Level 3," joked his mate, Bob Nixon.

The two Scots lads had landed on their feet with a boatbuilding apprentice position in Fremantle. Ten Pound Pohms they may have been, but they knew their way around town and for five weeks were to take up the challenge offered by segregation on the boat. In many ways that imposition on their freedom and leisure time was a reflection of the Maloja as a whole. It really did represent

Britain in the 1940s and 50s. The ship boasted first class and tourist class, rich and poor, professional and menial, families and singles and male and female. Ray along with the others was expected to muck in, but there were just too many damn divides. Still, all the inmates of Berth 77, Level 4, were happy to experiment with rules and prohibitions that were set up to be broken.

The food was fantastic! Much of it was stocked in Australia or at stops along the way in the Mediterranean and in Ceylon. Fresh fruit, vegetables and all types of meat, beef, lamb and chicken were served at the tables at every meal. Then there was booze, and although Ray was an astonished onlooker, he could only wonder at where these Scousers and 'Wegies put it all. The number of single women adventurers also surprised the occupants of Berth 77, many of whom treated their journey as an idealist escape from Britain for only £10. Their company just about compensated for the overwhelming number of kids, urban Brummies, Cockneys and Geordies, the scourge of a weather-beaten nation, all under one sail.

Luckily their mothers, along with liaison 'aunties' from the ship's staff just about kept them at bay. Ray had predicted correctly that they would soon be out of sight and away from 'The Daily Events Programme' as the liner entered the Bay of Biscay off the coast of south west France and northern Spain. Along with his cell mates, 85% of the ship's inhabitants were down for three days with seasickness, confined to their cabins. January was a tough month to travel in as the ship steamed ever closer to enter the calmer Mediterranean.

Ray had good sea legs, and was learning all the time. Just being about such a variety of exports with such recent colourful tales to tell was already feeding his hunger and thirst to see and get more from life. While traveling through the marvellous Suez Canal, both Port Said and Aden at each extreme had reminded him of the untold squalour that the Second World War had left behind. Yes, there was plenty of warmth, sun and light, but the human dimension there in the Middle East in 1950 was hardly in advance of the animal kingdom. Survival was the only thing that mattered.

However, this was all to change once they had entered the Indian Ocean, steering south-eastwards towards Colombo in Ceylon. The stifling oppressive heat of the Aden coastline gave way to more balmy trade winds before arriving in the capital, Colombo, for a shore leave of two days. Ray wanted more time to himself by now. Half the journey had gone in a whirl and he had lost precious time to work on his drawings and artwork.

The Bermondsey boy took leave ashore for an entire day of solitude. He desperately needed it. Out came his postcards as he took a ride in a Ceylonese rickshaw to a recommended picturesque fishing village north of the capital called Negombo. With palm and pineapple trees as a backdrop, he was able to put crayon to paper to depict local fishermen unloading their tiny boats. His first postcard would be sent to his mother's prefab: no words, no messages, just a phenomenal real life glimpse of the wondrous island in the sun of local fishermen at work.

He could never reproduce the colour though, and that frustrated him. He had left behind the grey of the sky and the English green of field. Now it was something that he had better get used to quickly. His new world would be dominated by blue, yellow and striking beige, the colours of the ocean, the fruits and the buildings. Ray just had to invest in some colour crayons for part of his work in future. Negombo would never be erased from his psyche, for he was yearning for colour in his life again.

The second half of the voyage did allow for more circumspection, more diary notes and a great deal of cross referencing with fellow intending expatriates. Time was moving on as long sunny days climatically were to be replaced in the mindset of the passengers by the oncoming destination of Western Australia. Once the liner was drawing near, days away from Fremantle and Perth, the atmosphere of a holiday ship merged more to that of a busy rail terminus. Approximately 20% of the assisted passengers with their families would disembark in Fremantle, and it would be time for many good lucks and bye-byes from newly acquainted friends. The ship had proved to be a sharing but transitory experience.

Ray had made a point of not getting too close to anyone during his journey. He knew it could only lead to further complications. Berth 77 had a bit of a drinks party the night before Colin and Bob were to start their new boatbuilding life. They would succeed, they were full of ambition. Once the human cargo was offloaded, the Maloja would steam ahead around the southern stretches of Australia. That air of expectation, of imminent arrival had continued for the entire occupancy, but for Ray with now a more spacious berth of three to the cabin, there was more time for thought. He was just a few days away from Botany Bay, then the Head of Sydney Harbour itself.

He was in a state of semi euphoria that could only be likened to the hour before midnight at a New Year's Eve party. Yet, even that did not contain the streak of stark uncertainty mixed with this futuristic equation. For the first and only time as he viewed afar the New South Wales coastline, he experienced images that flooded across his mind: bombs, food rationing, his volatile mother, hordes of refugees and prefabs filtered back to back across the memory glands. Overshadowing them all was the wash of the waves below him almost enticing the Maloja shoreward. Ray Bristowe, he murmured, you're on your way!

He couldn't wait to meet the Sykes family awaiting him in Darling Harbour. First however, he would relive the exhilaration of his forefathers on entering Sydney Harbour. The Maloja would steer a wide berth left, and there on a perfect early February summer's morning, was the panoramic view. From up high on deck, there it was, of one of the world's most natural harbours with all its nooks and crannies. The climax was to be sighting the glorious Sydney Harbour Bridge in the distance for the first time. He surmised, "From 'Paradise Street to the real thing, Paradise."

The Darling harbour terminal was packed with meet and greets, a cacophony of noise emanating from a relatively small building. It was, however, well sectored off with Ray scurrying off the boat into the immigration pen for singles. He had made it near to the front of the queue, and as mother had advised, all his documentation was held within his British passport. Normally young people were treated with some suspicion by surly officials, but not here. The migration officers backed by ever-present posters of colourful Australia on the walls, were all smiles as they welcomed the young British adventurers.

He was through in what seemed a moment, and once in the reception hall, all he had to do was spot a sign or placard with the name of Raymond Bristowe beckoning him to a new life. A myriad of eyes would be intent on recognition from reception parties, ever searching for a gesture of positivity from the five week ship dwellers.

Then, suddenly, a loud bark of a voice filled the hall dominating the airwaves. "Raymond, we're here, is that you?" he heard.

Ray changed direction to the booming voice clapping his eyes on a thick set, ruddy complexion that would introduce itself as Michael Sykes and then by his side, Martha, very obviously his partner for life. Both were beaming broad smiles as they had got their man!

"Please call me Ray, I'm only called Raymond when there's trouble afoot," joked the young pohm.

"In that case, Mick's the name," grinned Mr Sykes, clearly quite ready to drop formalities.

The trio, as Ray's travel bags on board would be transferred separately to Burwash Farm in Scone, readily pushed off to Sydney Central, a tram ride away just minutes from the quayside. Martha explained that they had

111

come down the previous day by train staying with relatives overnight, and were expecting to catch the midday train back northwards into the heart of New South Wales.

The trains were reliable but slow. The 160 mile journey would take close to six hours, maybe a wee bit longer as a change at Hamilton would be necessary to get to the Hunter Line for Scone.

"Blimey, that's a long way. D'ya think we'll make it before dark?" said Ray, placing surprise in his voice,

"You think that's far mate, it's only about one fifth the length of New South Wales, and the state's as broad as it's long!" quipped Mick.Early impressions had been good as they whiled away several hours in conversation. Martha bombarded the boy with questions about wartime London and about Ray's time as an evacuee. Mick, as sharp as a razor, would take in every syllable from the young Englishman. He had heard rumours that many of the English, as opposed to the rest of the Brits, were very snooty and particular in their manner. Admittedly those comments had been expressed to him about the hostel inmates stuck temporarily ensconced in spartan conditions, but Martha had heard similar accounts of married couples' reactions to their new Aussie environment.

However Mick reckoned on this boy being different. His voice was clear cut, no la-di-da, and he loved a bloke who could correct his name from Raymond to Ray as his first real words on Australian soil. At one point, when Ray excused himself to the wc, Martha remarked to Mick that what the lad needed was a good feed-up when they eventually would arrive home.

"What d'ya think of our dungees, Ray?" Mick smirked.

"Never done it before without water. Oh no, yes I have - when we used to nip out to the Anderson shelter at the end of the garden when the Doodlebugs were dropping," replied a thoughtful but mischievous Ray.

"Crikey mate, bombs dropping everywhere," Mick joked, "what d'ya use for loo paper?" he asked.

"The Daily Sketch," Ray responded.

"Hear that Mar, the boys got some dinkum Aussie humour 'bout him," Mick laughed.

Ray already was feeling liberated. The Sykeses seemed to be very down to earth people, but he was under no illusions that with the size of the dairy farm's acreage and Mr Sykes's evident interest in a local wine collaboration, that here was no country bumpkin. Several references were made in passing to the fact that Burwash was not just a family farm handed down the generations, but that it was a rural business enterprise. Martha had explained that milk, butter and cheese were the new staples for nearby distribution centres like Newcastle and Tamworth. These previously small towns were expanding rapidly, still small but enjoying their new role as food providers for Brisbane and Sydney.

She also stressed how the family had ties with the wine producing slopes of the Hunter Valley with her sister marrying a viticulturalist. Equally Martha had passed on her passion for horses to her daughter, Maggie.

"Don't know much about the nags, apart from Derby day," said Ray.

"That's gonna change, believe me boy. After church on a Sunday horses are our religion in Scone. Did ya know that Scone is the leading equestrian centre in the whole of 'Stralia!" informed Martha.

On returning home, she was soon to get to work on what she had promised, a slap up evening meal at Burwash. Ray was duly introduced to the grown-up children, Maggie and Mark, both now in their early twenties. The Londoner was not only treated to a sumptuous three course spread, but his first meal also displayed to him how rural Aussies approached the chores. The girls did all the cooking and preparation, the males all the washing up. Unless there was a barbie outside, that was the rule for every meal.

At this inaugural supper, Maggie introduced her fiancé Peter. Mark boasted of his sporting prowess, and in the kindest possible way the head of the household, Martha, laid down some house rules, which Peter and Maggie the future newly weds equally had to abide by.

"There are just two. No cohabiting and very simply, my hubbie is in charge outside the house, anything inside it's me," Martha ordered. That was interesting because Ray had been shown earlier his abode known as the cabin, which could only be described as an extension to the main farmhouse, an all-in lounge and bedroom with a tiny cubicle for a toilet. The furnishings were equally sparse, one single bed with a side table and lamp, one wardrobe and a sofa. Hardly the play pen for a budding young artist, but Ray's instincts told him that Martha meant it to be his alone, full sway. "It's all yours, decorate, add or subtract, just be ready for breakfast at six and evening meal at seven. The rest is up to you," she instructed.

That night, Ray slept for England. Then just before 6am Mark rushed into the cabin to supply his work dungarees. Ray had just been awoken by a burst of sunlight through a gap in the curtains. He had felt a new sensation which all the newly arrived Pohms would have experienced, an early morning sun that possessed both heat, glare and light. It had already penetrated the dark room he had climbed into so readily the night before. It wasn't just the light, he had also been disturbed by a very unfamiliar dawn chorus. What a racket! Aussie bird life had to be heard to be believed. Ray knew none of the varied squawks, whistles and shrieks, but he soon made the comment to Mark that he'd never need an alarm clock.

His first day revealed to him what a marvellous patch of the upper Hunter Valley he had landed in. Burwash seemed to be on a flood plain of the tributary that surrounded the farm on three sides as far as the eye could see. Pasture just seemed to roll down to the river's edge, which took an enlarged meander almost a quarter mile from the farmhouse. The farm boasted multiple rundown barns and a small stable block. After brekkie, Mick and Mark stuck Ray on the back of their farm truck and showed him the ropes. For the next two years Ray would be the latest farm labourer to take on the duties of milking, herding, feeding, cleaning, fencing and digging on the dairy farm. He also assisted Maggie and Martha with all things horsey at the stable block of four attention-seeking mares.

Mark really was to be his work supervisor, the duties being enhanced by Maggie's boyfriend Peter two days a week and of course Mick would override the lot of them. He had informed Ray that he had timed his two year stay perfectly as the year before was the year of the 1949 flood. The river had burst its banks and had come up almost to the farmhouse across the flood plain. Mick had cattle drowned overnight and many had to be roped to safety in dire conditions. Burwash had lost nearly fifteen percent of its dairy herd. Hence the Aussie's quest for more hands around the place as he had to implement some kind of diversity of income. They now introduced chickens and increased the number of mares at the stables for breeding purposes at the annual Scone horse fairs and markets.

For Ray, this was a different world. Even though the animals and the procedures would be governed by routine requirements, he knew that the work would never be dull over his time at Burwash. Over the coming summer and autumn months, he settled into a sunlit existence at one with nature. It was only when the so called winter approached four months later that he started to think what he could do on his weekend days off. He had precious little time for his art, despite sending two cards home to Bermondsey. His hunch that his charcoaled drawing of Tower Bridge and the docks, and his one of the Houses of Parliament would go down well with Martha and Maggie respectively, was well founded. Nevertheless, even though they framed the two, Ray never let on that art was his passion in life. It just seemed at this stage to be so incongruous amongst the raw-boned Aussies on the farm.

Then Mark, selected to play for the Scone Sports Club, suggested to Ray that he come down to the 'oval' to watch his team play against Aberdeen. What the Pohm couldn't understand was why they had to leave so early at 8am on their Saturday day off. The answer was clear. Scone played Aussie Rules in the morning and Rugby League in the afternoon against Aberdeen with exactly the same players, and on the adjoining pitch the women played hockey against their rivals. There were no leagues, just local rivalry at stake. The town's sports field, versatile in nature, could accommodate all three sports on the same paddock. Then the real festivities began.

There were no formalities after the sporting carnival. Beer flowed like no tomorrow and wine circulated out of bottles without labels. It seemed stronger, much more potent going by the number of drunken women and louder that loud sports-mad Aussie rules and rugby men. Then the music came on from an old radiogram set up in the corner, and mayhem broke out amongst nearly eighty party-mad inebriated Aussies. The women couldn't leave Ray alone. None of these raw prawn Aussie gals, most of them farmers' daughters, had ever seen a Pohm, let alone heard a true London boy. When he was on the dance floor, he was surrounded by girls eager to hear him just speak. Mark, well worse for wear, had introduced him all around with, "This is my farm mate, Ray, can't play sport, but fair dinkum bloke."

Earlier in the evening, the Bermondsey boy had explained to Mark and his mates that he was a qualified football referee. That night that boast was forgotten in the rush to go on a midnight kangaroo ride. Ray would be dragged along in an open backed farm vehicle just ten miles north of town where Mark's group toured the terrain to shine their lights on any poor troop of kangaroos caught in the headlights. It was a harmless local tradition, especially if they were entertaining a guest on their ride.

These winter Saturdays would be a regular feature in Ray's social life from that weekend on, especially when Maggie heard he was qualified as a sports referee. She immediately volunteered him for the hockey matches and after a few weeks, Ray was officiating the rugby games for the lads as well. In Scone, the definition of a sportsman was he or she could play any sport, and at least twice a day! So why shouldn't the Pohm become the town's leading referee!

True to form, Ray had procured rule books for rugby and hockey and even invested in a black and white striped uniform to ply his new trade all over the Hunter Valley. His Englishness really helped him be accepted as he was respected by all the Aussies as the establishment authority of colonial guidance. To be British was to be in charge, even though Bradman and the Aussies would thrash the Pohms every time!

Not only that but the Pohmie farmhand didn't mind getting his hands dirty either. In such a small town as Scone in the early 1950s New South Wales, Ray was a novelty and well liked, both by the elders who had fought in either of the World Wars and by his peers for his peculiar Pohmie ways. Ray had time off enough to purchase a full array of art utensils, paint, crayons and the necessary brushes to restart his talents. It had been a long time, nearly eighteen months before he seriously was to take to his unshakeable passion again.

There were good reasons for this development. Firstly on his days off he had the run of Mr. Sykes' truck. Secondly he now knew this pastoral landscape like the back of his hand and finally he had cheekily approached Maggie to supply a regular number of the female hockey players to act as models for his renewed interest in portrait painting. And not one of the girls would resist his approaches to have their picture done! Ray had earnestly drawn or painted a host of available girls, but although he had ventured out with two or three more physical than romantic clinches, his main leisure time activity was sidling off to Lake Glenbawn or the nearby Brushy Hill mountain range to develop his landscape work, notably during autumn weekends in March and April. He was particularly challenged here as the fauna and flora were totally fresh and novel to him. It was to his living memory a total pleasure to paint the colours and variations of trees, bush and tree lines during this period of time.

By now the Sykeses were becoming quite proud of their resident artist, and such was their involvement that once in a while they would pack off together for a picnic, the family and Ray, almost encouraging him to display his skills in the open air. Another more local joint pleasure was to spend time at Martha's sister's ever booming vineyard. Yes, of course there were many wine tastings of the principally white grape of either Chardonnay or Riesling variety shared by all, but Ray's more frequent visits represented a true interest in viticulture. Indeed Martha found it very easy to suggest to him that he should lend a hand at the wine harvest time in March and April.

Ray had made a mental note that the two farms, only six miles apart, were becoming more and more interdependent, notably on the labour side of affairs when the young men and women would act as extra pairs of hands when needed. Mick was clearly spending more time towards the end of Ray's tenure on the administrative side. He had hinted at many barbecues that he was instrumental in pulling together the local farms' produce in a form of an early cooperative in terms of both milk and wine production. He had seen the advantages of a number of farms collecting together rather than individuals competing against each other in the market place. To be frank, the two family farms combined through Martha and her sister and were heading to become an integrated unit. What really was to seal the knot was Maggie's wedding to Peter who was employed in the wine trade and distribution in nearby Murrurundi.

Maggie in just two years had doubled the size of her stables and was establishing herself in horse events as a major dressage competitor. She lived and breathed horses and it was clear that Scone attracted so many national and international shows and gymkhanas that one day her real ambition to become a breeder for the noble art would be realised. It would take time, application, know how and financial investment, but the latter would be the asset she would gain from her betrothal to Peter. Hunter Valley wines were taking off like a rocket as southern hemisphere wines from the Barossa and the Hunter were on every dinner table from Perth to Brisbane.

The young Englishman had worked his way through all these happy times and really had become part of the family and part of the town. What he had noticed most was what many on the Maloja had hoped for, that Australia did provide opportunity for all those willing to grasp it by the fruits of their labour. The Sykes, an ordinary family, had fully recovered from a disastrous flood of their land to being well on their way to creating something special of their own.

Yet what about Ray Bristowe?

It was more than timely when Mick Sykes in December 1951 drove Ray over to his sister-in-law's vineyard. He wanted to share a bottle on the terrace with his ten pound Pohm and 'shoot the breeze'. "Ray, we're coming to the end of our two years together. Enjoy it?" he quizzed.

"It's been the time of my life, Mick, great, just great," replied Ray.

"We've all liked having you. Never really had a man to man talk with you, the time's gone so fast. You know there are five types of bloke in this world: winners, grafters, drifters, posers and losers. Which are you Ray?"

"Never even thought of life in that way, Mick, you tell me," he replied.

"Well I will, I will. You are a grafter and a winner, but you do have the capacity to drift and pose. It'll be your choice," Mick suggested.

Ray was taken aback. He fell silent as Mick Sykes was to put forward an amazing proposal that would knock him for six. "Boy, I want you to stay on here in Scone til you get near your 21st birthday. We want you to work on the dairy farm and over at the vineyard; that way you can have two sponsors in essential farm industries. Once that time is up, you can get your Australian citizenship and you won't have to give up your Pohmie passport either. They will grant you citizenship if you can then do your national service here. It's only for six months full time and six part time. Complete that and you're an Aussie, free to do anything here, you could even go back to London as an Aussie or a Pohm!"

Ray worked it out he could work one more year in Scone, then after an army camp for basics, drills and skills training in 1953, he could make career decisions. He had known the score from one of the lads at Scone Sports Club who had just completed the compulsory one year military service. It didn't seem to have been that bad. He reminded himself he could then choose to pursue his life anywhere and it did mean no British army national service if he did return to England.

"Mick, you're on, stay with the family and witness Maggie's wedding of the decade with Peter. How could I possibly miss that?" he enthused.

"Spot on, mate, just one more thing, I'm gonna double your allowance for 1952. Hey, here comes Peter. Do us a favour Peter, pick us one of your best off the shelf in the tasting room along with a bottle of bubbly. Cheers mate, we have something to celebrate. You won't mind running us back to Burwash later on will ya?" Mick gave his son in law to be the orders.

122

Peter raised his eyebrows, shook his head, smiling and said,

"Whatever you say, Dad!"

Ray in turn, pondered asking himself what his mother would think. Her runaway boy might never come home.

CHAPTER 6

ART FOR RAY'S SAKE

"Gusto, Bristo, gusto, that's what you need."

Ray had heard these harsh words dozens of times from staff sergeant Delaney, nearly always at the end of a six mile yomp as his small group of army trainees staggered to the finish line.

"You can't take it, can you, you pommie poofter? God help us if we ever have to send you out to Korea," shrieked his army master.

Yomping, to Ray's disgust, was a physical form of torture imposed regularly on national service personnel to give them the discipline and backbone to survive a long distance group run with the load of rucksack, Enfield rifle and full army fatigues. The added weight was estimated to be an extra five to six kilos. What alarmed Ray the most was the Aussie army had inherited the mad form of stamina training from the Brits. Ray Bristowe was always at the rear of his ten man platoon. The underlying objective was to complete the course through the scant outback terrain beyond Wagga Wagga as a unit. The platoon was as strong as its weakest link and only Vivian 'Ginger' Rogers could rival Ray for that dubious distinction. The Pohm was eternally grateful that there was a recruit in his troop called Vivian. 'Ginger' got merciless stick, the army officer's word for outright derision just because his mother had decided on the name before the baby was born!

As for the Pohm, he had counted every day, now 153, since he had signed up for national service back in February 1953. As he was located with the Sykes as his given home in New South Wales, he was summarily despatched to the wilds of the state, deep down in the semi-arid south west at an outpost of an army base near Wagga. Mick Sykes had secured his route to acquiring Australian citizenship, but the catch was that Ray had to endure this purgatory for a full six months, 176 days to be exact, before being released back to the Hunter Valley. Yet, even then he would be expected to join the civil defence force for two days a week for a further six months.

Only then would he be fully confirmed as an Australian. Ray at the end of each weary Wagga day would collapse into his hard barracks bed exhausted. Yes, even with spending an extra year as a farm hand on the Sykes' dairy farm humping bales of hay and digging drainage ditches, he at least would have the respite at weekends. The demands of army service training were relentless. In his first month or two, he would endure recurring dreams of Scone and the idealised cheese and wine lifestyle of

125

Burwash. One night they would be still and concentrated as he would be perusing the beauty and splendours of Glenbawn Lake putting the final brush strokes to his latest landscape work. Another would be his fun and frolics with the hockey girls after another game at Scone Sports Club.

Then it was the most repetitive one of all, the wedding of Maggie and Peter, where he had been the best man to his newfound Aussie wine merchant mate. Bottles of Hunter Valley wine, the confetti, the magnificent reception at the vineyards were all images that flowed and faded as he emerged from the twilight of his dreams. Reveille was sounded and the stark reality of yet another Wagga marathon would kick in.

The sheer monotony overshadowed even the daily content of long runs, some yomping, drill on the parade grounds, obstacle courses, weapon maintenance and lectures on all aspects of army procedure. If there were to be light at the end of this long tunnel, it was on Wednesdays and Saturdays when the camp would indulge in organised sports, normally the two codes of rugby or Aussies rules. It was within the army training traditions to take note of any specific skills of the servicemen, for example, could they cook, pilot a light aircraft, drive an HGV, or even officiate at sports events?

Ray soon volunteered as an exponent of the latter, which at least spared him from the bone crunching tackles and occasional brawls of the sports fields. He just had to separate the miscreants, a skill he had acquired from his three years in Scone. This even impressed his staff sergeant Joe Delaney to such an extent that he would release Ray on the odd occasion to referee local club games in Wagga at weekends.

In fact, although Ray was hammered by his superior on the physical side of training, Joe was mightily impressed by the Pohm's abilities in the weaponry department, principally in the upkeep and condition of his Lee Enfield rifles and Stem guns. They were spotless following any session after a day at the rifle ranges. There was never any doubt that Ray would divulge his commitment to his art in an army camp of all places. It was because he was an artist with his propensity to take good care of pencils, brushes and all his accompanying materials that made Ray such an excellent caretaker of his weaponry, even though it was a regular daily chore.

Nevertheless, Joe Delaney still kept on his case, any slackening or drop in standards would be pounced upon with the threat of an ongoing plane ticket to the hell hole on the Korean peninsula. The Aussies were, along with the Kiwis and Brits, in full support of the Yanks in combatting the communist menace of Eastern Asia. Australia, after learning of Japanese intents from World War II was aware of the ongoing threat, and fully believed in the domino theory of Chinese conquest from South-East Asia to Australasia.

Still, it never really washed with Ray. By June 1953, the penultimate month before his release from full-time military induction, he believed that the Korean war was grinding to a halt, and anyway he knew that national service personnel were in the category of reservists. The full time army would carry all the load of deployment anywhere.

Apart from the unsettling nature of further nightmares with Joe Delaney and yomping, Ray was soon to end his basic training in July and although he would resume his continued army duties part-time at the Craighorn Barracks near Singleton till the end of the year, he had some hard thinking to perform. For a start, he had attended his citizenship ceremony a week after his 21st birthday in Newcastle. Now on completion of his military service, he was physically as fit as a fiddle, had experienced three years of solid work in a priority-labelled state occupation and he had paid his dues to Australia as a young military soldier to be.

Still, to Ray, 1953 was just delaying the inevitable. Apart from his Higher Certificates from Beckenham in London, he actually did not have any qualifications, but at least the one thing he did hold now, was an Australian passport along with a British one. He would now be able to claim any rights, benefits or options thrown up within Australia. He kept reminding himself that his greater skill and love was in his own hands. Why not explore the world of Aussie art, underdeveloped as it was in the 1950s? He was not to do this out on the streets, no, he desperately wanted to qualify as an artist and that meant a college degree.

Mick and Martha, offering the cabin for as long as he needed, were both keen for Ray to settle and make his long term future in Scone. Over several late evening dinners, Ray had the task, very reluctantly, of cutting his ties or at least loosening them. With Mick it was to be very difficult, but Martha knew in her bones that the boy had to transfer his natural talent of drawing and painting into something productive and potentially lucrative. That meant just one thing. He had to go to Sydney.

Throughout the spring, she would comb through the colleges and institutions to search out potential courses that had some pedigree or status. It was an arduous task. Art as a fully fledged university degree was thin on the ground. As a subsidiary yes, there were some options, but that was not really what Ray was aiming for. Then, one November day, Martha received a call from her own cousin whose house she had stayed in on the night before Ray's original arrival in Australia. She made the point that a small teacher training college, Montkeith, was inaugurating a full-time art degree which was affiliated to Sydney University.

The qualification was to be the potential forerunner to a future degree at the university. It was located in Glebe, basically in the centre of the city and it would be a resident course. Martha toyed with the possibility that there would be fees involved and she would immediately raise the subject with Ray. She noted that bursaries were available to cover part of the cost as long as the candidate would come to interview and produce two pieces of practical work. The Burwash mother of two now went into overdrive as she racked her brains considering how much the course would cost, and how the fees would be broken down? She just knew she already had irons in that fire!

Ray had always responded positively to his 'Aussie Mum'. Martha had that uncanny Aussie way of telling it like it was, but in the most polite and considered way. It was a trait that he had respected in one other person to date, in his own father, Freddie. He could lay his cards on the table with Martha, revealing that he had spent precious little money for the last four years. He had saved his allowance money from Mick and well, in the army, he was too cream-crackered to spend any.

"Cream what?" asked Martha, still not quite getting the London speak.

"Tired out, Ma, never had a car, got the Aussie gals to spend on me, didn't need any flash clothes. I've virtually saved the lot," said Ray.

"Well, you're gonna need it soon, my boy," smiled Martha.

Ray journeyed down to Sydney with Martha on the same trusted train that December with two canvas covers containing a portrait of Maggie on top of one of her favourite horses and an overview landscape painting of Lake Glenbawn. The interview would take an entire afternoon. Ray was nervous, but Martha exuded confidence in her boy.

The Sykeses loved both items of work as the Maggie portrait reflected, with the stables in the background, what was really going on at Burwash at this time. Equine matters were just pushing tiny Scone forward in the Aussie sporting calendar. As for the Lake Glenbawn painting, this was to be also a period piece. Since 1949, work had slowly started to build a giant dam to regulate the flow of the Hunter and its tributaries. The principle idea was to spread the water in a controlled manner for domestic, agricultural and stock use.

The Scone family was anxious for this project to increase pace after the minor flood at Burwash in 1949, costing the lives of a number of their cattle. Mick was acutely aware of the site of his farm on a flood plain, effectively surrounded by water. Martha wondered whether Ray's painting would be one of the last paintings of the lake which would be considered for its raw original vista. She had heard that the dam and its system would be operational, however, by 1956.

Ray sailed through the interview, explaining his aspirations in his foreign English accent for his time at the college, but in particular, his aims and objective and the story behind the two items of work he had submitted. His works would be given close scrutiny by the appropriate staff personnel at the college and duly marked on the student's potential.

Martha had been carefully deposited in the waiting room during the interview, but keenly had offered Burwash as Ray's home address. Ten days later, with a Sydney post mark, the letter arrived. Martha couldn't contain herself. "Well, Ray, what's the news?"

"Ma, I've made it, we've made it. I'm in, start in February!" he boasted.

Before Ray moved on down to Sydney, he had mutually agreed with the Sykes family that he would work on the farm during the long twelve weeks' summer vacations whilst he was still a student at art college. They were never going to give up on him that easily, and he for that matter would not forget how fantastically kind they had been since arrival day. Martha, as he suspected, would not only pay for his labour between December and March, but also arrange opportunities for Ray to exhibit and sell his paintings at festivals and galleries throughout the Hunter Valley in these summer months.

So, with his saved income, a nice little bar job in Glebe that Martha's cousin Louise had arranged and the income from the farm and his paintings, there was enough to meet Ray's residential and spending costs. The real bonus had been contained in the acceptance letter in that Montkeith had been so impressed by his two framed contributions that his tuition fees had been waived.

As a boy in Bermondsey, he had never known that getting educated would be so complicated and costly. One of the reasons for this was his dad had once told him that in England all fees were paid by the local council to send their more academic sons and daughters to further education. This was, of course, typical of Freddie, only partially correct.

In Australia, apart from some generous scholarships, bursaries and discounts for disadvantaged kids, it would be a matter of the state intervening to help with the fees. Luckily, New South Wales was also very sympathetic to newly arrived British youngsters to place them in universities as it would be a very positive inducement for them to remain for the long term. With Ray, he was in the box seats as he had already achieved both criteria with his recently acquired citizenship and national service under his belt.

Now it was time for term to start. If there could have been a polar opposite to the barracks at Wagga Wagga in its freezing cold winter nights and the riverine comforts of the Hunter Valley, it was Montkeith Art College in the heart of Sydney. Situated in a dense cluster of housing, the college was really the amalgamation of three four-storey buildings with connecting corridors at ground level only. Clearly the University of Sydney had purchased the private properties at an earlier date and converted them for educational use. Quaintly, the four buildings were renamed, Rembrandt, Monet, Picasso and Van Gogh. The latter was totally revamped into residential quarters for fifty students.

Ray was one of them. Lucky to have his own tiny room, he had been prepared well for communal living from his army stint. However, the clientele at Montkeith had to be seen to be believed. These students clearly had avoided the clutches of the likes of Joe Delaney. For here were roll neck sweaters, beads, American imported jeans, sandals and worst of all moustaches, beards and hair overlapping the ears. As for the girls, loose tops and tight bottoms were in vogue in mid 50s Sydney.

There was no turning back for Ray. He gazed at his contemporaries and found it ironic that they were all under the impression they were individual, sole artists. That was until they glanced at each other all wearing the same clobber of rebellious attire. They were merely a team of artists. Ray wondered how talented or inspirational they would be as students that had arrived at Montkeith from the fresh expanding suburbs of Sydney and Melbourne.

His mind for the first time switched to Mick's character classification. Ray inwardly laughed at those he thought would be drifters, losers and most numerous, posers amongst this throng. He was under no illusion that he had to muck in and engage with some of these spotty herberts who would dash to wear duffle coats as soon as the temperature dipped. No, this ten pound Pohm was at Montkeith to learn. After all, what did he know about art in the first place? He was totally self-taught and at this stage he could hardly tell a Rembrandt from a Monet.

Eagerly he launched himself into his first year studies which concentrated on the history of art and art in society for its lecture base. He would learn about impressionist, post-impressionist, cubism and the whole thread of conceptual art. Painting seemed to take on greater emphasis over either sculpture or ceramics, but he also had to take on a subsidiary to his main practical work in painting and that had to be ceramics. He never saw himself as a sculptor.

If anything, he was just a trifle disappointed that his ability to focus on producing practical art took a back seat in this first year. Nevertheless he was aware that the entire third year was devoted into producing practical assignments along with the teaching arm of this very broad art degree. In fact, he was just too busy and too motivated by all that he was absorbing on the theory and history of art to contemplate too much of what he was missing.

His daily involvement centred on his learning and his tutors. Ray was like a sponge, mightily impressed by the range of academic art historians to those tutors who clearly relished the more functional side of instruction and execution of the art form at hand. Ray Bristowe, for the first time in his life was being intellectually stimulated.

In the evenings, certainly for three per week, it was the opposite at the Globe bar in Glebe where he tended bar duties amongst a tough and ready but friendly crowd of locals. That autumn it seemed more intimate than ever inside a pine wood coated saloon. No one even ventured into the back veranda court and there was good reason. It rained virtually every night. Not here the sunny intervals with showers or damp foggy mists of London town, this was Sydney and it came down in torrents. October moved into November and Ray just needed a respite from the continual deluges and couldn't wait to get up to Burwash Farm for the long summer break.

The trouble was, that was where the incessant rains were coming from. One of the mysteries he had to get accustomed to in New South Wales, was the sun was moving right to left. It was incredibly high in the sky and, worst of all, it was dry in the winters and wetter in the summers, everything seemed upside down! Now he had to face one of the wettest springs on record in the Hunter Valley. So instead of gaining a nice bare backed sun tan in Scone, he was to experience heavy rains at least fours times a week.

Back in the cabin at Burwash, he had noticed a great increase in all forms of spiders and ground crawling insects, but far fewer flies than usual. The former loved the damp, the latter the rays of the sun. With Mick and Martha, there was an unease about the place in January summed up by Mick's constant worry about the height of the water table.

"It's getting quite a bit worse than '49," he would say.

Finally in early February with minor encroachment from the river onto his flood plain, Mick Sykes made the big decision. He along with the herding help of all the family would rawhide style usher all his cows onto the upper field, and some in addition would be transported to Maggie and Pete's vineyard where Martha's sister held sway. She had a fallow field with a barn alongside the terraced slopes of vines.

All hell let loose just the week after Ray retuned to college. He was listening to the wireless perched on the bar at the Globe. It was the evening of February the 23rd. The Aussie commentator stuttered out words like a wayward machine gun. "In the Upper Hunter, bridges are down and rivers have burst banks, 2000 cattle drowned, in Scone over 225mm have fallen in 24 hours, a wall of water is descending on Maitland, the situation is out of control!"

Updates occurred on the hour announcing thousands of homes and farms had been abandoned and worst of all, the forecast was for continued downpours from an amalgamation of low pressure systems over Queensland. Ray dashed to the bar's phone and as he knew the Scone number of Burwash off by heart, desperately wrapped his fingertips around the dials. It was pointless, the phone lines were down, indeed all communications including the mini airport and train lines were to be totally disrupted for the next four days.

Inwardly Ray did not panic, but he just had to know how Burwash had fared. From radio reports the next day, the scene from the air over that region was one of a gigantic lake of dimensions of 100 miles by 80. The Aussie army was called in with water-specific equipment to rescue thousands of inhabitants stranded on rooftops. It was the worst Australian flood disaster in history, the flood of 1955.

The Bristowe boy tried for two days by phone to trace the families. He even went down to Sydney Central that weekend to catch the train up, but all trains were cancelled as tracks were submerged and a muddy slimy debris was littering the rails, making any transit impossible. Finally on the Saturday afternoon, he made contact, not at Burwash, but at the vineyard. Thank God, the Sykes were together under one roof. Mick's crucial decision to move the dairy herd had saved his livelihood.

Yet, Burwash was under water. The lower floor of the house along with the cabin were inundated, the chickens had perished and the stable block was two feet under. Fortunately, Maggie had moved her precious livestock to a higher elevation east of Scone when the cattle had been transferred.

"There's nothing you can do Ray at this stage. The water is starting to subside, then it will take some time to take stock with the buildings at Burwash. I'm sure that when it is safe to rebuild, you can come up and help, but that looks like months away."

Ray faced reality yet again in his short life. He had lived through the bombing, he had witnessed the perils of winter freeze, and the desperation in Hamburg, now disaster for his nearest and dearest in Scone. He looked in his shared corridor bathroom's mirror and faced a very lucky man. He had to make the most of his time at Montkeith.

He had decided to stay on in house at the college through his second year, but would seriously consider an offer from 'Auntie' Lou to board with her at neighbouring Strathfield for his final year. His monies could see him through this middle year as he made tentative steps to see that there really was life in Sydney beyond Montkeith and Glebe. Academically by the end of the three terms, he had complete knowledge of artists and their biographies and work output from the old masters to the contemporary exploits of Pablo Picasso.

In the back of his mind, all he could think of was Burwash. It was to take the entirety of 1955 before Mick Sykes was to make the decision to rebuild some of the structures so badly damaged by the flood. His family had moved into the vineyard in this intervening period, essentially farming those spare fields with a reduced dairy herd. Ray was itching and atwitching at the end of his written papers' exams to get back to the farm.

He was also, now as a twenty three year old, wanting to spread his wings for the final year. To be exact, with the course's emphasis on practical work allied to the teaching of the subject, Ray was entering the sharp end. What he could achieve in this last year would definitely result in his career pathway. He had come to his professional crossroads. Would he make a go as a working artist or would he lean towards a penchant for teaching his most prized skill?

Ray was intent on gaining a distinction from his degree but he knew he was not the finished article yet, something was missing. He had nine months to discover exactly what it was.

* * *

Libby Hanks was a native of Tasmania. Originally a penal colony, the island was ideally suited to an almost separate development in Australia's history. When you mentioned Tassie to most Aussies, you would receive a knowing look really reminding you that the state's animal marsupial mascot was a devil.

She grew up in Hobart but frustrated at the slower pace there, soon migrated to Sydney to follow her undoubted talents in the field of painting. Rather than pursue an academic training, she was a social animal who was obsessed with the vibrant attractions of the bright lights. Libby succeeded in securing a series of part time locations at Circular Quay, Bondi and Woolloomaloo to exhibit her street art to tourists and local Sydneysiders alike.

The propensity to offer colourful scenes of harbour and water vista to the domestic population in post-war recovery was unique. She was one of the originals to prosper from her fees, boosted by her evening bar work up on the hill at The Cross, King's Cross, the Bohemian mecca for young trendsetters. There, she was plucked off the streets and out of the clubs and nurtured by another bright, young aspirant even rich before his stellar rise as a qualified accountant.

Libby's ticket had arrived. Jimmy and Libby tied the knot as Mr. and Mrs. when she was barely out of her teens. It was the attraction of opposites.

By 1956, Jimmy had built up a strong base for his advancement within the Spengler and Taylor partnership working out of Pitt Street and commuting from their first home via the daily ferry from Manly. His was a backslapping, hard drinking pole-climbing existence to gather in the high rollers of Sydney's fast expanding corporates. Libby with no thoughts on a family, built up a network of male and female friends and associates within a very comfortable marriage.

One of the offshoots of such connections was her continuation as a private artist for the walls of many of Jimmy's clients and affiliated companies. This in turn had led in 1952 to her landing a perfectly suitable post at Montkeith College in the city as the resident artist. Yes, with her tight white slacks and floppy Merino sweaters she could easily be mistaken for a post graduate student. Indeed, at the age of 28, Libby never presented an age barrier to her students, this fact being accentuated by her love of the new pounding rhythms of rock and roll and a popular quaint interest in the art of stained glass windows.

To the young artists to be, she was cool and her role as the tutor of continual assessment of final year students' practical work brought her even more into their daily orbit. Her classes were small, no more than seven or so who had chosen her area of specialism in painting landscapes and producing portraits. There was nothing abstract or ethereal about Libby Hanks' tutorials.

Ray had worked out the divides for his final year routine. The mornings were focused on art and education, the learning and methodology of how to teach and impart the essentials of art in the classroom and in the studio. The afternoons would, four days a week, be centred on project work. He was delighted to take up the option of landscapes and portraits with Mrs Hanks.

What he didn't expect was a blue-eyed blond with a glittering smile who exuded the newfound confidence of a modern Aussie woman. For decades, the antipodean female would only speak when she was spoken to. For the young 1950s woman challenging the sport obsessed, raw boned, hairy arsed Aussie male was a rare occurrence. Not with this one. Libby Hanks had that knowing look of familiarity with such an array of facial expressions. Ray could see that she has been around the block and was proud of the fact.

"Ray Bristowe, aren't you the guy that painted his girlfriend astride a racehorse?" she asked pointedly.

"Yes Mrs Hanks, but she ain't my girlfriend," said Ray slipping all too easily into his Bermondsey tones.

"Hear that class, we have a Pommie. This is going to be fun, and by the way, forget the Mrs, I'm known as Libby round here," she said.

So it was to Libby that he owed his bursary at the college. It was she who had assessed his earlier double contributions. From the start he understood where she was coming from as many of his classmates would continually remind him. They all recognised the students she highly rated by the excessive amount of repartee she would share with her victims. It was the case that whilst she shared her musing and ribaldry with particular individuals, a very productive partnership would ensue. Silence from her represented ambivalence or apathy.

Ray, still displaying some remnants of his cockney accent, was a sure fire hit for her. Not only did he draw attention from her in a communicative way, but she had rated his base talent with brush and crayon. His works were stark, brilliantly accurate but lacked the subtlety of brushstrokes, and there was an underdevelopment in the use of colour. It was to be in these areas that she had to influence him. His portraits needed a great deal of work in depicting human features, the shape and softness of the human form. His interpretation of a dominant feature would hit the eye dead on, too early in the observer. She could teach him how to represent such a feature more subtly by the nature of his brushstrokes.

Libby never would neglect Ray's fellow artists, she was simply too professional for that, but Ray was responding so rapidly. By the third month in April, his portraits of fellow students were impressive, so much so that his classmates would beg him to allow them to keep the images. Then a new development as she allowed Ray to stay after class.

"Ray, I would like you to join me up at Bondi at an adult class I run on Saturday mornings, every Saturday. We concentrate on cross-beach profiles there and autumn is the very best time of the year," she enthused.

All Ray had to do was catch the train up to Bondi Junction and walk the rest. All the utensils would be provided up there from a beach side art kiosk run by an associate of Libby's. An early morning start would be envisaged as the group would assemble close by the Bondi swimming pool and life guard facility on the south side of the headland. Libby had assembled her pitch, and as Ray arrived, she was ready to set out the programme of paint for the day.

"When are the other members of the group arriving?" he asked.

"Ah Mr and Mrs Dobson have been a late call-off, couldn't get a babysitter this morning," she offered gingerly.

That was that then, just the two of them, and that was how it was to be right through the next six months. Mrs Hanks was intent on grooming her protégé. Over the years she had from time to time given individual tuition, sometimes after the college day at evening classes, but normally on a Saturday when Jimmy would be playing Rugby Union for his old boys' team in winter. In summer, he would entertain prospective corporate clients at the SCG, Sydney's cricket mecca. Either way, he would come home worse for wear on a Saturday night, when the two of them would negotiate whatever was possible for the evening.

Ray had always wondered whether Mr. and Mrs. Dobson ever really existed. This was noticeably so as Libby was not only his art tutor, but his taxi service to and from a variety of Sydney venues. She would double as a tourist guide to Botany Bay, the North Shore and all points north and south of the harbour. The Londoner was becoming an expert on Sydney's nooks and crannies, and as he toured the southern suburbs of Putney, Mortlake,

Catford, Sydenham and Lewisham, it reminded him clearly that the city's original settlers were London boys like him.

Mrs Hanks now was incorporating business with pleasure. All visits for artistic wonder sites were now accompanied by an al fresco meal at fashionable harbourside restaurants or bars. To many an onlooker with his ruddy good looks and her chic outlook on appearance, they were a perfect modern couple. Ray was up for the journey because he had that distinction in mind. Yes she was an attractive woman but he was always aware of her marital status and his underlying passion for what a degree in art would bring to his world.

Libby pushed the boat out further as the summer arrived in October. Jimmy was up in Queensland for an end of season long weekend of rugby. It was a perfect opportunity to take Ray down to Batemans Bay, where a former female student had opened an art studio and shop. She thought it would be very appropriate for Ray to meet her as she was pursuing a full time occupation. Also, there were the added benefits of some detailed and specific sketching and drawing to be offered in the studio on Saturday.

Fran Oliver welcomed the pair on the Saturday morning at a nearby early brekkie venue on the beach. All was very orthodox until they returned to the studio at the back of Fran's shop. Libby sat Ray down and calmly suggested that he attempt something very new. She wanted him to go back to basics and charcoal sketch Fran, in the nude!

Evidently it was all arranged. Libby's friend was very comfortable with it as long as he was. From the art tutor's point of view, the completion of the most pleasant of tasks would be an indicator of how far Ray's expertise had come in the six months. One more rider which more than shocked Ray, was that Mrs Hanks would present the drawing as one of his three projected works for his final assessment.

Fran had posed before when she was not entirely happy with the outcome. By Sunday lunchtime, Ray's endeavours had produced elation between these two icons of art as far as his experience could tell.

"It's simply superb, no other student could achieve such levels in paint and charcoal as in your projects," said Libby.

"I am flattered, Ray, you seem to have captured all my lines!" replied Fran.

Ray had advanced and had a body of work throughout this period which he wanted to exhibit in two centres in December in Aberdeen in the Hunter Valley and there with Fran in the Bay later on in January. There was sound reasoning here. He felt that if there were very positive responses in both places, he seriously would follow Libby's advice into opening up his own studio after graduation in January. He was caught in two minds as his desire to teach was now coming to the fore.

He was also aware that teaching art was a marginal part of any school's curriculum. In Aussie levels of education, it was regarded as a mere pastime to be explored beyond the school gates. At best, there may be one lesson of art per class per week. If a young aspiring teacher wanted to teach art, it was as a minor subsidiary to a main academic subject. Ray never would have wanted that. He was noticing that as a result of his multiple visits with Libby to landscapes very varied in nature that he was intrigued by the geology and geomorphology of the land forms. Back in London, he had his higher certificate in geography, maybe, just maybe he might consider…..!?

His dreams were realised when he achieved his Honours with distinction, a Bachelor of Arts from Sydney University as results were announced in December. He made a point of a quick dash to see Libby on the term's final day to thank her for all she had done to inspire him to such heights.

"Remember, Ray, if you do go pro, just get down to Fran, she will point you in the right direction. You're ready for the challenge!" she confided.

To Ray it was a sad occasion to say goodbye. She hugged him tightly and he noticed the first drops of tears cascading down as she kissed him fully on the lips. Her dampened eyes were now fixed upon his in a disorientated stare. It slightly perturbed him.

Ray pushed open the gates of Montkeith for the final time as Auntie Lou would take him to Sydney Central, then reclaim her house again after a year of crayons, paper, paints and frames. He had always promised to put in a shift to help Mick return to normal at Burwash, but he would be back in Sydney in late January to collect his treasured degree at his formal graduation ceremony at City Hall. Mick was delighted to have Ray back as he was resurrecting the farm and converting it away from dairying to a fully fledged equine centre for Maggie. She was living her dreams. Mick and Martha now would concentrate more of their energies into assisting Pete expand the vineyard to provide wines to all outlets in Australia. The flood had made the Sykes recognise their commercial priorities, and it was a fact that wine and equine were the real profitable pursuits for the future in Scone.

Ray spent most of December and January digging drains and painting. This time the decorative side of house furnishing! He would need to return to Sydney for his graduation and to spend some time in Batemans Bay, which would allow him to assess his sales from the exhibits both in Aberdeen, and down there on the South Coast.

The ceremony was splendid. Graduation saw the formal side of the Aussie character with multi-coloured gowns adorning the hired suits of all the young men and women ready for the big, bad world. It was marvellous to see all the Sykes family come down to Ray's special day, a perfect hot sunny day with a garden party at the back of City Hall. Only one person was missing; he knew not why but Mrs Libby Hanks was nowhere to be seen. He was mystified!

* * *

Two days later, Libby Hanks would make her way up to an empty Montkeith College. Formally turned out in a trouser suit of beige, it was her second visit in a week during the summer vacation. This time she would hear the result of her professional appeal to the guardians and trustees of the college. She waited patiently in a side room before being admitted to face the tribunal. A series of remarks rebounded between Libby and the small entourage from the college elders. Finally, they submitted a statement to her, which read:

"Libby, we are relieving you of your duties here at the college with immediate effect. Over the last four years you have been warned of your inappropriate behaviour and lack of professional conduct on two previous occasions. You have continued to flaunt the strict line between staff and student. There has been put before you irrefutable evidence of an intimate relationship involving a final year student. For your sake and the interests of the student, let alone the reputation of the college, we have not involved him nor informed him of our decision taken today.

We will provide positive references for you but these will only be confined to the quality of your knowledge and the range of your expertise in the practical teaching of art. Equally we thank you for your four years' service here and wish you well."

Libby took it on the chin, lowered her head and retuning to the safety valve of the Hanks family, simply turned the page and entered the next chapter of her charmed life.

Auntie Lou was so kind to let Ray have her car for the week. Without further ado he put foot to the floor and was in Batemans Bay in four hours. No mucking about, but he was a bit nervous to see how the sale of his works including the overview of the one of Glenbawn Lake had fared at Fran's shop. She should by then have been exhibiting for over two months. Along the boardwalk he shuffled to find the place all boarded up, desolate, whilst there were plenty of signs of life all around. He popped into the ice parlour next door. All the answers to his questions were the same. Fran had shut up shop between Christmas and the New Year. The Aussie model had flown the nest never to be seen again, and with her went seven of Ray's most prized possessions.

He was devastated and soon realised he couldn't contact her through Libby. The college was not at all willing to pass her details on for obvious reasons. Ray used his reasoning for the first and only time to connect with the accountancy firm of her husband, and he was able to squeeze a modicum of information from the secretary. Jim was on sick leave and in a bad way.

"To be honest it's his wife I need to contact urgently," said Ray.

The secretary paused, clearly in two minds. "That's the problem, his wife's left him and ran off with another, another woman!" she added in a disapproving way and continuing, "No one can find her, he's in pieces!"

Ray knew little of Libby's private life, but surely it was too much of a coincidence. He added two and two together, and realised he'd been taken for a fool. With sales reaching only limited success in Aberdeen, he concluded that despite his academic award, the life of a commercial Aussie artist would be too precarious for him. The bad experience of his ménage a trois with his two Aussie sheilas was the clincher.

He returned to Lou's place to think things over. As far as he was concerned he was still rootless, despite discovering the belonging he yearned for with the Sykes family. They had given him so much in a very balanced family with genuine affection from his Aussie mother and father and a real sense of brotherhood from Mark and

Maggie. Every day up there was a delight where all the family worked hard for the common end.

Back in England, he was born into an antagonistic family, a true matriarchy, which was just intolerable, and it pervaded all aspects of the extended family. He had totally rid himself of it years ago, the fights, the arguments and the struggle. His only regret was isolating himself from his father who had battled bravely against the overwhelming regime of Janet and her infuriating sisters. His pitiful brother was welcome to the lot of them.

The trouble with the Sykeses, was they were rural, away from the main sway of life. As embracing as they all were, Ray was a city boy and he was desperate to find his own way in life, and indeed make a stab at creating his own family. Yet he was convincing himself that it would not be in Australia, despite his dual identity. He had found that 1950s Australia had lacked the scale of Britain. It was like the kid brother of England on the wrong side of the world, isolated from external influences as a result of its distance from the Americas and Europe. Sure, it was forging its way forward post war, but it still lagged behind in so many areas of cultural life compared to what he was hearing of the British revival.

He personally was caught now between two shores. What really clinched it in his mind was in the actual Aussie character itself. For Ray, it was too black and white, too harsh, too much of a "If you don't like it, then stuff you mate" mentality. He'd taken all the Pommie bashing with scant regard, but would they ever, especially in the competitive cities, accept as one of their own, the boy from Bermondsey?

Every February, through the consulate in Sydney and the city's university, the colleges of London would be conducting their milk round of colonial cities in Australia, New Zealand and South Africa. Their role was to attract young graduates for further study in London. In an ironic twist, it was the mother country's revenge for the ten pound Pohms. Yet here they were after the pick of the new world's brains.

Open interviews were being held for aspiring graduates with the tempting motivation of the single fare to be covered by the University of London. The only restriction was the applicant had to be an Australian citizen. Ray inwardly mused, he would be an Aussie today, tomorrow a Pohm!

With his graduate certificate handy alongside his Australian passport he applied more out of unreserved cheek than an absolute commitment to read Geography and Geology with no preference of college choice. Auntie Lou would hand him three weeks later the news that he had been accepted at King's College, London University later in the year.

It was the first week of May when his family came down for the last time to see him off. Ray simply did not have the heart to revisit Burwash and all around it. He had insisted that all farewells had to be made at Lou's place from where he would take a taxi back to Darling Harbour for the long voyage.

This time it was emotional. He kissed goodbye to his genuine family; his mum and dad, brother and sister and Lou and Peter. Ray left them with a large, flat rectangular package not to be opened until sail time at 6pm. He clambered into the cab, thinking one day maybe when he had kids of his own, he would return. He was convinced of that.

Meanwhile at precisely 6 o'clock, Mick and Martha opened their present. It was a huge framed, panoramic painting of Burwash, January 1957, resplendent in colour and with all the new buildings intricately included.

In the bottom right hand corner was signed, Ray S.

CHAPTER 7

YOU'VE NEVER HAD IT SO... WILD!

There was something familiar to Ray as he perused the watery landscape ahead of him. He had been there before, a long time ago, but Southampton Water and The Solent beckoned him home. On this occasion, as a fully-fledged Aussie with unruly beard, brown sandals and a flat hat with those fly-resistant togs draping down the edges, he had forsaken his birthright. He again contemplated that he had completed his overseas experience after nigh on ten years. When he left the agonies of post-war Britain, it was dark, drab and economically destroyed. Now he overlooked the quayside, ahead of Elvis and the rock and roll years. It was 1957.

For Phil, it was a very different story. Whilst his elder brother had run away from it all, it was he who had to endure the extended years at school, the winters and the shivering nature of his mother's prefab, and the rationing of anything you care to mention. Finally, he left the schoolyard behind in Bermondsey in the summer of '52, only to be bullied by his father to do his duty. The papers had arrived, and short of Phil taking up a working trade apprenticeship, it was the obligatory national service that loomed large for the next two to three years.

Freddie and Jan, starved of any meaningful contact through these years from Ray in Australia, were both realistic about the opportunities that lay ahead for Phil. He departed school with no paper qualifications, and their subsequent reaction was to push him into the army. He was physically well suited and there was a real chance for him to learn a trade or alternative skills in the services when ready for civvy street. There was another reason: they had been offered the chance to take up a newly constructed council flat in the neighbouring dockside community of Rotherhithe. Freddie had been given the green light following his application.

Jan was keen that with Phil now also maturing and away from the UK in potential postings, that there was at last a chance for Freddie and her to make a new start away from the temporary nature of the prefabs. Although the makeshift housing had been popular with many families, Jan always wanted something more solid in every sense. Five years within 'soft' walls had been enough.

Phil faced basic training well away in North Yorkshire and had been assigned to a local regiment. As was the tradition, regiments were geographically based and located in areas of training very much with relevance to the traditions of that branch of the army. In this case, he was to be nurtured within the infantry sector, and for the foreseeable future, he would go wherever queen and country would send him. The new monarch was to succeed King George during this period. Optimistically, it was to be a new Elizabethan Age. It certainly was a new world.

Asia had been exploding since World War 2. First there was independence for India, the Korean war, alongside considerable unrest in what was then called Indo-China, latterly the French colony of Vietnam. As a major colonial power, Britain in Malaya had to face communist insurgencies both on the peninsular and on the easterly extension into the tropical rain forest of Borneo. At this post-war stage, the areas were principally ruled by sultans and kings who had worked hand in glove with the British administrators. The latter had enormous influence in the commercial exploitation of palm oil and petroleum in Sarawak and Brunei, and most important of all, in rubber in mainland Malaya. The greatest proportion of vehicle tyres across the globe had originated in British Malaya. The motor car had arrived, everywhere!

Phil had taken some interest in the state of the world but mainly from the point of view of where he might be despatched to, and Malaya was at the bottom of his list for 1953. True to sod's law, within a month of basic training his group of rookie eighteen and nineteen year olds were offloaded on a military plane and ship heading for Kuala Lumpur. They were, for all intents and purposes, sent there to fight the communist insurgency, backed by China's Mao Tse-Tung. The Chinese connection was intent on destabilising the infrastructure of the differing states of

Malaya by essentially conducting guerrilla warfare and terrorist attacks on rubber plantations, rail centres and British military bases from Thailand in the north to Singapore in the south. Mao wanted the rubber for himself.

Phil eventually survived a ship journey to India, then on to Kuala Lumpur by military aircraft. He landed in a blanket, an overwhelming density of heat, close to 90°F, but it was the humidity that enveloped him that February night of 1953. His training had previously taken him on patrol across the Yorkshire Moors that autumn and early winter where the sun was hardly seen and at temperatures less than 40°F.

The orientation training of just two weeks in Malaya was supposed to condition him but nothing could prepare him for the jungle and the subsequent lines of patrol. He spent the first six months watching his patrol mates drop like flies with bouts of malaria and dysentery and a nasty strain of dengue fever which was a killer. The thin lines of infantry were periodically ambushed from the enemy's deep jungle hideouts and as for the guarding of the rubber plantations and oil dumps, the British soldiers were sitting ducks. Phil's natural physical prowess and aggression would not only prolong his survival, but also act as a foundation to lead. Within the year, gradually the Brits, with too high a proportion of newly conscripted national service men had, through the officers, learnt that smaller platoons operating in counter-attack tactical strategies were far more productive.

The security forces had to win the hearts and minds of the indigenous Malays to counter the terrorists, always hard to identify amongst the mass of villagers they were to encounter. Intelligence was the key with the aim to cultivate the friendship and cooperation of the native tribesmen. This could be achieved by the regular supply and accessibility of food and simple medicines, including penicillin. It also included the amalgamation of local volunteers into the special forces operating as scouts who were readily, along with the highly successful Gurkha regiments and platoons, acclimatised to dense jungle fighting. This approach hit the button. The Malays remembered the cruel treatment from the Japanese during World War 2, so they soon welcomed the white man who helped them with jobs, food and essential supplies.

After three or four years the tide of the campaign was turning. Phil was now being deployed in search and destroy missions. He operated within small detachments of no more than six soldiers. His platoon leader had been in the country since the start of the campaign back in 1949, a very seasoned Welsh veteran called Terry Jones. The gaffer, as he was nicknamed, had no rank, no serial number and no regiment, but he could speak Malay like a native and treated his fellow Gurkha fighters as blood brothers. He now was as pleased as punch as the extension of search and destroy was released from a previous position of a three mile limit from a fortified location.

For Terry and his handpicked unit of five reliables, this policy was to bear fruit. Yes they had to defend the plantations, the families, the tappers and labourers from the cruel murders of the terrorists. He knew his lads were equipped with bren guns, grenades and were receiving aerial support from helicopters with new abseiling equipment to augment rapid drops into firefighting zones. On one such mission east of Ipoh, in the state of Perak, Terry with two Gurkhas, one corporal infantry soldier and Phil landed to seek out the communist infiltrators. In hot pursuit, the two diminutive soldiers hit a trip wire which released embedded bamboo spikes and, in this case, booby trapped sacks which killed both on first contact and smashed into Terry's upper body. He was totally immobilised by the mass pounding which also glanced off the side of Phil's helmet.

Phil was stunned, but he had the willpower to radio one of the choppers for a rendezvous point. The helicopter was five miles away and was already ferrying extra troops into the vicinity. Phil and his fellow corporal were to carry Terry Jones back to the rendezvous, through water and mosquito infested jungle with only rats for company and the constant threat of communist ambush. Stripping themselves of all equipment except a radio on a backpack and two bren guns, they carried Terry, semi-conscious, for four hours towards the pick-up.

They made it, to their relief, before dark fell upon their journey from hell. Terry had suffered multiple fractures and dislocations that meant he could not carry anything for four months. After the rudimentary hospitalisation, Phil was to spend two months under observations in a British hospice in the community of Brickfields in central Kuala Lumpur. He wasn't to know it but he had received triple concussions to the head and worryingly, he showed scant signs of memory of the engagement back near Ipoh – and that was after two months.

Terry was wheelchaired in to visit Phil, and by his bedside, announced to him that he was up for commendations for bravery in the face of enemy fire and for saving the life and well-being of an officer.

"What about you, Tel? You made it from the dead. Without you, all three of us were scuppered," said Phil.

"Nah, Phil, in my unit, we don't take gongs," replied the Gaffer.

"In that case, nor do I. Put that in their report and smoke it, and what 'appened to the Corp?"

"He got a special! Promoted to Lieutenant in his reg. You know he went to Wellington College, you know," hinted Terry.

The two of them were to serve together again after a further month of leisure, and part of Phil's rehabilitation was a daily swimming session at the municipal pool of Petaling Jaya. Gradually he would get his aerobic fitness back with the aid of the poolside attendant, a Malay national called Puan. Life there in the suburbs of Petaling Jaya was relatively undisturbed by the troubles up country. Puan was a marvel and such was his empathy with the recuperating Brit, that he introduced Phil to a swimming partner for every morning of the 30 days of his recovery. The heroic Londoner would never forget it.

Why? Because Carolina Lee was a Eurasian beauty, only five foot three inches tall, but a model without parallel as far as Phil was concerned. Her diction was perfect as a result of her mother's instruction, spoken in such soft, generous tones of English, not Ingerlische! Her hair was shiny, her body so well-conditioned, but her curves were slender and soft. To start with, they would swim up and down both copying each other's strokes and soon they were sharing drinks, satay and nasi goreng by the pool, all cooked by their matchmaker Puan. It was a threesome made in heaven, but Carolina was smitten with the Bermondsey boy, once offloading her feelings about Phil to Puan.

"He's too good to eat, I can't get enough of him."

They were to share everything for that month. She apologised profusely for inviting Phil to Puan's on site quarters. It really wasn't much more than a changing room, but he had a soft couch, and it was, oh, so private. Phil had always admired, even leched after young Englishwomen, but he had decided years before that they were either all too pale or dominated by their mothers; and taking after their mums, were far too bossy. Carolina was the opposite. As he saw it, she was ultra-feminine, sultry and giving. Even though she had siblings and she still lived at home at the age of 26, she was independent enough to work as a travel assistant, so quite self-sufficient and business savvy at her afternoon office in Kuala Lumpur.

Phil was to return to Terry's unit for six more months having been passed for duty by the medical boys, but it would mean only seeing Carolina twice a month from thereon in. He would never ask to, nor see her home, right the way through to his demobilisation in 1956. They always met at the pool, sometimes escaping to one of the many bars, or eating alfresco in the hot Kuala Lumpur sun.

160

He had survived the Malayan Emergency. They had driven the Communists back and out, and within three years the federal states of Malaysia were born, a precursor to the state of Malaysia. Normally the National Servicemen would be transported home after their time but Phil had put in, with Terry's recommendation, for individual dispensation. He wanted to go the long way home. How, just how was he going to leave Carolina behind? His heart told him to stay but she would never leave Malaysia so his head held sway. He knew, despite all the efforts of Terry and others, that the army was never going to be a career for him. He was a London boy, through and through.

Carolina insisted they spend their final week together. She would reorganise his airfare and hotel to Cape Town, then to London delaying the trip by a full five days. Everything, places and timings, had to be on her terms over this last week. Their final night was at the Mandarin Hotel overlooking the Merdeka Stadium, a prominent national sports location. It was a perfect penthouse view of the vibrant city with champagne, caviar, even an advanced mosquito net. They made love like there was no tomorrow, and only slept just before light for three hours.

The next phase was the hardest. They had talked it all out over that week, there was no going back. Tears, tears and more tears, Carolina only wanted one last thing from Phil – an address, a contact address. He kept his own to himself, because he felt it right through that he should not be traced. So, he honoured a pact with Terry that she could use his P.O. Box number in an emergency.

Carolina had wanted a photograph, she already had several. She needed her memories, she had them so vividly, but she wanted most of all, that one point of contact, an address. Phil soon disappeared from view, the love of her life, but she knew one fact, one fact alone that had escaped the male-dominated existence and mind of Phil. That she, Carolina Lee could never leave her mother.

Phil convalesced in the open beauty that was Cape Town. The African sun was clear and dry and slowly his mind and body were recovering from the tempestuous moisture of the tropics. Sat out on the balcony of his Camps Bay lodging, he gathered his thoughts about his time as a national serviceman. There were so many pluses, despite the discomfort of his years in the army. He now was disciplined and had been put to the test in the ultimate conflict, his self-preservation. There were buddies along the way, but he had fought with his soul mate, the Gaffer, Terry Jones, a comrade for life.

He had also picked up vital skills. It did not matter what the machine, as he could prime it or dismantle it, and that included military hardware even down to bomb delivery. Equally, in the camps of the jungle, he came to understand the role and function of water, from makeshift domestic provision to surviving long days without it on patrol. Anything mobile he became master of, as he was now experienced in driving or controlling canoe, bicycle, car or military truck.

Yes, of course, he could offer these attributes once back in civilian life in London. His first priority, he thought, was a temporary one, to get fixed with a base. He chose to go back home, as mum and dad had welcomed him back with open arms to his own bedroom, alone and independent at last, and no more memories of sharing with an older brother. It would take him a while to settle back into a London that was undergoing enormous physical transition. He was to while away many evening hours at The Angel, and with a new winter approaching, he was to try all avenues for employment. It must have been near on three months since his demob, when Jim the barman handed him a scruffy envelope which had a Kuala Lumpur stamp on it, addressed to a P.O. Box number in London. Was it from Terry, he asked?

"A big Welsh bloke dropped it in at lunchtime," said Jim,

Phil in anguished trepidation, ripped it open. There was a colour postcard inside, a night picture of Selangor sports club, and on the back it read,

"Dearest Phil,

I trust you arrived back safe and sound in England and enjoyed your long journey. For the last few weeks I have been seriously sick, but it is the most lovely kind of sickness a young woman can have. Our love was forever,

Yours and mine, Carolina xx"

He had tried to get her out of his mind. He had to move on for both their sakes. What was this letter about? She spoke in riddles. What was a lovely kind of sickness? He was dumbfounded.

What Phil had never grasped was why Carolina had taken full control of their last days together, why she had insisted on delaying the dates of his trip, and why she insisted on an address? To foot soldiers like Phil one tropical week was just like another. For Carolina, each week represented distinct shifts in her biological calendar.

Philip Bristowe had never researched the culture of Carolina's South-East Asian background:- It was a mother's principal role to nurture and look after the children of their own daughters. She knew Phil wouldn't stand for that, and for her part, she would never abandon her own mother.

* * *

Freddie and Jan's council flat was part of a long block of brick dwellings only a five-minute walk from the Thames. On this Surrey side of the river, they had a great view across to what was then known as The Pool of London. Dockland London was ever present with the Surrey Quays on their side with Millwall Docks across a wide Thames where it begins with its huge U shape, inside of which was the original Isle of Dogs. There was water everywhere, so maybe it wasn't so surprising that Phil took up an engineer's mate position with the Metropolitan Water Board. The MWB label was on every drain and provided the provision of water in every form from across all the boroughs of the capital.

So, for Phil, all the bases seemed to have been covered. His twenty first birthday had been duly celebrated, but well before all that, something solid was missing. Every young man had always been in need of a role model. Normally he would look to his father, but in Phil's case, Freddie, like thousands of others, had been absent and more markedly would never be drawn into conversation on his experiences of World War 2. A personalised gap was yawning wide with the nearest person to breach that space being former military colleague, Terry Jones. Now, he was gone. His mum again understandably was only looking to the future but here was Phil destined to spend his young years family bound in a small flat in the same small neighbourhood of his childhood. Malaysia had given him the cut and thrust for adventure and the taste of success. One thing was for certain, the Metropolitan Water Board of the late 1950s was never going to fill that void. Nor was chasing after women, always eager for the ring around the finger and ever ready to start their own post war families and the inevitable struggle.

He would see posters, films and TV series that pushed all his generation to the glamour of one place....... America. Who could possibly resist at his age the lure of Marlon Brando's 'Waterfront', James Dean's 'East of Eden', Marilyn Monroe, Chuck Berry, Jerry Lee Lewis, Little Richard, Eddie Cochran, Buddy Holly and Elvis? What did Britain at this stage have to offer – skiffle bands and trad jazz clubs! Our country, according to Prime Minister Supermac had never had it so good. Phil would just surmise that all his folly was bull, as everything from washing machines to flashy painted winged Zodiac and Zephyr cars were imported from the USA.

Phil for the next four years lusted after just one thing that met all his urges for fun, risk, danger and freedom, and motorbikes were made and fully manufactured here in Britain. Maybe it was the connection to Brando or Elvis sat astride one with girls, music and freedom, but motor bikes had motivated a generation of teenagers and here in England they were mass produced at BSA and Triumph, the best and most sought after in the world.

Hitherto motor bikes had been all over the fringes of London, part of the day's functional routine to get to work and back in all the light engineering factories springing up in the suburbs like Hoover, Hawker Sidderley and the NPL. The blue-collar workers hadn't climbed into cars in any numbers yet, and they still clung to working and living in the same or adjoining neighbourhoods. A low cc 'pop-pop' motor bike or even a cycle was sufficient for their needs.

Triumph, BSA and the like dug these kids in their ribs and introduced the likes of Phil to motorbikes for leisure, for fun and freedom to get away. They would come with a set of leathers, a pair of jeans and that was his protection alone on the open road. Very few of 'the ton-up boys' bothered with helmets, after all they enjoyed that rush of speed and adrenaline pumping through the veins and their hair. From the start Phil pestered his Dad to lend him the extras he needed to add to his down payment, a brilliantly devised plan as a means to get to work at the MWB depot. It worked! Following a scope through the Exchange and Mart, he had picked up a Triumph 250 learner bike, sound as a pound, a little bit on the light side but with 4 speed and a solid frame.

He had a small indoor shed attached to the flat in Rotherhithe and for the next two years looked after the bike like a baby. He could strip it and reassemble it in just one morning, and living where he did, he was near the A2, the old Roman Road, which was as straight as a die and therefore allowed Phil to partake in weekend burn-ups down to Canterbury and Margate. When he wasn't down there in the summers, he would take the bike up west to the Serpentine lake in Kensington Gardens, park up and spend his Sundays swimming. Keeping fit was a priority for him, and especially as he spent most of his weekdays down holes or in cramped indoor places providing mechanical and technical solutions to water problems.

There were no steady girlfriends at this stage and ironically the reason for this had been there was not enough room or security on the pillion position, and with the external engine, it was both noisy and bulky. Only when he could upgrade to his dream, the Tiger 110, would he entertain a fellow passenger! That would happen down the line, but he would constantly be saving for that wish fulfilment.

Jan and Freddie were worried when that day arrived late in 1961. Their son had for nigh on five years been living under their roof. The Tiger machine rolled in with the parents recognising his appetite increasing for speed and thrills. At the same time, they were relieved at him gaining a regular local girlfriend, Joanne. She would calm him down, they thought, after all her folks knew Jan and both sets of parents were constantly trying to restrict her time on the back of 'that bike'. How do you make stick in an early

167

20s mind that a 650c.c. machine is a potential killer? The more they nagged the more numerous the burn ups and ton ups at weekends on his new power bike.

Phil had been a true rocker but principally in the sense of a bike and music fanatic. The American rock and roll stable had self-destructed by 1961: Eddie Cochran and Buddy Holly, both killed in car and air crashes, Jerry Lee and Chuck Berry locked up for misdemeanours and Elvis conscripted to the U.S. military. There were plenty of look alikes and wannabees, but the schmucky managers in the US were just producing pin-up 'Bobbies' and Britain was stuck in a copy Elvis competition. For two long years, Phil and Jo searched and searched for good live pumping music, but all they got was trad jazz live and soppy ballads or yodellers on the TV or radio.

One November Friday night, they were on their way back from a pub-club on the river in Barnes. Phil had been drinking earlier in the evening but the cold winter air did enough to sober him up. Joanne hopped on as he took the Hammersmith Bridge, Lillee Road route back through Fulham and onto the Embankment and Vauxhall Bridge. They never made it that far. Phil hit 50 into the sharp bend in Lillee Road, feeling the wobble that he knew was a warning. The Tiger was built for speed but there was always a question mark as to its manoeuvrability. The back wheel spun away from him on the wet surface as he broke fiercely. Then silence.

Both Jo and Phil had laid out on that pavement for a time before the ambulance arrived. They were both cut up badly, Jo's legs were a mess, but Phil was unconscious. His leathers had saved his body, but not his head. Neither went back to Rotherhithe that night, but Jo was able to get the hospital to make contact with her parents in the early hours of the morning.

Her father had put on a dressing gown, and walked the two blocks to rap on Jan and Freddie's door to set the alarm bells going.

"Phil's out for the count, he's badly concussed, but our girl is OK. She's wrecked all her clothing but she's getting patched up now."

Jan sobbed and sobbed, she was uncontrollable. Staggering back to her bedroom, she made an attempt to get dressed, to get ready.

"My boy, my only boy, we've got to stop him Freddie. You've got to take it away from him," she cried,

"Ok, my love, we'll go with Paul and Sue now. We'll get there by daybreak."

Neither set of parents blamed either of their kids or each other. They just prayed that the two tearaways could get through this trauma. It became better when Jo was released after observation later that weekend and Phil had also come round but was seriously groggy. He would have to stay in for at least a week. He had been lucky that the bike in the accident had ridden the pavement and careered onto a softer grass verge. His injuries were a broken ankle, a fractured kneecap, but the one that troubled him the most was the silent, almost invisible one to 1960s medicine, the concussion. He had experienced the symptoms before but when asked at the bedside of his condition, he always answered positively, all was fine.

Yet, it was not fine, at home. On his return he was oblivious to the stress he had caused the family. Phil was more concerned about the recovery of his Triumph than the tears and fears of his mother. There was only one thing for it. Jan, with Freddie's backing, just laid down an ultimatum to Phil. It was the Bristowes or the bike.

For the 26-year-old Phil, there was only one answer to that, the bike!

He had made off to a Battersea bedsit, having spent the worst Christmas of his life with no girlfriend, a bike in recovery and a pair of parents nagging him into oblivion. He didn't need any of that and anyhow, it was time to leave the nest and set out on his own. He had outgrown the Bristowe stranglehold, at last life could be enjoyed on his own terms.

Phil had heard from Jim down The Angel that his cousin needed a weekend evening's bartender not far from Battersea, in Shepherd's Bush called the Goldhawk Social Club. He had introduced Phil as a prominent former army man, a hard worker, who also could double up as a bouncer, a deterrent to the frequent rucks and brawls that were slowly destroying the club's reputation. Jim had tipped Phil the wink that it was well paid, and that the club's resident band on Friday nights was sensational, an outfit called The Detours that bent the walls with the new beat and rhythm and blues that was the talk of the clubs.

That summer of '62 introduced the Bermondsey boy to a new way of life. He moved jobs to an electrical engineering group called KLG that manufactured spark plugs on the edge of Putney and only four miles or ten minutes from the Goldhawk on his refurbished Tiger. His weekends consisted of serving beer, breaking up fights and mending some of the 'rice grinders', the pop-pop Lambretta and Vespa scooters that the Mods would pitch up with at the Goldhawk. Still it was worth it just to be there with The Detours, smacking it out with real aggressive music for the lads. There were girls there but they were just a sideshow. The Goldhawk shaped him and many of the crooks, brawlers and nutters of his generation pushing life to the limit. This was their generation.

The Detours had some older bloke on the drums, but there were three young frontmen, two big blokes, one with a huge nose, and the lead singer was a local tough nut. Their names were Pete Townshend, John Entwhistle and Roger Daltrey. Within 18 months they were to become world famous as The Who, whilst Philip Bristowe was their barman and bouncer! Alive again at last!

Within a year, the Detours had signed up the mercurial young Keith Moon on the drums and they were rolling as The Who. Everything about them and the stage performances was mobile. Twirling arms, crashing symbols, interchanging of roles and locations launched this band into pop and rock legends. Like Phil, they were just ordinary blokes from rundown Acton but they would forever be on the move all over the UK, scrambling around in old Bedford vans to get to the next slot.

Thus, by 1964, their mobility was enhanced by new motorways. Phil, but only in his case at weekends, could career up newly-laid stretches of the M1 and the M4. Life, supercharged by the emergence of BSAs and Triumphs and

171

to a lesser extent, Vespas and Lambrettas, was now accessible to the young. They could go anywhere, anyhow and anyway they chose. Trains with diesel engines were on the horizon as were twin and quadruple engine jet planes. The white heat of technology was simply blowing away steam and propellers.

Phil, in what he referred to as his second youth, had bought into a new fresh culture of speed. Soon after his national service he had bought into raw speed with the early power motorbikes and the excitement that was imported American rock and roll music. Now he was part of a movement, a British generation, a young culture that embraced speed and mobility in all its forms. Whether it was in music with the trim, three minute vinyl 45s, the 40 minute live sets on stage, or in England's fashionable motor industry which was pioneering the Mini and the Jaguar cars, it was true to note that they were all interconnected. Even welders like Phil were achieving enough money either to blow away at weekends or save for a rainy day. Read music, read cars, read fashion, all were Brit winners.

Before 1963, no teenager or for that matter no men or women in their twenties had ever heard of the phrase, disposable income. Yet, this was never taken to too kindly by the ruling gentry nor any parents that were of WW2 age and experience. Inevitably they were seeking something altogether different, a slower pace of life having survived the rigours of war and deprivation. Thus, it was an 'us' and 'them' conflict, young versus old, employees against entrenched bosses, liberal up against conservatives. It could be put no better than on the framed plaque that Phil had hung above his bed in Battersea, a four lined quote from The Who's anthem, 'My Generation'. It read;

'People try to put us down
Just because we get around
Things they do look awful cold
I hope I die before I get old'

Phil had bought into everything that the band had stood for; their lyrics and the image they expressed was as a force of challenge to the older generation. His father's generation could release their angst and frustrations in the theatre of war and conflict, not so for the likes of Phil's younger mates. National Service was abandoned in the early sixties amidst a declining British role in world affairs. The politicians had just weakly given away a huge chunk of the colonial land area and Britain's influence within it. The establishment was limping into the 60s. Phil frankly accepted these facts as gospel. Why shouldn't he? After all he was the one that had nearly been blown away in Malaya, all for nothing. He resented the buffoons at Westminster and was delighted by the antics of the modern youth challenging all that they had stood for.

Phil had never been a politician, but he had to sit every lunch hour in the KLG canteen listening to his elders complaining about the government of the day giving away the colonies to savage tribes and unappreciative natives. For those sipping back the lukewarm tea, it was whingeing about 'the good old days'. The young Bristowe had warned them that the current youngsters were breaking it all down.

They would laugh at him as he reminded them that young women were shocking their dowdy mothers with the revealing mini skirts and page boy hairstyles. These same women were earning money and prestige for Britain in fashion, just take a look at that model Twiggy. Magazines, journalism and the print industry were also opening to young entrepreneurs. New television stars were in the making as the BBC was opening up new channels in both radio and TV.

The shop stewards, admittedly not many of them existed at a private concern like KLG, at one point thought that Phil was becoming at best a valued union representative prospect and at worst a Commie agent! Underneath, they weren't blind as they would see the youthful Kennedy take on Krushchev and give the old Russian bear a bloody nose. Yes, and they were amazed at the impact that The Beatles were having as a pop music group worldwide. Yet the event which truly convinced them that Phil's younger generation was taking over was when the government and the upper-class establishment were brought to their knees by a sexually active girl about town called Christine Keeler. In what was to become infamous as The Profumo Affair she, as a working class girl, held the Conservative cabinet and foreign minister, John Profumo to ransom as their mutual liaison ended thirteen years of Tory rule and the old style patrician, Harold MacMillan, of 'You've never had it so good' fame.

If Britain had met its watershed, it was here in 1963. After Keeler's intrusion, there would seldom be any more grouse shooting aristocratic prime ministers around. The

174

young set were winning the battle for influencing a different kind of future for Britain, one that took little notice to deference and birthright, but more of what you could offer practically in a changing world of technology. Phil fitted in with this, but still was facing the uphill battle of no schooling. For him, the weekend was his zenith, his playground and his escape.

He could spend, spend and spend his wages and as a young shop floor worker, would raise the eyebrows of his colleagues. He was full of tales of spins down to Brighton, of legendary gigs he witnessed on Eel Pie Island or at the Half Moon in Putney. Even still he loyally followed The Who at their residency at the prestigious Marquee Club in Soho's Wardour Street. Yet he lived a two-tone life, based at his bed-sit in Battersea. He would bike it five days a week out towards the A3 to the KLG site to be another cog in the production of spark plugs for a variety of combustion engines. From Monday to Friday he would be conditioned along with hundreds of others by the starting hooter at 9am followed by the lunch break start and end drone and then finally what everyone had been waiting for, the knocking off hooter at 5.30pm.

Then there was the rush to leave for a multitude of cycle racks, motorbikes and small Morris Minor cars producing a daily traffic jam that only Piccadilly would have rivalled. He asked himself what was it all for? He did get some satisfaction from his job, at least he was productive and making things for a living. Pen pushing was something that he was never cut out for, but he had worked it out that he had to aspire to that in order to climb the ladder at factories like KLG. He would have to play the older generation's game of year after year of kow-towing to his elders.

On the weekend, it was the opposite. He had spent many months with Joanne but she inevitably was to turn out like all the rest of young women. Once they tired of the excitement of Phil's friends and lifestyle at weekends, these young women were becoming as tedious as the routine Monday to Friday empty heads. These females just wanted a ring, a nice house in the suburbs, a family with the inevitable extended family as their reinforcement. Such predictability appalled him!

So Phil just played the field, and now with the birth pill available, who was he not to indulge in the newfound freedoms for young women? As the mod music show, 'Ready, Steady, Go' was introduced at 6pm on Friday evenings, its caption said it all, 'The Weekend Starts Here', with live, mobile cameras amongst the smartly clad dancers and regular appearances of the Brit and Motown stars of these years. The programme acted as his anchor for a social life that never stopped until he collapsed after Sunday lunch into bed on Sunday afternoons.

If nothing else, for four years, south-west London had done him a power of good but as he stared at the peeling wallpaper at the flat on those Sunday afternoons, he was overtaken by the need to take stock and bring some individual control back into his life. He now regarded anything in London, south of the Thames, as his manor. A pleasant workplace like KLG was fine, but he was still stuck taking orders and held in a vacuum.

Phil Bristowe had work skills, knew mates and families from all the way upstream to Shepherd Bush and Wandsworth and down back past Tower Bridge to Blackheath in the East. He had his Triumph, he had his tools and more important, he had an uncompromising drive to prove he could make it on his own. After the Army, the MWB* and the KLG*, it was on the first day of 1966 to be PCB, Philip Charles Bristowe, the self-employed all-purpose plumber.

MWB – Metropolitan Water Board
KLG – Kenneth Lee Guinness

CHAPTER 8

DANCING WITH BLUE BLOODS

The London season had been in full swing that summer of 1957. Successive dances, cocktail parties and country house weekends had eaten into mid-September, but this one was the big one. Any debutante worth her salt would attend the Charlotte Anniversary Ball at 'The Grosvenor' on Park Lane. It really was not a matter of attending, more to whether you had been selected to demonstrate your virtues and assets at one of London's most glittering occasions.

"Oh, for heaven's sake, Sis, I don't think any of my shoes will go with this white dress aunt Deirdre has brought down. Can I please borrow those shiny high heels you wore at Cowdray Park?" said Sarah, only panicking slightly.

"Yes, of course," responded Rosie, her elder sibling. "Just a minute, I'll pop upstairs while auntie tucks that extra fabric in at the back. You've lost a few pounds, girl!"

Rosie clambered up the staircase which doubled back on itself in the deceptively sized mews cottage that the two nieces of Viscount Filby had shared for six months. Countess Deirdre, as she was widely known, had seen it all before both for herself back in the late 30s and with Rosie the previous two years and she knew, just knew that it would all go fine on the night. That would be the case, even though Sarah could be an awkward cuss, not a natural even though she was developing into a fine-looking young woman.

Deirdre reflected on the hours of deportment, bearing and elegance lessons at DeBrett's that Sarah had endured as the painful reminders of her late teenage years. Yes it was worth it, she would certainly reinforce the high esteem that the Filbys were held in the higher echelons of the peerage and court life. For tonight Sarah would be confirming her well-rehearsed curtsey in front of Prince Philip and Princess Margaret, if it were to be Margaret, as the Queen had gone down with a heavy cold.

Belgravia was perfectly placed for this titled family as their second home. For the Viscount, he was one of nigh on a hundred hereditary peers who would take up their position in the House of Lords for seven months of the year. The Lords was just a five-minute chauffeured drive away. As for the two girls and their debutante aspirations, Park Lane was just as near. The Filbys main residence was in deepest Sussex, a magnificent Victorian mansion with stables and land to spare.

How fortunate it was for these descendants that the Filbys had linked up in marriage to the Plantagenet dynasty that had ruled medieval England right through to the demise of Richard III at Bosworth Field in 1485. Even though they had lost access to the throne then, many generations of Filbys had sided with royalist causes and Britain's military prowess down the centuries. The military was prominent in the family history vaults and such was the notoriety of the Viscount Filbys that there was even a statue of one of the family in St Stephen's Hall in the House of Commons.

Now it was Sarah's turn for cultural advancement. Her aim was to attract a suitable male at the forthcoming dance to uphold the protocol and mannered traditions within a select circle. From acquiescing to the curtseyed training of Madame Vacari to her aristocratic comportment, she was part of a ritual as a means to focus and retain wealth and influence amongst a privileged few. Dear Deirdre had passed the baton down and had already perused the list of eligible suitors to be present that evening.

Yet, what would inevitably make Sarah's evening a great success was her quest for fun and experience. Auntie's generation would always have to look over their shoulders but she would almost ride into the valley of Mayfair undeterred by any external forces.

Amongst a gaggle of nervous young debutants, some as young as seventeen, she was ushered through from the waiting room as part of several hundred. A curtsey followed to the princess, a few steps back and sideways, then another for the prince. Shortly afterwards, the dance would follow with the appearance of the sprightly male heirs in their immaculate formal dress. How the evening proceeded from there was really down to the chemistry between the pairs of dancers. This was still the post war era of chivalry, of tradition and appropriate signals at the correct moment.

Never let it be forgotten that Sarah and her like, blond and beautiful, were expected to be married by their early twenties, and their pathway to marital and hereditary bliss was principally made possible by the debutante balls. Proof of their pre-eminence were the prestigious venues that supported the annual events held at The Dorchester, The Savoy and The Grosvenor Hotels, only the best for the best.

Sarah behaved impeccably and was the target for several embryonic peers that night. She knew that this would probably be her last, but even at nineteen she was keen to delay the advances, even fend off the inevitable future of her auntie's plans. Life was too short for such predictability and there was a streak in her that wanted to break free. The young Miss Filby rejecting academia, had already set her course in a medical direction. She had just won a place and was about to start nursing at University College Hospital, just north of London's bohemian quarter known as Soho. In fact, she had already begun three weeks before on an inset induction period in preparation for her three year training as a nurse.

The Countess was not best pleased but not at all surprised. She had enjoyed observing Sarah right through her teenage years and was amused and impressed by her enjoyment of life and her confidence to follow her own path whatever 'the slings and arrows of outrageous fortune'. She was a law unto herself!

That Saturday it was the peak of the Debutantes' Ball in Mayfair, the next weekend was to be a CND (Campaign for Nuclear Disarmament) house party hosted by King's College on the North End Road in Fulham. To her, more importantly in between, were the fetching, carrying, observing, and attending anatomy classes that made up her first term of student life in the autumn of 1957.

"Fancy a dance blondie?" asked a beer-motivated Australian, from what Sarah could tell, at her first house party,

"You have a nerve, at this late hour wearing that," Sarah pointed to a rather awkward looking outback hat. "Take it 'orf, and you may have a chance," she insisted.

"Crikey, the Aussie sheilas never make you work as hard as this, it's only a hop," complained the wayward antipodean, releasing the hat which revealed a thousand jet black curls.

"That's much better," approved Sarah whisking him away to the beat and twang of Hank Marvin's Shadows.

The room's capacity was no more than twenty, but even the walls were sweating as more than double that were energetically hopping and bopping between the beer barrel perched on the table at one end and the all inclusive single speaker Hacker Cavalier Record Reproducer under the window thirty feet away. This postgraduate outhouse was one of many commandeered in central London near enough for the students to do the tube run into college on weekdays. At weekends, Hornsea House was a cross between a Victorian tavern and the nearby Hammersmith Palais dance club arena.

The two of them, him certainly past his twenty fifth year, and her still a teenager at nineteen, could almost have been regarded as the odd couple as they danced right through to midnight. She hadn't a care except to catch the last District line train from Fulham Broadway to Sloane Square. Rather surprisingly, the roughly shaven Aussie, to the derision of his drinking mates, insisted on walking her to the station, down the wooden flight of stairs to the platform's edge. Just in time, the Upminster bound train ground to a halt. Sarah had forgotten the obvious.

"By the way, what's your name?"

"Ray, Raymond Bristowe," the Pohmie screamed.

The doors slammed shut and that was that. Ray was truly bowled over by this posher than posh girl, only remembering she was a nurse and lived very close to Sloane Square, probably one of the most exclusive parts of London in 1957. Still life had to move on as he was settling into his new digs as an undergraduate even though he was a well-qualified art grad in Sydney. He was to study Geography at one of the top departments for that discipline in the UK. His application had worked well, as he had stressed his interest in landforms and geology. King's College was world renowned for its concentration on Physical Geography and was at the forefront in welcoming adult students from overseas. Little did they know that Ray had spent his first experiences in life only one mile across the river on the South Bank!

Nevertheless, only such an intense course could keep his mind off the girl with the plum in the mouth accent and the golden hair. Both that and the social whirl that was

183

London coming out of the dark clouds of the war and into the bright new decade that was to be the 1960s. The reason students all over the world applied to University, King's and the LSE (London School of Economics) was their proximity, and we are talking walking distance, to all that was happening in one of the most vibrant capitals of the world. For Ray, yes, he was to live over there, across the river, the other side from his birthplace where there were theatres, cinemas, hotels, restaurants, sporting meccas, galleries, museums and nightclubs.

With all these draws, and with the colleges located as neighbours, he hoped one day he might bump into the girl of Hornsea House. Meanwhile, Ray was aiming to achieve some balance in his life between studies, his bohemian social life and his driving ambitions to develop his art in depicting as many scenes from the River Thames as he could find. Although he would set up riverside, focusing on the busy barge traffic with both skyline and dock areas as backdrops, it was really his feel for representing the motion of boats in relation to the flow of this magnificent river that caught the eye. For him there was nothing better than to venture out to Richmond Hill, Hampstead Heath or Blackheath to lofty perches to charcoal draw the vista from these prominent positions. The net result was his single room at Hornsea being cluttered with drawings and sketches on all walls and floors!

It was common for Kings to host periodic debates in liaison with the LSE and UCL, the 'This house believes that....' with proposers for and against the motion. A Hornsea mate introduced Ray to the excitingly eccentric evenings full of fun and inebriation. Near the end of his first year in June, they were both intrigued by the motion that,

'This house believes in Europe not America.' They entered the lecture chamber at the LSE and peering down the programme were some eminently posh names such as Timothy Ponsonby-Smythe supporting the motion with the seconder being the Hon. Sarah Plantagenet-Filby!

Ray fell about laughing at these public school prats taking the lion's share of the action again. That was until he got an eyeful of the female seconder, it was his Hornsea nurse! Honourable? Plantagenet! Ray could hardly spell it, let alone pronounce the name, and to add to the evening, both Ponsonby and Plantagenet won the debate.

At the bar he made a beeline for Sarah. This time he would make his intentions known, but would she give him the time of day? G and T's, the house reds and best bitter had passed between their mutual lips that evening. Sarah equally never forgot the rough Aussie, Raymond with the crinkly black hair. By midnight this time, they were an item with so much to explore together in their student days ahead.

First of all, they had to sort out their times available in both their second and final years as Sarah was constantly in nursing shift hours and Ray had lengthy periods of fieldwork for his dissertation.

They did have one common favourable pied a terre, and that was the mews cottage house at SW1, Burton Mews. Even though it was forbidden for them to cohabit in such a mutually convenient place, they were able to accommodate

Ray's visits and overnighters occasionally, but only when darling Uncle was not positioned in his safe seat in the House of Lords. Maybe the relationship blossomed because the Viscount and Rosie had gradually come to get used to Ray's blue-collar demeanour. Rather amusingly at one of the many dinner parties at Burton, with Ray in absentia, the Viscount would proclaim that his youngest Filby was on course for 'a morganatic marriage'. Only some of the guests that night appreciated his dexterity of language.

Such frivolity was reported back to Ray but always in good humour. Yet it riled him for little did Sarah, Rosie and family comprehend that he was on a determined mission to rid himself of the shackles of his common childhood. For a start, he seldom communicated with home and often in the most off hand and irregular way. Ray also answered an advertisement in one of Sarah's society mags to undertake elocution lessons. After eight years in New South Wales, his London echoes had now been enhanced by a nasal twang, enhanced only in a negative direction. He signed up for the entire autumn of 1959 for two lessons a week with the Blackmore-Brown agency off the Kings Road in Chelsea, very upmarket la-di-da.

It was to be years later that he was to discover that what attracted Sarah to the errant Londoner in the first place, were his unique tones, colloquialisms and rank bad language! It was well past that by the beginning of their final year at college. The pair were highly set on tying the knot, but Ray felt time would be ripe to pop the question after they had graduated in the July of 1960. It was down to him alone, both in the substance and the timing of the proposal. He would do the pleasure at hand and in the only way he could best express his love for Sarah.

Ray waited for September, booked a table at Langam's just off Piccadilly on the condition that he could supply an addition to the evening menu. Very simply put, it was a large white post card drawing meticulously detailed, almost engraved it was so exact, of a couple walking out of a church from their white wedding with a background of familiar faces and confetti scattered across the scene. On the back of the post card, were the immortal words

"Fancy a life together? Love you blondie."

The delicate artwork was well appreciated, even the Viscount and the Countess were there on the sides. Sarah's reply?

"Yes, please, Ray, you have more than a chance this time."

A society wedding set for springtime in Marylebone, and for the first time in his life for the Bristowe boy, in a church! The next six months were a whirlwind with graduation balls and a probationary two year teaching job for Ray in Richmond. As for Sarah, she was just too busy with Deirdre planning to bother with nursing just yet. So, the Viscount had got it right after all, a morganatic marriage!

The first buds welcomed an early spring in 1961 and found Ray just walking to the Embankment with his sketch pad. He set up with his fold-up chair, hesitated and stared down at the waters that had weened him, taken him away to foreign parts only to return to mother Thames to find the true love of his life. He stared across at Vauxhall to the left with adjoining Bermondsey and then switching right to the power station at Battersea. He had beaten all that muck, grime and the docks and he had cast off the limitations of terraced streets with narrow confines and even narrower minds; he had set himself free from a warring family and most of all, he had 'buried' his brother. Where was Phil now? No culture, no qualifications, no future for him, a simpleton. Ray Bristowe had made it. Sloane Square, Belgravia and now ready to marry a blue blood here on the only side of the Thames that mattered.

Instead of sketching the Thames that day, he conjured up yet another representation of the prospective wedding, a copy of the Langam's portrait to Sarah, but this time on the back it would just state the cold words from Raymond, "To Mum and Dad."

* * *

Across the river that morning, another young man drowsily gathered his thoughts together as he attacked the washing-up in a tiny bedsit in Battersea. Advertised as having a panoramic view of the Thames, it really was a bolt hole at best. So what was on the menu that sunny day, tea and toast like any other day? Phil Bristowe, if only he knew, looked out to the other side directly across to those posh embankment apartments. He was sat just two hundred yards from his nemesis for the first time in twelve years.

* * *

The morning of the wedding, Ray posted the card within the envelope to Rotherhithe. He didn't really want it to come to this, but deep down he had no nerve that projected feeling, certainly not for his own blood line. The shutters were firmly down. His wedding day was a boy's own story, but he would have to live with the fact that over a hundred Filbys and friends occupied one side of the aisle, whilst on the other side Ray enjoyed the company of a best man from Hornsea and three drinking mates from college.

Sarah said nothing, nor did Rosie, and certainly the Viscount and Deirdre seemed to be oblivious to the absence of any Bristowes. Clearly Ray had made some kind of reasons or sincere apologies. Surely there had to be a reason?

Jan, late for work on the Monday that followed, grabbed the post which came early but she would open this one envelope at her secretarial job at the office. Immediately she opened the envelope she hastily fixed her gaze and at first not quite comprehending what was in front of her, she started to quiver. Screaming at herself at the top of her pitch, "Why the little, who is she, who is she, what has he done?" Jan recognised Ray's unique style of communicating as he had never penned a written letter in his life. For him, a sketch always said a thousand words. The Bristowes had never been mentioned in Ray's relationship with the bride from the very outset. Now here it was for all to see, in a damn sketch.

For Jan, she could never forgive him, even Freddie might disown his eldest son. What were they to do as they had no up to date address or direct line to Ray. It was going to be a case of him calling the family. So that was the way he wanted it. She had lost him once to Australia, now what really hurt, she was to lose him again in London of all places. She sobbed, she thought again; she had kicked out her only loving boy Phil as well, all over a bloody motorbike. The Bermondsey matriarch had lost all that horrid day, she was heartbroken.

Freddie was never able to grasp what had prompted the two boys to turn out as they did. Whereas Jan in the ensuing years periodically would break down emotionally from the absence of her offspring, the dockyard father became very withdrawn as he approached retirement. By 1965, he had the pub with his Angel mates, a local allotment that he shared with his next door neighbour from the flats, and a Ford Anglia. Every other January since demob, he had spent a three week stay at the chest clinic following an injury he had suffered from a crash involving an American jeep in his last year back in Hamburg.

Even with regular recuperative visits to the army rest home in deepest Benenden in Kent, the tubes were getting tighter, no pains but periodic coughing. Jan was concerned, but was always relieved when he returned to Rotherhithe much rejuvenated from the break.

Then in early December an unseasonably sunny day as clear as a bell prompted Freddie's pride in himself and his Anglia into action. Out he ventured in his string vest vigorously sponging down the navy-blue Ford. Always having been in great shape, he wasn't used to losing his breath. That day he did. His legs buckled first as he felt more than dizzy, staggering to make it to a communal

190

public bench. He waited, it must have been at least ten minutes before he made the fifty paces to his front door. He said nothing to Jan, not then, and not even through Christmas until he boarded the army bus to hasten his annual escape to Benenden.

After a week away, Jan got the call. The regular house doctor who was always there for Freddie informed Jan that he would need to stay another month as he was bedridden with a severe bout of pneumonia, but fingers crossed, he was in the right place. By late February, Freddie was battling and the good doctor had called for Jan and her family to get to his bedside as soon as possible. Although she was clear not to contact Ray, she did get hold of Phil through Jim at the Angel who kindly drove the two of them down to see the stricken Freddie.

The Hospital at Benenden was small but spotless, and because of Freddie's condition he had an individual, separate room to himself. They were ushered to a side waiting room by a nurse who explained somebody who was in with her husband would be out soon. Jim and Phil comforted his mother for they knew this was going to be harsh. As they spoke, a tall pinstriped middle-aged man with a formal briefcase emerged from the room hardly noticing the 'family' trio, then accelerated away sternly down the corridor.

Phil wondered who the hell he was as Freddie never had nor entertained pinstripe suits in his whole life. Such formality was lost on him. On entering the small ward, Jan was not so subtle.

"Who was that, Freddie?"

Then as he responded in a low, hardly audible voice from a body that was unrecognisable such was his weight loss, Freddie reassured Jan that he was an old official that looked after his Union pension from the docks. When it came to money, the mother never asked questions. She had never needed to as Freddie was in complete control doling out the funds to her whenever and whatever she wanted. It was a tricky half hour before the old stevedore fell asleep, safe in the knowledge that he had given his pinstriped lawyer power of attorney. The secretive order and legally binding behest from Freddie was, after fees and expenses for a potential funeral and reception. All of his worldly goods would go to Jan, his wife of 36 years. Freddie had left her the princely sum of only £200.

The nurse and doctor reappeared and pulled Jan and Phil aside. It was shocking news. The pneumonia had spread to his kidneys, and at his age in particular, any attack on the body's vital organs could be critical. Freddie Bristowe was hanging on for dear life, four years short of his often quoted biblical reference of "Three score years and ten for me."

March the 8th was the day when Freddie lost his final battle. He had never even made the World Cup finals later that year to be played in his beloved hometown. Bristowe would never live to see Bobby and the boys lift the World Cup, just four months later. Jan didn't know which way to turn, except the doctor did explain that Freddie wished to be buried in Benenden Churchyard, and that between the Hospice and Mr Smailes, the man of pinstriped mystery, all would be paid for and taken care of. What a relief for her that was, but she never quite understood why Mr Smailes was involved, but if that was what the 'ole boy instructed, then fair enough.

Jan's duty was to announce the death and notify all friends and family of the funeral arrangements and subsequent reception. This time both Ray and Phil would be there. All responded as she expected with heartfelt sympathy and respect. Freddie had his own way about him, but wherever he went, he was a kind popular man and was truly liked whether in his docks and army days or within the Bermondsey families at large.

Benenden Parish Church rose up above an elongated recreation expanse of well-trimmed public ground which bordered the main road through the village. Conveniently the village pub,The Bull, where the reception was to be held, stood proudly on the corner there awaiting Freddie's people. Jan underestimated her husband's appeal. She recognised most of the crowd, all dressed in the appropriate black for a most reverent ceremony.

They were all there, Jim and the Angel crowd, motorbike Jo and her parents, some dressed in army uniform from Freddie's engineering buddies, and even mates under treatment with the nurses at the Hospice. Ray arrived with Sarah, but none of their three small kids were there, while Phil appeared looking very upset. Bringing up the rear as the procession entered the Norman church was old Mr Yates, minus Bilko, now with a walking stick all the way from Chandler's Ford. He was supported on his left arm by a middle-aged companion dressed elegantly in a knee length black frock with accompanying veil down her face.

John Yates, then a man of pensionable age was clinging to the lady in black. Such was the solemnity of the church service, he only exchanged words with her as they negotiated a slow walk up the aisle. He was at pains to explain that he was a neighbour of Freddie's during the early part of the war, and still enjoyed living in Chandler's Ford. By now, they had taken up the back pews for friends and associates on the left hand side. Almost speaking out of the side of her mouth, the lady quizzed him,

"And where would that be?" she whispered,

"Hampshire, down south and you, have you come far?" he asked,

"Oh a fair way further than you," she replied,

Mr Yates never did catch onto her response. With the start of the organ reverberating around the church, it was drowned out by divine intervention.

Few mourners that cold March afternoon shared many words until they made their way from the ceremony at St George's down the pathway to 'The Bull' public house.

To be frank, it was a sad occasion, only made more painful by an unforgiveable experience that occurred outside the pub reception. It seemed everyone was beginning a positive wake, when a noisy altercation of very strong words and threats was heard by all. History was repeating itself. Phil had accosted Ray in a verbal outburst. He promised that he would ruin his elder brother after his rejection of their parents at his own wedding five years earlier. Then he just disappeared, on the cherished motorbike he sped.

Jan ignored her sons, was upstanding in The Bull and thanked all for coming, especially Mr Yates, all the way from Hampshire,

"Where's your companion? Still life in the old dog yet," she joked."What companion? I never accompanied anyone."

"Then who was the lady in black, walking with you into the church?"

"Nothing to do with me, I thought she was family."

The helpful, trim woman had just vanished into thin air.

CHAPTER 9

THE GOOD LIFE

Ray was running late. His murky grey Morris Minor was starting to look old and colourless for a car of the psychedelic spring of 1967. What really didn't help him was the winding nature of the A22 dodging between the dips and peaks of the English Weald. Every little settlement seemed to end in the suffix of wood, den or hurst, no doubt reflecting the heavily wooded landscapes where tiny villages had sprung up with almost predictable regularity either side of this major trunk road by the Garden of England.

The picture postcard image he noted for future interest and engagement for his undying passion for paint. Currently that thought was relegated to the back of his mind. It was interview time. For five years now, he had bobbed around teaching in three British schools whilst accumulating no less than three children of his own with another on the production line. He had nipped in between state and private schools, and between the draw of his academic knowledge of geography and the pull of his first love, Art. It was time to decide.

For the sake of his young family as the eldest was now just starting in her first year of primary he had to provide a settled base. Sarah had sacrificed all her training to concentrate on nursing within the family in these early years and even to her surprise was thriving in her newfound involvement. Yet, she was tiring of Ray's inability to settle, he having been in three schools in the London area since their wedding in 1961.

However, Sandlehurst Preparatory School was different. They did not advertise in national newspapers or education magazines. Not at all, can you believe? Sarah's cousin had heard that the position of senior art master was open from a fellow teammate in his village cricket team and had duly volunteered the services of Ray Bristowe. Two days earlier, Ray had received the astonishing telephone call from a rather aristocratic sounding school secretary suggesting a meeting with the headmaster. What astounded Ray was the venue for the pow wow. It was not to be in a stuffy study of the senior master or in a governors' committee room, but in the public bar of their local village inn!

The King's Arms stood proudly set back along a tiny B road three miles from a bend in the A22. It was clearly a popular little pub with three bars and low ceilings whose main claim to fame was its association with the RAF and the Battle of Britain. Numerous portraits and memorabilia were dutifully paraded along the eye line, of airmen either shot down as heroic survivors or distinguished by triumphant returns from the conflicts of those heady days of 1940.

It was also clear that the King's had acted as their common room, a resting place between sorties and a gathering location to celebrate or drown their sorrows along with the locals. As Ray pulled into the car park, he made a note of the high number of cars already a fixture there at mid-day. Gingerly he stuttered into the nearest entrance, the public bar, definitely a place for workmen. One or two local farmers plus the older folk were already on their second pints with Smiths crisps acrunching!

Chiding himself, he realised that no self-respecting headmaster would frequent the blue-collar enclave. No, he exited hurriedly making a re-entry into the saloon which led on to the comfy seats and decorative wallpaper of the lounge. Vastly underpopulated, with the exception of two old prim and proper ladies drinking stout and a middle-aged clergyman with dog collar prominent, it was dead quiet.

Suddenly the Reverend Milton Smythe bounded up to Ray and with a welcoming smile said,"You must be Raymond Bristowe, our prospective artist."

The Bermondsey boy was somewhat taken aback by the informal approach but offered in an accent that Ray would need to cultivate beyond the elocution lessons of David Blackmore-Brown back in Belgravia if he wished to progress in this environment. There would be no room for 'you knows' or dropping the 'aitches' here,

"That would be me and to whom am I speaking?" Ray attempting his best practised English.

"I am the local Vicar of St Barnabas here in Sandlehurst and a governor of the preparatory school. My vicarage borders the King's Arms next door. I believe we will be going onto the school later on with JJ, when he eventually rolls in? It's only three quarters of a mile down the way. Incidentally, I'm known around these parts as 'Milt' or 'Smithey', note the 'e' in my name."

Almost on cue, a dashing busy fellow slammed the door behind him, and with the panache of a public speaker simultaneously announced, "Pint of the usual Smithey ole boy, and I believe Tony has prepared three ham rolls with some scotch eggs for lunch. Afternoon Raymondo, what's your poison, ole chap?" he asked with a fit of enthusiasm.

Ray just reeled from the shock. 'Ole boy, ole chap' and he had never been called Raymondo before; the prospective Head of the Art Department had just had his first taste of the infamous JJ banter.

"My name is JJ, honoured to meet you. Glad you like a little bit of the landlord's bitter, ironically a local brew of King and Barnes, what do you think of it?"

"Excellent Headmaster, thanks," answered Raymondo!

"Plenty more where that came from, and oh yes, let's forget the formalities, I am called JJ around here."

No one locally really knew if JJ was or were his initials, a nickname or an abbreviation, but Ray didn't care as he immediately took to the man that exuded enthusiasm and character. He realised that there was already a lifetime of varied experiences behind this headmaster, far and wide.

Also, just by the reaction to him by the landlord, the bar staff and Smithey and the locals, Ray knew this man was a winner.

JJ had kept much of his past to himself, but from what was rumoured and there were enough fabled stories, he had been nurtured in colonial East Africa as part of a British family in the inter-war years. During this time, he was educated in the Rift Valley of Kenya about an hour out of Nairobi in a British preparatory school at Gilgil. His father was to take in Italian prisoners of war from the desert campaign and rumour was that he had converted his livestock farm into a thriving centre for viticulture. The Italian prisoners had persuaded him that his land was ideal for the growing of both red and white grapes. By the end of WW2, JJ Senior was set to be the foremost producer of table wines in the whole of British East Africa!

Within a year or two, the son was to be packed off to the family's Cambridge college where the young JJ achieved a squash racquets 'Blue', but perhaps became more celebrated at the 'Hawks' Club as an investor on the stock market. Rather, he invested other well-heeled students' money with uncanny success. His real secret was his well-founded belief in American companies and their involvement in German and Japanese recovery schemes. This was allied to his confidence in South African gold and the wine industry itself, from which his family and he himself at such a start-up age, had procured a personal fortune and resulted in some very happy graduates at Cambridge.

By the early '50s JJ was well out of Cambridge and indeed out of Africa. He, since his birth in 1928, had witnessed the stages of colonial dominance, experiencing the extravagances of pre-WW2 Empire, and had essentially bypassed the worst ravages of wartime. He had the knack of assessing situations and options and extracting the bones of an argument, but notably of seeing the big picture. JJ was a visionary, he could predict what was to come in nearly every predicament.

Typically unconventional, he had entered teaching at the highest level in England's public boarding school system, a Classics master of high intellectual power. He not only motivated within the classroom but made sure he had developed a thorough grasp of what made the independent sector tick and provide the bedrock for the traditional ruling classes. In short, over the entire decade, he knew and could recite his Etons from his Winchesters, to his Marlboroughs.

He had learned from his father's experience with the Italians in Africa, the one phrase that would belong to him and those who worked for him, "Always seek the gap in the market!" JJ had foreseen by the end of the 1950s, "Never had it so good" decade, that the independent preparatory school was ripe for the picking!

Sandlehurst had originally been established soon after the First World War as a country house with over one hundred acres with the DeWitt family benefactor who valued the role of a small boarding school education. The family, like the Plantagenet-Filbys, were well founded as part of England's heritage, but this generation of the DeWitts was adamant that they wanted to pursue a role in traditional values to educate boys, and it was boys only, for the challenges of the world that Britain would encounter in the second half of the twentieth century.

Ray knew little of this before his meeting in the King's Arms that spring day. In fact, it was Smithey who had hopped into Ray's car after their lunch who had briefed him on some of the background. JJ had given him the impression that the Head of Art was pencilled in as his job for the taking. Still Ray was intrigued how JJ along with a similarly handpicked group of governors, had originally been entrusted with the running and financing of such an ambitious institution. All these background factors faded as he was given a school tour of classrooms, halls, sports fields, dormitories and of course, the art room.

JJ insisted that Ray would have full sway on all art classes and activities. The headmaster's definition of art, at this stage, was sketching and painting for the children up to thirteen years of age before going on to a senior public school. Ray made a point of relaying to JJ that art entailed a great deal more, entering into the horizons of sculpture, drama, music and nature. Did this sink in? Ray thought not but he was totally reassured that JJ would give him the tools to expand his department in the manner he saw fit. Ray was a perfect fit from both points of view. It was now just a matter of convincing Sarah. Their relationship was always built on team or collective decisions. Ray was sold on Sarah's liberal family history, even though there were dark eccentricities in her line of heritage. He simply had inhaled the lessons from Jan and Freddie who had, intentionally or not, paddled their own canoes irrespective of the feelings of each other and their children. He should know, he would never forget the childhood he endured, the ravages of the Blitz, Hamburg and the prison that was Bermondsey.

Their decision was made easy on two counts, with the overriding ethos of Sandlehurst. It was a welcoming place with a staff that was closely knit and sold on the high values of tradition set out by JJ. They would follow him to the ends of the earth. The first issue for Sarah was the proximity to the family home just outside of Eastbourne. The Filbys had their small estate there since Victorian times, an era when sea air was a privilege to be solely enjoyed by the upper classes. Equally for Sarah's uncles and grandparents, there was a very handy direct rail service to their customary seats in the House of Lords at Westminster.

In addition the one thing Sarah wanted was her own home, which would be dutifully covered financially by the Filby family, a home fit for a large family, detached with grounds, and of easy access to Sandlehurst and Eastbourne. They were to find their Shangri-La just outside of the town called Crowborough on the Weald. A private sale was affected. Poor old Ray just had to go with the flow, but he was a more than willing passenger!

In the late 60s, children could be seen and heard. Sarah and Ray's generation would be influenced as parents by the then current, groovy world of a new group of liberal educationalists, both in colleges and parliament. This was no surprise where Sarah was concerned, because all her forefathers had been liberal peers. As for Ray, and notably with Harold Wilson's labour government pushing the agenda for equal opportunities through comprehensive schooling, his family always had voted for the Labour Party. Thus, the newly-weds insisted on a state education for their kids Susan, Janet, Imogen and Peter on the way, in an open day school. Neither of the pair would settle for anything less than sending their kids off in the morning and seeing them again after school. The local primary and comprehensive would do them just fine!

Now, it was just a time to enjoy the summer of love with all its unfolding colour - even colour television was to be introduced within months - and settle into the world of the prosperous, the comfortable and the influential. At last, Ray was to embark on what he had craved for all these years. He and Sarah had made a stable, lovely life for themselves and their family. Settled at last!

From the very first day in September at Sandlehurst, Ray was welcomed as one of their own. The staff room was always a buzz with members talk of JJ's 'Thought for the Day', whether it be a point of educational principle, in Latin of course, or a congratulation or boot up the arse for one of the school's high achieving sports teams. The note was always pinned to a green soft board aside the list of permanent staff, which read:-

JJ - Headmaster – Classics

Mr R. Cranley – Deputy Head: English, History, Drama

Mr I. Easton – Modern Languages and Cricket

Rev'd M. Smythe – Divinity and Rugger

Mr K. Trimlett – Mathematics, Science and Cricket

Miss M. Poulson – Science

Mr M. Greatbatch – Music

Mr J. Boxell – General Studies and Football

Mr R. Bristowe – Art and Geography

Ray perused the list regularly though he never needed to as this core of plucky Brits would remain loyal to the school for the entirety of their careers. This indeed was an era when the teachers belonged to a school, it was their vocation. Over the ensuing years of his early time at Sandlehurst he compromised over a quarter of his timetable devoting it to Geography, or 'Joggers', as JJ termed the subject, but he soon realised that all the staff would muck in to cover each other. Underneath it all they relished the thought of starting the teaching day in a beautiful country house positioned on a split level site of stone rendered buildings set high above a lower plateau of games fields and woodland as far as the eye could see.

The start of each day would reveal a small sector of boarders at the school which was rapidly expanding its capacity of 150 boys. There was constant demand for more of the staff to live in with all its benefits, and Ray, along with his family, was target number one. For many years JJ, Dick Cranley, Keith Tremlett, Ian Easton and the mercurial Mary Poulson all lived on the grounds of Sandlehurst, either entertaining young families or just single men and women, like Ian and Mary, taking advantage of an expenses-free life style whilst they were young teachers.

Yes, the school through the 70s was expanding, and judging by the increasing number of scholarship names on the school boards in the Hall to prestigious public schools like Lancing, King's Canterbury and Millfield, it had gained a top academic reputation for this part of South East England. Swathes of families were moving out further from London to lead a healthier lifestyle, and JJ through his never ending network in East and South Africa, was a magnet for British colonial interest from parents who wanted their children educated in the motherland. Sandlehurst was in demand!

As Ray prospered within the school's family environment, he was very content that, despite many quaint practices and traditions and a host of eccentrics on the staff, this private enterprise worked. It was a functioning self-reliant body for good educational principles. What made it work without doubt was the relationship between JJ and the Deputy Head, Dick Cranley. The Headmaster had head hunted Dick, in the same way that Ray had been enticed through family connections. Richard Cranley was not only a damn good classroom teacher, but also a young liberal Conservative with a sharp eye for administration and organisation.

JJ delegated to Dick to run the school, the internal day to day staffing, timetabling and infrastructural elements. These vital areas did not in the slightest bit interest JJ. The Head was a consummate PR man, the shop window face of Sandlehurst: his was a world of overseas promotion trips with the return journey always touching down in Paris or Monaco. JJ had a decade's season ticket with Air France. On the home front JJ would convene several working lunches with the top men on the Headmasters' Conference, the body of senior public school headmasters and bursars. Let it not be said that he forgot his own staff who were regularly wined and dined at the School House on fortnightly Friday evenings hosted by his effervescent wife, Patricia.

Ray regularly would stay over after these 'dos', never comprehending why you needed four different types of wine with one meal. Whenever bottles were systematically emptied by the thirsty members of staff, JJ would sprint downstairs and hey presto, more vintage wine would appear. It was rightfully claimed that JJ had the best and biggest cellar of French wines in Sussex. Yet, although Ray held JJ with the deepest respect, it was another staff personality who had cultivated a lasting friendship with him. Dick Cranley, an artist and musician himself, had encouraged Ray's undoubted potential to flower at the school. They engaged in joint projects from concerts and exhibitions in paint to the staggering production of musicals and Christmas pantos. Dick, along with the former rock guitarist music master Mick Greatbatch, would write the music and Ray would take charge of the décor and artistic direction. It was a formula that all the kids and parents loved!

In fact the three of them were inseparable with the two single men famed for enticing Ray for many racy away days and evenings at the King's Arms. The Bristowe clan,

Ray always claimed, would be proud of his elevation here in the shires, all except Phil, but to hell with him. The art master was thriving professionally at a vibrant school, his young family were now at that age where they could be enjoyed by Sarah and himself and he had developed a strong bond of mainly male company as a kind of extended family. He would have liked more time in term to spend on his growing interest in watercolours to present some art works of his own but that could wait for the holidays. If it was security he was seeking, and for him it was the be all and end all, fifteen years and two generations of pupils had slid past in a whirl as the 1980s dawned on him. One more bolt from the blue for the new decade was Sarah producing, thirteen years after their fourth, Peter, another baby boy named Michael, born into their Sussex world of wonderment.

..*

Terry Jones didn't really know how to get round London but Waterloo station was world famous and he had a long evening ahead for his objective, a pub off Jamaica Road in Bermondsey. It was 4pm on July 28th 1966 and he was anxious to get there before the teeming millions would be heading out on their daily commuter trains to all points south, south-east and south-west. He still worked by the compass! At a news stand, he bought an Evening Standard and flipped to the back-page headline,

"Will Alf sideline Jimmy for the Final?" begged the question. Terry had noted the buzz around the town revolved around the England football team's chances at the

forthcoming World Cup Final at Wembley on the Saturday. He couldn't give a toss, as he hailed from the Welsh valleys, but he did get the paper man to give him walking directions to Bermondsey and the pub. Two and a bit miles was a walk in the park for Terry Jones. The walk was easy enough, across to London Bridge, along Tooley Street, then eventually onto Jamaica Road, he headed east to locate, and once there waited for opening time at 5.30 at The Angel.

The evening time had been allocated for his task, trusting that the Landlord had responded to his call the previous day to make contact with Phil. The Bermondsey boy these days was a midweek regular but normally appeared nearer chucking out time rather than opening doors. Terry ordered a pint of Courage Best and whiled away the time reacquainting himself with the dartboard in the public bar under the suspicious eyes of the regulars. It did not help that he sported a razor-cut military hairstyle in strict contrast with the locals' loose locks that hadn't seen a barber in months.

Phil had wondered what all the fuss was about when he was told at work to pop into his local to meet an old mate who did not leave his name. So he finally arrived after finishing off some work on a blocked drain, itching for a pint on a humid late afternoon. He pushed the doors open and hit the bar, eyeing up the vista of the Thames and Tower Bridge away to his left.

"His is a bottle of Anchor, cold. If you ain't got that, he'll take a Tiger," the trim looking stranger announced.

"Fuckin' 'ell, is that you Tel, whatcha doin' ere?" said Phil, very much recognising his company sergeant.

209

"Stand to attention when you're addressing an officer, you long haired git," barked the military man laughing with utter disdain.

The former comrades retired to the corner of the bar, spending the next twenty minutes bouncing stories of Ipoh, Kuala Lumpur and Petaling Jaya off each other. Terry Jones had never forgotten the night of the ambush, his Malay scouts and Phil's actions in the mosquito-infested jungle. There seemed already so much evidence of a lifelong bond between the two counter-insurgent comrades. Terry stared Phil out and reaching across the table grabbed his grey polo necked sweater and yanked the top down revealing a four-inch scar, a red vertical line of a wound.

"See you're still sensitive about that gash? After all we went through in the jungle, you couldn't even sort your brother out,"

Phil winced. "His time will come, I just gotta hurt him when it really will be curtains for him, payback time."

Sergeant Terry Jones gave him a nervous glance, the look from a man who knew what his comrade had been capable of, but he asked himself the big question, did Phil still have the itch, the twitch for real action? "Phil, why are you still fucking about cleaning wankers' bathrooms?"

"Piss off, Tel, I'll have you know I'm a qualified plumber and there's good money to be had round 'ere now that I'm self-employed,"

Terry gave his mate a rueful shrug, then struck hard, direct to the point,

"Phil, do you fancy some action, I want to give you the chance to do what you're really good at, are you still prepared to mix it and take 'em out?"

"It's been nearly ten years, what, back to the fighting game?"

There was a spark of interest which Terry would pounce on very quietly. He explained that he headed up a reservist unit that was neither attached to the Yanks nor Brits, but contained former specialised military from as far afield as Canada, Rhodesia, Australia, New Zealand and Nepal. He himself had devoted himself after his statutory national service to a command in the British Army for seven years. Terry's style of tactical application was unorthodox and this had been noticed in the echelons of the army's hierarchy.

He was promoted out of regular army duties in 1964 to form an ongoing unit which he would handpick to respond to the trouble spots in world conflicts. Terry was handsomely rewarded, but the work was intense, short term, dangerous and his unit would be task oriented, and highly specialised in nature. He knew that injury and even death was waiting around every corner.

"Are you up for it? Here's my phone number, mum's the word, you do not need to know nothing above us, just our force. Your boss will be me. You will answer to me only, but rest assured, we both know which side we'll be batting for!" exclaimed the former paratrooper.

"Hold it Tel, where will I be based, what about the money?"

"The force will get you a cover job so you'll be paid a regular wage with them, but where the real money comes in from us will depend upon the success of each specified operation. You are still in shape but you'll need six months retraining with the unit before your cover job will commence."

Terry stood up and heading for the door, pointed his finger at the mate who had once saved his life and said, "You have the weekend, then phone me."

Phil had already made up his mind, a command was a command.

Terry got the call, then had two further meetings with Phil to make him well aware of the six month's inhouse training. Only if he was up to scratch would he be allocated a cover post, a paramount position in a mundane job. It would be a case from thereon in that Terry would use a code word to Phil for an assignment to commence. It could be once a year or even once every three but it would always be only a short-term engagement. He would be issued with a passport for missions only and most important of all the termination of his employment would be exclusively on the say of one Terry Jones.

England had won the World Cup with the country now at fever pitch. Somebody invented a new phrase at the time that Phil had never heard before, it was 'the feel-good factor' of London town. What with the pop music, the fashion, the theatres and cinemas, who in their right mind would leave the place behind? The answer to that one was Phil Bristowe.

For him, the next six months were to prove hell on earth. He was to be conditioned in every respect. His flight on an unregistered Boeing 707 took him Stateside. That was all he knew as on arrival he was blindfolded and led off with no customs to another flight; this time it was a propeller job. The folds were lifted as the plane shuddered to a halt, the flight duration of no more than an hour, landing on a grass runway. At the tiny terminal building, there he was to greet him, the reassuring figure of Terry Jones.

Terry's jeep took the pair through nothing but forest from the landing strip of Eagles Meer. The vehicle sliced through deep cut valleys shrouded in dense deciduous forest, and Phil thought he spotted a road sign depicting the area was known as 'The World's End'.

So, it was to be, for the foreseeable future. He lived in a prefabricated farm hut on stilts, or was consigned to sleep rough in the forest. His war game training was interspersed with long periods of sleep or food deprivation, often of up to a week in duration. He was to work only in hot forested or open plain environments. Terry had made an early decision not to deploy Phil in water or urban settings. All modern weaponry was used with live ammunition and hand to hand fighting went up to the point of physical injury. Phil Bristowe enjoyed one day of leisure per month. Once the heat subsided in October, he was airlifted out of there to Asia, Sarawak to be exact, for final assimilation at 32°C for the remaining two months.

Phil knew two places, the Eagles Meer and a godforsaken small island virtually deserted in the back end of equatorial Asia. By the end of January his time was up. However, it was back to the vast Frankfurt-Main Air Base in Germany. Here Terry was joined, not by a posse of Yanks (Phil had had his fill with the staff commandoes for over five months) but by another rough and tough South African. Well that was what the Londoner thought. In fact, Patrick Rose was a Rhodesian, and more to the point, a Selous Scout, the unit across international militia with the highest of high reputations.

The pair debriefed Phil, acknowledging he was not to utilise his training immediately but to take the lead on the role as a warden for a supportive socio-religious organisation called Toc H Services. Stationed all over the British sector of Germany since WW2, these were outposts that supplied the British troops and their families with all the services that they would need in their communities to lead a normal, or near to normal a life in small barracks living aside the local Germans. Phil would lead Toc H in Munster in the Nord-Rhein Westfalen region and provide the village of squaddies with cafeterias, libraries, mobile shops, social and religious based support.

Toc H would be his cover. It was a charity-based organisation with grants from the British government in London. Thus, it was classified as non-military, even though it supplied vital services to army regulars and their families. Phil was to be in everyday contact with all levels of army personnel who regarded him purely as a civilian in every respect. His staff awaiting the new warden were all from civvy street, the vast majority full-time employees, but originally recruited from Toc H Central Office in London.

There was a religious base to Toc H, which was founded during the First World War by a pastor called Tubby Clayton, who had set up his charitable and voluntary outposts well back from the front to rehabilitate the traumatised British troops when rested from the atrocities of trench warfare. Their missionary work had extended post-war to broader social support and accommodation for non-military persons as well throughout the British Empire.

Now the self-employed plumber from Bermondsey was to take charge of a large central dwelling close to the army base which acted as a commercial entity. Phil had to provide budgets, rotas, inventories and quarterly reports on sales, services and personnel management to the head honchos of Toc H Central in London.

He had learned to run his own business and in addition he was working amongst people he knew and understood. The military mind set and way of life was engrained in him since the days of Freddie and Hamburg.

The challenge was within his own staff. What a bunch! He for sure, had noted through the previous minutes of reports that there was a very high turnover of personnel, that students were often used, sent out for temporary gap year periods. Most alarming of all was that there had been a disproportionate number of sackings due to mental and psychological factors allied to alcoholism.

His worst fears were soon to be realised. Many of these volunteer social workers, living off cheap alcohol (no British Services' taxes on hard liquor) and a propensity for either seeking low life German night clubs or homosexual companionship, had resulted in his first year of adopting the role of social worker to his own staff! The group was housed in an eight bedroomed manor in Werner Strasse along with a fully-fledged German residential staff including cooks, cleaners and handymen.

Phil recognised this was a cushy number for all employed, but one thing was for sure, that it was easy for him to keep his head down in the ensuing years. For six months, his masters had left him to settle down and get a grip on his surroundings. From his contract with Toc H, he was able to take two months clear per year. He took nothing, then in late August after delivering British newspapers around the base in the mobile van, he returned to the Werner to receive the call,

'Philip : Collingwood : Tel.'

The code was clear for him to make contact.

Welcome to all you Pohms to the land of opportunity. Posters adorn the walls of Sydney's migrant reception halls.

Libby's Saturday morning sketch class. A profile view of Bondi from her art kiosk.

Phil joins the Ton-up boys at weekends. All British Triumph bikes fascinated him.

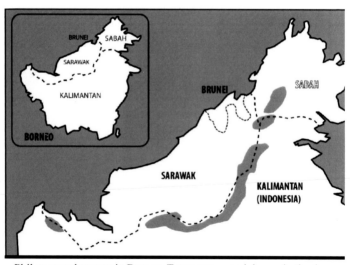

Phil goes undercover in Borneo. T company wreak havoc in the dense jungle (shaded)

CHAPTER 10

PERFECT ALIBI

Phil, in anticipation of his pre-operational briefing with Terry Jones, was jotting down some vital queries on his Toc H headed notepaper. He smiled to himself on the Munster to Luxembourg train at the Toc H mission statement at the head of the sheet.

"To love widely: to build bravely: to think fairly: to witness humbly."

Hardly the words of the unit's commander that very evening! Terry first took Phil aside as it was his first engagement. "Right Phil, in two days' time you'll be flying out on a civvy airline to Singapore. I can't tell you exactly the nature of how we'll be operating, but it will be a six-week engagement for the unit in an offensive operation in jungle conditions. On a successful return a deposit in pounds sterling will be placed into the account we'll open in the morning. You will travel under your unit's British passport to pass in transit to our destination, the oil rich state of Brunei."

"What about kit, chief?" asked Phil.

"You know the score. All of it is out there and one last thing, memorise to your dying day your passport ID number and the Luxembourg bank account number as well," insisted Terry, "and bon voyage, see you in the swamp."

Phil was relieved the money side was being looked after by the Gaffer. He still had no idea of the amount involved but working for nearly two months, both fighting and training other small units in a gilt rich state run by a Sultan in Brunei; The Bermondsey boy had to be in the money.

The quick trip to the bank with Terry was followed by a day and a half of tactical assessment and analysis by the Rhodesian boss, Patrick Rose. By then Terry had departed no doubt arriving at the meet point in Brunei under his own steam. Pat never left a stone unturned, down to the eating habits of the Iban tribe, who, as the original Borneo head hunters, were partial to the delights of human flesh! Phil was glad he was in the know of what background he was to be operating in, especially as his lone experience of tropical warfare had been in Malaya, albeit a decade ago.

The confrontation on the island of Borneo was between the Indonesian leader Sukarno and the oil-rich Crown dependencies of Sarawak, Brunei and Sabah. Indonesia had been ceded, nearly three quarters of this large island of Borneo, by the Dutch colonists. The border stretched horizontally west to east for nearly 900 miles merging into high mountains almost acting as a divide between the two sides. Since 1962 when hostilities began with Indonesian forces mounting incursions into the three territories mainly to target the oil fields, and police security forces. However, as in Malaya ten years before, the British backed forces had learned their lessons and had resisted well with custom-made modern equipment of helicopters and waterborne craft and with the expertise of Gurkha platoons, they had triumphed after five years of constant jungle engagement.

Many British, Malay and Gurkha regiments were deployed to fight in close quarter combat, ambush strategies and to make positive use of offensive patrols into every territory. The use of the Wessex helicopter squadrons was also vital in the carriage of heavy plant across the wide area of flashpoints. By the end of 1966 hostilities had ceased, with the Malaysian and Indonesian states signing a peace treaty reaffirming the territories of Sarawak, Brunei and Sabah to remain as independents within the orbit of East Malaysia. The threat of communism had been stopped in its tracks.

Of course, that was the official line. A number of highly specialised units, Terry and Phil's being one, now would get down to work. Terry outlined the task to his four Gurkhas and two Aussie colleagues. They were to infiltrate behind enemy lines linking up in a coordinated plan across the border into Indonesian held Borneo. They were armed with much improved jungle light specific Armalite assault rifles, 3.5 inch rocket launcher anti-tank weapons plus sophisticated seismic sensors which detected enemy presence within 50 metres by newly developed vibration signals.

Sabotage was the name of the game. Local intelligence by close links with the Iban tribesmen who held out no love for the Indonesian intruders cleared the way for locating staging camps and the river lines of communication used by the well organised Indonesian fighters. Phil had learned the technique of camouflage in hiding in the ground from the tribesmen in springing ambush after ambush. For nearly two months solid, with superior communications with parallel units, Terry's group selectively identified the river routes, the number and type of enemy boats and bases, and summarily wreaked havoc.

Following the official armistice, the undercover operations had mopped up any structure or area of mobility any future Indonesian group would hope to use, and not only that, with Terry's unit training up indigenous forces that were added to his unit, it was clear that any likelihood of friction from across the border was curtailed for some time.

Mission accomplished with this time both Terry and Phil hardly receiving a scratch. As was procedure, all of the unit returned unbeknown to each other or anyone else to their regular employ. It was the perfect alibi. Back to Luxembourg, Bristowe didn't even check his bank account.

In Phil's case, resuming duties at Toc H was just as unnerving a test as the Borneo jungle. Nearly eight weeks had passed since Barry Van Der Wilt had taken over the reins. It was either him or the highly eccentric Rupert Bentink-Budd. Barry was actually quite a reliable egg, if he would only stop flirting with the male of the species. Phil in short time had worked out that if you could allow Barry one clear long weekend off in four, he would elope to Berlin or Amsterdam for his dubious pleasures. Following those energetic interludes, he normally knuckled down to the variety of challenges that the Services Club would offer the British military in Munster. On arrival back he made up a thorough verbal check list for Phil,

"Love the tan, Phil, now where have YOU been?" he emphasised, "All quiet on the western front here, library well stocked, café is over-run, squaddies just love those new brown rolls, the mobile shop even with 'B Bee' driving it, is busy, and your idea of the young mothers' mornings is taking off a treat!"

Phil traditionally couldn't stand poofters, but Barry really was a laugh, and pretty harmless at that. He congratulated the 'blond bombshell' for filling in so well, so to speak.

"Ooo, yeah, just one more thing, Frau Kaessman has got her knickers in a twist for next Friday night. She wants to speak to you about the food budget as the Colonel is coming to dinner here at the Werner, along with Toc H personnel from London and Berlin."

"Right," said Phil "we'd better all be on our best behaviour including those two layabout students, what's their names again?"

"There's Noel of course, and the new arrival, young Bazelgette, he's off to Cambridge next year."

"How's Rupers been behaving?" Phil enquired,

"He's back on the cinzanos with you being away."

Phil knew that these so called dinners were periodic events, very festive, but he suspected they were just a means to check up on the natives, especially if General Secretary Gilbert Woodall would be there from London accompanied by the local garrison colonel along with the Scottish Berlin supremo, Fergus Laird. Then there were the wives too!

Everyone suited and booted, the next Friday came. He was certain of an impending disaster when former public schoolboy Rupert Bentinck-Budd, of prominent military family fame, volunteered to take charge of the cocktail party prior to the dinner, with cinzanos heavily on the menu! Small talk resonated across the room amongst dinner jackets and best frocks: of London, the troubles in Ireland, Berlin's night life and the Reds in the Beds. All thoughts turned away from the communist menace when the gong sounded for all to be served by the German house staff.

The evening was a smash hit. Certainly from the point of view of the personalities on site it was living up to expectations. Rupers' head began to swoon in ever decreasing circles as he divebombed directly into his oxtail soup. The recovery team of Barry and Phil carried him to bed upstairs to his cinzano bianco heaven. Meanwhile, under the table, lothario student Noel was playing an intense game of footsie with the colonel's wife, twenty-five years his senior. Quite clearly, she very much preferred the younger man. For Noel, just another phone number!

The carnal and bacchanalian desires apart, Toc H Munster had survived another bi-annual inspection very well. No doubt it would all be down there recorded as an item on the quarterly agenda back at HQ. Without a doubt, the star of the show had been Frau Kaessman, a large Deutsche Frau, a fact that always augered well for her Werner house dinners.

Phil was to settle into a six day a week regular routine and he really was getting the hang of producing balance sheets and budgets though he always could depend on Barry's eye for detail to check over all the facts and figures as he omitted something or forgot some element. Toc H Munster made three annual profits in a row, all with Phil described in London despatches as unassuming, shy, but relatively reluctant to delegate work. Bristowe, efficient, had kept his nose clean.

So it came as a bit of a shock to all the staff that he was, in 1970 to be transferred to Paderborn as the Chief Warden. Barry and the boys were sad to see him go, but onward and upward, Phil Bristowe packed his bags, climbed into his VW Beetle and headed east. On his arrival on a clear summer's day, he was introduced to the staff by Fergus Laird, down for the day from Berlin. Fergus did not brief him really at all on the ways and aspirations of the Paderborn station. He did, nevertheless, advise Phil that the further you ventured east, the less proficient the locals were in speaking English.

Fergus, a proud Scot, was not a modest man. He was in effect telling Phil to have a go at learning German, spoken German. Ironically enough, the Londoner had seen and witnessed how Terry had mesmerised the indigenous populations of Malaya with his command of the locals' language. If Laird was fluent, he thought, why not take a

223

course himself if one was available, preferably an evening class during the long winters.

Paderborn's Toc H had been run on very similar lines to Munster, but situated that bit closer to the East German border it seemed to Phil that bit busier with more military personnel. Fergus was right on the dearth of German speakers amongst his staff which included Edgar Prior, a close to pensionable age veteran of multiple campaigns, unfortunately leading a lifestyle that made Bentinck-Budd look like a sober judge. Equally disturbing was the assistance of Sophie Trescothick, a born again Christian who was the eldest daughter of the Commissioner in London. This meant there was a greater dependence on the local German staff in responsible roles both at the residential house and at Toc H central's facilities. For sure, Phil was wary of Sophie.

Therefore it was vital for Phil to make contact via a recommendation from Sophie to attend an open evening at Hillman's Language School in the centre of town. The relatively small converted house at least was close to all the town's facilities with decent car parking spaces at its frontage. Phil was welcomed warily amongst a small scattering of army wives and technicians attached to the Paderborn garrison. A shrewd move had been to invite Edgar to refresh his German, as the twice weekly evening classes had a real chance of keeping him off the booze.

The Hillman School was run by a husband and wife team called Franz and Sigrid who were ably supported by two more experienced teachers, Jurgen and Ingrid. Interestingly, the school offered base classes in English, both grammatical and conversational with Jurgen and 'Sigi', and starter classes in German along the same lines with Franz and Ingrid. All four tutors, as they were known, had graduated in modern languages or had big city practical experience in previous employment in further education or in the real world!

The German economic miracle, notably in industry and commerce took readily to the world language of English as a means to further business. After WW2, two dynamic decades pushed the German economy at a far faster rate than any other country and it was the German ability to embrace English as their second language which accelerated recovery in all areas. Compared to France, Belgium and Italy, the German Federal Republic outstripped those countries with the provision of learning English in school, but also to adults in outside work hours.

Franz had entered university back in 1959 leaving Brunswick his home town, to study English. His pushy parents were rather dubious as they would have preferred him to take on something more technical in response to the overwhelming number of opportunities in chemical and electrical engineering. Their son from the start knew his own mind, for it was always his intention to run his own business. With his flair for business management and languages it was just a matter of time. After graduating three years later, he joined a fresh and enterprising language school in the Hamburg suburb of Altona which was where he met his future wife, Sigrid.

Sigrid's mother was the founder of Altona EFL. Her business partner and Director Ralf Montag seemed to run the EFL (English as a Foreign Language) with a rod of iron and German efficiency. Being located near to the university and the port commercial centre enhanced the school's appeal. The group, right from its beginnings in the early 50s never seemed to be short of investment, sponsors or novel new schemes to push the cause of the English language to a thriving German populace.

Sigi grew up with the calming hand of a caring mother but she was doted upon by this managing director from a past that was rumoured to be closely associated with the pre war national socialists. The secretaries and junior teachers at the Altona school were never really sure if Sigi was his child or was he the guardian? Mother had never worn a wedding ring, but that was not unusual in the immediate aftermath of WW2 when Sigi came into the world. The itinerant mix of returning soldiers, refugees, overseas and foreign soldiers and unintended one night stands were tragically the norm during those early days after the war.

When Franz joined Altona straight from university in 1962, Sigi was about to celebrate her sixteenth birthday and leaving school. Rebellious from the start, she always yearned to break free from a controlling 'step father'. So for her later teenage years, she took up both hostess and modelling work down on Hamburg's infamous Reeperbahn. Inspired by the music scene and the resident bands from America and the embryonic years of the Beatles, she took up a secretarial job in St Paoli at a recording studio. Everyday language in the port was English; the musical tunes were all delivered in the words

226

of The Beatles. By 1965, she was fluent with a fabulous grasp of the colloquial. She was also in love at the age of eighteen. Her undying affection and regular daily attention was aimed at the handsome young teacher at her mum's school, Franz Hillman.

Sigi had won the prize, the prize of freedom that a young marriage would provide for her. Clearly they were meant for each other and importantly had mother's blessing. She knew that Sigi needed the security and stability of the older man, as Franz was then already approaching thirty years of age and he in turn would have an attractive resourceful young wife. They were always a team, and by 1968,with some parting finance from 'EFL', amicably broke away from Altona.They set up in the British garrison town of Paderborn, unfashionable but teeming with Germans that needed to learn English, and British personnel that were keen to speak the native tongue as a result of three year postings in Germany.

Phil Bristowe had signed up both himself and Edgar for the forthcoming winter course of 1970-71. Tuesdays were grammar and vocabulary days with Franz, and the highly enjoyable Thursdays 'Talkies with Ingrid'. Edgar was impressed by the professional way that Franz and Sigi had separated their duties to avoid the comfort of a 'hubby and darling' duo. These formal lessons, and the dialogue which passed between Phil and his German staff, notably the marvellous housekeeper Frau Sneyder, were a lifeline and a source of constant amusement to all at Toc H. They were working so well that Edgar inevitably invited their four tutors for Christmas Eve dinner celebrations.

Edgar insisted that all conversation between the staffs of Toc H and the Hillman school had to be in German for the first hour as he might just be sober at that point. Frau Sneyder cooked up a sumptuous meal which was readily enhanced by Phil taking up a table for ten positioned directly opposite Sigi. They laughed away the hours together eventually in English. Phil, taking in female company and drop dead gorgeous looking girls like Sigi, realised for the first time that he at thirty five was really a very lonely man.

Yes, he was enjoying life to the full, earning a salary with all home expenses covered and receiving unprecedented rewards from Terry's unit, but through Sigi he pondered to himself that something was missing, having eyeballed her all evening long. She was so very easy on the eye, in the way she glanced or turned her gaze to focus her attention that was universal but special. Somehow he felt so comfortable in her presence and though Sigi was never predictable he could almost sense her every move, smile or reaction.

He had never experienced these feelings for a woman before. The sensations were unique, but strangely Phil would never have thought of making a play for her. She with Franz were above all that. His respect for the young couple was immense. That 1970 Christmas had been the most joyful for the Londoner despite his inward loneliness and he was emphatically building up a very successful Toc H station.

This joie de vivre was compounded by a salary rise to £20 per week in 1971, but Phil's £20 was what he saved.

Unless he ventured beyond the gates of Paderborn, he never spent any money. Everything was provided. Another provision came later in the year through the hands of an unlikely source, that of Edgar! A hand scribbled envelope yielded a postcard within, then announcing:

"Phil:

Collingwood: Report Hannover Rail Terminal 22.7.71 at 09:00 hrs: T"

Patrick Rose was easy company in his E type 1964 Jaguar all the way to Luxembourg to board a Luxavia flight to Salisbury Airport. They sat with separate tickets in separate seats down to Africa but re-joined by car on their final leg to the city's northern suburbs. The Rhodie offered the younger man two weeks training with his own crack unit before deployment. Training in the Rhodesian bush country was hard core with Phil covering eight to ten kilometres a day laden with ten kilos on his back. The 'off' days concentrated on hand to hand combat and firearm drills, then the two days of para drops. On the final night, the former Selous Scout sat comfortably around a bush fire with a cold Castle beer to keep the freezing July winter out. He turned to Phil,

"This one's on me, but no more favours from here on in. You've trained with our unit and you're a Rhodie now. There'll be no Terry this time to wipe your arse for you. Tomorrow we move into Mozambique, do the damage, then retreat across into both Rhodie and SA territory. We will be yo-yoing for six weeks. Our ten-man unit will smash everything they've got."

Phil interrupted, "Are you sure we have the Intelligence to hit these Frelimo renegades? You know, as so called freedom fighters, they could pilfer Mozambique uniforms and dress up as government troops. Also what about turncoats, Pat, they're all black to me?"

"Don't you worry, our sorties will be swift and decisive."

For the next seven weeks, Pat's scouting unit was engaged with multiple firefights and ambushes against the Revolutionary 'freedom' fighters opposed to the decaying Portuguese colonial government. Surrounding encampments of enemy groups at night were their focus where the use of silent weapons was at a premium. Phil had been trained well and he soon became oblivious to killing. He was seeking, locating and destroying whatever and whoever came into his path. The unit on this deployment had another big advantage, even over small mobile enemy groups, and that was in the Scouts' ability to retreat back across the Umtali Hills over the border if pursued. Rhodesia was always near as a respite position.

The Frelimo forces were very reluctant to pursue Pat's insurgents back into Rhodesia. They had a fight of their own to look after within Mozambique at this stage in the battle for independence within Southern Africa. Multiple units, Portuguese, American, former Vietnam vets with a taste for action, and Pat's Selous units disrupted the pace of the onslaught of the Frelimo fighter, but these external soldiers couldn't prevent their inevitable victory. What even Phil gleaned from this operation was that once the Frelimo forces gravitated to power, they would be allied covertly with the black nationalist leader in Rhodesia, Robert Mugabe, and his 'ZANLA', the 'Zimbabwe Liberation Army'. Frelimo and Zanla were to be blood brothers.

Of the ten in Pat's sub unit, over the period they lost just one colleague, a young Rhodesian artillery lad who was caught and at first thought wounded but was soon finished off. Phil never dwelled on the possibility of capture or death and for that reason avoided close friendships with his colleagues. After one pitched engagement when grenades had saved the group's bacon, he had wiped out a Frelimo trench, well dug in, but, on return he had temporarily lost the hearing in his left ear. A tingling sensation followed him around for the rest of the day but gradually everything seemed to return to normal. He seldom gave it another thought.

Commander Rose had noticed though. On the debrief back in Salisbury, he ordered a period of two week convalescence for Phil in a unit outhouse. The Londoner could not believe his eyes when it not only was in England, not only in comfortable Hampshire, but in a village pub called The Greyhound in Longfield Green. All he had was one change of clothes, two long numbers of his passport and a number in Luxembourg and of course, a slightly sore ear. Still, he was told the landlord and his wife would look after him.

Mike and Debra had run The Greyhound as a tied tenancy to Courage beers for a couple of years occupying the flat above a popular pub in a self-contained village that was Longfield Green. Many of their locals were self employed in the trades, but the saloon bar boasted a fair scattering of professionals who commuted to both London and Southampton. It was ostensibly a quiet retreat, maybe except for Saturday evening when there was always a bit of a party atmosphere.

"Let me introduce you to my cousin, Mandy and her husband, David," Debra offered in her usual unpretentious manner.

David, a man of very similar build to Phil, but perhaps too many of those rugby evenings did show more of a central body stockiness, seemed friendly enough. His wife, Mandy, a very attractive blond, gave Phil a series of looks, stares and sideways glances. He immediately caught on as he moved to the bar to buy his round that she was giving him the head to toe inspection. That was the first of several G and T's and pints of Directors bitter that first evening of Phil's recuperation.

Debra had joined the threesome on and off throughout the evening leaving Mike and the bar staff to enjoy a very healthy set of takings.

"What's up for Sunday Cuz?" asked Debra of her cousin.

"Free as a bird, David's up in Aberdeen with the rigs for ten days or so," explained Mandy of her husband's contribution to the instalment of the burgeoning North Sea oil platforms. Engineers were a sought after commodity, with high salaries compensating for periods away from home.

"Why don't you come over for lunch? It's roast beef and all the trimmings tomorrow, and what about you, Sir, our new lodger, will you join us?"

Phil hadn't enjoyed a roast dinner for ages, but having answered in the affirmative enthusiastically just wondered where was the connection between the rough Rhodie, Pat Rose, Terry and this comfortable young social couple from Hampshire. As everyone vacated the pub, his curiosity got the better of him. He posed the question to Debra.

"That would be telling, wouldn't it?" she answered rustically.

He did enjoy his new found lie-ins. Never bothering to take the Sunday breakfast, he ventured downstairs from his room hastened by the fact that he had spotted a sporty navy-blue MG Midget pull into the pub's car park. It was Mandy wearing a headscarf and a sleek fitting trouser suit, perfect attire he thought for an open-top speedy sports car. She bounced along into the saloon clearly in a self-confident breeze of a stride. It was the female version of a strut, in no way arrogant but very self-contained.

Two hours later, she turned to Phil and in that same air of self-assurance posted the inevitable, "Fancy a spin, Phil?"

He knew what she meant. It was a mere drive in the country but it lasted from lunch until dusk. She was invigorated and initiated many areas of conversation to get to know this hell of a guy, an easy-going stranger with no ties.

"I'd love to go to Berlin, I've heard the night life is something else."

233

He responded very sharply that he only visited the city now and then as his role was to run a warehouse for imported British goods a hundred miles away.

Mandy didn't believe him. "I think you're telling me fibs, you rogue, I can tell a military man a mile away," as she rolled down his pale blue polo neck sweater. Her seductive stroll continued to stroke his neck revealing that long vertical scar,

"I suppose you got this humping jars of Branston pickle around the factory?"

Phil had been partly rumbled. He did not and could not reply, except only in one way, offering his lips to hers. They could not resist each other.

Mandy knew exactly what to do. She drove to a roadside motel just outside Winchester, the place of her work as a medical secretary. It was discreet well away from the village and her marital home. She booked in for a series of evenings and nights when she and David were never usually at The Greyhound. She would spend hours quizzing Phil on his life in Germany and his background,

"You're obviously a Londoner, what about your family? Where are your parents, have you any brothers and sisters?" Phil got the lot!

He just answered in that stark manner that would unintentionally prompt further questions. She seemed really interested in his mum. No harm telling her, he thought, that she'd had a difficult birth with him. Phil in the 1930s arrived in this world as a blue baby. And he had to have a complete blood transfusion at birth.

His auntie Edna had explained it to him once, something about he was born Rhesus Positive but mum's blood was Rhesus Negative, something about blood cells not mixing well.

"So what and whose blood did you end up with?"

"I think I'm in the 'O' category," he said with no confidence.

Mandy was, after all, a medical secretary. Maybe she could find out for him the accurate intricacies of blood and heritage but as far as he was concerned, he would always be the son of a cockney docker and of a mother who didn't take any crap from anyone.

She loved his nature but more so the pure physical release she could share with him, a trait that was diminishing within her marriage to David of seven years. Mandy could tell that Phil was not only a confident lover in himself but he exuded trust in her. There was something in the fact that she was a married woman that comforted him and even more with him being a single, foot loose and fancy free guy that excited her.

Their motel nights were coming to a close. They were private enough not to raise any suspicions though Debra did wonder, and asked Phil why he would disappear in the evening and night times so much. If anyone knew Mandy inside out, it was her cousin Debra, but she said nothing. Phil would actually take off back to Germany the morning of David's return from the rigours of the North Sea that September. It was such a shame they might never meet again.

It would be nine months later, on the nail, that The Greyhound would be packed full of the regular villagers in celebration. After trying so hard for seven years in and out of clinics and medical specialists, Mandy gave birth to a bouncing baby boy. David, a proud father, was ecstatic.

He was never to know. For that matter, nor was Phil.

CHAPTER 11

MONTE CARLO OR BUST

"I trust this vantage point is just what you want?" Milton Smythe suggested as he introduced Ray to his coastal haven overlooking Portsmouth Harbour.

"It's an amazing sight, this Armada, I just can't believe the number of warships, carriers and support craft we've put together. What a way to start a war!" Ray replied, more in awe than close scrutiny.

It was the back end of the Easter holidays in 1982 and Britain's 'task force' was setting sail for the Falkland Islands, now in the firm grip of the Argentine invaders. Prime Minister Thatcher made no bones about it, the assembled force with horns ablasting were to navigate the entire Atlantic to take on and take back the islands within weeks.

Both Ray and Milt were not men of war, the latter a deep pacifist steeped in religion, and the former had endured a bucket load in his troubled youth. Ray, however, was delighted to have a rare opportunity to view the event unfolding before his searching eyes. He was with canvas to record the scene from Milt's third floor balcony from the western side of the harbour. The view was uninterrupted, the elevation just perfect, and the light from a bright spring day unyielding.

Milt spent the day, tidying up his second 'retirement' home, regularly interrupted with trips to the kitchen to prepare his percolated coffee in the morning, Earl Grey tea for the afternoon and more than a drop of his favoured claret in the early evening. The two colleagues' situation could not be further in substance from the stern reality of the power and the violence of the Royal Navy finally by late afternoon disappearing from view to meet their impending fate.

Their conversation that sunny day was a backdrop to Ray's task at hand, to picture and record the scene but very much to reminisce comfortably on their mutual life at Sandlehurst. They were equally instrumental in their separate ways of channelling the spiritual and organisational platform for the school, to what JJ was to continually refer to as the Halcyon Years.

They were contented with their combined toil of fifteen years which now had resulted by 1982 in record numbers of boarders and day pupils. These young hopefuls had enjoyed the benefits of a very stable staffroom with the only additions being mainly confined to part-time teachers or highly specialised recruits. It was also fair to say that since the election of the Conservative Thatcher government, shortly to be re-elected for another four years, preparatory schools were a solid haven and were actively encouraged to offer an independent primary education option.

Indeed it was a good fit even though Milt and Ray would both be considered on the liberal side of conservatism that they thrived in their own separate disciplines and lifestyles. Ray's family was growing up fast and by the mid-decade with the exception of young Michael, all four were fleeing the nest to follow their own careers. Interestingly none of them were attracted to a university education, preferring the lure of apprenticeships in banking, design, electronics and travel. Sue, Janet, Peter and Imogen like their parents forged very separate interests into careers. Ray was proud of such diversity if rather disappointed that none of his children had blazed an academic path to a university education. Domestically both Sarah and Ray like so many parents were quietly relieved that the pull of the capital and independent living was strong in all four children.

Thus, it would not be long before the couple would be celebrating their silver 'jubilee', and with all the children bar Michael off their hands. Yes, Sarah quite rightly could expect to spend a lot more quality time with her husband in holidays, re-establishing former acquaintances and following potential new interests. With the school breaks and still living independently from the Sandlehurst premises they had one precious commodity, and that was time.

Yet, did they? Ray, without gleaning it himself, had taken on some specific traits from his father, Freddie. In middle age, he just evolved more into his job than into his family. Whereas Sarah saw more free time as an opportunity to relive their single years together, Ray had started to contemplate life as a series of projects to be taken on, developed and mastered.

Milt, who essentially was one of the bricks in the building that was Sandlehurst, instantly recognised Ray's journey throughout the school. The expansion of art as a subject matter into the realms of sculpture and design, the London trips for staff and pupils to notable galleries and exhibits and the introduction of adult evening classes at the school all propelled Ray's involvement as a central part of what Sandlehurst could offer current pupils, prospective parents and clearly beyond to the community at large.

His history, his own unique past as a trainee artist at school classes in Sydney, his infamous postcard communications and his infatuation with art décor and design were all opening doors and expanding horizons. Notably these skills were channelled inhouse and found natural avenues in linkages to other school departments like music and geography. Although they were in the planning stage, school trips to concerts, museums, cultural events and even by liaison with the language department, overseas visits were soon to be part of Ray's portfolio.

Twice weekly, informal strategic meetings to activate these aspirations were held with staff room stalwarts and close colleagues Mick, Rick, Ian and Mary. They were often joined by the friendly neighbour Milt, ostensibly to plan, but in reality to further their joint indulgence in the bacchanalian arts and sciences in the lounge bar of the King's Arms. They outpaced and outlasted a string of bartenders, who to a man and a woman, had followed the very English tradition of post-hours drinking for the locals by proclaiming they were hosting a private party after the eleven o' clock deadline. The Hurst crew, without doubt, had kept the pub afloat throughout the 80s as the 'Arms' itself was morphing towards the fine dining aspect of hospitality.

In many respects, that development even tightened the bond amongst the Hurst drinking set, as their own partners could be easily placated by a hearty and increasingly exclusive meal at the King's Arms. It became a very pleasant evening out for the other halves, as the culture of the local public house almost took on a stranglehold on the lives of these families. It also helped that the proprietor, Geoff, was a former butcher and his wife Wendy had early training as a chef. In the mid '80s it was unheard of for pubs to offer steak soirees or curry nights, but Geoff and Wendy were years ahead of their time in taking the British hostelry away from crisps, peanuts and pork scratchings.

Mick Greatbatch ever the musician inevitably was always to be tempted away to the public bar where a stone floor gave way to the simple pleasures of draught hand pulled ales, the customary Wurlitzer Juke Box and company more in line with his desires, that were of course, the local young women. He was always happier with the school's kitchen and secretarial staff along with the local village ladies, but probably this was not surprising as he ran a studio bachelor flat on the outskirts of Crowborough. So he hopped between bars often rather ungallantly leaving his regular partners, a pair of young twenty-something identical twins, Laura and Linda to their own devices. These two very resourceful ladies ran a mobile hot dog and burger van based in the carpark of the Crowborough rail station, but also were to be seen and valued along the south coast and at race meetings at Goodwood and Lingfield.

No one at the school could determine whether Laura or Linda, or both, was his 'special one'. Rick Cranley added the theory that neither did Mick! The rumour that floated around at the time that on many occasions the rock guitarist gave up on telling the difference, just took the two girls in turns!

To more sane propositions, the drinking set at the Arms had several projects on the agenda that Mick and all the others had to give their full attention to over the coming months and years.

Every meeting had an agenda and all such convenings were to be held at 'The Library' - the lounge bar of the King's Arms to anyone else. Hot on the list was the expansion of the activities of the school during these halcyon years, including the productions of Christmas pantomimes/nativity plays and the hiring out of the extensive playing fields in the school holidays to specialist courses for sport. In addition the commercial use of the school hall for musical functions and practice along with outside letting of the facilities for independent dinners, weddings and the like were also on the menu.

Sandlehurst was opening its doors after all these years. The public relations role was to increase, but step by step only. The altruistic stance of Rick Cranley and his 'Library' cronies was there to hide very individual, but social agendas of their own. In short, Ray wanted exhibitions of his art and pantos; Mick wanted to make a comeback by recording an LP at the school; Ian dreamed of his own 'Ian Easton Academy for Cricket'. Last but by no means least, Rick himself announced that he had just secured his engagement to Scottish distillery heiress Eileen McDowell and insisted that the marriage and reception be held at Sandlehurst with the Reverend Smythe as the minister!

Above this entourage stood fanatical support from one quarter, that of the carefree JJ. The Headmaster's personal interests beyond and within the school were in travel, promotion, cricket, fine wines including malt whiskies, and all manner of leisure and entertainment! The new accessibility of the school's vital assets, its grounds, manor house and the willingness of his staff to indulge in broad-based extracurricular pursuits were all exactly what the Head valued in a thriving, ambitious school.

Ironically, the break on all this expansion was the group of governors that acted with shrewd assessment on which projects could be classified as priorities. In this respect, there was a connection between Rick Cranley and one member of the De Vere family. Rick also needed a sounding board to bounce his ideas off and here he very privately confided in one Ray Bristowe. Both men had understood the governors' concerns of too much simultaneous expansion. Therefore, between them an informal five year plan was drawn up which prioritised one area of novel development over another.

Cranley acknowledged that behind every initiative the underlying motive was to achieve a measured growth in school numbers. Yes there was local competition aplenty but Sandlehurst had to be known throughout south-east England as always being one step ahead of the game. Shrewdly, he gave the green light to Ray's proposal for the Christmas of 1983 to embark upon a musical pantomime. He knew that this would embrace the staff, the parents, the children and the ancillary skills of Mick Greatbatch. The promotional value of such a venture shedding cultural light on top of quality academic performance at the school would enhance its reputation for offering an all round education.

The December performances of Cinderella also heralded one more significant element. That September, Sandlehurst was open to all classes, but mainly in the younger year groups, to....girls! The governors had tossed this subject around for some time but after one term and with the inclusion of girls as personnel in Rick, Ray and Mick's panto, all agreed it was a stellar move. After over half a century of primary education, Sandlehurst had gone co-ed.

The panto itself was well selected in the light of how the school was evolving with the audiences well versed in the irony of the girl portrayed as Cinders 'going to the Ball' as the clear parallel to girls reaching their ambition, to enter the gates of Sandlehurst. Ray's set and costumes, very much influenced by Sarah, added so much to a production that was brilliantly stage managed by Rick Cranley. Apart from the full houses on three separate evenings JJ, who was present at all three, noticed that the office in January was overwhelmed by applications to the school, principally from girls!

There was one other noticeable effect from the Christmas panto success, and that was in the status of music in the school. Up until December '83, Mick was only operating as a peripatetic music tutor who responded to demand in pupil requests mostly in out of school hours and at weekends. This was now to change.

His interpretation of the musical content of Cinderella was both intuitive and inventive as he caught the moods of the play, sad, bad and glad with individual and collective scores originally penned by his working with a Sussex five-piece band called 'Forbidden Fruit'. Armed with instrumentation which included an accordion and a fiddler the band produced an eclectic range of mood music. Their leader mysteriously named 'Bing' had played ten years earlier in Mick's heyday as a junior member of his group but was still very much part of the rocker's social entourage around Crowborough.

Henceforth, the music department was born and its home would be based around the old scout hut. This dilapidated building was to get more than a lick of paint, but what Mick was really attracted to was its low ceiling and subsequent sound quality. This could be widely exploited at will as the hut was conveniently located fifty yards downhill from the main school building. The sound at any pitch, was supremely self-contained – Mick was in heaven!

Cranley now got to work. Over the next eighteen months he passed through legislation as he fondly put it to open up the school for art classes for locals, adults that were keen to learn from Ray's thirty years' experience", all to be held in winter at evening times, whilst in summer, Mr Bristowe would entertain 'Art in the Fields'. Groups of Ray's followers would embark on day trips to chalk, riverine and coastal landscapes to join together in mutual projects.

If the local adults were not of an artistic bent, then they could sign up their children and offer themselves as mentors at Ian Easton's Cricket Academy which was active all through the summer holidays. For the dads, the highlight was for them to join Ian's midweek evening cricket invitational team that played limited over games all at home at Sandlehurst. Coaching for the sons in the daytime and beer for the dads on many a sunny summer's evening with 'The Invincibles' were twin pillars of the sport at the school.

Sandlehurst was sailing a very happy ship. This was no better illustrated than in 1986 with the marriage of Rick Cranley. His predisposition for taking golf breaks up in Scotland had not only improved his handicap but also had resulted in his meeting a vivacious young woman, ten years his junior, working as a public relations consultant for golf at St Andrews. They had enjoyed a long engagement back to 1984, but as was always his desire, he needed to bring her south and it was that which would take a long time.

His patience, only really seeing her properly in the long Sandlehurst holidays, had paid off, as the heiress to a small Scottish distillery would say yes to matrimony with all the trimmings of a "Garden of England" wedding in the April of 1986. It was a match made in heaven. Mick, normally late at night at the Kings Arms, would regularly ask the deputy headmaster why, by the mid-forties, he had never married. The answer Rick had offered was,"The right millionairess has not come along!!"

Well she had now. Sandlehurst hosted the wedding of the decade, officiated at that point by a very sober but joyous minister, the Reverend Smythe at the church of St Barnabas. Hundreds attended the event with a very healthy contingent from north of the border. The latter had a marked influence on the reception as it did seem, to everyone's delight, that the event was unofficially sponsored by Eileen's family products. Wine and whisky flowed amongst the second act of the Union! They were all there, JJ and his wine buffs, Ian's cricket squad, Geoff and Wendy's catering staff, Mick's 'twins', and the band of 'Forbidden Fruit', all ensconced in the spacious entertainment rooms, hosted as a wedding venue, with accommodation available for the very first time at Sandlehurst.

Even Ray, Sarah and the kids stayed on for that Saturday night and Sunday morning. Despite the elaborate merriment throughout the evening afforded by Bing's band of latter-day hippies and travelling minstrels, Ray had decided prior to the event to keep an even keel, to celebrate, but not to overindulge.

As the evening approached midnight, he may have been the one person there to have noticed a standout fact. His mind had easily clicked back to the church service where he had sat in a row of pews immediately behind the De Vere family. Yet, he had not noticed a single one of the revered ensemble attend the prolonged reception at Sandlehurst. Odd that, he thought. Over the coming months of 1987 and '88, the ghost of the De Veres was to prove to haunt him, but him alone at that juncture.

The final years of the decade reinforced earlier problems that had never been solved in England. Hooliganism at sports events, the growing chasm between rich and poor, resignations at the government's cabinet level over trade deals and the choice of whether to align with America or Europe were all symptoms of a political administration that had been in office too long. Was it always the case, Ray wondered, that the British could never sustain success for very long, ultimately giving way to complacency?

The 'feel' in the country was just not the same as earlier in the 80s with the positive lasting effects of the Falklands campaign and the rise subsequently in the economic fortunes of the nation. Confidence had come with the offshore flow of North Sea oil, but as time revealed, the benefit of the oil and gas boom was directed into the pockets of the big multinationals.

Ray had laboured hard to help in the process of establishing Sandlehurst near the very top of the educational tree. Yet was it his scepticism that observed an ageing Keith Tremlett nod off in classes, notably at staff meetings and often just retreat into a vacant stare into space in his familiar seat in the Common Room? Also, why was Rick Cranley sending too many apologies for missing 'library' sessions at the King's Arms? It was also a great shame that Mary was to leave and take up a new post, a headship in the summer of '88. Ray set himself down in the art room at the top of the stairs, and opened the window to peruse the scene outside around the school. The view was panoramic, he could see everything from up there, but that was the point, he saw nothing. It had dawned on him, even alarmed him, that there had been no new building in twenty years. Much had been promised but very little delivered. Time was starting to pass Sandlehurst by, and yes, since the middle of the decade the academic curriculum and examination results were stagnant at best.

Ray would confide in Sarah over his concerns, and had hinted that they must be aware of planning for their future. What really tipped the balance that summer of '88 were two incidents that would impact on the reputation of the school. Ian Easton, as master in charge of cricket, was ultra competitive as the coach and mentor to the boys. Yet he stringently believed in the traditions of fair play that was engrained in this most English of sports. Thus, the visit of rival Sussex school, Glengale, was the highlight of the season.

So with all the staff commandeered into support and Keith Tremlett's scoreboard ready to roll, Glengale won the toss and elected to bat at 2pm. They batted slowly only getting to 95 runs with 6 wickets down at 'Tea' time, 4pm, the all-important cultural break! Then instead of the time-honoured tradition of declaring their innings, they unbelievably continued on for twenty minutes more after tea until 4.30pm, only leaving Sandlehurst 80 minutes to chase their final total of 114. This was scandalous to all present, none more so than to Ian Easton who regrettably refused to send out his batsman for the Sandlehurst 'reply'. Game abandoned!

This unprecedented incident caused unsavoury comments between the coaches, the parents and between both headmasters attending the annual game. Headlines appeared in the mid-Sussex sports news, as the altercation was regarded as a public relations disaster. Although both Ray and JJ supported Ian's actions, the Headmaster became more sensitive to the reaction of the governors when a letter of strong reprimand appeared on his desk on the Monday morning.

Then Rick Cranley made the decision for the first time in five years not to produce the Christmas panto in 1988. In fact the annual extravaganza was cancelled. There followed a great deal of consternation the autumn following at that announcement, notably when on three evenings per week in November, the deputy head had thrown his hand in to cut a record, to produce a new CD along with Mick as the sound engineer for 'Forbidden Fruit'. It took the best part of November when the scout hut was not only out of bounds for pupils, but complaints from a variety of sources were aimed at this external development over the noise and the overall mess the 'recording studio' was left in after the numerous sessions.

The governors had appointed a new bursar in September that year, and his mission was to run a fine line of assessment through the finances and the day to day practices at the school. By December, he had already banned any further use of the facilities, notably the sports grounds and the scout hut, without his prior permission. These assets had to yield revenue. There were to be no more private arrangements, nor personal favours for preferential staff usage. Both Ian's cricket academy and the musical outlet of the scout hut would be under the bursar's control.

What was not under the Bursar's control was the First XI's impending cricket tour of Cape Town and the Western Province of South Africa. Scanned into the school calendar inevitably fixed by JJ, Sandlehurst was to participate in the annual Cape's Schools' Cricket Festival for junior and preparatory schools. The headmaster caused a bit of a furore earlier in the year by announcing it would take place over Christmas, but subsequent detail (i.e. wholesale complaints from the spouses of the staff males) revealed that the sixteen boy party with four lead masters would fly direct to the Cape on the day after Boxing Day.

Another solid reason for this was the selection of the Reverend Milton Smythe as team umpire. Inevitably he did have to face other pressing engagements at this time of year, notably the service at St. Barnabas over Christmas Eve and Christmas Day. With Ian Easton keen to resurrect the good name of Sandlehurst after the Glengale debacle earlier in the year it was still inevitable that he would lead the coaching but it was JJ who would ask one Raymond

Bristowe to manage the party. In true JJ style, he made the proposal back in August in The King's Arms,

"I say, ole boy, think it would be right for you to lead the group, leaving me to roam around, you know, a roving ambassadorial role amongst so many South African big hitters. I've got a colleague of mine to set up the tour organisation, specialist travel group for private schools. They even donate a kit bag for every one of the boys."

Yes, it was to be very much a trip for the boys, no females in sight. This would be cricket, loverly cricket with the intervening spaces taking advantage of tourism (Boden's Travel Group supplied their own courier for the entire trip of ten days) and for the adults, numerous tours of the winelands centred around Stellenbosch and nearby Paarl.

Ray was no fool, he just knew that December the 27th, Heathrow Airport, sixteen kids aged between 11 and 14 and the Christmas rush could well end up as a seasonal nightmare. As it transpired, the Travel Rep turned out to be one of those cricket geeks that even Keith Tremlett would have bowed before. So, no worries there then.

The underlying problems were within the staff. Ian Easton had to be on a short lead of control as the cricket tournament was essentially a festival with no overall winner, just a series of matches in the shadow of Table Mountain over a five day period in early January. Could he and would he curb those competitive juices? As for JJ, he would be a law unto himself as he just had too many contacts to reacquaint himself with and too many brochures to hand out to interested parties that were keen to send their young South Africans to an English education, a Sandlehurst education.

The umpire of the group, Milt, was the focus of Ray's attention during these sunny days. Milt had endured just too many days and nights at The King's Arms in recent years and had developed a frequent habit of unreliability, such as completely forgetting appointments even amongst his parishioners. The demon drink was winning his battle and here they all were with three days off before the opening of the festival. It was inevitable that he spent two days touring wine farms at Spier and his favourite Boschendaal. His other skeleton in the cupboard was his stance as a fervent anti-apartheid campaigner. Ray stuck to him like glue when in company with other South African umpires and officials. There could be fireworks at any opportunity to express his views that were vehemently opposed to the apartheid regime.

Apart from losing JJ for much of the time, although to be fair he was to be seen pacing around the boundary's edge sporting his slacks, sandals and bright red and yellow MCC tie at every game. The festival was a true gathering of cricket lovers played under a warm Cape summer sun on immaculately mowed fields. Milt luckily was to remark in Sandlehurst company that it was a disgrace that all the groundsmen and tea ladies were Cape coloured. It was still a very friendly atmosphere for the boys but apartheid South Africa was there for all to see. JJ oblivious to politics simply knew Africa too well.

Boden's travel rep, Howard Pollard, seemed to be as pleased as punch with the smooth running of the tour especially with so many young lads to control. Well that was the case until the last day when JJ casually announced that he would not be travelling back with the group. His reason: "Just thought I'd pop back via Nairobi and Gilgil, family matters!"

Howard clearly flustered with the disruption this would cause, eventually absorbed the omnipotence of the Headmaster. However, all hell let loose at D.F. Malan Airport when Milton Smythe arrived at the terminal as drunk as a skunk and was refused by British Airways to join the party to board the plane later that evening.

Evidently he, or so Ray and Ian thought, had been chosen to umpire the prestigious last match between two Cape schools from 12 to 5pm, then he was to taxi to the airport ready for the flight. This did not occur as on arrival at the Rondebosch school ground, he fell into an extreme altercation with the festival's organiser about the lack of non-white players, umpires and officials at the event. He simply refused to umpire and took off in a taxi to explore more wine farms for the afternoon.

To this day, with all the embarrassment for the boys and some of their parents, no one knew what got into Milt that day, but with the roving headmaster also in absentia, Boden's Tour Company took a very poor view of the Sandlehurst staff's lack of responsibility, despite all of Ray's sweet talking. It was another nail in the school's coffin, proven by the actions of Bodens who did write formally to the headmaster and bursar to issue a decree that the company did not wish to conduct any further business or collaboration with Sandlehurst Preparatory school!

Furthermore, there were to be no more cricket invitations from South Africa.

These were merely small fry when compared to the capers of JJ. The headmaster for as long as anyone could remember had insisted his Middle-Eastern and African promo interludes were paid for by the prospective clients, money up front in cash only as forward payments for the initial year of the boy's attendance. Nevertheless, with the new bursar following the paper trail, all of JJ's activities had to be accountable. After all, by the end of the 1980s, JJ had made the crucial error of claiming expenses from the school which produced an almighty row between bursar, governors and the headmaster.

Rumours were rife throughout 1989 that the Head had been rumbled, notably when it was leaked that his recruitment journeys were punctuated by returns via the gaming tables of Monte Carlo. No one could prove anything, because JJ simply for two decades had deposited cash payments into the school account with validated names of origin attached. No one had even dared or thought of questioning him. JJ now had passed his 60th birthday and sadly there were no birthday parties anymore, even his infamous Friday evening staff soirees were limited to two a term. He was clearly on the run and his wings had been abruptly clipped internally by an overzealous bursar and interfering governors.

It was not just an internal Sandlehurst phase. Not only were more modern methods of accounting applying to the school, but there were also more external rigorous checks and inspections of all kinds on health and safety, buildings

255

insurance, teacher qualifications and child protection. In short, even in the independent sector of education, the firm fist of the state and government agencies were directing their rules and regulations onto schools like Sandlehurst.

The pervading atmosphere at this bastion of traditional values now was tense, insecure and neurotic with nothing that the staff could do about it. The bubble had burst. Local reaction to the incidents of the previous year with the unwelcome publicity resulted in alarming drops in pupil application. Throughout the autumn term, it was noticeable that unknown official adult faces were visiting the school, never seen before. What indeed were they up to?

It was December 3rd, midmorning break, when JJ gave his daily address. Ray had noticed a watery-eyed headmaster, with lined skin complexion excessively pale almost with the bottom knocked out of a once proud vocal range, entered the staffroom and simply announced,

"Ladies and Gentlemen, fellow staff members and loyal colleagues, my time has come. I shall be taking early retirement as from immediate effect. Sandlehurst has been our lives, together we built something very special. All good things must come to an end."

At that, he shuffled away into the mists of time.

Twelve months later, the governors declared the cessation of educational provision at Sandlehurst. A multinational group of bankers had taken over the estate with further announcements to be made in the near future.

For the first time in his life, Ray Bristowe was without employment and salary at the age of fifty seven. He was devastated.

CHAPTER 12

TUBBY'S TASK FORCE

Phil was more than grateful for his time at The Greyhound with Mike and Debra, and inevitably as a busy woman, it was the landlady who would have the last word. As he climbed into the taxi to the station, she passed him a sellotaped brown envelope,

"You take care now, and follow the instructions inside," she ordered.

He opened the package. It read,

'Waterloo, Heathrow. Use this air ticket to Schipol, then taxi to De Ruyter Hotel, Amsterdamse-Weg, Amstelveen. See you for dinner this evening, T'

All this did not phase Phil Bristowe. When any communication ended with the letter T, he was disposed to follow orders, right down to the details of reciting his operational passport and Luxembourg bank identity numbers. The latter sometimes was a challenge as there were three more additional numbers, but he convinced himself it was no big deal as that account would only be used for a rainy day.

Short term journeys were water off a duck's back for him, so before he even blinked, he was in a Dutch taxi deep in conversation with a local taxi driver, all in English, debating whether the new football star Johan Cruyff was a better player than Bobby Charlton. It never ceased to amaze him how these uneducated continentals could speak his own mother tongue better than his London mates down at the docks!

"Room number 10, first floor sir, can I take your bags?" the bell boy asked. Phil followed him up one flight of stairs in this very elegant four-star hotel adjacent to yet another elongated canal. "Enjoy your stay at the De Ruyter," uttered the lad, as Phil opened his door to reveal a large room with a double bed and two decorative armchairs. All very high standard and orthodox, but with one exception. The armchairs were occupied!

"How the hell did you two get in here?" Phil screamed in total amazement.

"Never you mind, we have much to discuss," said Terry with a look for reassurance from Pat Rose.

"So you've brought out the heavy furniture, eh Tel," said Phil, shaking Paddy's hand, "It's been, what, only two or three weeks and I've missed you, you Rhodie rat!" he added.

After these greetings of mutual tomfoolery, Terry got down to business in a two hour long session with Phil on the subject and object of his latest engagement. He grilled the Londoner on every aspect of his time in Rhodesia and over the border in Mozambique. They talked at length on why and how they lost one, the only young soldier in their platoon. Then Paddy pushed him on the foxhole attack with grenades, asking whether his unit had completed the job and finished the Frelimo off. The 'Selous' never left any evidence behind as clearly Phil knew that their operations were under cover and top secret. Intelligence and information were crucial in the 'Bush' for both parties. No prisoner, no cry!

Phil answered these pointed questions as best he could, but under pressure there were holes in his recollection of events, not so much in his details but noticeably to his two inquisitors in his recall of the sequences of action. Then suddenly, Terry interjected,

"How's your left ear, still tingling a bit?"

As usual, Phil rejected any defect. What he had not absorbed was Patrick's seat position in relation to him adjacent to Phil's left-hand side. Then Paddy took on the role of information leader as he came to the point of the exercise.

"We want you to have a simple medical tomorrow, no big deal, just a few x-rays and ear assessments. You've been beaten up a bit in your past, and out there on duty in Africa. We have to assess all our top men once they're over 35 and you've been very good and have a real future with us but we must decide in what capacity," he suggested.

"I'm fit as a fiddle, is all that really necessary?" Phil added,

"Phil, of course we knew about our knocks in Malaya, the grenade attack in Rhodie and your scrape with death in Fulham. We have to be sure of you," said Terry.

"How d'ya know 'bout Fulham?" said an astounded Phil.

"Listen mate, we've got your Triumph's licence plate and the names of Joanne's parents!"

"Fuck me, what sort of a set up is this?" Phil interrupted.

"Go on then, tell Paddy your two lifelong numbers," asked Terry.

Phil hesitated not on his operational passport number but he just could not get the digits of his Lux. account in the correct order. He knew he had stumbled but Tel reassured him it would all be clear by the next day.

"Let's go eat. There is a marvellous Argentine steak house down the road called Bistro Buenos Aires. Paddy went on ahead solo followed two minutes later by Terry and Phil. Terry continued, "I take it that your hospitality at the Hound was warm and friendly," he added with what amounted to a knowing glance!

Phil unbelievably was picked up the next morning by his own VW Beetle, the chauffeur being one Patrick Rose. Just how did this Selous Scout obtain the vehicle? He was soon realising that his unit would always operate beyond the law. Terry was right, ask no questions, leave all considerations to him. That of course included a full medical at a private clinic out in a back street off the main square of the city of Haarlem. X-rays, more questions, an IQ test and multiple probes prodding both ears were the order of the day. One more detail shocked Phil when a tattoo artist came to the party and inserted two long numbers, independently, one on the left and one on the right forearm. That next evening, true to form, all personnel just made their independent way home wherever that was. Terry debriefed Phil by concluding that no news was good news but he should keep all the normal lines of communication open. He bade farewell with the ominous comment, "Heh, Phil, I understand Paderborn's going well!"

Yes, Tel was well informed but by whom he wondered. He frankly was to be too busy, with the ins and outs of running what he considered was a profit making concern for a café, a library, a social centre, a bar and a mobile van. Toc H was losing money at all the other German wards with the exception of the Fergus Berlin station. Nevertheless his experiences with Terry and the unit prompted him to become more interested in world affairs notably where military flashpoints were concerned.

He noted the rising tide of oil, nationhood and the Arab struggles in the Middle East, Israel's Entebbe raid in 73, the troubles in Northern Ireland, but his special attention would always turn to Southern Africa and the independence struggles of the blacks in Mozambique, Rhodesia and South Africa. Patrick Rose had left him in no doubt that there would be unfinished business for him in Rhodesia and he assumed that the Selous Scout had in mind a rather different role. How did he sense that? Well, why all the interrogation hassles in Holland? Phil knew he was soon approaching forty in 1975, and that was the normal cut off age for active on the ground service.

Maybe he was to be considered as one of the exceptions. It had not been lost on him that Terry must have been nigh on forty-five when he initially served his duty with Phil in Rhodesia. Many thoughts were running amok in his head about his future with the unit but as Terry had warned him that no news was good news he would bide his time in Paderborn for the next phase of his workload.

Phil didn't exactly want to enter into a routine in the garrison town but he settled into a six-day week on an expenses free lifestyle. Even his Sunday outing's petrol was all paid for by the B.A.O.R. (British Army of the Rhine). Professionally he had decided to delegate his various duties by allocating real responsibility to his Toc H employees. Edgar was to, of all things, run the bar which he did very successfully by adopting a no drinks policy while he was on duty. Sophie, with a plum public schoolgirl accent, was not only the 'library queen' but also would be a great hit with the young mothers' group as a sister superior.

That left Noel, the young twenty year old gap year student, who had found the extracurricular world of Toc H far too enticing to continue with his Oxford studies. He even seemed to boast to many an audience with a rather fake American west coast accent that "I've dropped out, man!" More likely he had dropped in to many a lonely army housewife on his daily rounds on the mobile. Still Phil did not care as Noel went out full and came back empty every single day. His sales, always high, were suspiciously numerous when it came to the offloading of Phil's new cultural magazines called Mayfair and Penthouse, sure-fire hits with the troops.

That pushed the Boss with his entourage of local Paderborn German fraus to run the café. Another shrewd move as the squaddie punters would quickly pass over their pay-packets for teas, coffees, breakfast, lunch and dinners with no chat up exchanges. It would be business first. Following Phil's conversational German classes at the Hillman Language school he had continued refresher and top up classes with both Franz and Sigi over the succeeding years as well as striking up a firm social relationship with Frau Sneyder and her family.

Phil had come to gain total respect for the German nation. He enjoyed their straightforward and logical approach to life and their ability to build, to secure and to make things work. Yes he would admit at times that they did lack on the lighter side of life but hell, did they ensure that all Germans would enjoy the basics in life. He knew where this had all come from, as it was their experience of rock bottom in the immediate post war years that created this reliable work ethic.

The trains ran on time, the hard winter frosts met the efficiency of gritter and snowploughs and the autobahns could take you anywhere. More than this, German businesses and suppliers ran like clockwork and bills were paid on time. On his days off Phil would visit Hannover, Hamburg, Cologne and West Berlin and on the weekends he embarked upon trips down the Rhine on river boat shuffles where he could depend upon fine local wines and spotlessly clean hotel rooms.

Without feeling it, these years in the 70s had transformed him into a Deutsche! Yes he was Bermondsey through and through but he lived in a world where there were no strikes, no class division, no snarled up traffic, no colonial ties, no migrants crapping all over the native culture, and where the trains did run on time! Phil, as a continental worker, was a part of the German economic miracle. He viewed Britain in the days of Ted Heath and Harold Wilson as a petty, small minded nation that was losing it and losing it bigtime.

After all he faced the frontline every day – he had sat down with all ranks in his Toc H facilities from colonels to squaddies and the one recurring theme was that they all felt they were taking on the world with one arm tied behind their back. Rules and regulations set by pompous politicians with no real world experience were the norm. Yet when any real international crisis materialised the Westminster set of party pricks, civil service lackies, bent lawyers and feckless feminists would turn to them every time to protect their liberties and do their dirty work.

Phil genuinely nodded his approval for they were never, none of them, to know they were preaching to the converted. The more they yielded in detail, the more he yearned to return to the action he was so badly missing. Paderborn station by 1976 could almost run itself. The quietly assertive warden Bristowe had retained a happy staff which was highly valued by both Fergus Laird's West Berlin operation and Toc H HQ in London.

Unbelievably Noel had lasted the course for five years and still on the mobile shop, was to hand over the keys to Phil for the VW's annual check up. His boss would speed it down to the base where some transport engineers would give it the once over. Turning on the ignition he noticed that Noel had left one of his girly magazines on the passenger side. Phil was not impressed. They were not meant for public viewing. He did quite naturally take a peek inside and on the inside cover was a postcard of Tower Bridge. On the back, it read;

"Downstream, you know where, first of the next month, 11am. T"

The next time he summoned Noel into his office asking the obvious question. The youngster pleaded he knew nothing of the 'mag' nor where it had come from. Phil knew T was taking a risk but there was no doubting that he sensed that 'Big Brother' was watching his every move. He needed this time to get things straight with Terry, that he wanted to control his own destiny on where and when he was to be deployed.

It wasn't to be. The Angel always opened its doors at eleven and that was the case on that August morning. There was a new bartender on duty, a lady clearly pissed off with Phil's punctuality and the cheek of the foreign bloke upstairs. Phil took the stairs two at a time.

"Blimey, never thought I'd see you in my own manor," said Phil,

It was the Selous Scout himself, Paddy Rose. "Phil, it's getting hot in the south, fucking steaming. We need you to command an entire unit until the end of the year."

"How'm I gonna get four months clear and where's Terry?"

"All that's been cleared, you're to have an ear operation here in the UK with appropriate recuperation time," he winked.

"What, down in Hampshire again? Can't wait," Phil replied.

"Nah, you idiot, that will be the cover for your job in Germany. Toc H should have received the letter by now and they will be appointing a Miss Trescothick to fill in for you during your medical leave. She will be informed tomorrow while you are on the first plane to Johannesburg. As for T he'll be at Jan Smuts to welcome you."

"Hold it, Paddy, what about all those tests back in Holland, you never got back to me?"

"No news was good news, you passed it with flying colours. This mission you'll be leading a sub-team, details from T."

Philip Bristowe had made the grade in this clandestine world, an underworld, and he was to go on in a leadership role alongside the tag of being a military adviser but still working covertly. His second tour of Rhodesian duty was a thankless task of protecting the oil route up through the Transvaal, Beit Bridge, and through Bulawayo into petrol sanctioned Rhodesia. Their mission was to deliver, by night covertly, millions of gallons of fuel to dumps across the southern section of Rhodesia. Officially to the world, South

266

Africa was not feeding the oil to the Smith Rhodesian Front government but the running of these supplies was paramount to the white controlled state's survival. The transit journeys would be perilous.

It was a fact that six, seven years on it was the Zanla guerrillas that were attacking these convoys within Rhodesia that was so dangerous to all combatants. Phil's group lost many drivers and guards as his group of counterinsurgents took on the ambushing guerrillas of Robert Mugabe. This time it was lethal, but with national service extended for all Rhodesian whites for two years, Phil knew it was crunch time and with the losses in personnel he undertook the training of regular Selous Scout replacements to smash the lines of the Zanla terrorists. By his age of forty he had become an Honorary Scout, but again sustaining injuries he won many battles but was never to win this war. South Africa eventually turned its back on the colonial rule of Ian Smith, and Zimbabwe with Korean, Russian and Chinese backing, would be formed as a new nation. Britain, naturally had sold out their settlers and would foolishly financially aid Mugabe's future prospects.

As for Phil he did recover after he had made the high fall from an oil tanker that he was riding side saddle for. The damage was a smashed-up shoulder and superficial sprains and tears but he was able to continue work as the chief warden at Paderborn. What became obvious to him was that active soldiering was passing him by and this was confirmed after 'Rhodesia 2's debrief. During those months out in the bush of Rhodesia he always wondered where

Terry disappeared to after the initial briefing at the Southern Sun Hotel at Jan Smuts Airport. There, his planning and intelligence were phenomenal but as for leading the front line in all the engagements Terry was nowhere to be seen.

There was a reason. Terry had gone 'upstairs' to planning, weapons and execution, seemingly the big brother to the conflict unit that he had served in since the early days of South East Asia. The news for Phil, post-operation, was equally clear and defined. He would be working again in specific deployments alongside now an ageing Terry Jones, but the Londoner's role was to be in weapon technology. His training, no passports needed, would be in Germany and within driving distance of Paderborn!

Ever since being a kid in Bermondsey, he had been fascinated by bombs, how they were detonated, indeed how they were put together and the varied tactical uses they were put to. Now as the unstable '70s decade drew to a violent close in Iran and Iraq and nearer to home in Northern Ireland, he was rallied to the side of Intelligence, and the technical knowledge associated with weaponry. Paderborn was his base, but he could command a five day working week with weekends free. He never discovered where Terry was based but as the new decade opened up he was spending training weekends across Luneburg Heath literally playing with and detonating missiles, reprogramming them and learning how to render new systems to be inoperable. He had to keep up with a fast-changing technology.

Some weekends, under cover, both of them would be taxied across the border into France to unknown installations to gain parallel expertise in the understanding of their weaponry development which was the most advanced of the western world outside of the USA. By early 1982 Terry was so regularly meeting Phil that he no longer needed any over the border rendezvous. They simply would diarise liaisons at popular cafes in civilian gear. It was early March when all their training over the previous five years was to come to fruition as they were to be the brains behind a commando group that was to be jetted into far away Santiago in Chile and then airlifted down to what did seem to be the last town of civilisation at the tip of the South American continent. This time their expertise was tied to a special forces group as Britain prepared their task force of thousands. Terry's unit, all ten of them, had specific instructions very simply to steal or to render inoperable the prized but limited in number Argentine deadly missiles, known as the French Exocet radar guided missile. The British government had secured a secret deal with Chilean dictator, Pinochet, to allow free passage to the Magellan Straits and the adjoining border territory into Argentina of small insurgent forces. Allied intelligence had revealed that all the Argentinian exocets would be deployed from airstrips in the deep south close to the Chilean border.

The Falklands crisis would kick off between April and the middle of June, giving just two to three months for Terry and his partner to do the damage. So secret were the missions that nobody knew of their intent nor means of gaining access to Argentinian airfields. Were they successful? Terry and Phil yet again survived but never were to say a word. It was, however, reported that two British ships hit in the Falklands Sound by exocets received direct fire damage but took over three days to sink. Evidently all naval personnel and experts on the scene claimed the missiles had not been detonated. No one knew why. Or how!

There were to be no Portsmouth welcome home parades for Terry and Phil. They, after all, belonged to a band of men that plied their trade in the shadows. There was time for conversation between the two on the long journey back to Germany. The two men were inseparable as Terry had become the blood brother that Phil never had. As they parted at Hanover airport, Phil back to his Paderborn fortress and Terry to God knew where, there was an air of finality, an atmosphere that pervaded the thoughts of the two men independent of each other. They were getting long in the tooth for these trials and tribulations. Only time would tell.

* * *

Phil collapsed onto the softness of his bed, sorely missed all these weeks. Then he noticed a note on the floor by the apartment front door. He jumped up and opened it. It was on one of those flowery headed notepaper sheets, popular with the girls. It was from Sophie, in pristine writing, "Glad to have you back – Dinner at my flat tomorrow night?"

Sophie Trescothick had slid into a man's world two years before by virtue of birth as the daughter of Toc H's Commissioner and by escape from a messy divorce. Out of the comfortable shires she flew into what was generally considered social work. As with Phil, Paderborn had provided the perfect hiding place. Now she was to make the first of a series of daring moves to further her political career within the structure of Toc H and it would directly impact Paderborn's chief warden.

Phil from the start distrusted her. She was not like his mother, Ingrid and Sigi, or even Carolina, all of whom would roll their sleeves up, put in a shift, then early in the evening spend thirty minutes in the bathroom and come out looking like a million dollars. How many men could do that?

Ms Trescothick, as she insisted on being addressed, was like the public-school head girl who would preach, do as I say, not as I do. She was the new kind of woman, who loved to be respected for her independent status but had been put through a private education costing thousands from daddy's pockets. When it came to any kind of problem or hardship she invariably would do a bunk leaving other mere mortals to clear up her mess.

"Well, Phil, what do you think of my pad?" she uttered as Frau Sneyder served the first course of prawn cocktail,

"Blimey, how did you get a housekeeper? Has she cooked the meal as well?"

"Oh yes, since your leave of absence, I have, how shall we say, co-opted her to help me in the flat at weekends." Cheeky bitch, Phil thought, who the hell did she think she

271

was? Sophie continued to drop the bombshell, "Phil, Toc H headquarters, have directed me to be the full time Paderborn Head Warden. Here is my letter of appointment," she said, thrusting the headed notepaper across to Phil.

He just sat there, waiting for further explanation.

"They have not forgotten you, Phil. I was informed you have been given a promotion too. Isn't that marvellous? Here is the letter to you, confirming the new post of roving Warden," she added.

The Bermondsey boy ripped open the communique, and yes there it was, the instruction from General Secretary, Gilbert Woodall, co-signed by the Chief Warden for Germany, Fergus Laird of West Berlin. The letter served as a commendation of Phil's earnest drive not only to broaden the scope of the social services provided, but also to achieve a healthy profit. It was Toc H's intention to re-evaluate their approach and they required Phil, as a single man, to spread his methods across the wards of West Germany.

He was to achieve this by spending a period of six months in each of the five stations at Bielefeld, Verden, Osnabruck, Munster and finally back at Paderborn. His next three years of employment had been mapped out for him without any consultation. So there he was staring Sophie in the face, yielding a decade's diligent application of budgeting, organising supplies and services and dealing with error prone personnel, all to hand it on a plate to a privileged example of mediocrity.

"Don't worry about me coping with the workload," she confided, "I will be working very closely with Fergus on supplies, and he will take a supporting role in the annual raising of accounts."

Phil, by then on his favourite 'Sneyder' dessert, nearly choked on his mousse chocolat, contemplating the cosy little arrangement. He had always thought that Fergus, over the years, had visited Paderborn a bit too often and now was beginning to realise why. His head was abuzz, something definitely was afoot. Was all this to be placed at Terry's doing as he had always suspected from the beginning that there was an indirect link between Toc H and the activities of the Unit. To his core, how could anyone imagine such linkage? For it was intangible to connect two such unlikely bedfellows, but that was why such covert action worked. His analysis at the meal with Sophie, and beyond, was that she was never to know these decisions had been made far above her realm. He was sure that Terry and Paddy were instrumental here so he just waited and waited for three long years. The roving role again was ideal for his security as he never really had enough time to get to know the various personnel at the wards. He did, however, have his work cut out as he launched into their mutual financial deficits and archaic work patterns and practices.

There were low assignments in the military towns of Bielefeld and Osnabruck but highlights at coastal Verden, pulsating times when he did briefly report in to 80s West Berlin with all the attractions of a world city steeped in intrigue, and he was never to forget his return to Munster.

The latter was particularly interesting as Barry Van Der Wilt was still running the show, but he had dispensed with Bentinck-Budd who had been another casualty of mental problems associated with his drinking. The irony of Munster's personnel was now that Barry had instigated his replacement to be his own live-in boyfriend! Ironic as Phil would spend six months observing the interaction of two effeminate work mates serving the interests of thousands of war-ready macho soldiers!

Yet, still the call never came. By 1985, finally back in Paderborn, it was all change there as well. Sophie had commandeered two new assistants, both female, one a former university friend of hers and the other a local German woman who doubled up as the café manager in the daytime and the resident housekeeper in the evenings. There was no room at the inn anymore for Frau Sneyder, pensioned off after twenty years service. That of course would not have bothered Sophie as her iron reign had been well enforced during Phil's sabbatical three years in the wilderness.

It was just the way she would look at Phil, let alone her part in his demotion to running the mobile (Noel was long gone after major rows with the Headmistress as he was prone to call her) that prompted a deep suspicion that all was not right. This allied to the continued presence of Fergus had Phil looking back over his shoulder. With no connection to Terry, Phil was called to an emergency meeting of wardens in West Berlin with Gilbert Woodall, Fergus Laird and the Toc H Commissioner himself all the way from London. When Phil entered the Berlin lair of

Fergus Laird and with no other wardens present, he smelt danger and adversity in the air. It wasn't the military kind, but a grilling of some nature was imminent. Woodall opened the proceedings.

"Philip, we have been looking over your accounts at Paderborn since 1980 and have discovered huge irregularities. Your stock taking figures simply do not add up, and we have discovered witnesses that will testify that you have been involved in black-market selling to local Germans at hugely inflated prices. Indeed, it would appear that you have personally benefited by those sales and compensating in the sales of other Toc H products by inflating their cost price to the military in our shops."

Fergus Laird then cut in by corroborating with Woodall that he with Sophie had collected the annual accounts over a period of five years and meticulously concluded that huge quantities of Black Label whisky, London gin and Russian vodka along with copious shipments of cigarettes had been side-lined off the order sheets and signed by one Philip Bristowe. The Scot then produced the accompanying sheet with Phil's signatures,

"What do you say to that?" he demanded.

"That is not my signature. Just who cooked up these lies? I worked as a Head Warden for ten years, over ten, then suddenly after 1982 when you pushed me out, to work out of Paderborn, you discover this? Do me a favour!"

"Just compare the accounts for Paderborn since Ms Trescothick took charge. They are real, no wonder she was actually able to drop prices and still break even," added the Laird.

"I bet she did, all with your little help on the side, eh Fergus," Phil stood up physically challenging the Berlin supremo.

"Now let's calm down, gentlemen. Philip, you have completed good service at Toc H," said the Commissioner, "but the proof is clear and the witnesses include a Brigadier here in Berlin who was amazed to be supplied from your sources at such an inflated cost that he reported the scandal to Mr Laird here immediately."

"Have you anything else to say?" The Commissioner had played his trump card by involving one of the highest military attachments in West Germany.

"Just, what do you intend to do about it?" added Phil.

"We are going to send you forthwith for a medical with an independent military doctor. As a result of that course of action, we will no doubt inform you. If you wish to appeal in any way, I must remind you that we have all the facts, evidence and witnesses to proceed with criminal prosecutions against you," the Commissioner warned.

Phil, having kept his head down deliberately to work singly and independently, was up the creek without a paddle. The only true character referees had either been sacked by Sophie (and Fergus!) or were of dubious association like Bentinck-Budd, Edgar and then Barry with his new boyfriend!

The official report was issued a month after the trumped up medical. Its conclusion was that Mr Bristowe had recurring absences of memory, indeed, had the effects present of cranial damage in the form of concussions received in his past. These lapses in memory meant that his

276

recollection of facts, events and happenings could not be relied upon over a period of time. The cranial impairment was exacerbated by severe damage to his left ear drum that had affected the efficiency of his hearing which could be considered operating only at 60% and deteriorating at a slow rate.

As a result of these problems which clearly had affected his work's reliability, it was with regret that Toc H services terminated his employment with three months of salary pending.

At the back of his mind, surely if there was a connection between Terry's Unit and Toc H, it would come then in February '86. The stitch-up was full proof, everyone was onside for Sophie: her dad the Commissioner, Fergus her confidant, the forged signatures, the Brigadier, and even the military medical examiner. Phil had to go with it. He would cut and run. No one would believe him against all those establishment voices. Besides, he had believed also that he had kept a secret from them all and that if they were aware of his activities within the Unit, that would just bury him six feet under.

He would head for home, but where in the hell was Terry?

Phil pondered over that question continually but he had no clue over the years if Terry had a possible home base. Even though they had fought hand in glove together in deadly theatres of war, he still knew very little personally about his loyal comrade. He never even issued any preferences for the Far East, continental USA, the Veld of Southern Africa or even nearer home anywhere in Europe.

The fact that Terry had made no semblance of a contact did worry Phil's thinking he had been put out to grass or even worse, had been eliminated altogether.

He had to turn his attention elsewhere. For Phil that was easy for a while as he was on salary and more pertinently, he was able to reside at the Toc H centre in Paderborn for another month. He had, over the years, gone beyond the simple acceptance of carrying out orders, now he regularly would ask the questions why and how? Thus, he had unfinished business in Germany. He knew that he would have to contend with the final outcome. He was out. Yet, it had left a very bitter taste in his mouth. Before returning to Blighty, he set himself two essential tasks for his own peace of mind.

Firstly, because he had kept the books as simple and straightforward as was possible, he professed to being innocent of the charges of any form of fraud or embezzlement. He was going to get to the bottom of this and his early vital clues revolved around Fergus in Berlin, the Commissioner in London and the bogus Brigadier. If he could establish a connection between the three and from there, investigate the volumes of strong alcohol and cigarettes that clearly were at the centre of this scam, then he would start to understand why and how this all happened. Clearly, Sophie had been the obvious beneficiary in terms of career progression, but Phil knew that there had to be more on offer for the Berlin supremo Fergus, and that would have been, money.

So, Phil went on a charm offensive whilst still in Paderborn. He mended fences by apologising in a note to

Sophie about his belligerent reaction in the meeting with her father and Fergus. She duly accepted his offer of dinner out in town. Although it was against his nature, he admitted he was out of order and perhaps after twenty years in the job, he was past his best. He even suggested to her that new ideas with a fresh approach was what Toc H's aim should be and that she surely was the best potential option. Sophie fielded Phil's humility with a certain amount of sympathy herself offering the possibility of her father writing an excellent reference for Phil for future employ in the UK.

"That's so kind of you, Sophie. Do you think he would do that?" asked Phil.

"The Trescothicks can be relied upon to help, we were all educated that way. Dad and my grandfather through the generations went to the same boarding school, Albemarle, in Norfolk, and I was in the first batch of girls back in '70 to attend the school. The actual school motto, in Latin of course, was "Work hard with humility.""

Phil stayed sober and continued in the same vein, one of respect and politeness. He had procured a potential reference for work, but more to the point, he had discovered a link point between the father and daughter, a common education.

Now, for the brigadier. It did not take him long to discover how many active brigadiers were in operation in the British Army of the Rhine and based in West Berlin in particular. In fact, from Phil's long list of army officer connections over the years, he produced a short list of just two at that time. His eventual collection of curriculum vitaes of their respective careers to date proved very interesting. One of them seemed to have spent his service career in far off places in Cyprus, Aden, and the Middle East in general, whilst the other had built up a formidable reputation of command on the streets of Belfast.

However, it was only the latter, who had attended Albemarle Public School and, at the same time period as the Toc H Commissioner, James Trescothick. Phil was now edging closer to the truth. He was well aware that Fergus in Berlin had been originally a squaddie, not a man of university education, but a facilitator without scruple. He had originally served in the late '60s in Ulster in the same Scottish regiment as Brigadier McNally, assigned to patrol West Belfast.

Once the Bristowe boy was back in England he would make a visit to Albemarle school as a 'guardian' to a friend's boy intending to go to that senior school. That occasion should confirm whether the two, if not three of them, as they say, went back a long time together. In simple terms his gut feelings pointed to the affirmative. He knew they were at it, but how?

Edgar, still in charge of the bar and its takings, shocked Phil into a proposal of one last night out for the boys. Phil had intended to one last throw of the dice with Paderborn's own baron of the bacchanalian arts. Yet again, Phil approached the evening as a learning experience, one in which he would allow Edgar to sing like a canary and reveal any untold gems. After two hours of inebriation at The Bitberg Beer Keller, the old timer was entering that phase of his, halfway between lucid sobriety and garrulous ineptitude.

During this no-man's land, Edgar dropped the bombshell that while Phil was absent during his own one week break each year, it was always then that Fergus or a Berlin Toc H representative would arrive to do a stock check with Edgar. He never really thought anything of it and considered it just regular procedure that Berlin needed extra stock, namely nearly always two dozen bottles of Scotch, London gin and Russian vodka along with copious numbers of cigarettes. Angus insisted on dealing with the consignment describing it as a readjustment of supplies from Head Office.

Phil was patently aware that Toc H Services were subject to virtually no tax, neither British nor German on these imported goods through Bremen or Hamburg from the UK. Only if the Berlin operation was selling these onto local Germans, was there a huge profit to be made. Phil knew one other factor, that an enormous profit would be achieved if Berlin station had the same arrangement at all the Toc H stations scattered around West Germany.

Edgar by midnight had forgotten what he had revealed to Phil earlier in the evening, inevitably continuing on imbibing until the taxi duly arrived. Phil in turn, wondered how long it would be before that taxi would become a hearse. He would see the old boy, however, right as rain, the next day's lunchtime.

Time was getting short before departure day. Phil had accumulated a great deal of gear or junk as most mothers would say. That all went off early in a trunk. His VW Passat would take him home via Barry Van der Wilt's Munster and lesser known, Billy Hughes at Bielefeld. Yes they were en route but he would instigate the same line of questioning to both of them as he had encountered with Edgar.

Before then, he needed to say his final good-bye to Frau Snyder and her family. That evening was to be a festive but in many ways sad occasion as Phil was well aware that this would be his last time with the Frau who had looked after him for so many years. Frau Snyder's daughter had married a young doctor, and it was to him that Phil directed his way late that afternoon before both would move onto dinner at the mother in law's.

Phil Bristowe was to search out for himself a full medical. A month later he would insist on another at his mother's health centre in Bermondsey. He needed a complete assessment as to his current health and potential for future demanding work. He would have both reports by both doctors within four weeks. Although he had acknowledged his left ear was forcing him to turn his head to his left on hearing in conversation, otherwise he had never felt better. He would await the news with his future at stake.

Munster beckoned with Barry ever-present with boyfriend Jules. Phil was to spend just a day each with Barry, then Billy at Bielefeld. To his delight, it was the same story. The Berlin mafia, as Barry called them, always would conduct an unannounced stock check when he was out of town with the less experienced and trusting Jules offering a very compliant welcome to the Berlin boys. One more day, and this time in Bielefeld it was Billy Hughes' turn to report that Fergus would often claim that Toc H had mistakenly overstocked the bar order and would relieve Billy of nearly one hundred bottles of hard liquor every year.

Phil remained schtuum, carefully navigating the conversations on a casual, chatty basis rather than in the form of an investigative journalist. He now knew their game and if Berlin was playing the same game with the other four Toc H stations, the ongoing profit could amount to a very healthy five figure sum per annum. It would work as long as the differing stations did not confer and Berlin knew that there was no reason in the world for them to do that. They all had their own separate internal organisation.

He had done it many times before, but Phil took the Hook of Holland car ferry to land early in the morning at Harwich, the East Anglian port that had grown into oversize since Britain's entry into the Common Market of Europe a decade earlier.

This route was convenient for another reason. Whilst in East Anglia he would now pop up to Norfolk to make that visit to Albemarle School. He had, prior to his journey, made all the arrangements to meet the school secretary late morning before his ongoing ride back to London town.

The school secretary, a Mrs Plummer, was the embodiment of a public school servant. As far as she was concerned, the world started and ended at the imposing gates of Albemarle. She clearly had been the Headmaster's right-hand woman for some time, and in effect, had preceded him. Surely she seemed to have been there shortly after the Second World War. Apologising for the Head's absence, she gave Phil the grand tour including all academic facilities and vast areas of ground for the school's emphasis on cricket and rugger.

The tour was terminated with tea and biscuits in the clubhouse. Phil couldn't believe his eyes as he perused wall to wall summer teams for cricket and on the opposite side, photographs of rugby first XV's going back to the end of the nineteenth century. Mrs Plummer drew his attention to the girls section which had begun in 1970 with a real sense of pride. It was obvious that she had had a part to play in the welcome introduction of the fairer sex.

Phil, as with all his detection work, remained coy only referring to the possibility of his nephew's intent to apply to Albemarle, and certainly not mentioning any association with former pupils. Nevertheless, there she was, an outstanding figure, the centre point of the front row, captain of the girls' hockey team 1973, the minikilted Sophie Trescothick. He wondered back just a few paces down memory lane to 1948, and the boys' rugby XV. Seven boys seated at the front, eight with the bespectacled master in charge in the back row.

The names of the boys in the backrow were listed below the team photograph. James Trescothick was the tall lad in the middle. Immediately below him, even then with that smug, military bearing, was the Berlin Brigadier McNally. The old school tie firmly entrenched there the year after the wicked winter of 1947. Albemarle was a quiet backwater but Phil smiled benignly, recognising that still waters did run deep.

He ran across a host of narrow country lanes before hitting the A11 never stopping, weighing up the links and possibilities between the three men and the prodigal daughter that had led to his demise. Then, his thoughts wandered to his own health, just what would come back from Germany and the Doc. in Bermondsey?

Phil would wait, and wait for both letters to arrive at his mum's flat. He was very confident of good news. He was not to be disappointed. Now in recommencing a new life in London, he could leave Toc H behind : He now knew the answers of how and why!

CHAPTER 13

CULTURE CLUB

Jan had installed a new bell system at number 12. It rang three times before she made it to the door.

"Sometimes you're worse than your brother, why didn't you tell me you were back? I could have got something ready,"

"Don't worry about that mum," Phil replied, whilst noticing that she had aged alarmingly. She appeared shorter and smaller and wearing glasses, a frail shadow from the days that were long gone. Phil had forgotten that she had passed her eightieth year, but he was soon reminded as he had to guide her into the living room. Living on your own in a damp council flat was no place for the elderly, he thought, as she put the kettle on. "Mum, I'm back, I've come back to look after you," he claimed. "I've thrown my cards in with Germany and they gave me a little pension.

It'll be like the old days again, but better than the prefabs," he lied.

His mother was shaking, and it was he that made the tea in the end. "Oh, son, are you sure, I can't believe it. You're sure you want to put up with an old woman with arthritis and the like?"

"I've only got one mother, it's my turn to look after you," he sighed.

It took some time and a great deal of patience, but new arrangements can work with a little help from the social services in Rotherhithe, the warm reception back at The Angel, and something that could drive Phil on as a motivation. The work he had ensconced himself in at Toc H really was a thorough preparation for looking after his mum, but his additional quest was to find Terry; was he still alive, in the Unit, or had he taken retirement?

Phil had successfully applied for unemployment benefit and had persuaded the local council that he was a full-time carer, so with money tight, he still had time to think about where he could trace Terry. First, he needed a base for all the gear he had transported from Germany including rejected stock and a huge number of musical artefacts including juke boxes, record players, Hi-Fi, speakers and a collection of over 800 LP vinyl records.

In his Battersea days, he had befriended a mate down The Goldhawk who owned a string of lock-ups near the river in south-west London. That would be perfect for him away from the prying eyes of his mother, well away up river from Bermondsey and Rotherhithe. He had contacted Joey who suggested he come down on a Sunday morning to scope out exactly what storage area he needed. Phil wanted to buy one, not rent, as that would be his security. So when they met up, Joey soon came up with the goods offering Phil a converted garage, just around the corner from Putney Bridge underground station.

The green flip-handle frontage of the garage was down a minor lane off the Fulham Road. Cash was required, and Phil could provide the reddies from the post office account he had retained from his Toc H savings. Luckily it was affordable in 1986 and Joey's paperwork was spot on. Phil Bristowe had bought his first property, a 20 foot by 14 foot garage. His first few months were spent carting gear back and forth between home and his lock-up. Joey was ace, he would help with every shift.

The two wheeler-dealers would always retire after disposal for an early breakfast at Lucianos, a favourite café of Phil's over the years. It had opened shortly after World War 2 with the owner, Antonio, who had been a prisoner of war being joined by his family to take on an Italian restaurant. By the late 80s, it served up the best English fry-up breakfast in London.

That morning Joey had to leave his pal early but Phil ordered yet another cappuccino, whilst alone staring at the comings and goings of the 85 and 93 buses outside. He was at a loss, where could he start to find out about Terry? His gaze moved from the window to the board on the wall for little adverts and business cards. The spread of small town Londoners making and scraping a living was all on there, including some announcement cards. One just hit him like lightning. It read:

"Old Rhodesians never die" : Every Monday at 11 – Eight Bells.

The notorious Eight Bells pub was just around the corner from the station. He thought, what if, yeah what if, he could trace Paddy Rose through a Rhodie connection. Surely he could lead him to Terry?

Phil wasted no time. The very next day, along with twenty or so others, including women, he joined one of the two long tables. The 'Bells' was awash with lager beer, biltong and loud banter, and it was only 11.30 on a Monday morning! He made a point of ingratiating himself with the group that referred to themselves mockingly as "Whenwees", short for when we were in Rhodesia. The Londoner made a bee line for the fit looking young to middle aged men and he found two that had fought through the campaigns of the 1970s.

He asked if they had ever served with a guy called Terry Jones or maybe a fellow countryman named Patrick Rose, who Phil believed came from just outside Bulawayo. The two gentlemen had no knowledge but pointed Phil to a very well coiffured fifty something lady they believed was from Matabeleland. She had only been in the UK for two years with her cattle farmer husband, both desperate to flee Mugabe's deathly purges on his opponents, black or white. Phil asked her the same question. After a long ten seconds silence, the tone of her voice lowered by responding with a question. "Did you fight with our boys?" Phil replied with recognisable detail of his engagements.

Then the farmer's wife described how one night Mugabe's henchmen came for both her farm and her neighbours. They set fire to all the outbuildings first, then the residential areas. Even their black workers were not spared along with all the farm's machinery. Her husband managed to get the bakkie farm truck out in time. As for her neighbours, they were not so lucky. The whole family was murdered in the cruellest of ways. The farm was owned by Patrick and Sylvia Rose.

"The local white farming community was in mourning but we all knew our time was up. All we have now are our memories, every Monday morning," she added.

"I am so sorry, how tragic." Both of them were close to tears.

"You mentioned another guy, never knew him, but a colleague of Pat's came out to visit a few times. Paddy invited us round for dinner once. Yeah, he was a big guy, but he wasn't English like you. He had a strong but lovely accent, was always joking about his injuries, loved rugby, and when we asked him where he had retired to, he was so funny, he said that it was a terrible place, "The World's End" where only eagles land!

Phil duly thanked her, then sidling away, just smiled and nodded to himself.

* * *

Far away the big guy with the monkey jacket threw the keys to his wife. She did all the driving these days around these parts where she was born and raised. Roll down Highway 154, in early autumn, it was a free run through the forest to the local store. He glimpsed all around, expecting to see bear, elk or skunk, but not this morning. Not even humans populated these dense woodlands.

Forksville's general store lay on the other side of the state's famous covered bridges, there the broad-shouldered trooper would treat her to the county's most popular brunch, a Phillie cheesesteak. A new college girl seated and served the couple respectfully,

"All the trimmings, ketchup, onions, fries for two and some of that coffee over yer," he ordered.

"Yeah, siree, coming up, hey, how'd you get to tark like that, I just love your accent!!"

* * *

Phil had survived his troubled youth, got through national service, endured the 'Beat Years' and most of all had defied the clutches of injury and death in real battles for survival in foreign fields. Yet nothing was to test him as much as having a front row seat over the next two years of watching his mother slowly slip away. In the end, he had valued the time and outings they would have together. They relived the market on a Saturday at The Blue and she especially seemed contented with the river trips and the odd summer bus trips to Hastings or Margate.

Yet time was passing them by, both of them, when they had to witness even the closure of the biscuit factory after all those years. She remembered everything, but when she outlined the good old days of working there, Phil just drew a blank. With Jan weakening by the month, her son just found it difficult to register clearly in his mind details from the past. He just thought it was what happened when you were getting on a bit. What was strange was he could remember people, friends and faces, but had a real problem in his memory of facts, actions and messages.

He had no association with Ray, and his mother forbade him. Jan had never forgiven him and all contacts had been lost decades before. She was hospitalised when Phil just couldn't cope any longer. Her mind was still there but whatever was eating away inside her would take her on the coldest January day of 1989. She had left her world of Freddie, docklands, her extended family and her darling, caring son Philip all to face a new London of computers, skyscrapers, financial houses in the sky and foreign faces.

Janet Bristowe's final wish was to be buried in Benenden alongside her loving husband. For one of the last matriarch's embedded in true London family life with all she went through, it was a quiet, humble ceremony.

* * *

It was the year's final day, indeed the decade was passing for the two figures who burst into the horseshoe shaped Pissarro's bar in Hastings. The elegant sounding name disguised the fact that this buzzing venue in East Sussex was more in the line of a music club than your average local boozer.

Ray and Mick had needed to make contact after the December upheavals at Sandlehurst. They could grab a spot of lunch, more like Christmas leftovers at this stage, before Mick could turn his attention to the sound system and acoustics for the New Year's bash. To every local's delight, 'Forbidden Fruit' were on the menu that very evening!

"You decided what you're gonna do?" asked Mick,

"Sarah and I have talked it through; I handed in my resignation two days ago, you know. I see little point continuing without JJ. He was right, it is the end of an era. Dick Cranley has been given the task of seeing through the transition period which at least gives all the remaining staff members some time and options. And you?"

"I'm going full time with 'The Fruit' as their sound engineer and manager. Much of the work will be in promoting the new CD and expanding the live gig circuit. I'm really up for it!" he mused.

"What about JJ?" asked Ray,

"Old soldiers and great statesmen never retire, they just fade away," Mick offered a line from literature.

"True, but the real winners here were the establishment, the governors and the DeVere family, even Sarah admits that. They all sold out to that bunch of multinationals. You know, Mick, they're even claiming now to replace Sandlehurst with an International Language School!"

The artist and the musician agreed on that and made a point of staying in contact, remaining big mates through their prospective futures. Both enjoyed their turkey sandwiches and chips with Mick popping a final question, "I trust you're coming to the gig tonight?"

"Pissarro's on New Decade's Eve? We wouldn't miss it for the world!" Ray added, but his world was about to change, and change vehemently. For a start, he was skint, and skint was not a word understood within the Plantagenet-Filby family.

Ray and Sarah, with an empty house barring young Michael had now to face facts, the dominant one of which was new to the couple that they had to venture into the big wide world and earn a living. Yes they owned their house but any disposable income had been all absorbed by bringing up and educating four needy children. Then there was Michael, the brightest and most academic of the lot. There were to be many debates as he completed his primary school final year concerning where he was to move on to. Against their earlier principles, they sensed between them that his academic potential had to be realised through the British boarding public school system.

Sarah didn't want him to be a child at home all on his own. Ray had fathomed it out that if they were to send Michael away for a private education it would cost, and that meant Sarah had to return to nursing and he had to make a commercial stab at the art world in all its facets. He had one other brainwave. He would network within the public school system remembering his great mentor JJ's success in that approach to education. He soon found Mary Poulson's contact details as the Principal of a co-educational boarding school across counties in Dorset. Would she take on Michael, and even consider an academic scholarship at Dalesmore Senior School?

Mary Poulson's school was situated in an archetypal English village, one of several surrounding the hilltop town of Shaftesbury. The family in visiting the well-established principal, immediately felt the warmth that she and the school exuded. In many ways this educational setting resembled something very special to Ray. It was a reincarnation, only bigger and more inclusive, of Sandlehurst. Michael, a confident child, took to the school for its emphasis on a newly built light library, including a specialised language laboratory. The boy was already excelling in his grasp of European languages.

Whilst a 'Common Entrance' pupil showed the young aspirant around the natural boundaries of such a green environment, Ray and Sarah faced the rather prickly subject of school fees. Mary, conscious of the competitive nature of independent senior education and the demands of tight financial control, simply suggested an aptitude test in English and foreign languages on his return from the tour.

"It will only take an hour and following that we'll have a very good idea of where Michael stands in his literacy and linguistic abilities. That done, we can offer quite possibly a half scholarship."

Ray and Sarah crossed their fingers all the way home, but left the more detailed assessment for the comfort of their own abode.

"Do you realise, Sarah, I have spent the last twenty seven years of my life confined to classrooms and then when home with you, we've brought up five of our own?"

"Yes, our lives have really been just about kids. The time has rather slipped away, but it has been fun. Darling, you don't regret it, do you?" Sarah said in some doubt,

"No, of course not, but I just feel I became institutionalised, and I dunno, but I can't help feeling I've restricted what you could have achieved, you know, in the medical world," he mused,

"We're happy, Ray, we've both sacrificed for the children but that can only be good and let's face it, you and I have broken free from our own upbringings. I never wanted to be an heiress with all that 19th century pomposity and we both know you were far too ambitious and talented to stay in Bermondsey and work in one of those dreadful factories or down at the dockside," said Sarah with some finality.

"You're right. I'm so proud of how you have brought up our kids, all of them are out there in the real world, working their way forward in what they want to give and take from the world," Ray beamed.

"Yes, Mr Bristowe, but now it's our turn again to move on, get Michael settled, and live our own lives again. Just think if we can make the most of our talents, we could actually spend some of the money on ourselves for a change!" she joked. "Still, with Michael's abilities, wouldn't it be great to get him into Oxford or Cambridge. He'll be the only one from our family, I know he can do it!"

"There you go again, another project. What would you be like without a project?" Sarah sighed in mock frustration.

Within the week, Mary had phoned to say that Michael would receive a half bursary in the following academic year entering it as one of the youngest in his class. His time at Dalesmore would be a seven year journey all pointing towards the halls of an Oxbridge college.

Sarah and Ray now got down to serious planning. Even to afford Michael's fees, they would have to register two separate incomes of self-employment: Sarah as a part-time agency nurse and Ray as a professional artist. They were both entering a brave new world. Neither had attached themselves to pension schemes, nor had either of them received any monies from beyond family entitlement or institutional allowances. Ray's taxes were taken off his earned income at source.

Ray realised at the age of nearly sixty, he never had to think about this aspect of life. Not only was he commercially naïve and inexperienced, he and Sarah had never really had to deal with adults as a part of their daily routine. The outside competitive and stress-laden world had passed them by. This hit Ray, in particular, where it hurt, in his inward sense of advancement. The adults he had encountered, Freddie, Farmer Sykes in Aussie, JJ, even Mick Greatbach, were all self-motivated, self-made men pushing the boundaries in their own fields. Compared to them, he just got stuck in a pleasant, comfortable institution that was happy in its little corner of England.

Ray's drive had always been within himself, but always from within an institution. Worst of all, in fleeting moments, he would think of his kid brother. For him, he'd have to face the world head on because Ray knew that the world would just crap all over Phil, taking advantage of his lack of education and ambition. Ray had indeed triumphed because he had climbed the ladder of life with solid qualifications for the modern age.

He also realised that now he had to diversify and pit his wits alongside a society that had entered the digital age, and a new tool for humanity, the world wide web, the

Internet. He knew nothing of these developments in their embryonic stage, after all, he was an artist, a people's person. That was the avenue he wished to explore, to offer services that he had dabbled in at Sandlehurst. There was in the 1990s so much scope for the specialist; he was to become a professional artist.

His mind was in overdrive. He would be ready to commission his paintings to galleries, offer evening classes to budding artists, work as a peripatetic teacher in schools and become embroiled in the auction world. Whilst Sarah would bring to the table her salaried agency pay based around health visits, both private and within the NHS, he would explore the equally lucrative world of the southern counties, where leisure time was in bountiful supply to both young and old alike.

Sussex and Hampshire, two affluent counties, full of the entitled minority, would ride along life's waves with the new 'nouveau riche' and those well-heeled enough for early retirement. Ray asked himself, what do they do with all this leisure time? The answers were in health, sport, art, music, vacations, cultural trips and if they had ailments, Sarah was at hand!

This resourceful couple were to rediscover themselves, certainly in terms of time well occupied, but would they be solvent, could they make it pay in the 1990s?

Ray had learned one big lesson back in Australia, and that was when life was closing in on you, the reaction had to be to get back to basics. The art school had driven that concept into his head. His art depicted artefacts, or the colourful representations of scenes or scenery. When he tired of colours, or was it really he was overcomplicating the juxtaposition of colours, he would return to monochrome to achieve the effect he so desired.

Back in Bingley, he had ridden miles to reproduce charcoal drawings of churches, cathedrals or imposing municipal buildings. His mastery of scale and perspective had been incredibly advanced at such a young age. The only area he seemed to struggle was in ceramics: indeed, it was the sole area at the Sydney Art School where he did not achieve a distinction. It was almost as if he should be confined to the outdoors to pursue now what was to become a semi-professional status in painting scenic landscapes and offering personal portraits.

He would travel by rail to such destinations as Chichester, Lancing, Winchester, Leeds Castle, Salisbury and Canterbury in the height of summers and set up to mass produce charcoal drawings. He would establish an unobtrusive pitch early in the morning and sketch a drawing continuously, often as many as half a dozen in three hours to be sold at £10 per item. To earn £60 per day as a self-employed artist would put the glint back in Sarah's eye very quickly. All travel and meal receipts, plus of course his materials would be set against tax at the end of the year. Yes, not quite Bondi Beach, but definitely a going concern.

Ray followed this course from the Easter break to October half-terms working Wednesdays through to Saturdays at these lucrative venues where church groupings, American tourists and day trippers were all keen to take tangible mementoes of their venture out on pleasant

English summer days. They would arrive individually, but the real earner for Ray were the coach loads of senior citizens, always impressed by the simplicity and originality of Ray's charcoal.

Still, he needed a further two days in an increasingly hectic weekly schedule to develop his landscape paintings. He had become a very seasonal animal and, rather like the grain farmer piling up his surplus in the summer for his winter feed, Ray accumulated varied but numerous landscape scenes on these two days a week in order to augment his winter income at local town exhibitions and auctions.

He was particularly fond of water scenes, perhaps first initiated at Portsmouth harbour a decade earlier with the Reverend Smythe. Streams and rivers in pastoral settings were his forte, seemingly obsessed by the River Thames and its tributaries. Later in the decade, for reasons that would become self-evident, he would paint scenes of Oxford and Cambridge students punting on the Isis and the Cam. Such was his prolific output that Sarah would convert one of the departed children's bedrooms into a workplace for Ray, and yet another bedroom for storage!

Sarah, in turn, had found a lovely little private health clinic that had the role of aftercare of mainly elderly patients following rigorous medical operations, based in the attractive small town of Pulborough. She would have the car as her means of transport for three days of the week. It really was a part-time heaven for her. They agreed that they would never work on Saturday evenings through to Tuesday mornings. Their combined income was enough to see them through to retirement, to support Michael in his education and pay their bills but after that there was precious little left.

As Sarah Bristowe expected, Rosie had inherited, with her own small family, the Burton Mews property. Yet Sarah really did not mind at all as Rosie was the sister who had bought into the Plantagenet-Filby heritage and lineage far more comfortably than she had. As for Sarah, she just loved being Mrs Bristowe, as wife in a stable loving family that had worked and paid for everything you saw. She was immensely proud of that fact. The family was now really Ray, herself and Michael progressing towards adult life. Just as she had hoped with their new existence another dimension was to emerge for them during these years up to and through the millennium, that of village life!

Wednespool from the start, the heady days of 1967, was always Sarah and Ray's idyll. A wee bit unorthodox as a hilltop village, the plateaued summit of which was occupied by adjoining farmland with a surrounding belt of 'C' roads circulating around the sides. Along these were a string of detached houses of all types from small cottages to large gardened dwellings, more like the estates of wealthy landowners.

The village was set there in mid Sussex for an eternity, a Saxon settlement whose name remained a mystery. No one for instance ever found a pool, and as for being launched on a Wednesday, forget it! Yet, for young couples intent on raising families, it was ideal with a tiny infants school and an 18th century parish church alongside a timber framed village hall. All provisions were gained from the nearest town, Crowborough and often by deliveries only.

Wednespool by 1995 had aged in parallel fashion to its inhabitants. Ray and Sarah were always aware of the fact that the majority were often their age sharing the interests at each and every stage of the family evolution. Their kids grew up together, the parents were God-fearing people who worked their varied passages in life and watched their families diminish as their children sought more from life than a pretty backwater.

Ray had been the quiet one in the village, for nigh on a quarter of a century he had focused on his career at Sandlehurst the other side of the A22. It was up to Sarah to correspond, mainly in the negative, to invitations to garden parties, whist drives, village fetes and vital community meetings. The two of them shared simply two priorities, that of Sandlehurst and their children.

Nevertheless, things had changed and they would have to adapt to very much more of a communal, cooperative way of life. Swapping services was rife and healthy, and the custom of farmers leaving small packages of boxed products at the entrance of their properties with a gratuity box was commonplace. Eggs, apples and all sorts of vegetables were available at whatever price the villager decided to pay. Rides to Crowborough were exchanged for hedge trimming or even haircutting! To Ray and Sarah, it was amazing how much a small village of two hundred country folk really did offer to everyone if you got involved. Their culture was one of mutual dependence.

Skills or pastimes were very quickly picked up by The Committee. In Ray's case monthly art exhibitions were the rule, and Sarah's counselling and medical application was much sought after as well. The village, however, had one big drawback: there was no public house! So the only way to remedy that was to open up the village hall on the first and last Friday of the month and throw a get together based around barrels of beers, copious wine and ample snacks. Coffee mornings were occurrences every Wednesday and country walks every alternative Sunday in summer time.

Whether the outlet was gardening, lectures, or theatre trips, just nothing was beyond the Committee. Those sturdy, but elderly types just reflected the wishes of their extended families, the villagers. Some were churchy on a Sunday, some were not, but all displayed the quintessential qualities of old England, values that were solid even in the context of their communal style of living.

Ray and Sarah just merged in, giving as much as they got. They particularly enjoyed the winter theatre trips to London with the thespian sector of Wednespool, reminding both of their December days at Sandlehurst, but now they were merely spectators. That could not be said about their involvement with the Wednespool Open Fete Day. The first weekend in August on the Village 'Rec' supported the largest sale of art, music, clothing and sporting goods in mid-Sussex. All were second hand of course, but with a projected income of thousands of pounds, it needed to be organised with military precision.

Cometh the hour, cometh the man. Brigadier Tony Devereux, a veteran from many campaigns, made light of such a task. Planned in the spring, two houses sporting large gardens were commandeered into action to be used as both depot and distribution points. One was Tony's and one was Sarah's! The Bristowes enthusiastically received all manner of antiques and throwaways which were erratically deposited on their extensive lawn and garage forecourt for the best part of July. Indeed, Ray even volunteered more of his time after the fete in collections and accounting for the profits made. Every year it was a roaring success, adding 50% more in receipts, all to be wisely spent by the Committee on the village, and to a variety of needy charities.

Ray and Sarah had become a fixture in Wednespool. You simply could not dream of such a place, so far removed from Paradise Street in Bermondsey. The next generation of Bristowe boys however was waiting in the wings, rather waiting for the post in mid August having helped his parents' friends lug all the gear around at the fete. Yes, it was 'A' level results time and Dalesmore would be sending out by first class mail what Michael needed and that was 3 'A' grades for entry into St Peter's College, Oxford.

He was upstairs when his mother brought a morning cup of tea with biscuits which were covered by a long white envelope with a Shaftesbury post mark on it. Ignoring the tea, he opened it and raised his eyebrows. He had won the game! Three A's in French, German and History. The day was his, but Sarah knew that there would be only one person who would be even more delighted!

Ray would always remember that day, August the 15th 1998. Michael never was allowed to forget that evening as Ray took the three of them off in a hired car to Pissarro's in Hastings, ordering a table for six. Somehow he had managed to track down three more revellers in the celebration. The six of them toasted the scholarship that Michael had just secured. "To Michael and Oxford!" they screamed, both Ray and Sarah, Mr and Mrs Dick Cranley and Mick Greatbatch.

It was champagne all the way to a very late bed upstairs at the night-restaurant that never disappointed.

The Bristowes had been equally proud of their first four children but Sarah knew that Michael's success was the cream of the crop to Ray. He had never forced his own academic background on to any of his four children, as he recognised their talents were just not in that direction. He was relieved that all four had pursued their interests into professional life and had settled into decent careers. What Ray could never cope with were wasters and, as far as he was concerned, he didn't have to look very far to recognise that type from his own upbringing.

Michael was a different ball game altogether. Self-motivated and prioritised, it was not just his parents who had noticed these qualities. Mary Poulson at parents' evenings had predicted this outcome. Knowing the boy inside out that his aim was to use his language skills as productively as possible, she had indicated to Ray that there was a future job and career waiting for Michael at Dalesmore!

Ray had made it as well. He had entered his official state pension years just months before. Health permitting, he had won another battle of adjustment from the Sandlehurst years. All his kids were now out of the door making their own journeys in life. His pride and joy had won a scholarship, as far as Ray was concerned to the most prestigious University in the world. He still had his loving wife by his side and the state was repaying him for all his years devoted to education and art.

He now could kick back with less engagements and commitments. Life would move him on to the golden years at Wednespool. Even without material gains from his decades of effort, he surely would be contented?

Ray's family settled into the most architypical of English villages.

THIS FRIDAY
IS
PUB NIGHT

Open to all, a first Friday of the month community run
local providing an ideal opportunity to meet up for a
drink and a natter.
Located in the village hall.
Open from 7.30 pm last orders 10.30 pm

Pub night in Wednespool : A barrel of beer provided and bring your
own wine brought the community together.

Raymond's wildest dreams. A son at Oxford University led to Michael's joining the educated elite.

London Soho. One of Shirley's favoured hunting and sleeping grounds in the doorways of 'The Cambridge'.

CHAPTER 14

SHIRLEY AND CO

From the back bar of the Angel pub, Phil stared down at the rippling waters of the Thames below. Only half a mile to his left was Tower Bridge, the symbol to all dockland folk of the old world, a world which had withstood Hitler's Luftwaffe, the Blitz and the growing changes of commerce. Yet by the early 90s it had eventually succumbed to the new structures that were to replace the specialised wharves that had handled cargo for generations.

To his right, the younger Bristowe, now getting on towards his late fifties, was raising his gaze to wonder at how the Isle of Dogs had given way to the Canary Wharf development with its high-rise banks in the skies. What Goering and his Heinkels had missed in WW2, the 1980s, and now into the 90s had completed the job on south east London and its people.

For Phil it meant much more than concrete and clay. The Angel was a daily respite but sadly was now harbouring fewer and fewer of the original dockland community. Many had passed on but even more had moved on taking advantage of selling their council flats that had originally sprung up to replace the bombed out areas of Bermondsey and Rotherhithe. Over the years these originals had scrimped enough money together to buy their own flats under Maggie Thatcher's scheme in the 80s. No more renting! Now they would sell in 1992 at the appropriate moment and bugger off to the coast, Essex, Kent or Sussex where property was cheap. Hordes of them departed, they had had enough.

Jan had never been one of them. She had lived a hand to mouth existence surviving off an old age pension and her savings in the Post Office. She had left whatever she had to Phil: some precious sentimental belongings and enough to see him through this transition. He still had the lock-up, that had been a wise move. So he could hardly have been considered a man of property. He placed all his mum's memorabilia in her second bedroom and because he only had a tiny concreted backyard he tried to brighten the place up with a collection of pot plants, including broad leaf varieties and cacti.

His neighbours in the block were increasingly from foreign climes, many from the West Indies, Africa and the Indian subcontinent. His potential isolation was there for all to see, as the migrants around him were building families with children of teenage years. There was unfortunately a high proportion of single parents, with basically hard pressed mothers attempting to keep unruly kids under control. The TV and video technology would be down their throats everyday pushing this and advertising that, so access was immediate whether they had the means to pay for it or not.

His generation of mums had brought their kids up on their own, but the 'war' was their fathers' war. There had to be discipline within the family just to survive in his days. Even the new locals often spoke in their differing mother tongues, notably the Asians who thrived in their ever increasing ghettoes in south and east London. Local crime, not like the post-war period when the 'firms' left joe public alone as theirs was a patch war, was becoming indiscriminate. Muggings were commonplace, hold-ups at stores, football nutters wrecking the place at the weekends, graffiti and vandalism all over the place, even old ladies weren't safe anymore. Phil was at odds with this environment. He could not adapt.

As for the cops, they didn't want to know. There were fewer on the beat, there was a relaxation even on their physical size, and all they did was buzz up Tooley Street and Jamaica Road in flash new cars talking over radios. If they took on any of the young hoodlums, many of whom were disenfranchised young second generation Jamaicans, they would be done for racism, open to the charge by the migrant minorities of deliberately targeting their communities. Those crooks that were sentenced by liberal judges, were handed out namby-pamby stretches inside of months in detention and let out with good behaviour after only half of the sentence served. 1990s Britain called that justice!

With such diversity of ethnic origin, the breakdown of the family unit was rife and religion seen as irrelevant. Any older Englishmen who had served as Phil had to protect the British way of life, were now severely compromised living in these central London boroughs. To Phil, who watched even the BBC surrender to the joke of multi culturalism, it was a case of sheer weakness of the prevailing middle classes and government. Of course, they would view this all from their far away Shangri-las in Hampstead, Islington and Surbiton, totally untouched.

Phil had a fortress he no longer belonged to nor was proud of. Yes, the Angel provided some solace but he was letting himself go, along with the maisonette. The walls were gaining in damp, the window frames failing and even the floorboards were giving way in the corner of rooms. His plants now had invaded his bathroom to such an extent that he could only use the downstairs toilet cubicle. His hygiene was down to hand washing and occasional deodorants.

As his maisonette was a downstairs, end flat of a red bricked block, other problems started to appear, as gaps in the brickwork and external ventilation pipes had created mice infestations and once in, mice colonies would be active across the entire block in winter time. As for the council estates, their upkeep and management were not a priority for the Tory local or central government, and it was not until the Blair administration in 1997 that some investment was placed into the local community.

By then, Phil was at ground zero. His clothing was the same as in 1987 overwashed in a kitchen sink, the same indoor slippers and his kitchen utensils comprising one frying pan off which he ate all of his meals. The floorboards had collapsed in the kitchen so he now would approach the cooker by a one-foot wide wooden plank. He had an uninterrupted view of the foundations, but still he would never deign to call the council. To him, they were the enemy, the establishment that was ripping him off for half his unemployment benefit, for rent and rates. He would never surrender.

Phil Bristowe now hoarded everything in his own bedroom where he hadn't slept for several years. He had endured his nights on the couch in a 'services' sleeping bag. Now at 60 years of age and the end of the century in sight, he would often pop out of this residential hell to stay the night in his lock up as he had bought a second hand camp bed, but he did confine this to the summer months only. Whilst there, he was something of a mind to consider a permanent move to the lock up.

After ten years he booked his first appointment at the local health centre, but really only did this as a result of his noisy sub-cultural neighbours complaining that his maisonette was the cause of frequent mice infestations and was a residence not fit for human occupation. It was he who was bringing down standards and property values! Phil knew there were crossroads in everyone's life and he recognised that on the day of his medical, he really was living in a foreign land. His Indian doctor pronounced him totally deaf in one ear and as a whole, his mental recall and

311

reasoning were impaired by evidence from X-rays and scans of cranial abnormalities. They all wanted him out.

An immediate inspection of his rented property was advised by the doctor and the local council would later send two female officers around for an assessment of the property. On entering the property, one of these hardnosed employees burst into tears, whilst her colleague was left wondering how could anyone live this way at the end of the twentieth century. Their report was damning. An overhaul of the complete maisonette would be required and Phil would have to pay out.

His ten-year tenure in Rotherhithe was up. His only remorse was that he had let the memory of his mother down, but what else do you expect of a true blue-blooded Englishman living in an environment taken away from him and so wickedly stolen by yuppies and foreigners of all origins? Phil even rejected all that the guilt laden social services would throw at him. He would let them house a bigger "more appropriate family" from the Indies. They would blend into their new neighbourhood very nicely. As for Phil, that July of '97, he would move up west, the lock-up was awaiting.

It only took him a day to transfer his worldly possessions, mainly thanks to Joey providing a pick-up from his base in Putney. The latter was dumbfounded,"You mean you're gonna live in this little space, Phil?"

"Till I get settled, but remember, it's all mine and paid for."

That summer and early autumn, Phil would use the money he would have regrettably paid out in rent as his spending money to get reacquainted with his hometown, London, as it approached the millennium. He was reminded when he visited the sights and famous landmarks that he had seen them sometime in his past, but he just couldn't recall who with and the circumstances involved.

Inevitably, most weekdays he walked and walked and at the weekend evenings he would invariably use up his spending money in Soho, Tottenham Court Road and the Strand drinking the pints at the cheapest outlets possible. He never did establish a local. Then, on one Friday evening at dusk about 9 o'clock as he leaned on the window outside, a fracas had started by the entrance to the public bar between the barman and two worse for wear customers,

"Get the fuck out of here and don't come back, and you can take this stinking trolley with ya," screamed an irate custodian.

Physically pushed to the floor, a demure middle-aged female with a slightly younger, but more volatile partner were laid out like scrambled eggs on toast on the narrow pavement. Phil was the only customer who turned and reacted in any way. He dusted the pair down, and calmed the situation taking the side of the underdogs as usual,

"Come on Shirley, that barman's a pillock, you know he's always out to get us. Let's move onto The Cambridge," cried the mistreated man.

"You've been so kind to help us, he's normally more brutal. You saved us from a kicking. Why don't you come along with Wyatt and me for a drink at The Cambridge?" she asked, quite formally.

How could Phil refuse?

Dark was approaching as Wyatt guided his new found friend into the chosen little hostelry just a stone's throw from Drury Lane. He fumbled through his pockets like an Aussie doing the All-Blacks Haka to find nothing of value as he proposed his round of drinks.

"Oh not that old chestnut, 'Wyatt', I'll get them in," said the lady parking her full Tesco trolley outside.

"Do I detect an American accent?" asked Phil.

"You sure do, honey, Californian born and bred, what's your poison?"

Philip Bristowe had just been introduced to Shirley Mauer on her terms, via a drink. She had been partial to one and other more adventurous substances ever since she ran away from her mother in Van Nuys, Los Angeles back in '68. Ironically to this chance meeting, her dear Mama was an Englishwoman who had fallen for an American sailor who had ship-leave from Portsmouth whilst on duty tour back in 1950. Her mother was as straight as a die, but her father's commitment to the US navy and tequila had sealed her fate as another statistic of a broken home. In her teenage years it was just to be mother and daughter.

Shirley dropped out to join a hippy commune at Big Sur up the Californian coast, and with the kind climate of the area survived in a tent for years. She lived as a mountain person, and whilst other group members possessed hunting, pastoral and cultivation skills, young Shirley could outdo all the alternatives by taking up the position of Head Cook. Her mother had taught her the benefits of an English breakfast, indoctrinating her with the message, 'You don't need another meal for the rest of the day.' That was just the start for her as she would learn and practise differing native dishes at her classes in High School in 'the Valley'. By the early years of hippiedom, she was fully involved with the music and self-sufficiency for nine to ten months of the year, whilst in winter she would work and live on site in breakfast joints in small town California. Normally she traded her skills for a bed and meals, sometimes when that was not possible, she would kip down in 24-hour laundromats and friendly stretches of either doorways or beaches.

In American terms, she was smart, slim with dark brown hair kind of caked, almost stuck down parted in the middle. She had learned from her parents by never getting hitched. This was made easy by literally spending her young life moving onto the next town. From Gilroy all the way down to south of Santa Barbara in Carpentaria, she had lived the life of her dreams on the edge of a culture she was essentially part of. Music festivals, food festivals and the sun would dominate large sections of her years. She had never owned a car, relying on rides and occasionally a bicycle, 'loaned', of course!

Shirley had one other personal tradition that was continued through her life, she made herself get cleaned up once a week. She recognised that Sunday or Monday evenings and nights were motel 'special offer' nights, so she could stay at almost 50% discount wherever she ventured. Another quirk right down to her bumping into Phil, was she would possess her own trolley, stolen from a major supermarket. It was like watching a young mother walking around with a pram, she looked naked without one!

In that trolley would always be a large, flattened cardboard 'home', temporarily outlined at the trolley's base with just one change of clothes, and her sole compromise to technology, a transistor radio. On the top of her 'house' was a small knapsack for smalls, toothbrush and soap. Her bathrooms were always available early in the mornings in the form of public conveniences or receptive coffee houses.

She had made her brave choices in life decades earlier and her demeanour was always one of calm and one in which she had accepted her responsibilities. 'Mountain Girl', as she often referred to herself from her days at Laurel Canyon above LA, was never taken up with religion. Her hopes were still fathomed in prayer and mutual communication with almost a desperate attachment to living for the day and striving for tomorrow.

Equally she did have her demons which in the main had been suppressed. The drugs were well gone in the rear-view mirror but like her weekly motel visits, there was often another night in the week where cheap grog normally in the form of rough cider or wine would take hold of her senses to await a wake-up call in a local hostel or hospital the next morning.

Phil wanted to know how long she had settled in England. She reminded him that from a young age that she had a British passport and dual nationality. By the end of the 80s she needed to have family near and sought out her elderly mother with multiple sclerosis who had been committed to a home down in Cornwall. So her first few years were down in St Ives, accessible to her, but never revealing to her mum that she was sleeping on beaches or rough in shelters.

Her move up to London coincided with her mother's passing four years previously. "So, how did you meet your partner?" Phil asked.

"Wyatt, my partner? That'll be the day, he is a drunk," with great emphasis on the 'is,' she said.

Wyatt just poo-pooed her away with a nonchalant flick of the wrist, complaining, "She's always been jealous of my superior education," he drawled, "Downing College, Cambridge and a distinction at the Guildford Law School. Shirley could never match that, could you my dear?"

"Then what? You frittered it all away with your kleptomania, absconding with clients' funds, banking legal funds into personal use, fraudulent transactions in real estate, do I need to remind you, and all for your desire to piss it away down the River Thames," she quipped, then continued, "Nah, we tend to hang around together. He's harmless but as you've seen tonight, once he gets a bee in his bonnet, he can upset a lot of folk especially with his high and mighty attitude."

"Where do you stay?" asked Phil.

"At this time of year, in there!" Shirley pointed to her cardboard and added, "In winter it's much more of a challenge. He buggers off to a church mission in Eastbourne, whilst I have a list of breakfast mobile vans I cook for that come with accommodation but that's usually only for January and February," she said.

Phil absorbed the fact that here were two educated and resourceful individuals with totally opposite backgrounds who had a different way of looking at life. There was so much history in both of them and that was what attracted him to them. Yes, they would lay out the cloth pouch for contributions to their lifestyle which were an extra bonus to their trips to the social every Thursday. They loved London, never tired of the great city whatever it threw at them. The Bristowe boy, by 11 o'clock was smitten and looking into Shirley's bespectacled blue eyes asked, "Can I join you tomorrow evening at eight?"

"But where will you stay?" she responded.

"For tonight I'm organised but from tomorrow night it's gonna be three's company for some time to come."

Shirley turned to Wyatt but he was asleep, all ready for his bed around the corner in a doorway down the street from Drury Lane Theatre. If he had tuned into Shirley and Phil that evening he would have been delighted to have on board a man who could stand his drinks.

Phil trudged off to Charing Cross down The Strand, jumped the barrier and caught the District line train to Putney Bridge, ten stations on. He only paid from Parsons Green, one single stop. For some reason that night, the lock-up was more inviting as he wrestled with his own thoughts. He even felt both physically and emotionally more comfortable than for years. Was it that he had rediscovered comradeship with Shirley and Wyatt? Maybe he had become more sensitive to the plight of others who had experienced the downturn in life. As he rumbled around in his sleeping bag, he was finalising his thoughts that, like himself, the American hippy and her downtrodden lawyer still looked life in the eye and pushed full throttle against any perceived hardship. Unlike the millions of Londoners who would journey to and then forsake the capital as evening fell, users the lot of them, Shirley and Wyatt were part of the fabric, an unbeatable urban pair. They had an identity, a quality that Phil was craving for inside out.

Shirley and Wyatt owned London, the others just loaned it. To Phil's way of thinking, he was of the same mind even though he conceded that he had already lost the battle for Bermondsey. The threesome met as planned the following evening at The Cambridge with Phil ready to adapt to whatever they would ask of him.

"Heh, let's just set up some ground rules here," said Shirley, "Yes we have to have 'em. We work as a trio on whatever stretch we settle on for the evening. Wyatt and me together as a couple who lost everything and you twenty yards along the same street using the maltreated veteran label. Ok, you comfortable with that, Phil?"

"Why separate?" he asked,

"Different punters feel sympathy for differing hardships. For us, it will invariably be couples who feel the guilt remorse, for you it'll be some of the older guys, maybe those that did national service."

"We'll pool the tips at the end of these warmer evenings. If we're lucky when Soho and Theatreland are really busy from 9 til midnight, we'll pick up £10 to £20 between us. Not bad, eh?"

"Will we use the same patch every night, right through the year?" the rookie posed the obvious question,

"Nah, summer season we'll work in Soho, the rail terminals and Berkeley Square depending on the day of the week. Once we hit the autumn months of September til the end of November, the location has to be the colleges. These students, especially in September and October are rich pickings when their pockets are laden with those fat grants. Ask Wyatt," she offered.

"Piece of cake, ole chap, especially with my accent. Even bring out the old college scarf, you know," laughed Wyatt.

"Why would you do that, for heaven's sake?" asked Phil.

"Dear boy, to open up a conversation. Once you've hooked a London student on the verbals, they're putty in your palms."

The conversation drifted after Phil bought his inaugural round, with Wyatt inquiring, after a shocking glance at Phil's outstretched arms,

"Talking of palms, hands and things, I noticed you have two long numbers inscribed on your lower forearms? You must tell me why and how they came about."

"In my past life, Wyatt, somebody gave them to me whilst I was young doing my services bit. Can't for the life of me remember why. Maybe it was for a bet or a dare, I dunno," Phil strained to tap into an empty box of recollection.

"He's a bit sensitive to numbers on arms, aren't you Wyatt? Tell Phil about your Pops," Shirley enthused,

"My father was a survivor from Belsen, you may have heard of it, ole boy, it was no Billy Butlins for him. They stamped a camp number onto his arm, first thing the SS required. How he survived, none of our family ever knew, nor told of the atrocity,"

"I'm so sorry, Wyatt, if I could erase them, I would, but they're impossible to shift," cried Phil at pains to soften the blow.

"No Phil, don't do that, one day they might mean something." Wyatt still had a legal bearing, a presence that demanded to be heard. Over the next few months and years, his experience of life's technicalities would be invaluable to Phil. That was of course, when he was sober. Once intoxicated, or even worse when he would give way to petty thieving and shoplifting, he was a liability to be around. Indeed, in 1999, 2001 and 2003, Wyatt was to spend time at her Majesty's Pleasure alternating six month stretches inside for drunk and disorderly with wanton damage charges and persistent shoplifting. As Shirley had always warned, Wyatt was habitual. He just couldn't resist kicking back against the society, in his terms, the Law Society, that had him struck off and destroyed his way of earning a living.

Wyatt enjoyed Phil's company over the years on the hoof, but mainly as a protective shield to the abuse he almost used to prompt from the angry members of the public. The number of aggressive passers-by were mainly confined to verbal confrontations which were water off a duck's back to Shirley but sooner or later Wyatt would bite back. On one occasion, in taking on a group of late-night inebriated football fans, the violence got out of hand as Wyatt ushered Shirley away to leave Phil to stand up to four regular nutters, all on his own.

His training still was with him but his ageing body was not. He could not deal with all four that brought him to the ground, sorely bruised and battered and needing crutches. As it turned out, the crutches proved a nice little earner over the following month from passers-by, sympathetic to a former serviceman and his injuries!

Shirley really did have her hands full with an ever increasingly erratic Wyatt and Phil, yes Phil. He was deteriorating, never having fully recovered from his beating and after the first three or four winters as part of her team, he would disappear himself for three months in early December. As she also would seek shelter at that time of year in her part-time mobile food outlets, she always would wonder where Phil would venture in absentia. He would never say. By 2003 late on, the Bristowe boy of 68 years was feeling the pinch, constantly falling asleep and worse, contracting light bouts of pneumonia. He could never sustain any decent periods of treatment as he always would check in to different hospitals. He would still, invariably, recover in April after his three month absence. That December, she wanted to insist that she must know where he was, in case of an emergency. She had already checked the University College Hospital, The Welbeck and other walk-in centres, but no trace.

Then much to her surprise, the next April, morning time, along with Wyatt, Phil had decided to invite them back to his winter hotel, the Bristowe lock-up!

"Three returns to Putney Bridge, one OAP please," Phil offered to subsidise his street mates of seven years.

Shirley took notice that Phil was full of beans again as he opened the lock-up's swing door to reveal one of the most remarkable spaces she had ever witnessed. Down the left-hand side were all manner of books, gardening utensils, ornaments and vases, whilst the right side included every type of recording equipment from radiograms to Hi-Fi, speakers, the lot. Balancing on top were over 800 LP records and what must have been the equivalent in 45 rpm singles. At the far end across Shirley's vision was a camp-bed, bordered by a clothes rack, one of those open temporary ones with two pairs of trousers and one old fashioned jacket drooping down from rusted hangers.

However, what startled the visiting pair was the emerging noise from a basket – the deep bark of a black coated dog that looked like a Labrador with a little bit of a cross about him.

"Oh yes, meet Bilko. I named him after a lab I once had. In fact, he's second-hand from Battersea Dogs Home just across the river. He looked just like the original Bilko, so I named him the same. He won't hurt you, he's just saying hello!" explained Phil.

As Phil continued waffling how he took the dog for daily walks over the recent three months ending up at the launderette where there was an outside tap that Bilko feasted upon, Shirley shuffled up the back of the cosy garage. She noticed there was the luxury of one electric power point but no sign of any area for food or sustenance, let alone sanitary requirements. She gazed at the corduroy brown jacket which had something slightly protruding from the single top pocket. Nosily she pulled it out, it was a ragged example of an old navy blue British passport! It hadn't been used nor even opened for at least fifteen years. She knew all that, after her move to Britain because the authorities insisted that she had to exchange her original 'beaut' for a downsized purple European Community one. So his was obsolete!

"Love to have a peep at that," said Wyatt

He scrolled his eye down the passport and before he could take anything in, Phil snatched it away from him.

"None of your business, Wyatt," screamed Phil, to which Wyatt replied seriously,

"Hang on a minute Phil, I won't look through it, just a scope at the cover. Hmm, interesting. Let's have your left arm again. Bingo, they match. Phil, we have a match!"

Philip Bristowe was nonplussed, staring at his arm and then the passport. It was true. Sometime in his past he must have allowed the tattoo insertion. He vaguely recollected being the recipient of anaesthetics, but tattoos never. He grabbed his valuable possession back very abruptly, checking the number again.

"Anything you can remember now, even to connect it to the other arm's number?" Wyatt cross-examined.

"I can't think of anything, my mind's a blank. So what do you think about my mate Bilko joining us this year? I'll take care of him and you watch, whole families won't pass him by without a pet, stroke and even a tip," suggested the new Barbara Woodhouse!

"You know you might have something there but you will have to pay for him out of your share," said Shirley.

"You're the boss, that's fine," Phil replied.

"Bilko can bark and chase away any bad vibes and nutters, can he bite as well?" asked Wyatt.

"Oh yes, but only cats, cops and retired lawyers, Wyatt!"

There was after all humour amongst thieves and there was undoubtedly a mutual care amongst these three miscreants that had bonded almost into a family feel with Shirley acting as the wise older sister to Wyatt and cousin to Phil. 2004 had been a true recovery year for the trio, with Wyatt back from custodial sentence, and Shirley more than pleased with the 'firm's' earnings. Berkeley Square over on the west side of Piccadilly and the two happy hunting grounds east of the Circus, Kings College and the LSE, had yielded such good returns that the trio could afford two public house night outs per week.

Yet Phil was not getting any younger. He reminded the pair of his dad's famous biblical quote, "A lifetime is Three Score and Ten", at the same time as informing them, that Christmas in 2004, that he was born in 1935! Shirley pulled Wyatt aside one day when Phil took time out to clean up the lock-up before winter set in for January.

"Look Wyatt, please, we must convince Phil that he has to set up a will. He has that hang-dog look about him, he's starting to walk with a limp, he's riddled with arthritis, but you know he'll never give in to doctors nor hospitals. That lock-up is his financial security, you know they're going for over ten thousand pounds these days. After all your connections, past and unfortunately present, you must get Phil to an associate friend of yours, who can help him," she suggested.

Ok, I agree, and I think I know the very practice. Leave it with me," said Wyatt.

Just before the three split apart that Christmas before their annual winter sabbatical break, the two good Samaritans put it to Phil.

"Phil, we are insisting, no more talk. You have to get a will."

The old soldier held up his hands to surrender but he made it clear that he would do so after the winter had passed in April.

CHAPTER 15

CROSSING THE RUBICON

The Principal of Dalesmore School,

Miss Mary Poulson

requests the pleasure of the company of

Raymond and Sarah Bristowe

at Drinks and Formal Dinner

on Saturday 3rd September 2005 at 7.00pm

Lounge Suits　　　　　*RSVP: School Secretary*

Sarah galloped through from the entrance of 'Acorns' in to the dining room where Ray was perusing his copy of The Times delivered earlier that morning. She plonked it directly on the crossword page enticing a glance of disapproval for the interruption from her husband. That was of course until he read the details of the invitation. His instant reaction was; "Michael never mentioned a word. It must be a very select gathering."

Ray's son by now was ensconced in the affairs of Dalesmore as he had been appointed Deputy Director of Modern Languages at the school over twelve months earlier. True to her promise, Mary Poulson snapped him up for his first post in English education after he had gained an upper second degree and a postgrad award in education at Oxford. Yet what had really impressed Mary was his two year stint as a French language assistant at an international lycée just outside Bordeaux.

He had lived life in a small settlement of medieval origin called Monsegur. Taking up a small apartment just off the main market place, he became a commuter of forty minutes duration each day, but would return to play a very active role in the splendid Aquitaine village at weekends. Michael insisted that whilst there he had picked up the region's 'entre deux mers' accent, and was proud of the fact he had only spoken the native language despite the increasing number of British ex-pats settling in this part of France.

However when a vacant post became available at the English boarding school with all the advantages of live-in accommodation, he jumped at the chance of crossing the Channel to return to his homeland. Both Sarah and Ray, inevitably, were delighted as their advancing years were really making it difficult to travel to visit Michael in deepest France. Two other factors affected this choice with

Ray now becoming very much a home bird at 'Acorns' and Wednespool, but more tellingly the truth was that since his withdrawal from the art world the year before in 2004, the couple were tight in terms of accessible funds.

They now were surviving on two paltry old age pensions, and neither was inclined to admit to their cash strapped, land rich existence. Ray had kept his beaten-up old Skoda car, but it now only spluttered into occasional action in local bursts. Another element that kept Sarah and Ray busy apart from their place on the village committee, was a recharged interest, almost obsession, with gardening. In olden days Ray had always mocked the Bermondsey wartime faithful for placing more value on their allotments than on their permanent residences. Still, he now saw it as his turn to cultivate his patch of English soil with an array of mixed vegetables, whilst Sarah opted for the upkeep of lawns and flower beds.

The penultimate Saturday before term started had heralded, at Mary's behest, a gathering on the terrace, superbly south-west facing for the evening sun. The school's kitchen staff acting as maids and butlers served never ending fill ups of Merlot and Chardonnay as the precursor to what was to be nothing short of a banquet. The make-up of attendees, nominally forty to fifty in number, naturally included the great majority of her staff, but notable were the exceptions to this rule. Michael, of course, was there gabbling to a small group with some animation. He broke away from the festive throng of men and women of pensionable age when he spotted Ray and Sarah in debate with the art master at the school,

"Can I tear you away for a moment, Dad? I have some people you may wish to meet," said Michael, grabbing his father.

As Ray scurried away with Michael he approached the group, some he immediately smiled at and recognised, others not. How could he not greet Dick Cranley and his Scottish heiress, then there was Mick who really was beginning to look like a cross between David Crosby of Crosby, Stills and Nash fame and the ponytailed Francis Rossi of Status Quo. Hugs were predictably exchanged as Mick introduced two ladies of similar appearance and demeanour, defying their middle forties age group with figure hugging outfits of pink and bright orange respectively,

"You remember Laura and Linda, Ray, surely?"

The Burger twins were back! They had pursued differing destinies with Laura settling after her wild days with Mick for an orthodox marriage with two children. The amazing one was Linda, who had escaped Mick's clutches to run a very modern restaurant in Brighton, and after nearly ten years with the pressure of being head chef and responsible for running the restaurant, she was beginning to look for a new challenge.

Then one day a rather elderly lady entered 'The Single Twin' continental auberge with what looked like her bank manager. They perused the menu, ordering four courses and at completion asked of the young waitress if they could have a word with the head chef.

Linda escaped from the demands of her kitchen to scream, "Blimey, after all these years, Mary how are you, how did you find my little abode here?"

Mary Poulson returned all pleasantries, very impressed with what she had experienced, enforcing Linda to hear what her companion, the Dalesmore bursar had to say for himself, when he asked the question,

"Linda, how would you like to take charge of our catering department at Dalesmore, starting in three months' time?"

Linda could see the ghost of JJ in all Mary's approaches that day, and here at the celebration party five years on, she had never had cause to regret her decision to take on such a marvellous opportunity in such a prestigious boarding school. Linda was set for life.

Mary had organised the meal with a head table seating eight, comprising herself, Mick, the two twins, Dick and Eilish, and Ray and Sarah. Cosily arranged around them were ten tables of four, which really that evening were to play the role of an audience to the Sandlehurst selection up top.

The meal was deliciously received. Then after the dessert, at the cries of speech, speech, speech, Mary stood up and toasted the assembled audience, the staff and the school, continuing, "Staff members and guests, I have invited you all here tonight, on the eve of the Autumn term 2005. It seems many moons ago now that I left college as a bright-eyed twenty two year old and began my long journey in the education of our young. This week I celebrate my 60th birthday. I have had a memorable double innings, first at Sandlehurst, then here as Head at Dalesmore. During that period I had only one regret and that was that the staff at Sandlehurst, several of whom are here on top table tonight, never were able to recognise and celebrate the role and contribution that our mentor, JJ, had played in our lives. He is now bedridden and too sick to come from his residential care home tonight, but he has sent his heartfelt best wishes. He taught me many things, the most vital was to depart while you're still ahead. Tonight, I can announce my retirement at the end of this term!"

The room was silent in a state of shock. Then suddenly Dick Cranley arose and offered a double toast, to Mary Poulson and JJ. The whole entirety of the room applauded for three minutes, at which Mary invited young Michael Bristowe to the top table for an announcement.

"Ladies and gentlemen, Mary has asked for one final request and it is my duty and pleasure to approach the members of this top table; Will you on behalf of Dalesmore School, Dick Cranley, Mick Greatbatch and you, Ray Bristowe, present to public and school audiences two successive nights of pantomime at the school hall in December? Mary is keen for you to perform a modern, updated version of Cinderella. It would be her swan song. It really would be her swan song. It's got to be yes or no, tonight, your answer gentlemen please!"

'The Three Musketeers' arose simultaneously, giving each other a cursory glance, then with a nod and a final flourish, toasted the health of Cinderella 2005! Thus it became a busy autumn for the Bristowe family commuting three times a week between Wednespool and Dalesmore, and much was the same for Dick Cranley. Mick inevitably was the exception in taking up the musical residency at the school at the grand old age of fifty four, the oldest rocker in town! For him, it was a temporary respite from a damp squat in Bexhill.

With Mary concocting changes to the timetable to accommodate extra classes for drama, music and art design, the future participants for the panto definitely made up the time required to present a spectacular for the weekend of December the 17th. Nothing was to get in their way. For Mick, these days a virtual recluse living in Bexhill on state benefits, it was to be a release from the obscurity of a mundane existence. Now at Dalesmore he was, maybe for the final time, back on centre stage again composing and cajoling the new young cast as well as utilising the services of the music scholars at the school.

Even part of half-term was set aside for hastening the construction of props for the set and the delivery of costumes. Mary's publicity team was put into action as posters had been designed by the art department under Ray's stringent tutelage. Ray indeed had learned a great deal from his Wednespool village experience in how to coordinate with Dick in bringing together all of the talents that Dalesmore had to offer.

Such was the confidence that the scheduled dress rehearsal was ready for Sunday, the 11th of December. Mary brought the cast and the staff together in the early days of the month and duly announced;

"You have all worked so hard that through my contacts around the county's theatrical outlets, I have been able to treat you all and hopefully it will motivate you further. We will be in the audience at a top London production the night before our own rehearsal. Our own school bus can transport us to the venue in time for a slap-up meal before one of the capital's most stunning productions. The name of the play and theatre will be kept secret until we arrive at the doors on Saturday evening."

Miss Poulson would never do things by half. December was to be a whirl for all the cast and staff whether on or off the stage. The three weekends for them were all fully booked. That was the case for the audiences as projected ticket sales for Cinderella had surpassed all expectations. The school hall would be packed on both nights.

* * *

Phil Bristowe had survived. It was already April and his annual hibernation had tested him to the full. The winter of 2005 was severe, so bad that for the first time he had acquired a two-bar electric garage heater to work off the one electric plug point. That one investment plus intermittent trips at peak periods to the A and E over at Putney Hospital had saved him. Psychologically his father's voice kept echoing in his head, 'Life's a three score and ten, son,' as he was to celebrate his 70th that summer.

He soon met up in Berkeley Square with his two entrusted street colleagues. April for the group was always a positive, hopeful time as the temperatures rose, and matched the positivity of London's populace yet again emerging, slowly from a long winter. Phil along with new recruit Bilko, was eager to discover what difference the doe-eyed four legged addition would make to the weekly tips.

Both Shirley and Wyatt had yet again forlornly put on hold their badgering of Phil to get a will sorted once and for all. Yet, having still mentioned to him that a meeting with Wyatt's solicitor friend had been set for the time of Phil's birthday in early September, the Bristowe boy finally had consented. The trio were to enjoy their best summer on record with their takings reflecting the stability of a third term in office for the Labour Blair government. Money was out there on the streets, the theatres and clubs were full to capacity, and the long days of Berkeley Square followed by Drury Lane at night had reinforced to all three of them that London was the world's, as Wyatt would put it, 'nice little earner.'

The September week of Phil's 70th was also to be his first interview with David Westbourne of the partners of the same name. How Wyatt was able to gain his services was a mystery, but Shirley had got the distinct impression that when they were at Cambridge together, Wyatt had something on him. Honour amongst thieves, she thought.

Shirley also had her own wiles. In buying Phil a celebratory night out, she was able to drink so excessively that she, for the first time in eight years, ended up sleeping in the lock-up. Phil, also oblivious to the situation that night, had just let his 'firm's leader' through the front entrance. So with the interview with Westbourne the following afternoon, she got to work. Wyatt had informed her that to obtain the partner's services, she needed to obtain as much documented information from Phil as possible. Only that course of action would confirm the role of chief executor for the probate. In simple terms, Phil had to make a written undertaking that his will would be totally controlled and directed by Westbournes.

She was up by seven o'clock whilst Phil was comatose to the world. Then Shirley conducted her search on tip toe, as silently as she could. All she could pull out from his corduroy jacket was the old British passport, an old moth-eaten neck tie and a piece of paper in the lining with a P.O. Box number but no name. She wondered whether it was his or not, then pocketing it, she just stared at this enigma, Phil Bristowe fast asleep with an outstretched arm revealing that tattooed ten-digit number. The elderly hippy always carried a pen, surely the number had to correspond to something or somebody. She scrawled down the number in haste.

Later that day, Wyatt met the pair outside the offices of Westbournes, just off Russell Square. Phil had recovered, patting himself on the back that he had after all reached seventy, and proceeded to attend the appointment which required Wyatt to be present as the interpreter to all the legalistic mumbo jumbo that David had to adhere to in such circumstances. The long and short of it was that Phil did sign everything over to the lawyer, pending any further notices including the known paltry details of his estate and wishes to be carried out in the event of his demise.

After one hour, Wyatt led Phil outside to be greeted by Shirley patiently waiting for the news. Wyatt gave her the nod, and then she simply asked if she could use the ladies 'boudoir' at the practice. He pointed her inside and instead of going left she went right, into Mr Westbourne's office.

"Sir, you may be in need of these items of paperwork. They will help in your instructions to have all the facts together," she offered.

David Westbourne had been briefed of the make up of 'Wyatt's firm' and the role that Shirley had played in resurrecting Phil's life. She handed David the navy British passport from distant days, the P.O. Box number and address and finally her handwritten reproduction of the ten-digit tattoo and the red tie decorated with some kind of vegetable motif.

"Oh yes, I did ask him about that indented number," said David, "but he had no recollection at all of its significance."

Shirley insisted he spend ample time on the matter. He, with some depth of sincerity, assured her that Westbournes would get to the bottom of the matter but it might take time especially if there were international implications.

"David, I'm worried he won't last another winter," she added.

The exact adherence to Phil's instructions could only be made after the solicitor's searches were complete. The full details of the estate and the manner in which the will would be conveyed to interested parties would be fully confirmed at a second meeting.

As Phil, Wyatt and Shirley retreated that early autumn afternoon to their patch along Kingsway by London's colleges, they really thought they would be back in Westbourne's offices by the end of the month. It was not to be. It was to take nigh on a full three months until the end of November before Phil was summoned to return, this time all by himself.

He hurried past Luciano's, but even that was at a snail's pace. Drips were hanging off the end of his nose as yet another morning passed without him shrugging off a November cold that had gone straight to his chest. He had made the decision, as Wyatt had termed it, "to become a day boy". Living permanently in the lock-up, his normal routine with bus pass in hand was to catch the Routemaster bus, but today he would bypass the Eight Bells pub, and take the tiny underpass walkaway below Putney Bridge, then up the stairs for the number 30 bus. The amble was only four hundred yards, but it still had taken his breath away.

Russell Square was a haven for the professions, a focal point for lawyers, doctors, accountants and consultants. This presumably, he thought, would have been Wyatt's world had he not been caught with his fingers in the till. He knew he had to be at the top of his game, mentally alert, to deal with the Westbournes a deep rooted family of public school toffs. Arrogant to the core from the day Mumee and Dadee had laid down oodles of money to launch their precious ones into Oxbridge to follow careers that the Square would provide for them, their rules and regulations had run the country for centuries but not for this boy from Bermondsey.

"Marvellous to see you, Philip, cup of tea?" was his welcome.

"We have finalised and drawn up the bare bones for any potential probate we can disperse on your behalf. You know you really didn't give us much to work with, but Shirley's intervention proved critical."

"In what way?" replied Phil, intrigued at this unknown.

"Well, she deposited your extinct British passport, a P.O. Box number with address and a grubby old tie. Believe it or not, it was the latter that led us to a full appraisal of the extent of your estate's value."

Phil admitted that he had big holes in his memory bank, particularly on details of places, timings and details of arrangements but he seldom forgot a name or a face. It seemed that he now just lacked the capacity to slot the person to a specific place or time.

"Well you'll be glad to know that we at Westbourne's have been able to do just that. You have already supplied us with your current residential details and estimates of both property value and contents. You will see from Paragraph 1 that we have accounted for that. Paragraph 2 accounts for your monetary worth, all things considered, which you must allocate today. Have a cuppa, take it all in and in say twenty minutes, you can give us your final dispersements and instructions. You will note that the Introductory Summary reflects the conversations we had in our first meeting, and the Addenda displays any further expenses or outlays that you have intended to defray.

Phil studied Paragraph 2's details intently. It took two cups of sweet tea before he had reviewed every aspect to his satisfaction. He was unambiguous in every instruction and definite in all allocations. That November day, Phil

Bristowe was fully in charge of his faculties and cognisant of signing over all his affairs on the dotted line to David Westbourne.

"Thank you, Philip, we trust it will be still many years to come before we put your Last Will and Testament into action."

"Incidentally, David," Phil changing the subject matter, "how did you meet Wyatt in the first place?" he continued.

"Up at Cambridge, we studied together. James was the Marshall at Arms of our social group of undergraduate lawyers,"

Phil left the Georgian building none the wiser for his enquiry! Maybe Shirley would know. The time was tight for Phil as he had promised her he would be there at the LSE by 4pm. The students had again come up trumps that autumn term and it was from their generosity that he was now able to commute from the relative obscurity of Putney each day.

Shirley was there with Wyatt and spotted Phil as he stood out as the old geezer amongst a sea of fresh faced students scurrying around the courtyard entrances of the School of Economics. It was ironic that she would suggest a board meeting on that very subject. The three regulars at WC2 settled into a relatively empty student coffee house with Shirley leading the debate.

"Gentlemen, we are moving house for two weeks before the winter break, assuming you're both organised for that period. The students are now low on funds but I have an idea to cross the river to London Bridge station. Along the road from there a new theatre is packing them in at this

340

time of year. I've done my homework, it's a children's exclusive theatre called 'The Unicorn'. It used to be over here, but the Arts Council have put together a huge grant for a grand new building to celebrate one of the first performances in London of Caryl Jenner's pioneering work for kids in theatre."

"Sounds pleasant enough, but children don't have money," advised Wyatt, not really up with orthodox family life in 2005.

"No, but their parents do and if they are accompanying them, they are well off and eager enough to spend money on a night out with their precious ones," Shirley enthused.

"Are you sure? South of the Thames is not known for donating spare cash to even decent charitable causes like ours. It would be like crossing the Rubicon from our little operation here in Theatreland," Wyatt added, completely foxing Phil with classical references.

Phil was keen to give it a try as it would only be a two week task, and with Bilko there to attract the kids, surely it would be a winner. Shirley turned to him gently suggesting her only doubt was whether he could last it out, as he had had to withdraw with pneumonic bouts earlier in the month. He looked very pale to her and with just a donkey jacket and a roll neck sweater, she had already supplied him with an extra blanket for the long haul. As she nervously viewed more drips from his nose that were becoming a regular source of anxiety, Phil piped up,

"Shirley, you know I was born just along the road from Tooley Street where this new theatre now stands. I can remember Dad once took us down there for a Christmas panto, but I've forgotten where, or was it a football match, but it was a happy time, all colour and singing, I loved it," he reminisced.

"That seals the deal because the production company are to be performing a glittering musical. The atmosphere round the theatre with all those kids will be something special for the couple of weeks leading up to Christmas," Shirley concluded.

"So, first night will be the Friday, then the big one the Saturday, the 10th," confirmed Wyatt.

Phil grimacing slightly, took their leave that afternoon. It had been a long day and he was physically, mentally and medically drained.

* * *

The happy cast clambered aboard the bus and for some adolescent reason the fact that Michael was driving added to the overall excitement. The fourteen girls and seven boys clearly felt that his relative youthfulness as a teacher would provide a journey up to London akin to a frivolous safari. Predictably their effervescence was cooled as Mary Poulson took up her front seat with the Cranleys and Mick Greatbatch. An announcement was duly made that there would be a stop en route at Wednespool to pick up Ray, Sarah and another village notable who was the theatre buff for all the local enthusiasts. She was steeped in rural Sussex with her greatest claim to fame back in the 1960s when she was the manager of a tour party for the England Women's Cricket team! Her name, Eleanor Dalliance, seemed to reflect that era.

It was a quick pick-up, no time for tea and buns, as Michael made good headway towards Croydon and South London. Mary was in her element pointing out notable landmarks on the way, safe in the knowledge that she had 29 Unicorn Theatre tickets in her handbag for the show and just as important, a first floor exclusive booking for 5.30pm at the equally newly located Nando's restaurant at London Bridge. Originally a South African chain, it was establishing a great number of outlets across London for its chicken open hearth meals. These were to prove very popular with the youngsters as they created a hubbub of excited noise upstairs in the restaurant. For the waiters, it was sheer pandemonium!

The only action that could interrupt the sumptuous grazing of her flock was a loud bang on the table from Miss Poulson. She was able to dominate the airwaves shortly before seven o'clock by announcing that her cast would be watching an all children's production of the musical 'Smike'. This interpretation of a part of Dickens's Nicholas Nickleby was to be a fine example of how children and adults could interact both on and off the stage but most of all she pointed her cast's attention to Smike's universal appeal to all ages and backgrounds. In strict organisational tones, she urged all her cast to walk from the London Bridge Nando's along Tooley Street in a group. Michael, having parked the bus earlier in an underground car park, would lead the procession of excited teenagers to the theatre, set back off the street. It was just a three hundred yard walk and maybe it was the heightened anticipation, but it was obvious that the cast and the staff of 'Cinders' were oblivious to anybody or anything else other than their own buzz of conversation and expectation.

For sure, they hurried past shop windows paying no attention to their contents and as for the other members of the public in their way, well, they were an irritating irrelevance, a barrier set up to frustrate them getting to their destination. They certainly had no recollection of passing in the doorways the bedraggled forms of old men and women crouching down for the night in their sleeping bags.

"There's another gang disappeared on us," cried Wyatt, as not one of the Dalesmore set had even slowed to see his plight.

"Don't you worry, just like last night, they'll be back towards ten o'clock, that's when we must be proactive. Let's face it, the three of us and the dog look like something out of Dickensian London, and that's what they will have just seen with 'Smike' on at the Unicorn," she quipped.

Inwardly, Shirley was very anxious. The evening before, Phil had regularly dozed off at his pitch and it seemed the only prop which could keep him active was brandy which he kept in his inside jacket pocket for the colder evenings. The one fact she understood was if the punters felt they were passing by a group of drunks the tips would not be flowing. Phil was erratically treading a fine line. She was to watch him and Bilko like a hawk that night as the dog's noises, barking, growling and whining were all at times signals to Phil's health and activity level. They were indeed a double act.

At one point of the evening both Wyatt and Shirley left their stand and sidled the thirty yards between them and Phil. He gave the impression to them of not quite being with it, being more concerned with when they would pack up for the night. He was shivering and his complexion was sallow. Shirley passed him a hot tea from her flask. Phil, yet again, seemed to perk up as she impressed upon him that it was all hands to the deck as the advanced parties of theatre lovers were on their way back.

Ray was one of them as he brought up the rear of a scattered bunch of adolescents. He had thoroughly enjoyed the production with Sarah at his side. He had always had a soft spot for Dickensian London and its heritage, including Smike. The only drawback was the plush brand new concrete structure, which from his childhood recollection, seemed totally out of character with Tooley Street and SE1.

All his musings of the old days of Caryl Jenner and the Olaf Grammar School pantos were set aside ahead of his stride by a noisy commotion involving the girls from his own cast. They seemed to be stroking and getting involved with a stray labrador dog by a shop window. As he approached the scene, they were tugging at a tramp, a street beggar whilst the dog continued to whine at a deafening pitch.

"We're only trying to give the man a Christmas box but he won't wake up, sir," the trio's leader complained, "Do you think there's something wrong with him?"

From nowhere, Shirley had dashed from the next window in a state of panic, screaming, "Bilko, be quiet, calm down, let me have a look at him."

Ray's curly hair almost stood on end as he reminded himself that Bilko was such an unusual name for a dog. He knew that Mr Yates had a black lab of the same name. Now Sarah was on the scene and Ray made it clear it was her job to dispel the anxious girls and give this poor man some breathing space.

"Sarah, take a look, what do you think, he's ghostly white?" asked a crouching Ray.

There was something about the stillness, the shape of the nose and forehead that tilted the head backwards against the shop window that was vaguely familiar to Ray. He now bent his knees, a full extension to get level with the man's head. Nervously he placed his shaking hand onto the stagnant chest of the beggar, pulling back the top of his roll neck sweater to reveal a four inch scar. Ray had been here before; the flashing image of him bending over his kid brother consumed his every reaction.

"Hurry, Ted, run, get some help, find the lifeguard," he screamed.

Sarah looked aghast at Shirley and she in turn was shocked and confused at what was unfolding before their very eyes,

"His name's not Ted, it's Phil," shouted Shirley.

"I know, I know, I know, Sarah get an ambulance, he's collapsed, see if you can find a pulse, woman?"

Then Shirley asked softly, almost under her breath, "How do you know his name?"

"He's my only brother, my own flesh and blood," the tears were now streaming through his empty stare.

Sarah had never witnessed her husband weep. Inconsolable, he tilted his head onto her shoulder. He was trembling out of control, his words rambling into a high pitched rant,

"What have I done? It's been forty years. I was never there for him. Now look at the state he's in, Mum will never forgive me. I'll stay with my brother, I must be with Phil. Sarah, you go on home, take the children to Michael. What's your name, love?" he asked of Shirley.

"Shirley Mauer, and you're Ray, aren't you? Hey Wyatt you look after Bilko. Ray, I must also stay with Phil, OK?" she insisted.

Ray, almost regaining a semblance of control said, "You know we used to have a lab called Bilko. Phil loved that dog like nothing else."

Within five minutes, the ambulance from nearby St Thomas' Hospital arrived with flashing blue lights swamping the London Bridge skyline. It was too late. Phil had died in Ray's arms.

Once inseparable as little boys of the Blitz, then a lifetime detached and divided, it took Tooley Street to bring them together again. This time, the Bermondsey brothers had become one.

CHAPTER 16

THREE SCORE YEARS AND TEN

At the fifth ring, David Westbourne answered the phone.

"Hello, Westbourne Solicitors here."

"David, is that you?" A firm vocal range posed the question.

"Yes, indeed, who's speaking please, how can I help?" said David.

"It must have been the leek that gave me away," stated the far away voice, clearly communicating from across the miles,

"Pardon, I'm not with you, can you enlighten me?"

"The regimental tie, scarlet, with the leek emboldened," informed the caller, still with those up and down tones,

"Oh, my God, it's you Commander, marvellous. Have you been able to make the connections for the day?"

"Yes siree, every single one of them, some by P.O. Box, others by email. Can you believe a number by telephone

348

and a fair proportion by connections with breweries and the Foreign Office!"

"Phil certainly knew who he could rely on. Have you given them the venue, the time and date, and of course, where necessary their expenses will be covered?" asked the solicitor,

The Commander did not need to answer but for confirmation's sake, he repeated down the phone that the Philip Bristowe Memorial Day's celebration was to be held from midday on Friday the 25th of February 2006 at Da Luciano's in London SW6. The total number attending would be twenty four at the last count. The celebrations would be conducted by the commander but at a poignant time nearing conclusion, David Westbourne would formally recount the details of the last will and testament of Philip Bristowe.

The first of Phil's requests, not eligible within the official will, was for there to be no funeral. Within three days of the post-mortem, he was to be committed to rest and his ashes to be dispersed from the height of Tower Bridge into the River Thames. David Westbourne was to spend much of his time throughout the ensuing January and February connecting the details and the potential beneficiaries of the will. Whatever the estate was worth, his specific instruction was for the information therein not to be divulged in any way until the memorial service in late February. Every aspect of this process was to be unorthodox, hardly surprising that, as Phil could never be labelled as anything other than enigmatic.

Yet, there was a trusting nature to the relationship that was built up through their meetings between the renegade and the Russell Square solicitor. Phil always had high regard for expertise borne out of practical experience and David had climbed the legal pole for two decades since his Cambridge days with Wyatt. Originally a family firm with traditional networks, even such an establishment was under siege to the all inclusive push of society to promote diversity and inclusion into the boardrooms of the legal profession, whatever the abilities and experience of the chosen ones.

David understood all these trends but for him, it was a matter of offering a top service and retaining the highest possible standards. Achieving government imposed numbers and percentages were just ill-informed dictates of not just political correctness, but of functional lunacy. Maybe that stance was why at first Phil thought he was dealing with yet another public school toff, a reaction that was soon to be overtaken by a mutual rapport and respect in their exchanges.

The flexible nature of this legal mind ensured that all the right people, those that Phil really wanted, would be there on the day and those weeks leading up to the event would require the skills of a detective as well as a diplomat and lawyer. As the day got closer, he had zoned in with the aid of the commander, and their organisation was to be completed by the confirmation call on the Friday, the week before.

David had worked tirelessly throughout that autumn to uncover the dilemma of the numbers tattooed on one of

Phil's forearms. It took him some time with international banking enquiries, but it was the number of digits and its last two which corresponded to a foreign country that had given the game away. He had, indeed, traced the account number to Luxembourg, a high interest bond. The instruction for this specific account was that it would maintain its set annual percentage interest as long as it remained intact with no withdrawals. The monies would simply roll over. Philip Bristowe had never touched it since its inception in 1967.

At this stage, the detective solicitor had not liaised with anyone except the bank in Luxembourg and as he had power of attorney and was the chief executor, he was able to gain access to the account. With that acquired knowledge he could not fathom how Phil had come into these funds. David's one brainwave was to link the passport number of one forearm with the bank's account number on the other arm.

Philip's original British passport was in his possession from Wyatt's kind intervention. David now began to sift and he didn't have to sift for very long. There were only five deposits in his account, equally there were only five overseas stamps in his original passport. He put the two pieces of information together and hey presto, they matched. To the day, within one month later, the deposit was transferred into his account after the very clear passport stamps of departures. They were:

Venue	Arrival	Departure	Deposit
Pittsburgh, USA	Aug 66	Jan 67	Feb 67
Sarawak, Borneo	Aug 67	Oct 67	Nov 67
Salisbury, Rhodesia	Jul 71	Sep 71	Oct 71
Johannesburg, South Africa	Aug 76	Dec 76	Feb 77
Santiago, Chile	Mar 82	May 82	Jun 82

Once he had made contact with the man with the scarlet tie of a noted British regiment, the arrangement with no questions asked was wholeheartedly confirmed. Philip Bristowe had been the recipient of separately sourced income but his internal injuries had precluded all knowledge of them.

This was where Terry Jones came in. In his first telephone collaboration with David, he had admitted to being the delivery source of these periodic credit notes into the Luxembourg account but he would go no further into divulging why, how, when and how much. The solicitor, from a wealth of tracing experience, recognised that here were lines that should never be crossed and in most cases there were good reasons for these limitations.

Yet David did hold the ace card in one area. He was the sole possessor of Philip Bristowe's blue passport, knowing exactly when and where Philip had ventured over the years. He put two and two together and they had made four. Nevertheless, he had not complied with the deceased's wishes for an early committal as a result of the state's law that a coroner was required to perform a post-mortem before issuing the death certificate. The Bristowe boy left this world beyond a settled home, and therefore a detailed coroner's examination was law.

Westbournes had made the eventual contact to discover that pneumonia was the direct cause of death but secondary breakdowns of vital organs contributed to the finality. The coroner, known to David, had incidentally made several observations to the solicitor that there was evidence of cranial abnormalities consistent with multiple concussions, a huge number of fractures to both upper and lower body. Interestingly enough, there was a trace by virtue of a noticeable intravenous insertion in his right wrist that suggested he had been subjected to a post-natal exchange of blood, almost definitely at birth. In the 1930s that had meant he was born Rhesus Positive and that it would have then been an unholy battle for mother and child to survive.

David was to realise that Philip's life had, from the first few seconds of birth to lying in a crumpled heap in Tooley Street, been one long battle. There was just one more call he had to return, that was to the commander before re-joining the more mundane organisation of Phil's Memorial Day.

"Terry, just one more thought before you make your journey across the pond next week. You know I have Phil's passport displaying his trips overseas etc, but it is not that area I wish to explore any further. However, any comments under the 'distinguishing marks' that he could be recognised by? Was that a Unit directive?"

Terry hesitated to reply, quite deliberately, with the comment, "I never knew he had any," he lied.

353

David then enlightened the old soldier, not about the childhood scar of the neck, but of the complications of a very singular birth. "No one knew about that. How could anyone possibly have known, apart from his mother?" he genuinely replied.

Terry Jones, as so often, was right officially. How was he to know, however, that there was to be one guest that next Friday who would beg to differ and had tangible proof!

* * *

That done now, it was David's duty to secure the venue with Luciano, and to collect together the vital documents. Although he had been in communication with his former student leader, Wyatt, in the process, it was to be a very selective, secret gathering which would arrive with bated breath at the Italian restaurant on what was to be a very premature spring like day.

Luciano was a past master at hosting family events and celebrations. His family hailed from Calabria in the south of Italy where family bonds were the bedrock of tightly knit communities. Yet, of all of his regulars, he had a special place in his heart for Phil. Never really knowing the details of his past, Luciano suspected through his connections up the road at the Eight Bells, that his past lifestyle had been full of action. Luca was an anglophile, indeed he was born an Englishman, whose parents had been liberated by the Allies as they surged through Italy in late 1944. He in turn was therefore a specialist in Italian cuisine and English full breakfasts.

It was Phil's instruction that both would be part of the enormous buffet which not only would feature home made pizzas visibly prepared in front of the customers, the finest pasta with freshly made sauces, but also scrambled eggs, bacon, sausages, the works! His weakness for Piedmont's Gavi di Gavi wines was there by the rackful, and he had even laid on a barrel of Courage beer direct from the Angel pub in Bermondsey. When it came to food and bevvies, Luciano left nothing to chance.

The 'Italian Stallion', as Phil called him, closed his restaurant to outsiders for the day with a red, white and green poster affixed to the door stating 'Family celebration in progress'. Indeed, brother Silvio and sister Franca joined his elderly Mama in hosting what was to prove a mixing together of nations in this cosy intimate bar-restaurant in a small corner of south-west London.

Even the lay out of the single storey hostelry was superb with the usual tables and chairs cleared out to make way for an ample floor space with the buffet at the 'Fulham' end, and a short platform with a quaint speech desk supporting the 'Putney' wall. Around the edges and by the windows opening up onto the main road, Franca had positioned tables for two and four persons.

The bells from the All Saints church alongside Putney Bridge and the river tolled loud and clear, twelve monotoned notes. Only two hundred yards away, there was a conscious movement of people off of the pavement and into the colour of Da Luciano's. Unlike many of the adjoining shops with their goods and services aimed at specific genders or ages, those that marched into the

355

restaurant that lunch time were of an incredibly diverse nature. They ranged from early twenties to some in their eighties who were struggling on their pins.

There also seemed to be a fair split of men and women but the one eccentric feature was in the variety of dress codes. Included in this distinguished or motley crew, depending on how you saw them, were top Saville Row suits, street people in not much better than rags, military top brass jackets, local workmen in Levi's and Doc Martins, high fashion ladies in high heels and even a ridiculous black labrador dog in a body warmer!

David welcomed this amazing collection calmly but at times he was bewildered by the number that would all be classified as speaking in a form of English nowhere near familiar with his plum Cambridge vowels. There were, what he thought were, Glaswegians, clipped Afrikaans South Africans, high German, Dutch, Californian drawls, wide boy cockneys, oriental soft spoken Chinese, and a boyo from the Rhondda Valley of South Wales!

With every individual served a generous opening glass of red or white wine, it was the Rhondda veteran who took to the platform first to engage the audience that had already settled into a party atmosphere. The atmosphere was prospering through the kindest social service and interaction of Luca, Silvio and Franca around the room.

The big guy clambered up on to the platform, his regimental tunic lighting up the stage. For him, with white shirt and scarlet tie, this occasion did need to have a backbone of formality. He would provide that at its outset, and no doubt the Westbournes would conclude similarly in appropriate legal fashion. Just for ten seconds, he glanced across at Carolina Lee with her daughter Phillippa, and he, Terry Jones was back again in the jungle on Phil's shoulder. He paused and gathered his senses,

"Welcome here to you all in Phil's backyard, his home was in Bermondsey just seven miles downstream. He loved this river as he loved life. Today I stand privileged to share with you one exceptional man. It is a fact that, between you, thousands of miles have been covered from four different continents to celebrate this amazing life story.

It is likely that you are, many of you, unknown to each other. Believe me, you all played an enormous part in his life. Whether you be friend, family, mistress, boss, colleague or comrade, you will have been touched by or instrumental in Phil's remarkable life that was uniquely his, his three score years and ten.

Why am I here, Terry Jones from the Welsh Guards and T Company? I'll tell you why, because Philip saved my life from a cruel death. Not just me, he saved countless more in the work we shared. All at his own personal expense and sacrifice, and do you know, those hundreds out there never even knew him. Phil lived in the shadows and if you think you knew him or had him taped, dream on you fool."

You could have cut the air with a knife. Bewildered guests nervously were on tenterhooks, not knowing what was coming next. Terry continued, wishing now to introduce some levity.

"I cannot share openly with you our mutual times together, but let's just say they started over fifty years ago. Yet I would be the first and last to enlighten you all that,

357

for richer or poorer, in glory or anonymity, Phil served and lived for other people. You here at Luciano's today have been the lucky ones, because you can say that you once knew Philip Bristowe.

So, my friends, I ask you to mix and piece together your parts and experiences in his life. I feel certain that it will prove enjoyable and entertaining, but even more than that, it may answer many questions you may have wanted to ask of Phil himself. He was a man of many parts. It's also clear in my mind that he would have loved to have been here on this occasion to have introduced you all to each other! Please, can you do just that today?

Here's to Phil! Raise your glasses to Philip Bristowe."

The chinks of wine glasses resounded across Da Luciano's, followed by a crescendo of natter, chatter and a double bark from Bilko! The party was to officially begin. A disorderly line at the 'Fulham' end eagerly surged forward to devour the extensive spread, some enticed by the continental pasta and pizza, some traditionalists heading for the bacon and eggs, but yes, many, filling up their plates with a combination platter!

David Westbourne stood motionless, perusing the scene. He was dumbfounded, thinking to himself that at last he was witness to a cockney beano, and he was going to enjoy it too! Then he pinched himself to remember he had a formal duty to perform later in the afternoon. Judging by the assembled throng, he was sure that it might even be nearer evening time!

It took the guests five or so minutes to select their choices of sustenance, and almost by mutual consent settled into filling the tables of four. You could tell, maybe because of the advancing years of most of them, that the invitees preferred the early opportunity to enjoy the buffet sitting down. More poignantly, David eyeballed the division of the personalities as they were seated effectively in such groups. At this stage in the proceedings, he made a point of being at the back of the line with Terry. He was very aware that 'The Commander' would have interacted at some point in time with at least half of the attendees.

What David wasn't party to was the extent to which Terry had participated in Phil's association with the groups that on this mutual day, were covering six decades. He wondered whether Terry could even recognise physically many of those now sat down for luncheon. David's mind was slightly put to rest as the Welsh Guard was attempting a running commentary as the individuals became small groups of four at the adjoining tables. For some Terry nodded his head as if not to know. With others he began a description with the comment, "That must be 'x' from the 1980s" or whatever decade came to mind. Then there were the clear favourites with whom he had shared time and the corresponding mutual venues in far off places.

The lawyer at almost a subconscious level, scanned the restaurant wondering how one person could have been so closely attached to such a variety of humanity, and this led him down the path to how they would all react to the details of the impending will. He allowed Terry to join Fergus Laird and Gilbert Woodall at their table which was headed up by the affable Luciano. There was already a hint of bon viveur about that table, of men who enjoyed the

359

trappings and rewards of life that a little bit of authority had ensured.

Next along the line of tables was almost the opposite as Phil's London boys, Joe and Jim along with ex-London landlord of The Greyhound, Mike, were already teaching an enthralled German from Hillman's Language School, Jurgen, the subtleties of cockney rhyming slang. The latter somehow got the impression that cockney, or a good knowledge of the dialect, was the equivalent of Germany's 'haute Deutsche'!

David now could see that the tables had been filling up quite rapidly as he nodded positively at Ray Bristowe's table mates. Of all the people present, Ray was one of those that David had wanted to meet, being the deceased's brother. Ray, always well mannered, courteously rose to introduce his wife Sarah, then Sophie, one of Phil's work colleagues from Paderborn, and finally to the eldest prim and proper lady in the room, who Ray claimed had been his nanny in Hamburg. Helga smiled sweetly, clearly overwhelmed by the attention she was given in such friendly, but unfamiliar company.

Frankly, David could hardly hear a word she said as a result of the din and racket coming from the next table. The entire room not only had to contend with Toc H stalwarts Barry Van de Wilt and old Edgar, the latter now in his mid 80s, going at the wine at full throttle, but also tolerating Wyatt's pathetic attempts to pacify his new partner in life, Bilko the black lab. This errant dog, just couldn't resist the pungent aromas of sausages and pizza which were being thrown his way. It was a relief to all that at least Shirley was there to calm the overexuberance of old men behaving very badly!

The solicitor could finally see where he was heading. It was the far table by the window. Before he could arrive at that destination, a group of three women presumably with one of their husbands discontinued eating to thank David for being the focal point of organisation and administration of the memorial. Two of the ladies bore an obvious resemblance, maybe sisters, both beautifully turned out with immaculately coiffured hair. They introduced themselves as Debra and her cuz, whatever that was, Mandy.

Simultaneously, the second pair, obviously partners, introduced themselves as Franz and Sigrid Hillman. Franz boasted in ever such a detectable German English accent that it was they who had taught Philip his immaculate German at their language school. The foursome already in such a short time were getting well acquainted to such an extent that Debra and Mandy had already invited the Paderborn couple to visit their quaint little English pub, The Greyhound down in deepest Hampshire. Franz was intrigued to know why it was called after that type of a dog?

David, eager now to eat, joined the young table or what appeared to be so, as youthful Michael politely introduced himself as the nephew of Phil. He was Ray's youngest child, but he quickly added that he had never met Philip. Ever the Oxbridge gentleman, he was to reassure David that in just 15 minutes he had learned more about Phil from the mother and daughter at his table than he had ever gleaned from his father!

The Russell Square devotee turned his attention to the pair. The mother, Carolina, spoke impeccable English, a lady of colourful dress sense that reflected her partial Chinese roots. She wore one of those high necked multi decorated blouses that were very familiar to David as he had spent a six month secondment in a Hong Kong practice in his graduate years. He did ask whether she had origins in Hong Kong. Undeterred, the elderly lady replied, "Oh no, I was brought up in an Anglo-Chinese family in the days of Malaya. Phil was out there on national service for several years. He was my sweetheart. They were hard times in Kuala Lumpur in those days. Let me introduce my daughter, Phillippa."

David glanced then embarrassingly broke into a stare. There were a small number of the guests that day who eerily took on some of his deceased client's features. He could see the family features, even in Michael sitting opposite him, but this girl had Phil's nose and eyes set in a Eurasian frame. He hesitated in their flowing conversation from asking the obvious sensitive question but her name said everything. This revealing confidence was just one of many that would be divulged amongst the long lines of tables that afternoon.

By 3.30pm, Luciano's desserts, cappuccinos and aperitifs had just added that touch of order to the proceedings that, even within the context of a memorial service, had lasted over three hours. Then finally there was the period of reflection as David Westbourne vacated his

362

conversations and approached the lectern to prepare his speech. The earlier courses of English and Italian cuisine had given way to what could only be considered an after meal drinks party. Mild background music filled the air for some time whilst the guests were keen to stretch their legs and mingle with more of Phil's closest and dearest over his lifetime.

On the stroke of four o'clock, it was inevitably the Master of Ceremonies, Terry Jones, who would take the stand for the very last time. Accompanying him was the man that Phil had entrusted with all the detail and legal reinforcement that he felt his own life had merited. David Westbourne was not to let his most celebrated client down. He had kept his confidences to the letter of the law.

"Prey, be seated, for David Westbourne and the reading of the Last Will and Testament of our Philip Bristowe," boomed the voice, the appropriate order of Terry Jones.

David Westbourne, attaching his glasses and then gingerly opened a wide dossier with one headed sheet bolding stating,

THE LAST WILL AND TESTAMENT OF
PHILIP CHARLES BRISTOWE

I, Philip Charles Bristowe of sound body and mind have herein granted the Power to the Executor of my Estate, David Westbourne of Westbourne Solicitors to issue my Will as follows:

363

My residence at 5 Raglan Yard SW6 will be transferred in its entirety to the ownership of one Shirley Mauer.

The contents and value of all items within the lock-up of 5 Raglan Yard to become the property of one James Earp, commonly known as 'Wyatt'. This includes my housemate, Bilko the dog.

The remaining value of the Estate including all holdings in banks and entitlements will be transferred.

The sum of 2.1 million pounds.

To my sister Sigrid Hillman, born Sigrid Semmler.

Daughter of Helga and Freddie Bristowe.

Silence, there followed an interlude of silence, maybe no more than twenty seconds, as the world of Philip Bristowe cascaded down onto every human emotion. Shock, horror, astonishment, tears of joy and tears of emptiness filled the restaurant. No one could credit what they had just heard. Surely those last few lines so formally dispensed by David Westbourne were some kind of fantasy?

Only David knew better. Phil's final pronouncements were all rock solid. As several of the guests sidled away to the exit doors including the family of Ray Bristowe, there was just one more instruction that had to be informally carried out by the Russell Square devotee. He was to hand a note contained in a soft brown envelope, addressed to one:

Ray Bristowe, 'Lyndhurst', Park Road, BINGLEY.

Inside it in Phil's best handwritten scroll was a message. It read:-

To Ray Bristowe,

Once upon a time, I told you:- "One day, I'll get you for this."

Today has been that day.

Phil.